Jeni Wood.
8 : VIII : 58.

A CITY OF BELLS

By the same Author

ISLAND MAGIC
THE MIDDLE WINDOW
TOWERS IN THE MIST
THE BIRD IN THE TREE
THE CASTLE ON THE HILL
A PEDLAR'S PACK (Stories)
THE GOLDEN SKYLARK (Stories)
THE IKON ON THE WALL (Stories)
SMOKY HOUSE
SISTER OF THE ANGELS
THREE PLAYS
SONGS AND VERSES
MAKE BELIEVE

A City of Bells

by

ELIZABETH GOUDGE

O joy, O joy,
For the humming street, and the child with its toy.
For the priest, and the bell, and the holy well.

MATTHEW ARNOLD

GERALD DUCKWORTH & CO. LTD.
3 Henrietta Street, London, W.C.2

First Published April 1936
Reprinted 1936, 1937, 1939, 1941,
1945, 1947, 1948 *and* 1949
All rights reserved

PRINTED IN GREAT BRITAIN BY
WYMAN AND SONS, LTD., LONDON, FAKENHAM AND READING

DEDICATED TO
M. L. O. C.

CHAPTER I

I

JOCELYN IRVIN, sitting in a corner seat in a third-class railway-carriage and watching the green and gold of England in the spring slip past the windows, meditated gloomily upon Life with a capital L. A funny business, he came to the conclusion, consisting in climbing painfully to the tops of ladders and falling even more painfully to the bottom of them again.

Looking back over his past career of slow ascents and sudden descents he remembered with amusement the years of hectic scrambling in ink and mud that had finally raised him to the exalted position of captain of the school. . . . Never again would he be so glorious, never again so revered. . . . But the eminence had not lasted and as an undergraduate in his first term his glory had caused no one to blink.

At the end of three years his good sense and good looks and good temper had made their mark, but then had come the Boer War and no one took any notice, except unfavourably and with strong language, of a junior subaltern who did not as yet know his job.

In time he knew it and, as the urgency of war sent him up his third ladder at headlong speed, the army knew his worth. So well did it know it that the final humiliation of death might have seized upon a portly general so armoured with clinking medals, and richly coloured by red tape, that it would have been hard to distinguish him from a boiled lobster.

7

But the fate that controls our destinies had thought otherwise, and a bursting shell had sent Jocelyn home to England again with an incurably lamed leg and a future that consisted of nothing but an immense question mark.

What to do with him his large and impecunious family couldn't imagine. It was the beginning of the twentieth century, a moment in the history of the English upper middle class when the things that a gentleman couldn't do far outnumbered the things that he could do. When Jocelyn suggested humbly that he thought he might be a commercial traveller his father blew down his nose contemptuously, and when he said gently that he'd always thought it would be great fun to be a bookie his brother Hubert implored him not to be more of a fool than he could help. His proposal that he should keep a hotel was received in chilly silence and the attractive idea of going round the country with a barrel-organ he dared not even express.

His family's own ideas for him, such as shutting him up in somebody's office in Whitehall, or planting him out as somebody else's secretary in the House of Commons, seemed to him detestable. He loathed London, and in any case he was in that state of fatigue of mind and body when all well-meant suggestions immediately make the sufferer want to do the opposite. He was being difficult, and knew it. So difficult did he know he was being that in pity for his family he decided to go and stay with his grandfather, Canon Fordyce of Torminster, and relieve them of his presence.

The family did not think it was a good idea. Torminster was a small Cathedral town in the depths of the country. so far away from everywhere and so difficult to get at that it could hardly be said to belong to the contemporary world at all, and it surely did not hold out much hope of advancement to a young man in search of a profession.

Grandfather, too, was hardly likely to be helpful. To begin with he was seventy-eight years old and to go on with he was one of the saints of God, and as such tragically lacking in sound financial judgment and that taking of thought for the morrow that produces a fat balance at the bank and the ability to assist impecunious relations.

"Anyhow Grandfather is restful," said Jocelyn to his protesting family, "and a Cathedral town is at least quiet. . . . Not all this beastly traffic thundering by outside the window so that you can't even hear yourself curse. . . . No, I tell you that I do *not* want help in packing my bag. Hang it all, I'm not blind, lunatic and incapable because I have a game leg."

His temper, always so sunny in the past, was now distinctly overcast, and when he had taken it and himself and his bag off in a cab to the station his exhausted family heaved sighs of relief and took tickets for the theatre to celebrate his departure.

II

And now, after a railway journey of unbelievable slowness and intricacy, Jocelyn was nearly at Torminster. He had never been there before, for Grandfather's working life had been spent in the slums of a North Country town, and the thought of seeing old friends in a new place, like a prized jewel in a fresh setting, was sufficiently exciting to pierce like a shaft of light into his dark mind.

There would be Grandfather himself, and Grandmother, a forcible old lady who had spent a busy and exhausting life trying to counteract the effect upon the family finances of Grandfather's saintliness, and the orphaned grandson who lived with them, Jocelyn's cousin Hugh Anthony whom he had seen last as a baby, and the little girl they had adopted to keep him company. . . . Just like the lovable stupidity of Grandfather to adopt yet another child in his old age. . . . And there would be the elderly servants, Ellen and Sarah, who had spoilt him so when he was a boy, suffering his booby-traps with admirable patience and letting him lick the jam-spoons after breakfast.

And these beloved people would be living not in the middle of smoke and noise and poverty, but in peace and beauty, in a setting that matched the personalities they had created through their years of hard work. That was as it should be, Jocelyn thought, for who should dare to live in the middle of peace and beauty who has not earned it?

As though to prepare him for the city that lay at its heart the country was becoming more and more beautiful. It was that moment of spring when the world is pink and blue in the distance and yellow and white close at hand. Blue hills were piled against the sky in shapes more lovely than a man can build and the woods that lay at their feet or crept up their sides had all flushed rosily at the kiss of the spring. The gorse was in riotous bloom and each green field broke at its edge into a froth of blossoming blackthorn. The primroses were in flower and the larks were singing. It was a still, warm day after rain, and delicious smells came to Jocelyn through the window, the smell of the gorse and the wallflowers in the cottage gardens, the smell of wood smoke and freshly turned earth and rain-washed grass and fresh beginnings. A pity to be tired of life in such a world, thought Jocelyn. If the old earth could wash herself and begin again so often and so humbly why could not a man do the same?

The train swung round a bend, the blue hills parted like a curtain and the city of Torminster was visible. Seen from a little distance it had a curiously unsubstantial air, as though it were something real yet intangible, a thing you could see but not touch. It lay in a hollow of the hills like a child in its mother's lap, and it seemed that as it lay there it slept. It looked so quiet that it was hard to believe the ordinary life of men and women went on in its streets. Rather it seemed a buried city sunk at the bottom of the sea, where no life stirred and no sound was heard but the ringing of the bells as the tide surged through forgotten towers and steeples. Jocelyn could see a confused mass of roofs and chimneys and church-spires, some high and some low, weather-stained and twisted by age into fantastic shapes. The smoke from the chimneys went straight up into the windless air and then seemed to dissolve into a mist that lay over the city like the waves of the sea that had drowned it, and out of this sea rose a grey rock with three towers. . . . The Cathedral. . . . It stood there gloriously, its majesty softened by the warm day but not diminished, its towers a little withdrawn in the sky yet no less watchful.

III

Jocelyn realized with something of a shock that the train was standing still in a perfectly ordinary station. Machines holding matches and chocolates faced him, and a beery porter was obligingly withdrawing his bag from beneath his legs. He had for a moment seen the real Torminster, the spiritual thing that the love of man for a certain spot of earth had created through long centuries, but now he was back again in the outward seeming of the place. Torminster, he supposed, would have dustbins like other towns, and a horrible network of drains beneath it, and tax collectors and public-houses. It might even look ugly in a March east wind and smell abominably stuffy on an August night, but these unpleasant things would now never matter much to him for he would feel towards Torminster as one feels towards a human being when one has, if only once, seen the soul flickering in the eyes.

"Take the bus," Grandfather had said and Jocelyn accordingly took it. The Torminster bus, once experienced, was never forgotten. In shape and colour it was like a pumpkin and its designer had apparently derived inspiration from the immortal conveyance that took Cinderella to the ball. It was pulled by two stout bay horses and driven by Mr. Gotobed, a corpulent gentleman clothed in bottle-green with a wonderful top-hat poised adroitly on the back of the head. His face was red, his whiskers pronounced and his language rich. . . . He and the Dean together were the outstanding figures of Torminster.

"Get in, sir," he said genially to Jocelyn. "I was ordered for you by the reverend gentleman. Fine day. Come on with that luggage, 'Erb. One gentleman for the Close and four buff orpingtons for The Green Dragon."

Jocelyn was established on one of the two wooden seats that ran the length of the bus, with the buff orpingtons complaining of their lot and straining agitated necks through the slats of their crate on the seat opposite him.

"All aboard?" continued Mr. Gotobed, as though they were bound for the North Pole. "'Eave up the gentleman's bag, 'Erb; we can't sit 'ere all night while you calculate 'ow many drinks you've 'ad since Christmas."

'Erb heaved up the bag and slammed the door while Mr. Gotobed climbed to the box, flourished his whip, laid it across the backs of the horses, told 'Erb what he thought of his ancestry and set the pumpkin in violent motion.

The outcry of the buff orpingtons was now drowned for the wheels of the bus were solid and the streets of Torminster in many places cobbled. Jolting through it, and shut away from the subdued hum of its life by the walls of the bus, Torminster once more seemed to Jocelyn to lack

everyday reality. The soft, moist air was the atmosphere
of dreams and the old houses that lined the streets seemed
to be leaning forward a little, as though drowsily nodding.
The bus made such a noise that the few vehicles that passed
them went by unheard and the handful of passers-by,
though their lips moved and their feet trod the quiet pave-
ments, were silent as the dead. Down the side of the sloping
High Street, as they climbed up it, a little stream came
hurrying down to meet them and Jocelyn gazed at it enchanted. Its water was clear and sparkling as crystal and
it must have come down from the hills that surrounded
Torminster. The bus stopped for a brief, respectful
moment, to let the Archdeacon's plum-pudding dog cross
the street, and he could hear the stream's ripple and
gurgle. . . . What bliss, he thought, to keep a shop in Torminster and do business to the sound of running water and
the chiming of bells.

The High Street ended abruptly and they were in the
Market Place, a wide, open square surrounded by tall old
houses with shops below them. There was no one in the
Market Place, except one old gentleman and two cats, and
the peace of this centre of industrial life was complete.
In the centre was a holy well that had been there before
either the city or the Cathedral had come into being. A
high parapet had been built round it, with a canopy overhead, and if you wanted to look inside the well you had to
mount a flight of steps. The water, that welled up no one
knew how far down in the earth, was always inky black
and when you leaned over to look in you could see your
own face looking back at you. Sometimes it stirred with a
mysterious movement and then the sunlight that pierced
through the carved canopy touched it with shifting, broken
points of light like stars. There were always pigeons
wheeling round the holy well, the reflection of their wings
passing over it like light. There were pigeons there now,

and it seemed to Jocelyn that their wings splintered the veiled sunshine into falling showers.

The bus clattered round the Market Place and stopped with a flourish in front of The Green Dragon. It was a small hotel and public-house combined, its old woodwork glistening with new paint and its windows shining with prosperity. The dragon, his scales painted emerald green, and scarlet fire belching from his nostrils, pranced upon an azure ground over the porch. Here it seemed that they would wait a long time, for Mr. Gotobed, after the exhaustion of carrying in the buff orpingtons, stopped inside to refresh himself.

Jocelyn got out and strolled a little way up the pavement, and then stopped stock still and stared. The most important moments of a lifetime seem always to arrive out of the blue and it was here that Jocelyn, his thoughts objectively busy with this Hans Andersen city, experienced a subjective moment that startled him like a thunderclap.

Between the tall Green Dragon and the equally tall bakery two doors off was wedged a little house only two stories high. Its walls were plastered and pale pink in colour and its gabled roof was tiled with wavy tiles and ornamented with cushions of green moss. There were two gables, with a small window in each, and under them was a green door with two white, worn steps leading up to it. A large bow-window was to the right of the door and a smaller one to the left. There was something particularly attractive about the bow-window. It reflected the light in every pane, so that it looked alive and dancing, and it bulged in a way that suggested that the room behind was crammed so full of treasures that they were trying to press their way out. But yet it was in reality quite empty, for Jocelyn could see the bare floor and the walls papered with a pattern of rose-sprigs. Behind the house he thought that there must be a garden for the top of a tall apple-tree was just visible behind the wavy roof.

The house affected him oddly. He was first vividly conscious of it and then overwhelmingly conscious of himself. His own personality seemed enriched by it and he felt less painfully aware of his own shortcomings, less afraid of the business of living that lay in front of him. He had felt like this once before, at the beginning of an important friendship.

"Why is that house empty?" he asked Mr. Gotobed, when that worthy returned to his duties wiping his mouth with the back of his hand.

"Because the gentleman what 'ad it 'as gone away and no one else ain't taken it, sir," explained Mr. Gotobed patiently.

"But why has no one taken it?"

"No drains," said Mr. Gotobed briefly, and climbed to his box.

Jocelyn was now the only passenger left in the bus as they completed the circuit of the Market Place and turned to their right up a steep street at a smart pace. Then they turned to their right a second time and passed under a stone archway into the Close.

Instantly it seemed that they had come to the very centre of peace. In the town beyond the archway there had been the peacefulness of laziness, but here there was the peace of an ordered life that had continued for so long in exactly the same way that its activity had become effortless. Outside in the town new methods of buying and selling might conceivably be drowsily adopted, or some slight modernization of the lighting system might take place after a year's slow discussion of the same, but inside the Close the word "new" was unknown. Modernity had not so far touched it and even to admit the fear that it might do so seemed sacrilege.

Jocelyn, as the bus rolled along, looked across a space of

green grass, elm-bordered, to the grey mass of the Cathedral. Its towers rose four-square against the sky and the wide expanse of the west front, rising like a precipice, was crowded with sculptured figures. They stood in their ranks, rising higher and higher, kings and queens and saints and angels, remote and still. About them the rooks were beating slowly and over their heads the bells were ringing for five o'clock evensong. Behind the Cathedral rose a wooded hill, brilliantly green now with its spring leaves, the Tor from which the city took its name.

"What a place!" ejaculated Jocelyn, and held on to the seat in delighted excitement. To his left, on the opposite side of the road to the Cathedral, was another, smaller mass of grey masonry, the Deanery, and in front of him was a second archway.

Once through it they were in a discreet road blocked on each side with gracious old houses standing back in walled gardens. Here dwelt the Canons of the Cathedral with their respective wives and families, and the few elderly ladies of respectable antecedents, blameless life and orthodox belief who were considered worthy to be on intimate terms with them.

The bus stopped with a jolt at Number Two the Close and Jocelyn got out in front of a blue door in a wall so high that only a grey roof and the tops of some trees could be seen above the wallflowers that grew on top of it. He felt the thrill of excitement inseparable from a walled house and garden; for a house behind railings has no secrets, but a home behind walls holds one knows not what. He opened the door and went in, and Mr. Gotobed, following him with his bag, banged it shut. There was something irrevocable in its clanging and Jocelyn felt that the old life was now dead indeed. Something new was beginning for him and this lovely garden was its starting point.

IV

He stood on a flagged path bordered with pink and white hyacinths and all round him spread a glory of colour and scent. The Torminster gardens had been tended and loved for generations and they all had an amazing luxuriance. Red wallflowers, red and yellow primulas, forget-me-nots, squat apple-trees studded with coral buds, flowering cherry-trees, lilacs and laburnums and syringa bushes were all jumbled together in glorious confusion. On a little patch of lawn to the right grew a mulberry-tree as old as time, its heavy, weary limbs propped up by stakes, and behind the house, where the kitchen-garden was, a cedar-tree towered up against the sky like a blue-black mountain.

The house faced Jocelyn as he walked up the path. It was old and grey and solid, its walls half hidden by creepers and its small, diamond-paned windows so withdrawn among them that nothing could be seen of the rooms inside. It would have looked like a farmhouse but for the extraordinary apparition of a tall grey tower that shot up at one side of it.

It was an astonishing house. When Jocelyn had walked up the flagged path between the flower-beds, and stooped beneath the branches of an apple-tree, he found himself under the porch in front of the open door looking down a flight of steps into what seemed a dark cellar. The walls of the house, he noticed, were three feet thick and the smell of damp was overpowering. He rang the bell and, as his eyes grew accustomed to the darkness, he saw that the cellar was a large, stone-paved, vaulted hall, with no light in it except what filtered through the curtain of wistaria that hung down over the porch. Pots of flowers stood in the corners, their scent unsuccessfully fighting the smell of damp, and a row of candles stood on an oak chest.

"What a place!" murmured Jocelyn again. "Like a chapel."

"The 'ouse is Norman in parts, they say," said Mr. Gotobed. "Full of 'istoric interest if damp. I wouldn't live 'ere meself if you paid me for it, dammit, no. But the gentry are different. They don't object to the rheumatics if caused by 'istory."

A door opened at the farther end of the hall and Sarah appeared, her purple silk apron a glorious splash of colour in the shadows. Sarah was tall and gaunt, with grey hair strained back from a grim, determined countenance. She had a heart of gold, though she kept it hidden, and her preference was for the gloomy side of life rather than the sunny one.

"Mr. Jocelyn," she exclaimed sepulchrally, but there was a gleam of affection behind her glasses.

"How well you look, Sarah," said Jocelyn cheerfully, shaking hands. "Years younger than when I saw you last." The temptation to annoy Sarah by taking an optimistic view was one he had never been able to resist.

"I'm far from well, sir," said Sarah, "the damp of this 'ouse being something cruel, but I keep up for the sake of others. . . . You can take that bag the 'ole way up the back stairs, Gotobed, and not 'alf-way up, as you did last time we 'ad a visitor. . . . Come this way, sir, tea's ready. You'll find the master and mistress much aged, but you must expect that."

She unlatched a door on the left that opened on a flight of uncarpeted stairs and led him up, stumbling in the half-dark, until they reached a landing and the door to the drawing-room.

It was a small, square room panelled in dark wood, with windows looking on the garden. It was Grandmother's room and held the battered treasures that had accompanied her through her arduous working life; her Victorian chairs with their scratched legs and cross-stitch seats worked by herself when young, her miniatures and books and faded antimacassars, her few bits of old china and the two shells that sounded like the sea when you held them to your ears. Not a very beautiful collection, perhaps, but part of Grandmother and therefore priceless.

She sat bolt upright in her arm-chair on one side of the wood fire that was burning in the grate, knitting woollen stockings for the heathen, with Grandfather opposite her in his arm-chair with his hands folded across his stomach, and at sight of them the love that Jocelyn had for them both, compounded of gratitude and amusement and reverence, burnt up as freshly as though he had seen them last only yesterday.

Grandmother was small and withered and gave the impression of having shed everything in her passage through life except the essence of herself, and that a sharp, decided, wholesome essence. Her twinkling black eyes were like a bird's, and as sharp as needles, and her little parchment-coloured face was wrinkled into a thousand lines of humour and decision and common-sensible strong-mindedness. Her iron-grey hair was arranged in corkscrew curls, the fashion of a past age, and on her head was a cap with purple bows. Her grey dress was of great age and made of alpaca so stiff that it could surely stand by itself, and her hands were mittened. She was eighty years old but neither age nor bereavement nor hard work had in the least dimmed her vitality or stemmed the flow of her fluent, emphatic talk.

Grandfather, who was only seventy-eight and the youngest of the Canons, was quite different. He, too, was very short, but he was the reverse of withered. He was very round indeed. Yet the curves of his person did not suggest either indolence or laziness, they suggested rather a tolerant mind and a large heart, and his round, rosy face bore the unmistakable stamp of personal control and austerity, a stamp that is like clarity in the atmosphere, a thing that you cannot describe but only rejoice in. The eyes behind his powerful, double-lensed glasses were pale blue and slightly astonished, as though he had never ceased to be surprised at the beauty of the world. . . . He was as bald as an egg, but had a little white jutting beard of the type that is usually seen upon the chins of gnomes.

Yet there were a few people in Torminster who did not like him, for he had developed the habit of unconsciously speaking his thoughts aloud, a trait which endeared him to none but those rare lovers of sincerity who really enjoy hearing the truth about themselves. His life in the slums had implanted in him a slight tendency to think that the well-to-do exaggerated the trials of their existence, and also a tendency to get a little impatient if the Cathedral Chapter at its Chapter meetings talked for more than one hour on the subject of Canon Roderick's right of way through Canon Elphinstone's seakale bed, which Canon Roderick said existed and Canon Elphinstone said did not. "Bless my soul!" he would say suddenly in the middle of a Chapter meeting, "what a fuss about nothing! Send 'em all down a coal-mine, dear God, send 'em all down a coal-mine." And then he would smile sweetly at the sudden silence that fell, blissfully unaware that he had given tongue. And it was the same at tea-parties, when he might remark *sotto voce* on the poorness of the tea, and sometimes it was the same in the middle of the Sunday morning anthem at the Cathedral, when he would ejaculate loudly, "Is this what they call modern music? Dreadful! Dreadful!"

v

"Mr. Jocelyn," said Sarah, and left them together.

The welcome that the two old people gave to their grandson was typical of them. Grandfather bounced to his feet and hurried forward delightedly, his hand out and his whole face beaming. Here, his manner implied, was the one person whom of all others he was most anxious to see and in whose welfare he was most interested. And there was no insincerity in his welcome. His interest in his fellow-creatures was so deep that whoever was with him at the moment seemed to him to be the very best of God's creatures. . . . And Jocelyn was his favourite grandson.

Grandmother, meanwhile, sat in her chair very stiffly, her hands folded on her knitting, and waited to see how Jocelyn had developed before committing herself. Her bright eyes darted critically over him, noting his fair, close-cut hair and moustache, his trim figure, well-brushed clothes and slight air of fatigue.

"Humph," she said, "you're improved. More like your dear mother and less like your father, thank God. I never could take to your father, good man of business though he is."

"Dear Jane," murmured Grandfather, "there is good in all."

"I didn't say there wasn't," said Grandmother, "I merely said that I don't take to the good in Thomas. . . . You dress better than you did, Jocelyn. When you were at Oxford you were a radical, I remember, and dressed accordingly. I told your mother what I thought about it at the time but she said she had no influence. I will say for the Army that it teaches the compatibility of a sense of duty with a crease in the trousers. . . . You may kiss me, Jocelyn."

His kiss produced one of her rare moments of softening and she touched his cheek gently with one of her dainty, mittened hands. "You look tired, dear boy," she said. "You'd better be fed up. I'm sorry about your leg but, as I said to your grandfather, it's a mercy it wasn't your stomach or your brain. Given belief in God, a good digestion and a mind in working order life's still a thing to be grateful for."

She abruptly stopped talking and became engrossed in the ritual of tea-making, her little hands hovering over the old silver and Worcester cups and saucers. A hush fell, the steam from the tea-kettle rose into the air like incense and the fragrance of China tea mingled with the scent of flowers. Jocelyn leant back restfully in his chair, feeling life halt a little and its grip on him relax. It seemed no longer a river in spate, whirling him along without time for thought or feeling, but a calm backwater where the opening of a flower and the song of a bird would be important and significant.

"Does time ever pass in Torminster?" he asked Grand-father.

"Dear me, no, dear boy, nothing ever passes here. The past steps into the background, of course, but it never seems to disappear. . . . I think, dear Jane, that you are putting too much milk in Jocelyn's tea."

"It's a sleepy place," pronounced Grandmother. "I've started two working parties for Missions to wake them up a bit, but I never saw women make flannel petticoats so slowly in all my life. . . . Thank you, Theobald, but I am quite capable, at my age, of making a drinkable cup of tea. . . . Help yourself to bread and dripping, Jocelyn."

It was not perhaps usual to eat bread and dripping at afternoon tea but Grandfather liked bread and dripping and insisted upon having it, in spite of Grandmother's repeated assurances that it "was not done." It was his habit to do what he liked, whether it was "done" or not, provided that what he liked was compatible with his religion. . . . He did not eat dripping in Lent.

"Where's Hugh Anthony?" asked Jocelyn.

"Having his tea downstairs," said Grandfather. "We

find that best. He's eight years old and exhausting, though a dear boy. We've adopted a little girl to keep him company, thinking female influence might quiet him down, but there's little improvement noticeable as yet."

"Your grandfather's latest," said Grandmother in resigned tones. "He saw the child at that orphanage he's on the board of, liked her eyes and brought her straight home with nothing to her name but a Bible, three pinafores and a couple of vests. Did you ever hear anything so ridiculous?"

"I was guided to do it," said Grandfather.

"Well, all I can say is I hope someone will be guided to care for the poor children after our death," said Grandmother forcibly, and sighed. She had been married to a saint for fifty years but still found it as difficult to adjust herself as she had done in the first month of her marriage, when he had given away their bed to a woman whose need, he felt, was greater than theirs.

"When that dear child's eyes met mine," said Grandfather, "I knew that her welfare was my responsibility. . . . I have sometimes thought, dear Jane, that, should Jocelyn marry, he might, after our death, feel guided to take upon him the fatherhood of both those dear children."

"Well," said Jocelyn doubtfully, "you never know."

"Not until the time comes," said Grandfather happily. "So, as I say to your dear grandmother, why worry beforehand?"

The atmosphere felt a little tense and to lighten it Jocelyn asked them about the house in the Market Place. "Who lived there?" he asked. "It's a jolly little house. It's a crime it should be empty."

All the happiness drained away from Grandfather's face, leaving him looking stricken and old, and it was Grandmother who answered.

"A young man called Gabriel Ferranti lived there," she

said. "He looked like an organ-grinder and wrote books
that nobody could make head or tail of, and was considered
to be clever for those reasons, though why untidy hair and
an inability to make oneself understood should be the hall-
mark of genius I have never been able to understand. Your
grandfather took a great fancy to him; what for I don't
know."

"There was great good in him," murmured Grandfather
sadly.

"What happened to him?" asked Jocelyn.

"He got into the financial difficulties that were only to
be expected of a young man with a name like that," said
Grandmother, "and disappeared just as your poor grandfather was trying to bring out the good in him. Your
grandfather naturally took it all very much to heart, for
goodness only knows what has become of the young man
now, or of the good that your poor grandfather thought
he was bringing out."

"If he had only told me about his difficulties," mourned
Grandfather, "I could have relieved them."

"What with?" asked Grandmother a little sharply. "I'm
thankful the young person had the good taste to disappear
before you'd given him our last halfpenny. . . . If Jocelyn's
finished his tea take him to his room while I get on with my
knitting."

The two men went out together while Grandmother's
voice drifted after them in its habitual chant of, "Knit
one, purl one, knit two together."

VI

Jocelyn followed Grandfather's squat black figure and
bald head up to the final stairs to the spare-room. It was a
perfect panelled room with three windows looking out on

the garden. Old oak beams crossed the white-washed ceiling and in each of the four corners of the room was a carved wooden seraph with two wings covering his feet, two folded across his breast and two outspread behind him. There was no carpet on the oak floor that rose and fell like the waves of the sea, and no pictures on the walls, and the furniture was limited to the barest necessities.

"This is perhaps more of a monk's room than a soldier's," said Grandfather, "but you must remember that Torminster was once a monastery and the Close is the coffin that holds its bones. Some people find this house frightening. The bones of the skeleton show through too clearly, they say, and the damp smell makes them think of death."

"How old is this house?" asked Jocelyn.

"It belongs to all time. The hall and kitchen and larder are Norman, the tower is fifteenth century and this room has an eighteenth-century powdering closet. . . . But my greenhouse is pure Victorian. . . . Have you everything you want?"

"Everything but peace of mind," said Jocelyn unexpectedly and blushed crimson.

He remembered of old that Grandfather's effect upon him was always to make him say exactly what was in his mind. . . . An embarrassing effect. . . . Such people as Grandfather, possessed of a sincerity as catching as measles, shouldn't be allowed about loose in a world where the wearing of a mask was good form.

Grandfather sat down at the foot of the bed and folded his hands across his stomach, always a sign that he was giving a subject his serious consideration. The expression of his face changed from one of trouble to one of deep attention, as Ferranti's disappearance passed from his mind and Jocelyn's mental condition took its place.

"Peace is as essential to mental health, dear boy, as light to human life. What has happened to yours?"

"Mislaid it in South Africa," said Jocelyn bitterly. "My work's gone and I don't know what to do. How can a man be peaceful when he has no future?"

"Don't talk nonsense," said Grandfather almost sharply. "We've all a future. You don't know in what direction yours lies, that's all, and you've not the patience to wait and see which way the wind blows."

"The wind?" asked Jocelyn.

"Our destiny is like a wind blowing," said Grandfather. "It carries us along. But now and again the wind seems to drop. We don't know what to do next. Then it may be that a blade of grass growing in the road beside us bends slightly. It is a tiny movement, slight as a whim, but enough to show us which way to take."

Jocelyn smiled at Grandfather affectionately. "If we were all to yield to our whims," he said, "we'd do some pretty crazy things. I, for instance, would start a shop in Torminster."

"Would you like to start a shop in Torminster?"

"It's an idea that occurred to me as I drove up the High Street."

"Then start it."

Jocelyn laughed. "I was only joking, Grandfather. How could I start a shop with no capital and no experience and no business capacity?"

Grandfather unclasped his hands and rose sighing to his feet. He feared that Jocelyn was in a difficult frame of mind, depressed and restless, and this was hardly the moment to induce him to see reason.

"Stay here and do nothing," he advised him. "Stay a year if you like. What does it matter? It's often necessary in life to do nothing, but so few people do it nicely. And as for peace, there's plenty of it in this house and in this town. They are so weighted with age that they have, as it were, fallen below the surface of time, like a buried city below the sea. ... Fall with them. ... Dear me, I must go and say evensong or I shall be late for dinner, and that distresses your dear grandmother."

Left alone Jocelyn unpacked slowly, discovered the powdering closet, hardly bigger than a cupboard, where long ago some hooped and panniered lady had silvered her hair with powder, put a round black patch on her chin, rouge on her cheeks and rings on her fingers. ... What a fuss about nothing her toilet must have been! ... But perhaps she was one of those people who do nothing so nicely that it becomes something. As he arranged his books on the shelf in the closet he pictured her to himself, slim and golden-haired, clothed in silk that rustled like autumn leaves, tremendously absorbed, as she powdered and patched and laced, in the creation of beauty.

And longer ago still his room was part of the monastery. Some monk sat here, perhaps, making a missal, painting into it purple pansies and ivory roses and queer little animals with long legs and scarlet tongues, the great-grandfathers of the dragons who pranced on the signboard in the Market Place. And the monk, as he painted a blue sky behind his ivory roses and put golden scrolls round the animals' legs, would have been as absorbed in the making of a beautiful thing as the lady with her rouge-pot and her jewel-case. ... And on them both the winged seraphim would have looked down, and for them both the time that in Torminster did not pass away but only stepped into the background would have been measured into golden lengths by the chiming of bells.

Jocelyn realized that for him too bells were ringing, for the Cathedral clock was striking seven and he must change for dinner. On the last stroke Sarah knocked at his door and entered with hot water. She did everything by the Cathedral clock. When it chimed half-past six she put the kettle on. When it chimed a quarter to seven she slowly filled the cans and toiled up the stairs to the room where Grandfather and Grandmother slept, where she laid out their evening things on their fourposter and dumped their hot water into the basins with resounding bangs, just as the first stroke of seven rang out. . . . On the last stroke of seven she knocked at the spare-room door. . . . It was all a very serious ritual and she stumped across the room to Jocelyn's washstand with the solemnity of a priest approaching the shrine of the oracle.

"You've laid out your own things," she said severely. "*I* do that."

"I'm sorry, Sarah," said Jocelyn meekly. "But you see I was unpacking and I thought it would save you trouble."

"Trouble!" snorted Sarah. "That's what I'm here for. Life's made up of trouble. You must expect that. . . . I expect you find the master and mistress sadly changed?"

"I don't see the slightest difference in them, Sarah," said Jocelyn. "They never change."

"Ah," said Sarah, "you don't live with them as I do and see them going down 'ill steady. I 'ope the dinner will be eatable but Ellen's very 'eavy-'anded with the pastry owing to 'aving been thrown over by the butcher which, as I tell 'er, it's not to be expected that a man should keep faithful to a woman of 'er age, but it takes a light 'eart to make light pastry and it's we that are the sufferers, as is only to be expected when you remember that in this world the innocent suffer for the guilty. . . . Dinner's at a quarter to eight, sir."

She stalked away again and Jocelyn was left to embark upon the second shave of the day. It was quite unnecessary but he was fastidious, one of those people whose private as well as whose public moments are controlled and decorous. Without consciously realizing it he liked to make each trivial act of life a thing of individual perfection, and in this he was linked to the monk and the lady.

He was immersed in white lather when there was a

sudden pattering of bare feet outside his door, which burst
open with no preliminary knock to admit a small boy with
freckles and flaming red hair. He cast one glance at Jocelyn
and dashed out again, leaving the door open and shouting
at the full force of his lungs, "Come on, Henrietta, he's
shaving!"

Before Jocelyn had time to draw breath Hugh Anthony
was back again with Henrietta. They had evidently arisen
from their beds for they were clothed in white nightgown
and nightshirt and were barefooted. They leapt on to his
bed with the agility of young rabbits and leant over its foot
as though it were the front rail of the dress circle, their eyes
bulging and their mouths ajar. Jocelyn realized that, for
the first time in his life, he was an exciting entertainment.
The parental toilet was, he had heard, as good as a circus
to the Edwardian young, but these children, fatherless and
with a bearded grandfather, had up till now missed one of
the chief thrills in life. He flourished his razor and prepared to do his best. While he did it there was no sound but
deep, ecstatic breathing, and when he had finished there was
a long-drawn sigh of satisfaction.

"There! He's done!" said Hugh Anthony. "Did you
think it would be like that, Henrietta?"

"I thought it would make more noise," said Henrietta,
"like when Bates cuts the grass."

"I expect he hadn't got enough beard," said Hugh
Anthony. "Now if Grandfather started shaving I dare say
it would be more noisy."

Jocelyn put on his coat and turned round to survey the
couple.

Hugh Anthony at eight years old was compact and
rounded like his grandfather. His blue, astonished eyes
were also like his grandfather's, but his circular face, dusted
all over with golden freckles, his turned-up nose and flaming
red hair were all his own. Quite his own too was his look

B

of perpetual inquiry. His whole body seemed at times to be curved into the shape of a question-mark and the word "why?" was seldom off his lips. The house rang with it from the moment he woke up in the morning until the he fell asleep with his final question still vibrating in the air of the silent, unanswering night.

"Why don't you grow a beard?" he asked Jocelyn.

"I've been a soldier," said Jocelyn, "and in the Army it is the fashion to have a moustache only."

"Why?"

"To distinguish soldiers from sailors, who are either clean-shaven or have beards."

"Why?"

"It's just the fashion."

"Why?"

"I don't know."

"Why don't you know?"

Henrietta pushed Hugh Anthony face downward on the bed and seated herself upon the small of his back where, enthroned in grace, she smiled sweetly at Jocelyn. She was a child of few words but all her actions were quick, decisive and to the point.

She was an astonishing creature, not conventionally beautiful but with a grace and a certain luminous quality that were far more arresting than the usual nine-year-old female chubbiness. She was small and thin with long-fingered hands and slender feet. Her brown eyes were curiously changeable with her moods, sometimes blazing with light and sometimes opaquely dark, as though the spirit behind them were a newly lit flame so sensitive that a breath of joy or sorrow could fan it into a blaze or extinguish it altogether. Her face, small and pointed, rising from the toby frill of her nightgown like a flower from its calyx and very pale against her straight dark hair, made Jocelyn think of white jasmine.

"I hope we are not intruding," she said politely to Jocelyn. Her voice was curiously deep for a child, with a ringing note in it that was very beautiful.

"Not at all," said Jocelyn. "I am honoured."

"Grandfather says Hugh Anthony is to call you uncle," she said. "Do I call you uncle too even though I'm only adopted?"

"Please," said Jocelyn. "Until now I have had no niece. It's a dreadful thing, you know, to have no niece."

He came close to the bed and smiled down at her, and instantly, with her answering smile, her whole being seemed to come flooding into her face. She was giving him her friendship with the lovely abandonment of childhood that has not learned yet to hold back for fear the love given should be scorned. Jocelyn, in this his first close contact with a child, felt not so much touched as stabbed. This trustfulness and fragility were almost terrifying, for how in the world, as children grew from childhood to maturity and the bloom was rubbed off them, did the sensitive spirit itself escape destruction? . . . Well, sometimes it did but sometimes it did not. . . . And the man who destroyed it? "It were better for him that a millstone were hanged about his neck, and that he were drowned in the depth of the sea." Heaven above, what an alarming thing it must be to be a parent!

But at this moment Hugh Anthony, whose ordinary temperament was always a relief after Henrietta's emotional one, became tired of lying on his face with his mouth full of eiderdown and abruptly heaved up his posterior. Henrietta rolled off the bed to the floor on one side and Hugh Anthony on the other.

"Did you bring your sword?" he asked, while still in a recumbent position.

"No," said Jocelyn.

"Why not?"

"I didn't think I should have any use for it."

"But we could have played at St. George and the Dragon with it, you being the Dragon and me George."

"I'm sorry," said Jocelyn. "I never thought of that."

"Then you should have," said Hugh Anthony severely. "You should have remembered when you packed that I should have wanted to see your sword. Grandfather says that every morning in one's cold bath one should say to oneself, 'Now what can I do for others to-day?'"

The gong rang.

"Hadn't you two kids better go to bed?" inquired Jocelyn.

"We don't go properly to bed till it's dark," said Henrietta, sitting up on the floor and re-plaiting her hair. "We're put there and then we get out again. Come on, Hugh Anthony, we'll go up to the top of the tower and see the stars come out. We'll take Uncle Jocelyn's eiderdown."

They departed as suddenly as they had come, trailing the eiderdown after them like clouds of glory.

VII

Dinner was eaten placidly in the dim old dining-room downstairs. Grandfather wore his dinner-jacket, which had been new twenty years ago and had had to be let out considerably since with new material that did not match the old, so that Grandfather had a very odd striped appearance. Grandmother wore her black silk, which had been recently turned by Sarah so that it looked as good as new, the lace fichu that had belonged to her grandmother and her gold locket containing a lock of the golden hair that Grandfather had, astonishingly, once had.

They ate boiled fowl, a rhubarb tart that was all that

could be expected of Ellen in her jilted state, water-biscuits and bananas.

After dinner Grandfather and Grandmother slept in their arm-chairs, waking up now and again to ask Jocelyn if his poor mother had found a cook yet. Jocelyn read a *Punch* that was several months old, said no, his mother hadn't got a cook yet and the kitchen-maid was leaving, and wondered if the time would come when he might find the peace of Torminster a little monotonous. . . . It might, but it had not done so yet.

When ten o'clock struck Grandfather and Grandmother woke up abruptly, said to each other, "Was that ten, dear?" and got up. Jocelyn lit the bedroom candles that stood on a table outside the drawing-room door and gave his arm to Grandmother, who was a little tottery with sleep. She would, if the truth were told, have liked to go to bed every night at nine but she never had gone to bed before ten and felt that, unless she was unwell, it would be self-indulgent to indulge the wish. The notes of the clock rang out one by one into the silence as the procession mounted the stairs, Grandfather bringing up the rear with the best silver teapot in a green baize bag. . . . Grandmother kept it by day beside her in her work-basket in the drawing-room, and by night under her bed. . . . The last note was sounding as Jocelyn kissed her good night.

"Good night, dear," she murmured sleepily. "See that the lamp in the drawing-room is properly out. Your poor grandfather is not to be trusted."

Grandfather was oblivious of either of them. Though the teapot was dangling from one hand and his lighted candle, held askew and dropping grease on the floor, was in the other, he was already saying the last office of the day. "Turn Thou us, oh God our Saviour," he murmured, "and let Thine anger cease from us. Oh God, make speed to save us; oh Lord, make haste to help us."

Jocelyn, having piloted him in and shut the door on him, stood outside on the stairs listening.

"Hear me when I call, oh God of my righteousness: Thou hast set me at liberty when I was in trouble; have mercy upon me and hearken unto my prayer."

It pleased him to imagine that the voice was no longer the voice of Grandfather but that of the painting monk of his fancy. Then it seemed to him that the sound swelled and became not one voice but many. Not far away, perhaps in the chapel-like hall, the light of tapers gleamed on brown habits and tonsured heads and a carved crucifix that hung in the shadows.

"I will lay me down in peace and take my rest, for it is Thou, Lord, only, that makest me dwell in safety."

He strolled happily to his room but on beholding his bed his peaceful mood turned to rage, for the children had come back in his absence and denuded it of everything except the sheets and the mattress. There was nothing for it but to sally forth with his candle into the dark and find the young demons.

And finding anything in this house was not easy for it seemed to have no geographical plan. Odd flights of steps ended at locked doors, twisting passages with wavy floors led apparently nowhere, and it was not until he had been barking his shins on sharp corners for ten minutes that Jocelyn opened a door leading into a spiral stone staircase that evidently wound up from the kitchen regions to the top of the tower.

He toiled up, cursing the fate that made a lame man go for a ten-mile walk to find his bedclothes, until a gleam of light through an open door told him that he was at the top and he stepped out on to a flat, leaded space surrounded by a stone parapet.

And there, lying on his blankets and pillows and covered with his eiderdown, were Henrietta and Hugh Anthony, sleeping the sleep of an easy conscience.

They looked so delicious, with dark lashes lying on starlit faces and parted lips a little appealing in their relaxation, that Jocelyn postponed waking them to hear his avuncular remarks. Instead he sat down on the edge of the parapet, lit his pipe and drifted away again into the dreams that seemed to be a necessary part of existence in Torminster.

It was such a night as the gods in their niggardliness do not give often, so still that the sound of his own breathing seemed to him a desecration. The bowl of the sky was a deep blue, golden at its rim where the lights of the city stained it and hung across with a silver cord of stars. The towers of the Cathedral were black against it, like the crags of a mountain, and down in the dark garden the white hyacinths were stars in a reflected sky. The beauty was so unearthly that the thought of its passing was a pain. "Or ever the silver cord be loosed or the golden bowl be broken," muttered Jocelyn, and wished it were possible to draw beauty into oneself and preserve it unfadingly for ever.

If only, he thought, one could preserve as part of oneself the scenes and the events that were beautiful and get rid of all the others. His own memory now was a thing that he did not much care to look into. The horror of war, its futility and bestial cruelty, had injured his mind as a bursting shell had injured his body, leaving it sickened and vaguely aching. He wished he could forget South Africa. Looking back on his life in the Army it seemed to him now nothing but a wilderness of heat and bewilderment, and but for the emptiness and uncertainty of the future he thought that he would not have been sorry that it had ended. He had not, he thought, in spite of his wartime success, been a particularly good soldier. His bent of mind was a scholarly one and his outlook on life that of an artist. Regulations had irked him, and red tape, and that life of routine that so often stifles imagination.

Yet what was he to do with himself? His sense of beauty,

though deep, was not sufficiently strong to make an artist of him. It was not a sword driving him on to express it in poetry or music or painting, lest he die, it was rather that faculty of critical appreciation that can separate gold from dross. He had it in him to be a valuable friend both to creators blinded by the sweat of their own effort and to the wistful multitude who need an interpreter in the courts of the spirit. But he knew this only vaguely and the half-knowledge offered no solution to the problem of his future.

"I must be the worst sort of idiot," he said to himself bitterly. "A parasite and a drifter."

He watched the curls of smoke from his pipe wreathing aimlessly away and thought how like they were to his own life, drifting out into the night as he had drifted to this quiet town, and to that empty house and Henrietta.

His figure grew tense. Why had he thought of the house and Henrietta like that? Vividly, and connecting them together in his mind? He felt as though two threads that he must follow had been put into his hands. He was reminded of a game that they had played when they were children, a game they called "treasure hunt." They stood in the lighted hall and the end of a long coloured ribbon was given to each of them. They followed their ribbon all over the house, winding it into a ball as they went, up creaking stairs, through ghostly rooms and down terrifying passages, until at last the persevering and the courageous reached the end of their ribbon and found their treasure, a ball or a box of soldiers or a sugar pig.

Smiling to himself, suddenly hopeful and light-hearted, he knocked out his pipe and tweaked the eiderdown off Hugh Anthony.

CHAPTER II

I

REAL life had begun for Henrietta on the day that she came to Torminster. She had, of course, existed at the orphanage, she had slept and eaten and learnt her tables up to twelve times nine, but it had all seemed dark and queer and now, a year later, she could remember very little of it all except a lot of noise and hurry, the smell of boiled cod and windsor soap and the wart on Matron's chin. She had not been unhappy but she had not been alive. She had been like a jack-in-the-box inside his prison, with the lid smacked down on top, and it was not until Grandfather had lifted the lid that she had shot up into life and power and thought.

Never would she forget the first time that she saw Grandfather. She was sitting with the other children learning about the capes of England, where they stuck out far into the sea and where they did not stick out so far, what towns sat upon them and what towns did not, what counties they stuck out of and what seas they stuck out into, and Henrietta, like Galileo, cared for none of these things. . . . She was bored and though she did not know it she was starved. . . . And then the door had opened and Matron had come in, followed by Grandfather engaged in a tour of inspection. He sat on the board, they told her later, though what the board was and why he sat on it they omitted to explain. Henrietta for ever after had a mental vision of a see-saw and Grandfather sitting on one end of it with the Mayor, who was also on the board, on the other, and soaring to heaven and sinking again to earth with delighted chuckles.

When he and Matron came in Henrietta had been at first completely absorbed by the wart on Matron's chin, which always fascinated her, and then, suddenly, she was aware of Grandfather and her inside turned upside down.

The children had risen to their feet at a word from Matron and stood behind their desks with their hands at their sides, clothed all alike in hideous black overalls, with their hair tightly plaited in plaits that stuck out in horizontal lines at the sides of their heads. Henrietta was at the back of the room and so she was able to gaze at Grandfather as he walked between the lines of children, saying what Matron called "a kind word" to each. She gazed at his rounded form, his bald head, his white beard like a gnome's, his astonished blue eyes behind their powerful glasses, and she loved him.

Henrietta had a startling capacity for falling in love at first sight, but, though she was at this time eight years old, it had never before been used. Love was now flaming in her for the first time, a volcano in eruption. Would he, when he got to her desk, speak to her? What would he say? With her soul in her eyes she watched his every movement, his every fleeting expression and, as he came nearer to her, though he smiled and nodded and pinched the rosy cheeks of the orphans with every appearance of joviality, she had a feeling that he was unhappy.

Henrietta's instinct was, all her life, unerring, and it was not at fault now, for the orphanage always reduced Grandfather to complete misery. The dear little girls were happy, of course, well fed and well cared for and well educated, and later on they were planted out in situations of the utmost respectability, but yet . . . All those black pinafores. . . . And the unbecoming style of hairdressing. . . . Every child the same. . . . Flowers needed individual care, some wanting one sort of soil, some another, some wanting sun, some shade. Was it perhaps the same with children? If you treated them like so many ninepins in a row what happened to their individuality?

Mechanically pinching and smiling and saying kind words, but inwardly entirely wretched, he arrived at Henrietta and neither pinched nor smiled nor spoke, for Henrietta, her face luminous, was presenting him with her friendship. The effect upon him was much the same as it had been on Jocelyn and he felt not so much touched as stabbed. Then he pulled himself together, located the position of her desk and went on down the line pinching and smiling, and finally followed Matron out of the room, leaving Henrietta in a world where the sun had gone in and no birds sang.

But at the end of the lesson she was sent for to Matron's room and told that she must put on her hat at once and accompany Grandfather to the station, for he had adopted her.

Matron was in a frightful state, and no wonder. People had often told her that Canon Fordyce was "original," "eccentric," "a little touched in the upper story," "saintly," and so on, but this was the first time that she and his practical Christianity had come to a head-on crash.

"Most of Henrietta's clothes are at the wash," she said despairingly.

"I want the child, not her clothes."

"The case ought to go before the whole board for consideration."

"I'll deal with the board."

"I've never had such a thing happen before."

"Then it's high time it did. Routine will be the ruin of you good people," and Grandfather produced his watch and mentioned the time of his train, for the orphanage, though it was in the nearest big town to Torminster, was yet a long way from it, and the last train missed meant a night in the horrible place.

Though undoubtedly a saint Grandfather had the devil's own obstinacy, and Matron was annihilated. A cab was hastily fetched and Henrietta hurled in after him, together with her Bible, three pinafores and a couple of vests, the only bits of her portable property that Matron could seem to lay her hand on in the hurry of the moment.

Henrietta was perfectly serene about the whole business, too serene, Matron thought. Though she kissed Matron very politely on parting from her she showed no sorrow at leaving the institution that had sheltered her infancy. On the contrary, as the cab moved off, she was seen by Matron to be giving one of the ecstatic wriggles with which she always greeted the major joys of life, such as sausages for breakfast or the appearance of the first butterfly of the season.

But the wriggle over she gave no further sign of emotion and sat very still beside Grandfather as the cab rolled off to the station, so still that he was afraid she might be unhappy and looked anxiously down at her. She still wore her black overall, with black stockings and black button boots, her horizontal plaits stuck out on each side of her head, the hard black sailor hat which was at that time the fashionable headgear for orphans was tilted forward over her nose, and her hands were folded placidly on the Bible and underclothes that lay in her lap. . . . He was dreadfully afraid she was unhappy but he could not see if her eyes were wet because of her hideous hat. . . . He took it off, flinging it contemptuously on to the opposite seat, and then with his rheumaticky old hands he unplaited those detestable plaits. She looked up at him, waves of delight rippling over her face, and he saw that she was silent only from excess of joy.

The railway journey to Torminster was a delight to both of them, though their fellow-passengers thought they had never seen such a peculiar couple in all their days.

II

No words can describe what Henrietta felt about Torminster. She arrived, as a year later Jocelyn arrived, in the
spring, and if this was not Paradise she would have liked
to be told what was. The dreaming city, the west front
of the Cathedral with the rows of kings and queens and
saints, the wooded Tor, the gardens full of flowers, the
singing birds and chiming bells, the old house with its
carved angels, the humming High Street and the holy well,
these things did not belong to the world as Henrietta had
hitherto known it, the world of a cod-and-windsor-soap-
smelling orphanage in a big town, and she felt like one born
anew on a different planet.

And the people, too, she loved. When she and Grandfather presented themselves before Grandmother, on that
amazing day of the adoption, she was not in the least upset
by Grandmother's rather sharp greeting of, "And what in
the name of goodness have you got hold of this time,
Theobald?" Grandmother's bark, she saw at once, was a
great deal worse than her bite, and she very soon discovered
the intensely grandmotherly heart that operated within
Grandmother.

Sarah and Ellen were nice also, though rosy Ellen who
made her dough babies with currant eyes and let her wipe
out the mixing basin with her finger after a cake had been
made, was perhaps nicer than gaunt, gloomy Sarah.

Then there was Bates the gardener, who sometimes
allowed her to assist him in his labours, and Gotobed who
brought them their visitors in a yellow pumpkin and used
rich-sounding words such as "damn" and "blast" whose
meaning she did not know but whose solid sound gave her
a great deal of pleasure, and gentle Miss Lavender who
taught her and Hugh Anthony in the mornings, and the
Dean with his beautiful whiskers, and lots of others.

But Hugh Anthony was the best of all. She had up till now had nothing to do with the male young, for at the orphanage the sexes had been kept in watertight compartments, so that friendship with a little boy was a new experience for her and she found in it something that her friendships with little girls had never given her. She found his questioning mind, so different from her own, very stimulating, and his instinctively protecting attitude towards her was new and sweet. His rare kisses, too, were different from the kisses of little girls, more exciting and more worth while. He was her mate, her fairy lover, her perfect complement. She could not analyse her feelings but she knew that she loved him with her whole heart and soul and would until she died.

And then there were her lovely clothes. Those she had arrived in, the black hat and black pinafore, the button boots, the black serge bloomers, the thick woollen scratchy combinations that buttoned up under her chin and descended —having become distressingly elongated in the wash— half-way down her legs beneath the black woollen stockings, together with the three pinafores and two vests—the Bible was retained—were returned to Matron with Grandmother's compliments and in their place came clothes that seemed to Henrietta fit for a princess.

Smocks of periwinkle blue and rose-pink for everyday, with white muslin for Sundays, a soft white sailor hat, white socks and little brown sandals, petticoats with scalloped borders and combinations that were soft to the skin and descended no farther than the knee. Grandfather did not allow her to plait her hair, except at night; it hung loose, confined only by snoods of ribbon of the style affected by Alice in Wonderland.

And then there was her bedroom. It was a tiny room over the porch, as monastically furnished as Jocelyn's but with a population of six carved angels instead of four.

They were, however, baby angels, not stately seraphim. They had two wings only apiece and no bodies, poor little dears. Henrietta wondered what the originals up in heaven did about their food, stomachless as they were, but supposed God fed them somehow since these prototypes on earth, who had presumably been copied from the originals, were very fat in the face and jolly-looking. . . . Sometimes at night Henrietta would hear a rustling of wings in the dark and think they were flying round and round her bed, giggling and trying to catch each other. . . . It was probably only a bat.

But this little room, though it was meagrely supplied with the luxuries of life, always excepting angels, was rich in good smells. Wistaria covered the wall outside the window, and in the summer great bunches of blossoms, heavy and pendulous as grapes, filled the world with scent. But even when the wistaria was not in bloom the smells were delicious. In spring there were the hyacinths and all the summer through there were roses, in autumn came the sharp smell of chrysanthemums and the pungent scent of wood smoke and fallen leaves, and in winter there were perhaps the best smells of all, the faint scent of the very earth itself and that delicate perfume of the frost that is hardly a perfume at all, but rather a distillation of crystal cleanliness.

Just at first Henrietta had been frightened of sleeping by herself. At the orphanage she had slept in a dormitory with other little girls and worked and played and eaten in a seething horde, never knowing a moment's privacy day or night, and that had seemed so natural to her that loneliness, when it came, was terrifying. When Sarah took away her candle and left her to the dark she had hardly known how to bear it. She had lain awake hour after hour, shaking with fear, her round black head turned sideways on the pillow towards the place where she knew the window was and her eyes straining through the dark for the first glimpse of the dawn.

But quite soon her fear had left her and she knew that the most precious possession she had was her room and the privacy it gave her. She was immensely proud of it. She dusted it herself every day and Grandmother allowed her, under the supervision of Bates the gardener, to pick flowers for the blue pot on the window-sill.

In it she dreamed dreams and saw visions. While she slept it seemed to her that strong arms were carrying her from place to place, showing her ivory palaces where the wind whispered through the pillars like violins playing very softly, and crystal mountains full of musical streams, and green lawns where rose-petals fell with a sound like rain, and she enjoyed it all immensely. And when she woke up she tried, by the exercise of her own will and imagination, to create other lovely things. She built white towers beside gold sands and blue sea and tipped the crest of each wave with curling snow, making them very tall so that as they curved and broke on the sand they made a sound like the organ in the Cathedral. And she planted gardens full of roses and hollyhocks and set singing birds in every bush, and she built caverns under the sea of emerald and mother-of-pearl and put mermaids singing sad songs in them.

For in every dream that Henrietta dreamed music had its place. She even thought that colours and scents had their sounds. Red was a trumpet blast and green was the sound of fairy flutes, and the scent of the wistaria was a tune played by the violins that made one want to sit down on a cushion and never do any work any more.

It was important, because the only memory that Henrietta had of the days before she went to the orphanage was a memory of music. A woman in a blue dress had sat at the piano singing and Henrietta had danced as she sang, her bare feet going pitter-patter on a shiny floor. The woman had sung faster and faster, her voice gay like a blackbird's, and the baby Henrietta had danced and danced, her toes

getting pinker and pinker with the effort, until at last her
legs had got entangled with each other and she had fallen
over with a bump. The woman had run to her and picked
her up and they had sat on the floor and laughed. Henrietta
could only remember what the woman had looked like,
she could only remember the sound of her, her singing and
her laughter and her deep, ringing voice. The memory of
this woman and her music had become almost submerged
at the orphanage, but in the quiet of Henrietta's bedroom
at Torminster it came back to her very vividly.

All these things and people combined acted upon her like
sunshine on a folded flower. She expanded and the essence
of her, the flower's scent, that had been too tightly bottled
up to live, came out into the open.

And the essence of Henrietta was a dreamer of dreams.
Her mind was not inquiring, like Hugh Anthony's, but it
was intensely appreciative. She noticed that certain things
were lovely and she stored them in her memory, taking them
out later and fastening them together to make a dream, as
a woman will embroider a posy of flowers with coloured
silks. Later on in her life, when she grew up, she realized
that dreams cannot be hoarded selfishly in the mind, lying
piled one upon the other, getting dog-eared and faded, but
must be generously spilt out into the world, and she learnt
how to paint her dreams with a brush on canvas so that
other people saw them too. . . . But Henrietta the famous
artist was still far in the future, her powers guessed at by no
one except Gabriel Ferranti, the man who had lived in the
house with the green door.

III

It was Henrietta who had discovered him in the first
place, and all because of the stuffed owl in the parlour at
The Green Dragon. . . . Afterwards it was extraordinary

to think of the effect that owl had had upon the lives of them all, and pathetic to think that the poor thing was dead all the time and could take no pleasure in the fuss and to-do it created.

The discovery of Ferranti by Henrietta was in this wise. When she first came to Torminster it was ordained by Grandfather and Grandmother that in the mornings she should share Hugh Anthony's lessons with Miss Lavender, but that in the afternoons, when Hugh Anthony was playing cricket with the boys at the choir-school, she and Sarah should take a short walk for the good of the health.

But Sarah was not keen on walking. It made her corns jump, she said, and, though corns were only to be expected at her age, she saw no sense in making them jump unnecessarily. So instead of patrolling the lanes where the white violets grew, as Grandmother thought they were doing, Sarah and Henrietta went to The Green Dragon and sat in the parlour and talked to Mrs. Wilks, the proprietress of The Green Dragon, who was a great friend of Sarah's, being in fact Sarah's brother-in-law's second cousin on his mother's side.

Mrs. Wilks was very beautiful, with wonderful golden hair, a bulging figure and a blinding magenta blouse, but Henrietta did not like her. She did not like her loud laugh, nor her well-meant but smacking kisses, nor her jet earrings, nor the way she asked questions. Still less did Henrietta like her parlour, which was hot and smelt of lamp-oil and last Sunday's dinner, and least of all did she like the stuffed owl.

It was rather moth-eaten and it had glass eyes that glared and in one of its claws it held a very realistic dead mouse. Henrietta, sitting one day on the edge of a hard chair with her legs dangling, gazed at that mouse and wondered if it had cried when the owl caught it. . . . And if owls eat mice. . . . And who had killed the owl. . . . And whether it had cried. . . . And suddenly she could not bear it any more and slipped off her chair.

"Could I go out in the garden, please?" she asked Mrs. Wilks.

Mrs. Wilks, who had a kind heart in spite of her blouse, said, "To be sure, lovey, you hop along out." So Henrietta hopped.

The garden was at the back of The Green Dragon and was not particularly interesting, for there was nothing in it but a water-butt, a cinder path and Mr. Wilks's nightshirts hanging out to dry on the line, but there was no terrible moth-eaten owl gazing at you out of baleful eyes so Henrietta preferred it to the parlour.

The only source of amusement available was kicking cinders up and down the path, so for a solid ten minutes Henrietta kicked and then, quite suddenly, she became aware of the next door garden over the wall.

Someone was gardening there for she could hear the soft thud of a spade being driven into earth. Henrietta loved to watch people digging, for the disinterred worms fascinated her. She liked watching them clinging to the earth with their heads and their tails while they heaved their middle parts up into the air like a railway-arch. She thought it was wonderful of them to be able to move along like that, without legs or wings, and wonderful of God to have invented so many different ways of progression for His creatures. The wall between the two gardens was low and Henrietta, hoping for worms, put her hands on the top of it, gave a little jump, dug in her toes and heaved herself up so that her chin just came above the level of the wall.

She saw a wild, tangled strip of garden, a confused jumble of apple-trees, currant-bushes, weeds, rose-bushes, cabbages and long grass. A tall, thin man was gardening quite close to her. He had untidy black hair and a white face and a torn blue shirt and Henrietta liked him, though he was not in

the least like any of the people who came to Grandmother's.

"Hullo," she said.

Gabriel Ferranti started and looked up. He saw the
face of a child framed in a sailor hat which had slipped backwards and encircled the back of her head like a halo. Ten
finger-tips were gripping the top of the wall, but he could
see no more of her. She looked like one of the bodiless
little angels in her own room, or like their Italian cousins
who float about in pictures of the Madonna. Her dark
eyes had the same gravity and her lips the same sweet
earnestness.

He stared at her for a moment and then came over to her,
smiling at her and pulling down his shirt-sleeves. She saw
when he came close to her that he had deep lines scored
across his forehead and round his mouth and somehow, for
a brief moment, they made her feel sad. She did not know
that the man in front of her was living through that difficult
moment when the scarred and dying beauty of youth is
putting up its last fight before the approach of age, and so
she did not know why she felt sad.

The sight of her saddened him too, but he knew why.
He was a natural pessimist and the sight of the young
always depressed him. . . . They seemed to expect so much
of life that life would never give them and so soon their
smooth flesh would be wrinkled and ugly.

"Hullo," he said. "Are you bodiless, or are you just
hung up on the other side like a bat?"

"I've my toes in cracks," said Henrietta.

He reached a long arm over the wall and gripped her
blue linen smock in the small of the back. Henrietta on
her side scrambled with her toes and in a minute she was
on top of the wall and he had lifted her down.

"So you *have* got a body," he said. "I'm sorry."

"Why?" asked Henrietta.

"I had hoped you were a celestial apparition, and so exempt from the troubles of this world."

Henrietta did not know what he was talking about and asked if he had dug up any worms. He said he had and they looked at them together and marvelled at the way they got about. Hugh Anthony, had he been present, would have wanted to know why God made them without legs, and if Ferranti had admitted to ignorance of the divine purpose regarding worms Hugh Anthony would have wanted to know why Ferranti didn't know why God didn't say in the Bible why it was that worms hadn't got legs? But on this occasion Hugh Anthony was not present and Ferranti and Henrietta just marvelled quietly together, storing up a wriggly memory in their very similar minds. . . . That night he wrote a strange poem called "Convolutions" that was afterwards famous, and years later she painted a picture full of queer spirals that created a great sensation in artistic circles but was never completely understood.

When they had exhausted the charms of worms they sat on the grass and Henrietta made daisy chains, while Ferranti told her a story of how he had sailed in a golden gondola in a city where the streets were not paved with noisy cobbles but with silent, silver water, and where the sun was so hot that it could melt the ice out of your heart and the pain out of your mind. No one ever grew old in that city, he told her, and love never died, and Henrietta, gazing at him spellbound, believed every word he said. It was years since anyone had believed anything he said and he found her faith entrancing. . . . Here at last, after years wasted in writing books and poetry that no one would read, was an appreciative audience. . . . They were both completely happy, Ferranti for the first time in years. Two of Nature's oddities as they were they fitted each other like hand and glove.

And then, just as Ferranti was describing the meal of pomegranates and red wine that he had partaken of in the watery city, eating off a blue glass plate and drinking out of a crystal cup, Sarah came out into The Green Dragon garden calling for Henrietta. They could see her gaunt head and shoulders as she stalked up the cinder path, looking for Henrietta behind the water-butt and amongst Mr. Wilks's nightshirts.

"Sssh!" said Henrietta to Ferranti, but he, with that heartless loyalty to each other's discipline that seems to afflict even the best of grown-ups, immediately got up and handed her back over the wall.

"Well, I never," said Sarah, "I didn't expect *that*!"

Henrietta, usually a moderately good child, behaved abominably. She yelled and stamped her foot on the cinder path and wrenched at her hat elastic so that it snapped and her halo fell off. "I won't go home!" she stormed. "I won't! I won't!"

"I never saw such an exhibition in all my life," said Sarah.

"Stop that row!" said Ferranti sternly, from the other side of the wall. "With your face screwed up like that you are no longer beautiful."

Henrietta seemed to know without being told that he cared for nothing that was not beautiful. She choked back her yells and composure came back to her white, starry face. "Please may I come again?" she asked.

"Don't choke like that," said Ferranti, "it spoils the timbre of your voice." And then to Sarah he said, humbly and pleadingly, "May she come again? I will take good care of her."

But Sarah, murmuring something vague about "not knowing, she was sure," hurried Henrietta away, employing the homeward journey in telling her what she thought of her. Henrietta was a naughty girl, she said, to get over walls and talk to strange men like that, strange men who wrote poetry and were erratic about their meals, so Mrs.

Wilks said, and though pleasant-spoken enough were probably no better than they should be, as Mrs. Wilks said and should know, living next door and baking him an apple-pie once a week as she did, and Sarah never had trusted men with long hair and never would, and Henrietta must not tell her grandfather what she had done or he would be very angry, and this sort of thing was only to be expected when an old couple as should know better took to adopting children with one foot in the grave, and she'd said the same to Ellen only last Wednesday.

But Henrietta, who always lost her way in Sarah's remarks and hardly ever emerged at the other end with any clear idea of what she was to do or not to do, failed to grasp the fact that she was not to tell Grandfather, and told him all about it that evening while they watered the tulips.

Grandfather, far from being angry, was highly interested. He had heard that some unknown young man who wrote books had come to live in the house with the green door, but had also heard that the young man did not wish to be called upon and so had not called, for Grandfather in his humility was always careful not to push himself in where he might not be wanted.

But Henrietta's story made him feel quite differently. She made Ferranti appear as a fairy-tale man, a teller of tales, tall and thin, with a blue shirt and black hair and a white face with lines upon it, a person of such attraction that it seemed little children would follow him to the world's end.

"Dear me," said Grandfather. "The Pied Piper of Hamelin."

And it was this thought of the Pied Piper that made him decide that he would go and see Ferranti that night, for Grandfather had always felt sorry for the Pied Piper. . . . A bitter man. . . . A disillusioned man. . . . A man whose faith in human nature had been so shaken that he had disappeared inside a mountain and been no more seen. . . .

Poor fellow. . . . Grandfather would go and see him, he told Henrietta, and if he turned out satisfactory of course Henrietta should continue her friendship with him.

So after dinner, disregarding Grandmother's wishes that he should let well alone lest the person turn out peculiar, Grandfather placed his round clerical hat on his bald head, clasped his plump hands behind his back and strolled off under the stars to the house with the green door. . . . Returning home again, to the intense annoyance of Grandmother at the—for him, at his age, as she pointed out for three-quarters of an hour before they slept—disgraceful hour of midnight.

All through that summer the three-cornered friendship between Grandfather, Ferranti and Henrietta flourished like a green bay-tree. Grandmother, though she once met Ferranti at the butcher's and was introduced by Henrietta, thought little of him. The person was, as she had expected, peculiar, and though she asked him to tea from a sense of duty, and bestowed upon him the rather frigid smile that she kept for those unfortunates whom as a Christian she must love but as a human being intensely disliked, she found herself incapable of going farther. Hugh Anthony, too, did not much like Ferranti; his knowledge of cricket was negligible and he always lost his temper if asked more than one question per minute. . . . But Grandfather and Henrietta loved him.

He would hardly ever go to see them at the Close, being afflicted with the misanthrope's "house-bound" attachment to the sorrows of his own roof tree in a very acute form, but they went to see him. To Henrietta he revealed one side of the Pied Piper character, the piping side, that opened to her a new world of fairy-tale enchantment, but with Grandfather he ceased to pipe and became just pied, a poor parti-coloured creature whose original bright hues of romance and idealism had been dimmed by failure and disillusionment. He was, as Grandfather had suspected, a bitter man, a man whose faith in human nature had been so shaken that he had elected to disappear from the world as he knew it. The house with the green door was his Pied Piper's mountain, whither he had withdrawn with his unwanted dreams.

Grandfather, though he loved him, could do nothing with him. Their arguments usually ended with Ferranti's parrot cry of, "Religion. . . . Bosh. . . . I've seen through all that." Grandfather, scratching his bald head in perplexity, seemed to remember that George Eliot had once remarked that when people said they had seen through a thing they usually meant they hadn't seen it at all, but this remark, though shrewd, did not help Grandfather in the difficult task of trying to make a man see what to him is invisible. . . . Grandfather knew of nothing harder, except trying to bring home to a wasp or butterfly the existence of a pane of glass in a window.

And then Ferranti disappeared.

IV

It had been Henrietta who had discovered he was there and it was Henrietta who discovered he was not there.

It was a windy Saturday in early November, when the red and yellow leaves were drifting through the streets of the city and torn wisps of grey cloud sailed across the stormy sky behind the Cathedral towers. Every now and then a scurry of rain swept by on the wind and the cry of the bells as they rang for matins, now loud and now faint as the gusts carried the sound and then dropped it again, was inexpressibly sad.

She felt restless and depressed. It was Saturday, and a whole holiday, but Hugh Anthony was in one of his

tiresome moods and wouldn't play with her. Instead he
lay flat on his stomach on the dining-room floor and studied
football, a pursuit from which nothing roused him but the
periodical need of going to the kitchen and refreshing the
inner man, which seemed to become very empty when lain
upon. She decided that she would go and see Ferranti.
He never lay on his stomach and studied football, a game
he heartily detested, and could always be relied upon to
leave his writing, or gardening, or whatever he was engaged
upon at the moment, and come into the garden and tell her
stories.

Like a flash she ran out of the house, down the garden and
out into the Close, just as she was, in her red serge dress and
white pinafore, with the rain stinging her cheeks and her
hair flying out behind her in the wind.

When she got to the Cathedral she turned to her left
on to the Green by the west front, for it was possible for
pedestrians to get from the Green to the Market Place
through a little tunnel that bored through one of the houses.
Hardly anything was still on the Green and it was wildly
beautiful. The elm-trees were swaying and creaking and their
leaves were falling and drifting and bowling over the grass
in golden battalions. The few people who were about were
clutching their hats and billowing skirts and breaking every
now and then into absurd little runs when the wind caught
them. The rooks, storm buffeted, were cawing angrily
and flapping protesting wings. Only the carved figures on
the west front were still, those kings and queens and saints
and angels who had faced a thousand such days and would
face a thousand more. The clock struck as Henrietta went
by, booming out over her head, but she was in too much of a
hurry to look up at the carved baby over the west door, as
she usually did, always hoping that he would jump and
crow in his mother's arms at the sound of the bell.

She ran across the Market Place to the house with the

green door, but she saw at once that it had a very shut-up appearance, and she thought that Ferranti must be in his garden, so she went in through The Green Dragon, pushing past the astonished Mrs. Wilks and running down the passage to the cinder path. She scaled the wall and clung on with fingers and toes, but there was nobody in the other garden and the roses were gone and the cabbage-stalks looked limp and desolate. She ran back through The Green Dragon and out into the Market Place again and round to the front door of the house. She mounted the two worn steps and beat on the door with her hands. She went on beating, a wild tattoo of brown fists on hard wood, but no footsteps came down the passage inside to answer her, and the windows, shut and clouded with raindrops, were like closed eyes with tears trickling out under the lids.

So he had gone. The Pied Piper had disappeared and would perhaps never be seen again. She had no doubt that he had gone for good and a terrible feeling of desolation overwhelmed her. She ran back across the Market Place and the Green, so blinded by her tears that it was not until she had actually bumped into him that she saw Grandfather, bobbing along to matins with his hands clasped in the small of his back and the wind bulging out his surplice so that he looked like a white balloon.

"Henrietta, dear child!" he exclaimed in horror.

The relief of finding him was so great that Henrietta's tears, which until now had been a mere sprinkling, became a positive niagara, and Grandfather had to pat and soothe her and mop up her face with his handkerchief before he could make head or tail of her story. But when he did understand he was, though grave, by no means despairing.

"He's just out," he comforted her. "I expect he's gone to the bank."

"He hardly ever goes to the bank," sobbed Henrietta.

"He hates the bank because there's never anything in it. And you can see that he's left the house because it's crying."

"Now, dear child, don't be fanciful," said Grandfather, but her distress was so great that he decided to leave matins, which was his responsibility this morning, to the tender mercies of the Dean and the Precentor, risking what the Dean would have to say about it afterwards, and look into this disappearance of Ferranti's at once. . . . He could not bear Henrietta to suffer and her capacity for doing so seemed to him alarming.

So they went together to the Market Place and looking at Ferranti's house Grandfather saw that Henrietta was quite right, for it had that indefinable air of desolation that an abandoned house always wears.

They stood together in the gutter and looked at it sadly and at that moment out came Mrs. Wilks, followed by Mr. Wilks, a large person with a ginger moustache whose waxed ends stood out further than one would have believed possible.

"Do you know where Mr. Ferranti is?" asked Grandfather politely.

"Flitted," said Mr. Wilks, and he said it with such grimness that Henrietta's heart sank.

"How do you mean, Mr. Wilks?" said Grandfather. . . . He said it a little sharply for he did not like Mr. Wilks.

"Gorn," said Mr. Wilks. "In the night. And owes me a bill for beer as long as your arm."

"And that not the only bill owing," said Mrs. Wilks. "It's no wonder he's taken himself off. He'd better. He's done away with himself, you may be sure."

"That's enough, Mrs. Wilks," said Grandfather with, for him, extraordinary sharpness, and turning round he marched abruptly away across the Market Place with Henrietta pattering after him. He was very angry, she saw to

her surprise, and talking to himself. "Saying a thing like
that before the child!" he muttered. "Pray God she didn't
understand!" She did not, so it was all right.

But at the west door of the Cathedral his rage seemed
to evaporate. "We'd better go inside, Henrietta," he said,
"and ask God about it."

"Yes, Grandfather," said Henrietta forlornly. Her ideas
about God were at this time extremely hazy but correct as
far as they went. He lived in the Cathedral, she imagined,
much as Grandfather lived in Number Two the Close, and
was kind and good like Grandfather, only more so. He
had made her, so she understood, and provided her with
her dinner daily so as to perpetuate His work, and He must
be great and beautiful because His house was like that.

Grandfather pushed open the heavy swing-door and
they were inside and in spite of her grief she thrilled a little,
as she always did, to its grandeur and loveliness.

From where they stood at the west door it stretched
from their feet away into the shadows in the distance so
that they could not see where it ended. Great pillars stood
in ordered ranks all the way up the nave, so tall that it gave
one a crick in the neck to look up to the place where their
straightness curved into lovely dim arching shapes that
went up and up into the roof and criss-crossed high over
your head like the branches of trees in a forest.

It always seemed to Henrietta that there were flowers
growing in the forest, for on sunshiny days the sun shone
through the stained-glass windows and spread patches of
colour over the floor of the Cathedral, and on wet days the
candles lit in the shadows shone like daffodils.

The nave and the choir were separated by a carved screen
where angels and saints stood in their ranks as they did on
the west front, and when the choirboys were hidden behind
it and singing, as they were now, it seemed to listeners in
the nave that the angels themselves were singing.

Grandfather and Henrietta walked up the nave towards the first row of chairs but when they got there they remembered suddenly that St. Paul had very strong feelings about little girls who went into church without their hats, and Grandfather made Henrietta fasten his handkerchief round her head with a safety-pin that she fished up out of her underclothes for the purpose.

This little matter attended to they knelt down side by side and Grandfather in his absentmindedness began to join in with the choir. "I will sing and give praise," he sang in his cracked old voice. "Awake up, my glory, awake, lute and harp, I myself will awake right early."

Henrietta, who could see nothing at all to awake a lute and harp about in their present situation, prodded him gently. "We're going to tell God about Mr. Ferranti," she reminded him.

"Dear me, yes, so we are," said Grandfather, and began to ask God if He would be so kind as to look after Mr. Ferranti and see that no harm came to him.

Henrietta prodded Grandfather again. "But God doesn't know what's happened," she said. "Couldn't you explain it all from the beginning?"

"God knows everything," said Grandfather gravely.

"But He might have been looking the other way when Mr. Ferranti went off," said Henrietta desperately. "I want God to know about the house crying, and what Mr. Wilks said, and everything."

Grandfather, scratching his head in perplexity and wondering if this was, or was not, the time to try to explain the omnipotence of God to Henrietta, decided it was not, and going back to the beginning again explained the situation to God down to the smallest detail. Henrietta, leaning against Grandfather and gazing up into the soaring arches above her head, was comforted. God, she felt, was now in possession of all the facts and, if He was anything like this wonderful house of His, was quite capable of dealing with them adequately.

Then they walked home together and Grandfather told Henrietta that she must try not to be unhappy because Mr. Ferranti had gone away. She had prayed and must continue to pray, and Grandfather would make inquiries of the police as well as pray, and that was all they could do. . . . In this beautiful world that God had made joy was a duty.

So Henrietta tried very hard to be happy again, and succeeded, but she did not forget Ferranti and the thought of his disappearance was a wound in her mind that never quite healed.

As the months went by and he was not found in spite of all Grandfather's efforts the past of which he was a part stepped into the background. Henrietta found it quite hard to remember exactly what he had looked like, but she never forgot the stories that he had told her. The pictures that they had created in her imagination linked themselves to the music that a woman in a blue dress had once sung to her and became one with it in her memory.

CHAPTER III

I

THE morning after Jocelyn's arrival dawned blue and lovely.

Grandfather and Grandmother were the only ones who talked during the early stages of breakfast. Jocelyn, who came down a little late, was silent from fatigue and the necessity of catching up, and the tongues of Hugh Anthony and Henrietta were fully employed in dealing with porridge, bacon and egg, milk and water, toast and marmalade.

What, asked Grandfather of Grandmother as the meal drew to an end, was to be done with the dear children this afternoon? The choirboys were on holiday, it was Sarah's afternoon out and Grandfather had a Chapter meeting. . . . In the suggestive pause that followed Jocelyn said nothing. . . . Though in search of a profession he did not feel much drawn to that of nursery governess.

Henrietta bolted a mouthful and, following a rule of life implanted in her by Matron, wiped her mouth before she spoke. "I should like," she said, "to go with Uncle Jocelyn to the house with the green door."

"Why?" asked Hugh Anthony with unwiped mouth.

"Because I dreamed I did. I dreamed that I couldn't get the door open, but Uncle Jocelyn opened it with a big golden key."

"What did you do inside the house?" asked Hugh Anthony.

"I didn't do anything," said Henrietta, "because I woke

up before I got inside. But I dreamed all sorts of other things first. There was a tall, thin man who piped, and who looked like Mr. Ferranti, and dancing children in coloured cloaks and houses with red roofs."

"What do these children have for supper, dear?" said Grandfather to Grandmother.

"Milk and biscuits, dear," said Grandmother rather sharply, for she disliked interference with her domestic arrangements.

"Before we go to the house we'll show Uncle Jocelyn the sweet-shop," said Hugh Anthony.

Jocelyn, yielding to fate, squared his shoulders and accepted the responsibilities of resident nursery governess. At half-past two that afternoon, he declared bravely, he would be ready.

The breakfast finished Henrietta and Hugh Anthony asked to get down and raced upstairs to get ready for morning school with Miss Lavender. They put on their brown strap shoes, attached the immense sailor hats that were then fashionable for the young to the backs of their heads with the help of elastic under the chin, and slung their satchels over their shoulders. Their grandparents, watching through the dining-room window, saw them go jauntily down the garden path and smiled affectionately. Hugh Anthony wore a dark blue sailor suit and Henrietta a rose-pink smock and they looked very nice if perhaps not as studious as could be wished.

The garden door slammed behind them and they were out in the Close. A blossoming tree that leaned over the garden wall dropped petals on their heads, the sun shone and they were happy. They walked along the pavement hand in hand, being careful to put their feet down in the centre of each paving-stone and not on the cracks, and at every sixth step they gave a little jump. This not walking on the cracks of the paving-stones was part of the ritual

c

of the walk to school and was always observed with great
solemnity.

Then they passed under the archway that separated the
Close from the Cathedral Green and planted themselves
in front of the clock on the north wall of the Cathedral to
watch it strike nine. This also was part of the ritual.

It was a wonderful clock. A great bell hung between
the life-size figures of two gentlemen sitting down. They
had bushy hair and square caps on their heads, and held
sticks in their hands, and for most of the day they sat
perfectly still gazing at each other with every appearance
of acute boredom. But at each hour they suddenly came
to agitated life and made savage onslaughts on the bell.
They struck it with their sticks and kicked it with their
feet and made a great deal of noise indeed. Henrietta and
Hugh Anthony adored these two gentlemen and it was one
of the griefs of their life that owing to other engagements
they could not be present every time they came to life.
When they were grown up, they had decided, they would
always be present, for to watch that clock was a life's work
in itself.

But nine o'clock was good and lasted a long time.
Nine kicks and nine blows and a glorious great boom at
each. They stood perfectly still, their mouths ajar and
their heads thrown back, listening and watching as though
they had never seen the thing before.

When it was over they sighed, walked on a little way
and descended the steps to the Cathedral Green, where
they stopped again to look up at the west front. It did
not look to-day as though it were built of stone. The
blue air and golden sunlight of the misty spring day seemed
to have soaked into it and dissolved its hardness of colour
and outline, so that it seemed an apparition that might
at any moment vanish. The rows of sculptured figures
were not statues to-day, they were ghosts, an army of

spirits stepping silently through the veil of mist hanging between earth and heaven.

"I do wish He'd laugh," said Henrietta, looking up at the Christ Child. "If I could reach I'd pinch His toes and then I'm sure He'd laugh."

"Don't be silly," said Hugh Anthony. "He's only stone. Come on. Run."

Having taken as long as they possibly could to get from home to the west front they then took to their heels and raced each other across the Green to Miss Lavender's house, arriving in a most impressive state of perspiring eagerness for learning that Miss Lavender found very touching.

A half-circle of old houses stood round the Green, back to back with the houses in the Market Place, and Miss Lavender had lodgings in one of them. She was very poor, so poor that she could never tell anyone just how poor she was, and it had been Grandfather's idea that she should eke out her tiny income by teaching Henrietta and Hugh Anthony. She had never done any teaching before, except Sunday-school teaching, and she had no idea how much she ought to be paid for it, so Grandfather was able to pay her too much without her knowing.

Her parlour was on the first floor, a little room looking straight out into the branches of the elm-trees that pressed close up to the window. There were two wooden desks for her pupils, a table with a globe on it, behind which Miss Lavender sat, a bookcase full of books, one shabby arm-chair, photos of Miss Lavender's relations on the mantelpiece and a picture of "The Soul's Awakening" over the tiny sideboard. That was all there was, except the canary and the cat.

Miss Lavender herself was tall and thin, with grey hair and a kind, meek face. She always wore grey alpaca, and steel-rimmed glasses, and her beautiful voice was never raised either in reproof or anger.

Her method of education was very much ahead of her time, for she employed the modern method of self-government and allowed her pupils to study whatever subject they felt most drawn to at the moment. But in employing this method she was not actuated by a study of child psychology but by a desire for peace and quiet. As she suffered from headaches, and it was quite impossible to induce Hugh Anthony to do what he did not want to do without a frightful row, she was obliged to let him do what he did want to do, and the same in a lesser degree with Henrietta.

The result was not too unsatisfactory for they were neither of them lazy and let loose in the field of learning, Hugh Anthony with his inquiring mind and Henrietta with her contemplative one, they made each of them for the food that suited them best and munched away like a couple of young heifers, one devouring buttercups and the other daisies.

"I shall do geography," announced Hugh Anthony that morning, when they had hung their sailor hats on the pegs in the hall and clattered up the stairs to Miss Lavender's room. He loved geography, for the questions that could be asked about it were endless. Why were some people black in the face, for instance, and others yellow and others white, and why was there snow at the North Pole, and was it hotter in India than it was in England, and if so why? Miss Lavender, when asked, never had the slightest idea, but she had a very good geography book provided by Grandfather and Hugh Anthony was able to find these things out for himself to his entire satisfaction.

"I shall do literature," said Henrietta. She did not like geography, for she had had enough of the capes of England at the orphanage to last her a lifetime, and her explorations were all made in that realm of knowledge rather vaguely described by Miss Lavender as "English literature." This included reading, writing, dictation, learning by heart "Be good, sweet maid, and let who will be clever," and looking out of the window.

Henrietta loved words, both the shape and the sound of them. She had not yet discovered her own powers as a picture-maker—for Miss Lavender did not attempt to teach painting—but she had discovered through words the symbolism of sound and shape and their relationship, just as in her dreams she had learnt to link colour and movement with music. "Silver" was a word that she especially loved. She thought it was the loveliest of words because it was so cool. If it gave her pleasure to hear Mr. Gotobed say "damn," as though the word were a fine, strong fist crashed down on a hard table, it gave her even more pleasure to hear Miss Lavender say "silver," for she immediately thought of fountains playing and a long, cool drink on a hot day. It was a satisfactory word to write too, with its capital S flowing like a river, its l tall as a silver spear and the v like an arrowhead upside down. Yellow was another good word because of that glorious capital Y that was like a man standing on a mountain-top at dawn praying to God, with his arms stretched out, his figure black against a sky the colour of buttercups. . . . All her life yellow was her favourite colour and the one that symbolized the divine to her.

From the delight of forming letters into words Henrietta went on to the intoxication of forming words into sentences and here her instinct was unerring. She seemed to know just what words to choose and how to arrange them so that they sounded like a bar of music and not like the tea-things falling downstairs. Miss Lavender, unaware how early a feeling for poetry awakes in children, was astonished at Henrietta's sensitive ear. She had, a few days ago, read them Shelley's "To a

Skylark." She had thought it far above their heads, but the larks were just in the middle of their spring ecstasy and Henrietta had demanded "something about larks," and Miss Lavender had not at the moment been able to lay her hand upon any literary lark except Shelley's. She was astonished, as she read, at the hush that fell upon her schoolroom. Henrietta never moved and even Hugh Anthony, who was carving a portrait of the Dean on his desk with a penknife, neglected his activities to listen, leaving the Dean whiskered on one side and not on the other.

"That's nice," said Henrietta when the poem was finished. "That's lots nicer than 'Be good sweet maid,' or 'How doth the little.'"

"But you didn't understand it, dear, did you?" asked Miss Lavender.

Hugh Anthony, who had gone back to the Dean's whiskers, did not reply, but Henrietta said, "It sounded good. It jumped up and up like the lark and it sang all the time."

"Well!" said Miss Lavender. "Dear me!"

And now, this spring morning, Hugh Anthony being provided with a chapter on coal and why it behaved in such a peculiar way when set alight to, Henrietta was presented by Miss Lavender with *Verses for the Little Ones*.

She flung it into the corner of the room.

"Henrietta!" exclaimed Miss Lavender in horror.

"I don't like it," said Henrietta. "I'm not little and I want that lark man."

"Not if you behave like that," said Miss Lavender, and began to shake nervously, for occasionally, mercifully very occasionally, Henrietta could be extremely naughty.

Henrietta saw Miss Lavender shaking and she was sorry, for she was not one of those demon children who enjoy tormenting. . . . She liked power as much as anyone else but Grandfather had already taught her that in this world you may lay violent hands upon no personality but your own; other people's, if you dare to touch them at all, must be handled with a touch as light as a butterfly's. . . . So she picked up *Verses for the Little Ones* and apologized for her disgraceful conduct. "Though I'm not going to read it," she ended firmly.

Miss Lavender gave in and produced Shelley.

There was silence in the schoolroom, Hugh Anthony engrossed in coal, Henrietta in turning the pages of Shelley and Miss Lavender in the knitting that she was able to take up when the dear children were good.

The light in the room was a green light for outside the windows the elm-trees were covered with new leaves and the sunlight had to filter through a green mist before it reached them. . . . Leaves. . . . The thought of them was in the minds of both children, for Hugh Anthony was discovering to his astonishment that buried forests turn into coal and Henrietta was thinking that the pages of Shelley as she turned them rustled like autumn leaves.

"Leaves." The words suddenly danced up at her from the page and caught her eye.

> "O wild west wind, thou breath of Autumn's being,
>   Thou from whose unseen presence the leaves dead
>   Are driven like ghosts from an enchanter fleeing,
>   Yellow, and black, and pale, and hectic red,
>   Pestilence stricken multitudes!"

Suddenly she remembered that autumn day when she had run across the Green to look for Ferranti and the leaves were falling and drifting and bowling over the grass in golden battalions.

"Thou on whose stream, 'mid the steep sky's commotion,
  Loose clouds like earth's decaying leaves are shed,
  Shook from the tangled boughs of heaven and ocean."

She did not quite understand that but she had a vision
of the sky as it had been that day, with torn wisps of
cloud sailing along behind the Cathedral towers, leaf-
shaped clouds that blew before the wind just as the leaves
did. She read on eagerly, uncomprehending but pounc-
ing eagerly on beautiful individual sentences. "And saw
in sleep old palaces and towers" . . . "And flowers so
sweet the sense faints picturing them." . . . Yes, she too
could dream of beautiful things and picture them to herself when she woke up. . . . And here were the leaves
again.

"Drive my dead thoughts over the universe,
  Like withered leaves, to quicken a new birth;
  And, by the incantation of this verse,
  Scatter, as from an unextinguished hearth,
  Ashes and sparks, my words among mankind."

"Miss Lavender," said Hugh Anthony suddenly. "Is
it really true that the flame that comes out of coal is the
sunshine that got shut up in the leaves of the forests that
were buried?"

"If it says so in that book," said Miss Lavender
guardedly.

"It does say so."

"Then it's true," said Miss Lavender, "because your dear
Grandfather bought that book and he would never buy a
book that made incorrect statements."

Hugh Anthony thought hard, and his thinking powers
were considerable. "Then when the flames come out of the
coal the sunlight that was buried comes alive again."

"Yes," said Miss Lavender, and remembering that Easter was only just past hastened to improve the occasion. "A new birth," she said slowly and reverently, her knitting in mid-air with the heel half turned, "a resurrection."

Henrietta puzzled over the last verse of the poem with knitted brows, saying it over and over so that she had it by heart. "Do all things that have gone away come back again?" she asked.

"Yes," said Miss Lavender.

"Why?" asked Hugh Anthony.

"Because it's a law of life."

"Why?"

"Because God ordained that it should be."

"Why?"

"It is not for us to question the will of God."

"Why not?"

"Hugh Anthony, I don't know."

"Why don't you know?"

Henrietta arose and fell upon him. They rolled over and over together on the floor. They upset an inkpot and frightened the cat and gave the canary, who was elderly, a heart attack. By the time Miss Lavender had quieted the cat and the canary and got the ink out of the carpet with milk and lemon it was, to her great relief, time for the dear children to go home.

When they had gone she wondered for the hundredth time if teaching the young was really her vocation and what, if anything, the dear children had learnt that morning.

They had, as it happened, learnt a good deal. The fact of resurrection had been brought home to them, some facts about coal were now a part of their mental equipment and Henrietta had memorized some words of a great poem. . . . It was the latter attainment that later turned out of great importance to them all.

c*

II

Henrietta, during lunch, had to be reproved three times by Grandmother for bolting her food. The fact was that she was in a tearing hurry to get Jocelyn to the house with the green door. Things always came back, she had learnt that morning, the spring, the sunshine that had been buried under the earth and, as she had been given to understand at Easter, dead people too. And if dead people then why not live people? Why should not Ferranti come back? Couldn't Uncle Jocelyn make him come back? In her dream, when she could not get inside his house, it had been Jocelyn who had opened it with a golden key.

"Oh, hurry up, Uncle Jocelyn," she cried impatiently. The meditative way in which he was spreading butter on his biscuit was almost unbearable to watch.

Jocelyn ate a bit of biscuit very slowly and remarked sweetly that it was now a quarter to two and he did not propose leaving the house until two-thirty, as had been stated clearly at breakfast.

After lunch Grandfather went to his Chapter meeting, which had been arranged by the Dean to take place at the sleepiest hour of the day so that all the Canons should go to sleep and he should get his own way in a matter of some dispute, Grandmother to her room to rest and the rest of them to the lawn. Jocelyn and Hugh Anthony established themselves under the mulberry-tree and shared *The Times* between them, Hugh Anthony lying flat on his front with the cricket and Jocelyn sitting upon a deck-chair with the state of Europe. Henrietta sat on the wheelbarrow at a little distance from them, swinging her legs and suggesting at short intervals that it must be nearly half-past two now, of which remarks they took no notice whatsoever. . . . There were times when Henrietta almost disliked men. Their capacity for silently refusing to do what you wanted them to do could be very irritating, far more so than the voluble reasons invented by a woman to account for the fact that she just did not happen to want to do it. . . . Henrietta was of too tender an age to analyse her annoyance, she just knew she was annoyed.

But the Cathedral clock struck two-thirty at last and Jocelyn, who was at least a man of his word, rose to his feet and put his hat on.

"But I've not finished this cricket," objected Hugh Anthony.

"Come along, old chap," said Jocelyn. "You must never break your word to a lady."

"Why not?" asked Hugh Anthony.

No one seemed to know why not and they sallied forth, Jocelyn holding the garden door open for Henrietta with as much courtesy as though she had been the Queen of England. She was at once mollified and slipped her hand into his as she walked along beside him, being careful not to tread on the cracks of the paving-stones.

"We're going to the sweet-shop first, remember," said Hugh Anthony.

They crossed the Green and went through the tunnel into the Market Place. The sweet-shop was on the opposite side of the Market Place from The Green Dragon and was twin sister to the one that Miss Matty kept at Cranford. Its window was as gay as a flower-bed with glass jars of coloured sweets, striped sticks of peppermint-rock and families of white sugar mice and pigs with pink noses and string tails. It was kept by Martha and Mary Carroway and their niece 'Arriet Kate.

Martha was in the shop when they went in, a charming little old lady made out of Dresden china, with bright eyes that darted over Jocelyn with burning curiosity.

"Relative of Canon Fordyce?" she murmured audibly and with a worried look.

"My name is Irvin," said Jocelyn obligingly.

"Ah! The Canon's daughter's son from London," said Martha, and was happy. Torminster was one of those small cities where it is a torment to the inhabitants not to know every detail of each other's goings-on and ancestry. It was small enough to make this knowledge possible yet big enough to make it difficult to come by, so there was great ardour in the chase.

"Now then," said Jocelyn, "what shall we buy?"

Hugh Anthony believed in striking while the iron was hot. Uncles, he had discovered, were always filled with avuncular ardour at the beginning of their visit but as time went on they were apt to cool a little. It might be that Jocelyn would not want to visit the sweet-shop a second time so he felt it would be as well to lay in a stock of necessities now. He would like two pigs, he said, two mice, an ounce of bullseyes, a stick of rock and some liquorice.

"And you, Henrietta?" asked Jocelyn.

She asked modestly for some hundreds-and-thousands, which she adored. They were coloured sugar-balls the size of pins' heads and were delicious eaten between slices of bread and butter. First you bit through the soft sponginess of the bread and then your teeth crunched gloriously into the sweet grittiness of the rainbow-coloured balls. The contrast was curiously exhilarating, adding a very special savour to life.

"Nothing else, Henrietta?" asked Jocelyn.

Henrietta shook her head. She disliked excess. Things were much more enjoyable, she thought, if you took them singly and in small quantities. Hugh Anthony could never see eye to eye with her in this.

Martha weighed out the sweets in her shiny scales,

added an extra one or two in the tradition of Miss Matty, and put them into cone-shaped pink paper bags which were placed in Jocelyn's pockets.

"Good afternoon," he said politely and limped to the door.

Martha, in the excitement of his entry, had not noticed his limp but now she adjusted her glasses and had a good look at it.

"The step of that bus is very treacherous," she murmured.

Although she seemed to be making a statement there was a world of pleading in her tone and Jocelyn paused before closing the shop door to say, "I injured my leg in Africa. Good day."

Martha gathered up her skirts and fled out of the shop to the back room beyond, where dwelt her elder sister, aged eighty-nine, with the cat and a constant supply of its offspring.

"Mary!" she cried, tripping over a basket of kittens in her excitement, "who do you think I've had in the shop? Canon Fordyce's daughter's son from London. Been telling me all about himself, he has, Mary. Turned out of the army, poor young gentleman, because of having his leg bitten by a tiger. . . . What'll he do now?"

"I couldn't say, Martha, I'm sure," said Mary in her faint, piping treble. "Was it a large tiger?"

She was a beautiful, saintly old person, with white hair curtained on either side of a transparent face. She was so thin and fragile that she could hardly be said to be there but her figure was given solidity by the fact that she wore, one over the other, out of affection for the dead, every single one of the petticoats once owned by her deceased mother and aunts.

"As to the tiger, Mary, I couldn't say, but could he go into the Church?" asked Martha, looking worried again.

"Where did he go when he left here?" piped Mary. "If he turned towards the Palace he'd have been going to ask the Bishop if his lordship considered him suitable."

"There! I never thought to look!" cried Martha, clacking her tongue in annoyance, and gathering up her skirts she ran back to the shop again.

On her reappearance she was able to report that Jocelyn and the children were standing on the pavement outside Gabriel Ferranti's house and staring in through the window.

"Ah," said Mary, "he'll be taking the house and setting up for himself in business."

"Go on with you, Mary!" expostulated Martha. "Young gentlemen don't go into trade."

"He's maybe not such a gentleman as he looks," said Mary. "Canon Fordyce's daughter in London married beneath her, so I've heard. It'll be books. Books are very genteel.'

By nine o'clock that night it was all over Torminster that Canon Fordyce's grandson from London had taken Gabriel Ferranti's house and was turning it into a book-shop.

III

As though drawn by a magnet Jocelyn and the children had crossed the Market Place to the house with the green door. The paint was cracked now and the two worn steps very dirty because no one had washed them for so long. There were cobwebs in the corners of the window-panes and a few of the wavy tiles had slipped out of place.

But nothing could dim the beauty of the little house, it was no more ugly than a lovely child is ugly because it has smuts on its nose and mud on its pinafore. Yet the house cried out, as the child would not have done, to be washed and tidied. It seemed to Jocelyn to be holding out hands to him, beseeching him to help it.

"How imaginative being with children makes one," he thought, and bent a little nearer to peer through the window at the empty room and the rose-sprig wall-paper. In places it had come away from the wall and hung in strips, and the sight vexed him.

Hugh Anthony was eating a sugar mouse, beginning at its pink nose and working backwards, and so was not much interested in the house, but Henrietta was leaning so close to the window that her nose was flattened out into a white button against the panes and her breath, that came rather pantingly, dimmed the glass and obscured her vision.

"It's all empty," she mourned. "He's not come back yet."

"No," said Jocelyn absently, and stepped back a few paces to see just where the tiles had slipped.

"It's not empty!" cried Henrietta suddenly, her voice rising sharply. "Quick! Look! Someone's come in!"

Her excitement communicated itself to Jocelyn. He stepped quickly forward and bent to look, then exclaimed under his breath and pulled out his handkerchief to polish up the panes that Henrietta had obscured with her breathing.

"No, it's not him," said Henrietta, and let out her breath with a deep sigh.

"It's only that lady who comes to stay in the Close," said Hugh Anthony contemptuously. Everyone was making a lot of fuss about a woman, he thought. It was often done and he could see no sense in it.

Jocelyn did not even hear him, he was too much occupied in gazing at the most enchanting back view he had ever seen. It was that of a slim girl with an aureole of short, curly golden hair that stuck out all round like the petals of a sunflower. She wore a childish cotton frock of delphinium blue, with short sleeves and no collar, that showed the warm, creamy colour of her skin and the lovely moulding of her arms and slender neck. At the beginning of the twentieth century unadorned clothes and short hair were not the fashion for the grown-up and the deliberate simplicity of this girl was somehow arresting, as arresting as her attitude.

She stood with her back to the window and her head thrown back, quite still, poised and attentive, as though she were listening and watching. . . . Listening apparently only to the silence and watching the sunlight on the patterned wall-paper.

"Let us in! Let us in!" cried Henrietta imperatively, and drummed with her finger-tips on the window-panes.

The girl swung round and Jocelyn, entirely forgetting his usually excellent manners, rubbed almost feverishly at the window with his handkerchief, so as to see her face perfectly. It was the most alive face he had ever seen. Her eyes were tawny and full of light and her heart-shaped face, with its delicate yet determined features, had a transparency that made it seem like a window through which she herself could be seen with a delicious clearness. Jocelyn felt that he was looking through two windows at the most courageous, generous person he had ever encountered. She was pale, but not with the moon-light paleness that was Henrietta's, for she looked sun-kissed and warmly loving, and somehow she was familiar. Somewhere else, Jocelyn felt, he had encountered that vivid personality.

"Let us in! Let us in!" cried Henrietta again, and the girl nodded and smiled and ran out of the room.

In a moment the green door creaked and squeaked and then slowly opened.

"The bolt sticks," said a clear voice. "I got in through the scullery window myself."

"Did you go through The Green Dragon and then over the wall into the garden?" asked Henrietta.

"Yes, I did. I was paying a bill to The Dragon and I, told them I must get into this house or die, so they showed me the way over the wall and through the window."

Jocelyn had shut the door behind him and they were standing in a dark passage that smelt of damp and rotting wood. Two doors were on their right and one on their left and in front of them narrow stairs crept away into darkness.

"Come into the back room," said the girl. "If we go into the front one they can see us from the Market Place."

She opened the second door on the right and they were in a small, panelled room. It had a beautiful old fireplace and a window with a window-seat looking into the garden.

"It's a bigger house than you'd think," said the girl. "There's another small room downstairs, with a kitchen and scullery behind it, and there are four bedrooms upstairs, all of them old and crooked, the kind of rooms that Hans Andersen's people lived in."

"Don't you think the whole of this city is Hans Andersenish?" asked Jocelyn.

"Yes, I do," she said. "That's why I love it. To come on a visit here is like walking into a fairy story."

"So you're on a visit here too?"

"Yes. My name is Felicity Summers and I'm staying with my godmother, Mrs. Jameson."

"She lives next door to us," explained Hugh Anthony thickly, through mouse. "Sarah says she's wanting in the upper story."

"Hush!" reproved Henrietta. "Grandfather says she is not like other people because her husband was a very noble missionary and was killed by cannibals."

"Hold your tongues, both of you," said Jocelyn embarrassed. "How about running out into the garden?"

He opened the window and they willingly ran. Henrietta wanted nothing better than to go out into the garden of her dreams and Hugh Anthony had got to the mouse's tail and wanted to spit out the string.

"I beg your pardon," said Jocelyn to Felicity.

She laughed. "Aunt Adelaide isn't really mad," she explained. "She's just a little fantastic. . . . I suppose you're yet another of Canon Fordyce's grandsons?"

Jocelyn pleaded guilty and they sat down together on the window-seat.

"What were you doing staring in through the window like that?" she asked.

"What were you doing breaking in through the scullery?"

"Is there anything in this world so attractive as an empty house? Does any normal human being ever pass one without wanting to go all over it?"

"Then let's go all over it. I've not been yet, remember."

They went. The little box of a room on the other side of the front door was not very exciting but the kitchen behind, with its oak beams and its red-brick floor, was beautiful, and the bedrooms were, as she had said, crooked and enchanted. Two looked out across the dreaming Market Place to the towers of the Cathedral and two looked over the garden to the hills and woods beyond. They explored them in a fascinated silence and then came back to the panelled room and sat down in its window-seat. They both felt thoughtful, and a little sad.

"Why is an empty house so attractive?" asked Felicity.

Jocelyn pondered, looking out into the beautiful garden where the untrimmed flowers and grass and blossoming apple-trees had run riot to such an extent that they were woven tightly together like a tapestry.

"How can we help loving houses when they stand to us for so much?" he said. "Warmth and protection and a means of expressing ourselves. You love a new house because it stands there waiting to be good to human beings and an old one because it has been."

"And an old house is a sort of history book," said Felicity. "All that people thought and did in it must be written in it somewhere. . . . Only the ink's invisible."

"Were you trying to read the invisible writing when I looked at you through the window?" asked Jocelyn. "You looked as though you were listening and watching."

"I was wishing that I knew the story of the man who used to live here and then disappeared. Gabriel Ferranti."

"Why? Did you know him?"

"Only by sight, but a man who looked so odd and had such a fantastic name must have had an interesting story."

"Not necessarily. Some people are obliged to be fantastic because their lives are so dull that otherwise no one would notice them."

"Well, I think he had, and it's written in this house. If I were free to do what I liked I think I should come and live here and learn how to read the invisible writing."

"What did you say your name was?" asked Jocelyn suddenly.

"Felicity Summers."

The name had a familiar ring and at once Jocelyn knew where he had seen this girl before. A picture rose in his mind of a crowded theatre gone mad with enthusiasm, of men and women cheering and clapping and waving their programmes while a slim figure came through the parted curtains again and again to take her calls. He could see her now, clothed in elaborate white and silver and with the eager vivacity of her face heightened by rouge and powder, curtsying and smiling enchantingly at stalls and pit and gallery.

"Now I know you," he said.

"No, you don't, because in Torminster I'm not Felicity Summers the actress, I'm only Felicity."

"You're right about being a different person divorced from one's profession," said Jocelyn. "One's work is what binds one to the world, isn't it? Without it one shrinks, as though one had no point of contact. . . . A cat without whiskers."

"Have you lost your whiskers?" she asked sympathetically.

"Yes, I was a soldier till I caught a lame leg in South Africa."

"Then for the moment we're both workless. That means that we're left with our essential, untrimmed selves. No make-up on me, no spurs on you. That ought to make it easier to make friends, and I'd like to be friends. Will you bring the children to tea on Wednesday?"

Jocelyn, who as a rule loathed tea-parties, accepted with alacrity.

IV

After dinner that night he found himself unable to keep quiet and look at *Punch* while his grandparents slept. He kept waking them up to talk about Felicity.

"I saw Felicity Summers at Ferranti's house, Grandmother," he announced.

"Oh," said Grandmother. "An actress. She stays with that peculiar woman, Mrs. Jameson, who very frequently has very odd people staying there."

"Have you met her, Grandmother?"

"No, dear, I haven't. I make a point of not going there when Mrs. Jameson has her odd people staying. I may be old-fashioned, I dare say I am, but to see that girl, with no chaperon and no hat, riding through the

Close on that old grey pony of Mrs. Jameson's, the one that pulls the mowing-machine, with everything in trousers for miles round following after, sets my teeth on edge."

"Oh come, Grandmother, I don't suppose she can help what follows after," said Jocelyn, grinning. "Beautiful actresses are like a street accident; it's not their fault if crowds collect."

"They need not smile backwards over their shoulders."

"But that's much nicer than frowning frontwards."

Grandmother said it was very warm to-night and went to sleep again, leaving Jocelyn to continue the conversation with Grandfather.

"Is Mrs. Jameson really very odd, Grandfather?"

Grandfather sighed and woke up. "Yes, dear boy, very odd, but there is great good in her. She has money and uses it well. I don't know why, but a small cathedral town always seems to attract peculiar elderly ladies. . . . Of course, no doubt we are all of us much more peculiar than we have any idea of. . . . It may be that I am considered odd myself." And he went to sleep again.

"You've not met Felicity, Grandfather?" said Jocelyn presently. There was a note of interest in his voice that this time woke Grandfather right up.

"No, dear boy, but I should much like to do so. Dear me, yes. A very beautiful young woman."

"She's asked me to take the children to tea there on Wednesday."

"Dear me, I envy you. I should like to see Felicity and Henrietta together. . . . Sunshine and moonlight."

Grandfather looked at Jocelyn attentively and with satisfaction. He noticed that he was looking different; younger, more alive, with a warmth in him that communicated itself to Grandfather and made him, too, feel different. Perhaps this warmth came from yet another love story set burning in the old city. . . . Yet another added to all the hundreds that must have . . . must have . . . When ten o'clock struck Grandfather found he had been dozing again.

v

As Jocelyn passed the door of Henrietta's room, always kept ajar in case she should want to yell for Grandmother in the night, he heard her voice. She wanted assurances that there was nothing under the bed, he supposed, and he went in to give them.

But Henrietta was only talking in her sleep, a habit of hers when over-excited.

"Leaves," she said. "Yellow and black and pale and hectic red."

Then there were confused mutterings and then she came out suddenly and clearly with a whole consecutive verse.

"Drive my dead thoughts over the universe,
　　Like withered leaves to quicken a new birth;
　　And, by the incantation of this verse,
　　Scatter, as from an unextinguished hearth,
　　Ashes and sparks, my words among mankind."

As he undressed and got into bed the words haunted Jocelyn, and when he drifted towards sleep he thought again of Felicity and of the house in the Market Place. The story of a man's life was written in it, she had said, and she thought it would be possible to learn how to read the invisible writing.

Thoughts became deep sleep, and sleep the dream that

comes before waking, and he was standing in one of the bedrooms at the little house, the big one that looked out over the hills and woods, and staring at the blank wall opposite the window. Words were written on the wall and he was reading them. He read on and on and when he got to the end he knew the story of Ferranti's life. Then a sudden beam of light swept across the wall, wiping the words away, and he woke up to find Sarah pulling his curtains.

"Wet to-day," she said. "But we must expect that after all the fine weather we've 'ad."

Jocelyn, sitting up in bed and pouring out his early tea, found that the story he had read in his dream had gone from him. He could not even remember what it had been about. The words of it had been swept away like dead leaves before a wind.

CHAPTER IV

I

WEDNESDAY came and Jocelyn and the children once more sallied forth watched from the front door by Grandfather and Grandmother and from an upper window by Sarah and Ellen. In the placid life of Torminster tea-parties were of importance. They lay on the surface of existence like the markings of the hours on a clock face, measuring the slow movement of time. Events were remembered in relation to tea-parties. "It was the day I went to the Archdeacon's in my blue silk," a Torminster lady would say if asked when her cook gave notice. Or, "We made twelve pounds of crab-apple jelly that year. I counted the pots when I came back from Canon Roderick's. . . . I wore my puce."

So it was important that Jocelyn and the children should go to tea with Mrs. Jameson. Sarah gave Jocelyn's suit an extra pressing and Ellen sewed new elastic in the children's sailor hats, put a white collar on Henrietta's smock and bought her a new pair of strap shoes.

Jocelyn, apart from the fact that he wanted to see Felicity again, felt that the event was epoch-making. He put the feeling down to the fact that the Torminster houses stood in walled gardens, so that when you went to tea next door you seemed to be going a journey into a foreign country.

In Torminster there was no looking over a low fence to see what the butcher was taking next door for dinner, and no watching the road outside through railings to see who attended next door's tea-party to which you had not been invited. No. High walls enclosed you as in a moated fortress and you could know nothing at all of the goings-on of next door except by a system of espionage carried on through the agency of whichever of the trades-men happened at the moment to be walking out with cook.

From this followed the feeling that next door was a long way off. You went out through the door in your wall and banged it shut behind you. You were now separated from your own citadel. Your hollyhocks and your roses were hidden from you and if you could see any-thing of your house it was only the top of a crinkled roof; the eyes of the house, the windows, could no longer meet yours and you felt as though the house had turned its back on you. Abandoned, you turned to your right, advanced a few paces and found yourself opposite another closed door in a high wall. . . . Next door. . . . You could see nothing of it and for all you knew anything might have happened beyond that wall since you were there last. The house might have been painted magenta, or peacocks might have been introduced in the kitchen-garden and mock-turtles in the front garden, they might have a new lawn-mower or a bird-bath, or simply anything. You laid your hand upon the door handle with an expectant heart, like a sailor who has sailed from across the seas and lets down his anchor in a foreign harbour.

Savouring this feeling Jocelyn paused for a moment at Mrs. Jameson's door. It was scarlet, with a brass handle, and over the top of the wall looked white lilac-trees already in blossom. The green and white and red made him think of a Chinese plate picturing that enchanting world of bridges and pagodas and lovers who never grow tired.

"Hurry! Hurry!" whispered Henrietta, alternately

raising herself on her toes and swinging back on to her heels again, to get the stiffness out of her new, squeaking strap shoes.

The promise of something fantastic contained in Mrs. Jameson's scarlet garden door was fulfilled when one got inside, for her garden was like the palette of a child's paintbox, a confused jumble of all the brightest colours on earth. It was too early for the geraniums and calceolarias that she loved but there were red tulips, golden marigolds and blue irises in profusion. There were also a sundial, a pond with goldfish in it and a hammock of striped red and green, all of them looking rather odd against the formal dignity of the Queen Anne house behind them.

It was one of the charms of Torminster that though the houses were all of them old they were of different periods, so that Queen Anne jostled William the Conqueror and Queen Elizabeth patronized the Georges. They all had different atmospheres, too, Grandfather's being monastic and Mrs. Jameson's mad Chinese.

Jocelyn and the children mounted the steps to the front door and rang the bell. It was answered by Felicity, who wore her simple blue frock and looked extremely out of place against the assortment of bric-à-brac that the hall contained. Tiger skins lay on the floor, bamboo tables stood about loaded with every kind of silver ornament, and the shields and spears of savages covered every space on the walls not already occupied by sticky oil-paintings and photographs of Mrs. Jameson's relations.

There was a twinkle in Felicity's eye as she ushered them in. "I thought I'd better let you in myself," she said, "so as to explain things. Come upstairs and mind the thistles."

Jocelyn saw to his amazement that the banisters had bunches of thistles tied on to them.

"There are no back-stairs for the maids to use," explained Felicity, "and so Aunt Adelaide ties thistles to the banisters so that the maids shan't put their hands on them."

She walked prancingly up a few stairs, Jocelyn toiling after, and then stopped again. "I'd better explain Aunt Adelaide's clothes. She always dresses in the colours of the Church's seasons, stockings and all. She wears purple in Lent, red at Whitsun, white during festivals and green the rest of the year." She pranced on a little farther, stopping again to give her final instructions. "Whatever you do don't contradict Aunt Adelaide because that upsets her. And if you don't like parrots pretend you do."

"Why?" asked Hugh Anthony.

"Don't ask questions, Hugh Anthony," Jocelyn whispered hoarsely.

The drawing-room was a lovely room, curtained, carpeted and furnished in scarlet. There were so many chairs and tables and china ornaments and photographs that it was almost impossible to move and in each of the four corners of the room was a green parrot in a cage.

Mrs. Jameson rose at their entry and came graciously to meet them. She was a tall and very dignified old woman clothed from head to foot in snow white, it being still the season of Easter, and scintillating with jewels. Her fingers were covered with them, and her wrists, and the bodice of her silk dress, and a string of pearls was even twisted in her white hair. She looked like some superb, barbaric princess until one looked at her face, which was that of a bewildered child.

"Good afternoon," she said in her deep tones. "Sit down. And are these the dear children? I have seen them in the Cathedral at divine service, but I have never yet had the pleasure of receiving them in my house."

She shook hands graciously with Jocelyn and the children, who were mercifully struck dumb with astonishment, while the parrots yelled, "Good-bye, dear," in chorus. Then they all sat down before a silver tea-tray and quantities of plates containing every kind of sugar cake.

When she had poured out the tea, and asked them if they liked milk and sugar, Mrs. Jameson seemed to drift off into a dream and became silent. Felicity and Jocelyn chatted with some constraint about London and the weather, and the children, still overwhelmed, just ate. Only the four parrots were really voluble. "Give us a kiss," said one, "Scratch Poll," said another. "Good-bye," said the third firmly, while the fourth hinted over and over again, "Must you really go now?"

Half-way through tea Mrs. Jameson came to life. "I am sure you are interested in missions," she said to Jocelyn.

Remembering that she must not be contradicted he said that he was.

"Then you will like to hear," she said, "that on the spot where my dear husband was killed there is now a Christian church and school; so you see his death was not wasted."

"No, indeed," said Jocelyn gently.

"There's nothing I hate more than waste," went on Mrs. Jameson, her mind swinging off to another topic. "But for me there'd have been a great deal of waste when that young man who lived in the Market Place ran away. What was his name? Ferranti."

"How do you mean, Aunt?" inquired Felicity with interest.

"His effects were sold, dear, to pay his bills, and I was the first arrival at the sale. I always go to sales. I always say it's wonderful what one can pick up at them. . . .

Well, yes. . . . When I arrived there were piles of papers, newspapers and magazines and so on, lying stacked on the floor in a corner of the room. 'What are you going to do with those, Mr. Jones?' I said to the auctioneer. 'Burn them, ma'am,' he said, 'they're no use to no one.' 'What waste, Mr. Jones!' I said. 'I'll buy them to light my fires with.' And I did. I hate waste."

"And are they all used up?" asked Jocelyn.

"Not yet," said Mrs. Jameson, "for I had a good deal of paper of my own laid by, but I'm getting through them gradually."

"I think it was very foreseeing of you to buy those papers," said Jocelyn gravely.

Felicity beamed at him. He was being sweet to Mrs. Jameson and she liked him more than ever for it, for she loved her godmother. She was no more mad, Felicity always maintained, than Felicity herself. She had suffered a great grief and the effect of it upon her had been to make her a child again. Womanhood with its sorrows had been too much for her and subconsciously refusing to face it she had turned backwards into her childhood. But she was always perfectly rational, she never told lies, she never had delusions. She was amazingly generous, giving of herself and her money to every good cause that came along, she was loving and deeply religious and pathetically trusting.

"I should like to play spillikins with the children," she said to Felicity when tea was over. "You can take Captain Irvin into the garden."

Behind the house there was a walled vegetable-garden and down the middle of it ran a wide, moss-grown path arched over by nut-trees, and here Felicity and Jocelyn strolled up and down. The thick moss deadened the sound of their footsteps and the interlaced bright green leaves made Jocelyn think of carved, lacquered Chinese screens obligingly put up by Nature to ensure privacy while his friendship with Felicity put out its first timid leaves.

But only Jocelyn was conscious of timidity for Felicity did not know the meaning of the word. She had been given the happy gift of a spirit that faced outward and she bothered about herself and her feelings as little as it is possible for a human being to do. Artist though she was the thought of self-expression was hardly ever in her mind except as a gift that was hers to give. When she acted it was of the waiting audience in the dark auditorium that she thought, not of herself. They wanted something of her and her response was as fresh and natural as the reply of the trees to spring sunshine.

And so now it was Jocelyn of whom she thought. He had given her a moment of rather strange experience that had seemed to bring him very close to her. When he had stood in the Market Place and looked at her through the window of Ferranti's house he had seemed to see her herself, the essential untrimmed person whom she had told him was not Felicity Summers but only Felicity, and his look had thrilled her and comforted the lonely place that cries out for help deep inside every human being. Until that moment she had hardly realized that the place existed, but the sudden touch of healing applied to the ache and then withdrawn again had woken her up to awareness. Conscious now of this empty room at the centre of her being it had been with almost a fellow-feeling that she had learnt from the cook that Jocelyn had taken that house in the Market Place. . . . The poor thing would not be forlorn any more, and neither would Jocelyn.

"I'm so glad about your house," she said impulsively.

"What house?" said Jocelyn.

"That house of Ferranti's that you are turning into a bookshop."

"But I didn't know I was," said the bewildered Jocelyn.

"What?"

"Whoever told you I was?"

"Aunt Adelaide's cook. Everyone in Torminster knows about your bookshop and we're all so pleased."

"But how can everyone in Torminster know about it when I don't know about it myself?"

Felicity began to laugh. "In Torminster everyone knows much more about one than one does oneself, you'll find."

"But I haven't said a word about it to a soul!"

"But perhaps you've thought a thought about it to yourself?"

"Well, it did just cross my mind that it would be fun to keep a shop in Torminster, but it was only an idea——"

"That's enough for Torminster. It's one of those places where thoughts blow from one mind to another and then sprout. It's the quiet, you know. Quiet is to thoughts what air is to seeds. It's wonderful what receptive minds Torminster people have. Now Keziah, the cook, only has to walk past a person's house and she knows all their family history, especially the parts they wouldn't want her to know. It just blows out of their minds and sprouts in hers." A note of anxiety crept into her voice. "You don't mean to tell me that you *aren't* going to open that shop?"

"But of course not. Why should I?"

All the happiness went out of Felicity's face and she looked like a lovely child whose toy has been snatched away. "Oh, I *am* so disappointed!"

"But why?" said Jocelyn gently.

"Because Torminster needs a good bookshop so badly. What with the relaxing climate and the soporific effect of the bells Torminster people have minds like Tennyson's lotus-eaters."

"But a bookshop wouldn't alter the climate or stop the bells."

"No, but it might counteract their mental effect. . . . And I hate that darling house to be empty. I love it as though it were a person and I want it to be lived in."

"Someone else will take it if I don't."

"No, they won't, because of there being no drains."

"I don't see why it should be me to suffer a drainless existence for the sake of the minds of Torminster."

"Oh, please! Please!" begged Felicity, and Jocelyn saw to his astonishment that she was near tears. He had yet to discover the passionate energy which she bestowed on any new idea.

"But I've no capital," he pleaded.

"You must have your pension, and your Grandfather would help."

"But who would buy the books?"

"The Dean and Chapter. And you could have a circulating library. And we'd have a special department for the children and it would all be perfectly lovely."

"I couldn't let Grandfather lend me money," said Jocelyn firmly.

"If that isn't just like a man!" said Felicity with a sudden flash of the temper that was a part of her temperament. "I thought you had more sense than most but you're just like all the rest, as proud as Lucifer. You'll disappoint us all and leave that house to its loneliness and prevent the Dean and Chapter learning a little something rather than stoop to a bit of humility!"

Jocelyn tried to change the topic of conversation, not knowing yet that Felicity could never be got to talk of something else until she had said the last word on the first subject, but was entirely unsuccessful. . . . In sheer self-defence he found himself discussing the books that should be bought and the style of furniture best suited to the house with the green door.

II

When he wanted to go home the children would not come. Their awe had evaporated under the influence of spillikins and they had discovered that the house was an enchanted Chinese palace and that Mrs. Jameson was a child like themselves. When Jocelyn went upstairs to fetch them he found Henrietta telling Mrs. Jameson one of Ferranti's fairy stories. She was listening in open-mouthed delight while the parrots, whom Hugh Anthony was feeding with sugar, said, "Oh, my!" at intervals. When requested by Jocelyn to come home they refused point-blank and with regrettable rudeness.

"Leave them," whispered Felicity. "It's so lovely for Aunt Adelaide to have someone of her own sort to talk to. . . . I'll see they get home in time for their baths. . . . I'm so glad you've given in about that shop."

"But I don't think I have, have I?" said Jocelyn, and went downstairs in such a whirl of bewilderment that he put his hand on the banisters and pricked himself severely.

And when he got home things were no better.

Grandfather and Grandmother were both out on the lawn, Grandfather walking up and down and saying evensong and Grandmother sitting under the mulberry tree and knitting for the heathen.

"Well, Jocelyn!" she said in tones of severe reproach, "I don't think you should have left me to hear of your arrangements from my own parlour-maid. I may be old-fashioned, I dare say I am, but in my young days elders were not so treated by the young."

D

Grandfather paused in the middle of the psalms to beam. "What does it matter whom we hear it from, dear Jane? I think the course Jocelyn has decided on is most sensible. Dear me, yes. . . . Thou visitest the earth and blessest it, Thou makest it very plenteous. The river of God is full of water. Thou preparest their corn, for so Thou providest for the earth. . . . We all need to have our minds broadened, especially the Dean."

"What exactly has Sarah told you, Grandmother?" inquired Jocelyn.

"I have never heard anything so ridiculous in all my life," said Grandmother. "I can't imagine what your poor mother will say. Or your father either, for that matter. I will say for Thomas that he knows what employment is suited to a gentleman and what not."

"All employment that is compatible with his religion is suited to a gentleman," announced Grandfather. "Do not forget, dear Jane, that the Apostles themselves were in trade. . . . Fish."

"What's that got to do with it?" asked Grandmother. "The Apostles were not my grandsons."

"Thou waterest her furrows," said Grandfather, continuing his perambulations. "Thou sendest rain into the little valleys thereof, Thou makest it soft with the drops of rain, and blessest the increase of it. . . . My dear Jane, just as God sends corn to feed our bodies so He sends books to feed our minds, and the farmer and the bookseller who act as intermediaries are the most blessed among men."

"We've never yet had a shopkeeper in the family," said Grandmother to Jocelyn. "And there are no drains in that house. And who's to provide the capital? Your poor Grandfather, I suppose."

"Who told Sarah I was going to open a shop?" demanded Jocelyn.

"The grocer, who had it from Martha Carroway at the sweet-shop."

"And how did she know?"

"That's neither here nor there, Jocelyn. The point is that you did not inform your Grandmother of your intentions, as you should have done, before informing the whole town."

"But, Grandmother, I haven't the slightest intention of keeping a bookshop. The whole thing is a canard. They abound in Torminster, Felicity Summers tells me."

"What's that?" said Grandmother.

Jocelyn said it again.

"I never heard of such a thing in all my life," said Grandmother when she understood the situation. "And who, I should like to know, is responsible for spreading these lies about my grandson? I'm going in now, Theobald, to talk to Sarah. This is not the first time I have had to reprimand her for listening to idle gossip."

Jocelyn gave Grandmother his arm across the lawn and then came back to Grandfather.

"Thou crownest the year with Thy goodness and the clouds drop fatness," said Grandfather, but he said it very sadly.

"Grandfather!" exclaimed Jocelyn. "Did you want me to open that bookshop?"

"Yes, Jocelyn, I did. Nothing could have given me greater pleasure. Dear me, yes. Just the thing."

"But why, Grandfather?"

"I thought you so suited to the vocation of a bookseller, Jocelyn. You have sympathy and tact. You would have understood the individual needs of your customers. . . . And then I should have liked you to live in Ferranti's house."

"But why?"

"You might have been able to discover what has happened to him."

"But how?"

"A man always leaves the print of his personality on his dwelling-place. I thought that living there you might have got to understand what manner of man he was and then, aided by your knowledge, you might have been able to think what we ought to do to find out what has become of him."

"Grandfather, aren't you being rather fantastic?"

"I dare say," said Grandfather forlornly. "I'm old."

"I'm so sorry to disappoint you," murmured Jocelyn.

"Yes, it's a disappointment," said Grandfather. "The moment I heard about it I felt you had been guided. It would have been a joy to me to find the little capital that would have been needed to start you." He sneezed sadly. "It's getting chilly. I think I'll go indoors. Have you any idea, dear boy, where I had got to in evensong?"

"You were somewhere in the psalms."

"Thank you. I shall have to go back to the beginning again now for fear I missed any out."

He walked sadly away, his shoulders a little bowed. His attitude seemed to beseech Jocelyn like Felicity's, "Please! Please!"

"I'll think about it, Grandfather," he said suddenly. Grandfather swung round, beaming. "That's right, dear boy, that's right. But mind you *do* think. Don't just take out your feelings and look at them, which is what passes for thought with most of us pitiful, self-centred creatures. Look at the question from everyone's point of view, not forgetting that of this illiterate city."

He went indoors, leaving Jocelyn to pace backwards and forwards on the lawn. He was under the impression that he was thinking things out, but in reality he was only reiterating the one idea that was uppermost in his mind. . . . His pride would not allow Grandfather to finance him. . . . The old man was not wealthy. He would have to take up capital that would be needed later on for Henrietta and Hugh Anthony. The whole idea was preposterous.

The garden door flew open and Henrietta burst in. Her hat had as usual slipped off backwards and dangled by its elastic, her face was flushed and her eyes shining. She looked so lovely that Jocelyn stopped dead with astonishment and allowed his one idea to evaporate.

She careered straight through Grandmother's best flower-bed and flung herself upon him. "I'm so glad! I'm so glad!" she panted.

"What about, Henrietta?" he asked, holding her by her thin elbows and looking down at her transfigured face.

"That you are to live in that little house."

"Who told you I was to live in that little house?"

"Felicity. . . . Now it won't be lonely any more and I shall help you sell in the shop."

Jocelyn let go of her elbows and thrust his hands ruefully into his pockets. "*Et tu, Brute!*" he remarked.

His tone chilled Henrietta and fright seized her. "But you are? You are?" she asked wildly.

"But why should you care so much, Henrietta?"

"I do! You must! I want to sell in the shop!" she cried, and began hammering him with her fists. All the joy had left her face and she looked like one of the furies in infancy.

"You will? You will?" she demanded.

He could not endure to see that look on her face and he took hold of her pummelling fists reassuringly.

"Yes, Henrietta, I will," he said.

CHAPTER V

I

IN the difficult weeks that followed Jocelyn consoled himself by thinking that none of it was his responsibility. Torminster had decided that the empty house in the Market Place must be turned into a bookshop and that he must keep it, and he had no choice but to obey.

But it was all very difficult. Grandmother and Jocelyn's family detested the idea. They had never yet had a shop-keeper in the family and it had been their earnest hope that they never would. . . . It was not gentlemanly. . . . Jocelyn reminded them that the family fortunes had been laid by an Irvin who kept a tannery in the reign of Queen Anne and lost by an Irvin in the reign of George the Fourth who thought that tanning was too smelly to be gentlemanly and exchanged it for card-playing in good society.

"Playing games in good society doesn't pay," said Jocelyn, "so I'd better go back to the leather."

But his family snorted and pished and produced for his inspection just what he had been afraid they would produce, a job in an office in Whitehall or a secretaryship to someone who sat about in the House of Commons when he felt like it and dictated his autobiography to his secretary when he did not. The promise of both these positions had been procured for Jocelyn by his family by much hard work, and the giving of several little dinners that they couldn't afford, and they were rightly incensed when he refused them.

"I'd die in an office," said Jocelyn, "and if that old idiot Enderby-Wetherby started dictating his past life to me I should start telling him what I thought of it. . . . No. . . . I shall keep that bookshop."

His father once more blew down his nose contemptuously and his brother Hubert for the thousandth time implored him not to be more of a fool than he could help, further remarking that if he liked to behave like a lunatic he could not expect financial assistance from the family along the road to Broadmoor.

"I don't," said Jocelyn. "Torminster wants me, so Torminster shall lend me a hand."

But it was Grandmother who was perhaps more outraged than anyone else. The rest of the family would have Jocelyn making a fool of himself at a comfortable distance but she would have him doing it at her very door. Every time she bought a leg of mutton from Mr. Atkins the butcher she would be obliged to remember that her own grandson was a colleague of Mr. Atkins, and Mr. Atkins would remember it too and the mutton would probably be tough in consequence. And every time she bought a reel of cotton from Mr. Bell the draper she would remember that just behind her, across the Market Place, Jocelyn was selling *Eric, or Little by Little* to Canon Elphinstone for Canon Elphinstone's grandson's birthday present. . . . The same wooden counter that separated her from Mr. Bell, emphasizing the gulf between them, would be separating Canon Elphinstone from her own grandson. . . . And Canon Elphinstone, whose blood, people said, was not nearly so blue as he gave one to understand, would be very patronizing about it.

But though Grandmother was outraged she was bountiful. There was a strain of generosity in her that shot up every now and then like a volcano. It had erupted when she acquiesced in the adoption of Henrietta and it erupted now when she announced, in the middle of telling Jocelyn what she thought of him, that though Grandfather was paying for the books she, out of her own money, intended to pay the first month's rent.

"Grandmother!" gasped Jocelyn, overwhelmed.

"You may be an idiot, Jocelyn," she snapped, "but at least you shall not be a starving idiot. . . . Not while I live, that is. . . . I'm fond of you, Jocelyn," she finished suddenly.

Jocelyn kissed her and thanked her and apologized a little desperately for the burden that he was to everybody who had anything to do with him.

For Jocelyn was not enjoying himself. Grandfather and Grandmother seemed pouring out a mint of money on top of him and he felt suffocated beneath it. And he felt humiliated, for who knew if the shop would pay, and if it did not how could he ever hold up his head again?

Yet he persevered, for he did not seem able to help himself. When he tried to think how it had all come about he found that he had not the slightest idea; but one thing he did know; he had been carried to the place where he found himself by something other than his own will. . . . It was almost as though the wind of destiny that Grandfather had spoken of had suddenly arisen and lifted him off his feet.

II

But if Jocelyn was not altogether enjoying himself Felicity was. She was taking several months' rest from the stage and had meant to pay a round of visits to adoring friends, but the shop fascinated her so much that she threw over the adoring friends and remained on the spot to help with the books.

Hugh Anthony was enjoying himself too, asking questions about shopkeeping, and Henrietta and Grandfather, and old Martha of the sweet-shop, who had taken such a fancy to Jocelyn that she announced she would come every morning and "do" for him, leaving the sweets to the care of old Mary and their niece 'Arriet Kate, who though a little wanting in the top story could always manage the change if the kind customers told her what to give. . . . In fact they were all enjoying themselves, except Jocelyn.

Yet even he felt happy sometimes for he already had for the house with the green door an almost passionate love, and in preparing it for its duties he imagined he felt as a mother must do who dresses her daughter for her bridal.

The front room with the bow window made a perfect shop. Mr. Loveday, the carpenter and undertaker, very kindly gave them a lot of coffin wood for the shelves quite cheaply. Something about the misty atmosphere of Torminster made everyone live till a hundred and ten, and poor Mr. Loveday, who had only come to the city recently and had been unaware of the preservative quality of its atmosphere, found the coffin trade not what he had expected and was only too thankful for the work of erecting the shelves. There were curved tiers of them in the window, taking the curve of the bow in a most artistic way but not high, so as not to obscure the charming view of Jocelyn inside behind the counter. The walls of the room, and of the little room on the other side of the passage that was to house the library books, were lined from floor to ceiling with shelves and the floorboards were varnished and polished till they shone like ebony.

The green door was given a coat of new emerald paint and the doors and window-frames inside the front rooms were painted scarlet. It was Henrietta's taste. Jocelyn thought it too bright but was not listened to.

Felicity was enchanted by the beautiful old kitchen with its beams and rose-red tiles, which had been scrubbed till they took on an almost velvety softness. She bought copper pots and rose-sprigged china, and Grandmother, with another outburst of generosity, unearthed some lovely old silver that she did not use and gave it to Jocelyn for a present.

Jocelyn's mother who, though she dared not say so to Thomas her husband and Hubert her son, was thrilled by the whole thing, bought lengths of Liberty material out of money she ought to have been buying new blankets with and sent them to Jocelyn for curtains and cushion-covers. Sarah cut them out and Felicity and Henrietta made them, sitting on Grandmother's drawing-room floor and stitching away under her sharp eye.

Felicity was an expert sewer. Her seams were straight as the high road and her neat stitches marched along them at regular intervals like well-drilled soldiers. She never pricked her finger, she kept her cotton clean and she sang as she worked. . . . Henrietta watched her sew in marvelling adoration.

For with Henrietta it was otherwise. Her stitches progressed along her seams like poor little hunchbacks crawling up twisted country lanes. Somehow her cotton, though it might start life blue or pink or green, was always jet black by the time she had been sewing with it for five minutes, and the progress of its journey was marked by dots of blood. But she would not give in. Felicity, Grandmother, Miss Lavender, Ellen and Sarah all offered to relieve her of her pair of curtains but she would not hear of it. She sewed on and on, hour after hour, breathing heavily, and now and then, when no one saw her, crying a little because her pricked finger was so sore. When at last the labour of love was completed Felicity hung the curtains in the post of honour, the window of Jocelyn's sitting-room looking on the garden. And she did not wash out Henrietta's bloodstains, instead she pointed them out to Jocelyn. "Not every man," she said to him severely, "can say that a woman has literally bled for him."

This sitting-room was the only room in which Jocelyn did not allow himself to be dominated by feminine taste. He sent to London for his few personal treasures and locked the door on the inside while he arranged them. He hung school and regimental groups and a few etchings against the old panelling of the room and spread a shabby but beautiful Persian rug on the floor. He stacked his pipes on the mantelpiece and bought a table and bookcases for his books and two comfortable but modern arm-chairs from Mr. Bell across the way, who furnished as well as draped. He heaped his walking-sticks in one corner and his fishing tackle in another and put hooks in a third to hang his mackintosh and gardening hat on.

"It won't do, Jocelyn," said Felicity, when admitted. "It simply won't do. The rug is lovely, but it clashes with the curtains, and the chairs are too modern. You want period pieces in a house like this. Look how lovely your bedroom looks, with the little four-poster and the old chest-of-drawers. . . . You oughtn't to mix etchings with dreadful groups of moustached soldiers and school-boys don't look right on panelling."

"They are my friends," Jocelyn told her gently, "and it's my panelling. You know, Felicity, I care about beautiful things as much as you do but everyone needs one room where they can heap up their past regardless of beauty. Every picture and stick and pipe in this room reminds me a bit of the past that I liked. One can relax in one's past. One hasn't got to do anything about it any more. . . . And it's companionable, too."

Felicity looked up at him anxiously. "Will you be lonely here? Will you regret coming here and hate me for helping to make you come?"

The June sunshine lay in patches on the floor, outside in the garden the roses were in bud and Felicity in her blue frock looked entrancing. . . . Jocelyn laughed, for loneliness seemed as far away as last night's dreams.

"I don't think I shall ever regret coming," he said. "I haven't enjoyed humbling myself to do it, and perhaps I shall go through times in this house that I shan't enjoy either, but I promise you that I'll never regret."

His last word seemed to fall into the stillness of the room like a stone flung into a well. It seemed to Felicity that its falling sent ripples outwards to the walls that broke in echo. "Regret." She could hear the sound of the spoken word fading away into silence yet living on in every room of the house. She walked to the door and then came suddenly back to Jocelyn, seizing his hands impetuously. "Don't regret!" she implored him. "Don't! There's been too much of it here. Regret for the past must be awful to bear. . . . One can't do anything about it any more. . . . You said that yourself."

"Felicity, what's the matter with you?" Jocelyn rallied her. "Come into the shop and see the till for the filthy lucre."

They went out and the room was left with only the word regret alive in it.

III

But the greatest excitement of all was the arrival of the books. Second-hand books for the library and glossy new volumes for the shop, red and blue and green and purple and black, with golden lettering and sometimes leaves edged with gold, so that when the books were closed it seemed as though wise words were enclosed in golden caskets.

Jocelyn, Felicity, Grandfather and the two children unpacked and arranged them. Jocelyn and Felicity did the unpacking and sorting and Henrietta and Hugh Anthony ran backwards and forwards from the counter to the shelves putting the books in their places. Grandfather did the same, arranging one book per half-hour because he always had to stop and read some of it before he put it away.

Half-way through the afternoon he stopped stock-still in the middle of the floor, *Pride and Prejudice* in one hand and *Wuthering Heights* in the other, to deliver a homily on the profession of a bookseller.

"It is the most friendly vocation in the world," he announced.

"Why?" asked Jocelyn. "Leave a hole just there, Henrietta, for Jane when Grandfather has finished holding her."

"A bookseller," said Grandfather, "is the link between mind and mind, the feeder of the hungry, very often the binder up of wounds. There he sits, your bookseller, surrounded by a thousand minds all done up neatly in cardboard cases; beautiful minds, courageous minds, strong minds, wise minds, all sorts and conditions. And there come into him other minds, hungry for beauty, for knowledge, for truth, for love, and to the best of his ability he satisfies them all. . . . Yes. . . . It's a great vocation."

"Greater than a writer's?" asked Felicity. "Yes, Hugh Anthony, leave a space for poor Emily on the third shelf."

"Immeasurably," said Grandfather. "A writer has to spin his work out of himself and the effect upon the character is often disastrous. It inflates the ego. Now your bookseller sinks his own ego in the thousand different egos that he introduces one to the other. . . . Yes. . . . Moreover, his life is one of wide horizons. He deals in the stuff of eternity and there's no death in a bookseller's shop. Plato and Jane Austen and Keats sit side by side behind his back, Shakespeare is on his right hand and Shelley on his left." He paused for a moment while Felicity took *Pride and Prejudice* and *Wuthering Heights* gently away from him. "Yes. Writers, from what I've seen of them, are a very queer lot, but booksellers are the salt of the earth."

"Mr. Ferranti was a writer," said Henrietta.

"He was," said Grandfather sadly. "Poor fellow. The ego was terribly inflated. . . . Dear me, where did I put Jane and Emily?"

IV

It was the evening of the day before the shop was to open. The last book had been put in its place and the shop blind had been lowered to hide the glories within from the inquisitive gaze of Torminster. All his helpers had gone home and Jocelyn was alone in his house for the first time. He ate the supper that old Martha had left for him, cold ham and pickles and blancmange so hard that it needed a hatchet, in the kitchen with the rose-red floor. The copper pans that Felicity had arranged on the mantelpiece winked in such a charming way and reflected the red tiles with such a warm glow that they seemed alive, and such good company that he did not notice his loneliness.

But when he went into his sitting-room, the back room that had also been Ferranti's sitting-room, he did not feel so companioned. He was tired and the peculiar feelings that lie in wait to pounce upon those who are both tired and alone proceeded to pounce. The bits of his own past that surrounded him seemed to have receded very far away. His friends hanging on the walls seemed to be looking at him through a veil, and that veil, he felt, was another man's past. It was hanging all round him, obscuring his own, and like a mist it was closing in on him.

He had sat down in an arm-chair with a book but suddenly he felt that he could not sit still. . . . And he was so cold. . . . The sunny June had given place to a wet July and outside his window the garden was wrapped in a cloak of soft, steady rain that never ceased for an instant. There was no wind and all day long there had not been one rent visible in the muffling pall that shrouded the world. The damp was awful. It penetrated every cranny and it seemed to Jocelyn that the atmosphere inside the house was as saturated with it as the atmosphere outside. It was the sort of weather that Torminster specialized in and its inhabitants were quite used to it, but to Jocelyn, on this his first introduction to its clamminess, it seemed unspeakably depressing.

He put on his mackintosh and went out to the shed in the garden where he had stored the chopped-up wood of a dead apple-tree. He carried the logs into his sitting-room, fetched paper and matches and lit a fire. The lovely yellow flames burst into flower in the grate and the exquisite smell of burning apple-wood filled the room, as though it were the fragrance of the flame petals.

Jocelyn lit a pipe and drew thankfully nearer to the golden comfort. The damp of the room seemed conquered and the mist that had been closing in on him drew back. . . . He was reminded of a man who lights a fire in a jungle to keep the wild beasts at bay.

He was deep in his book when a knock at the front door startled him. He went down the dark, damp little passage and opened the door almost apprehensively, but outside in the dripping Market Place was no one more alarming than Grandfather, muffled in his voluminous cloak and with his immense old green umbrella erected over his round hat.

"Come in," cried Jocelyn. "Whatever made you come out again in all this wet?"

"I thought you might be lonely," said Grandfather. "Yes. Depressing sort of evening for your first night. I'm lonely myself. Your dear grandmother has gone to bed early with a cold and Felicity is up in London. Coming back by the late train. Thank you, my dear boy, if you could manage to put the umbrella down."

In the passage Grandfather tenderly uncovered a parcel of books that he was carrying under his cloak. "Ferranti's books," he said. "After his disappearance there was a sale and I bought these—all he had left, poor fellow, that he had not already sold. I did not want them to fall into unsympathetic hands. . . . Yes. . . . They are yours now."

"Do you want to give them to me?" asked Jocelyn.

"Yes. They belong here."

Jocelyn hung up Grandfather's cloak in the passage and led the way into the fire-lit sitting-room. He pulled up a second chair to the fire and then went to the kitchen to get hot coffee. Only when two cups of it were steaming on the table between them did he look at the books. There were only three of them, Shakespeare, Byron and Shelley.

"Did he only have these three left at the time of his disappearance?" he asked, holding the shabby volumes between his hands.

"That's all. He had parted with nearly all his possessions. . . . What excellent coffee. Did Martha make it?"

"Yes," said Jocelyn. "But I think that old saint Mary must have made the blancmange I had for supper. It was the kind of blancmange," he added vindictively, "that only a spiritually minded woman would make."

"Mary," said Grandfather, "was once the Archdeacon's cook, but though her influence on the household was very great her beef-and-kidney pudding did not agree with the Archdeacon and he pensioned her off."

Jocelyn carried Ferranti's books to the bookcase and put them with his own. He did not question the gift of them, he did not even say thank you, for it seemed to him quite right that the only tangible things left from Ferranti's past should live here with his. Coming back to the fire he piled on more logs and settled himself in front of Grandfather.

"Tell me about Ferranti," he said.

"There's so little to tell," sighed Grandfather. "That was the trouble with Ferranti, he could tell one nothing. He was an egoist who could not let himself loose in words. The poison of self-absorption had no outlet, if you understand me, and I am afraid that it may have drowned him."

"He lived to himself?" asked Jocelyn.

"Entirely. He was here for two years and as far as I know made no single intimate friend."

"Not even yourself?"

"I tried," said the old man humbly, "but I failed. I was a friend, but not intimate. I came to see him often, and he came to see me, and we talked of books and music and the fair beauties of this world, but of intimate things he would never speak. I could never get near him. It is difficult to take the citadel of another man's being by storm, dear me, yes, but my failure there I count the worst of the sins I have committed against my God."

He stretched out his hands to the fire and Jocelyn saw to his astonishment that they were trembling. "Sin?" he questioned smiling. "Do you call it a sin that you could not force the confidence of a reserved egoist?"

The old man raised troubled eyes. "When a life is

shipwrecked," he said, "one asks oneself, what were those near at hand doing that they did not prevent it?"

"Some ships," said Jocelyn gently, "sail so far away by themselves that no one can get to them when they sink. In a case like that the only man to blame is the man who owns the ship and sets the course."

"I cannot accept your comfort without adding the sin of self-deception to the sin of my failure," said Grandfather. "I know quite well that if after seventy-eight years of the enjoyment of God's goodness I cannot at the end of it kindle a spark of belief in a fellow-creature then I am not worthy of the bounty I have received."

Grandfather's self-scourging was pitiful to see and Jocelyn tried hard to comfort him. "You attempted the impossible," he said. "Some of us are lucky enough to find a causeway for our feet across the slough of this world; belief in God, belief in love, belief in a sound core at the heart of seeming rottenness; something or other. But we find it for ourselves. It's the tragedy of life that we can't communicate it."

"It is to our shame if we cannot."

"Not always. For what can we do? We can cry aloud and hold out a hand to another man, but even though he may take our hand and come nearer to us we have no way of forcing his feet to find rock. That he must do for himself. If he's too lazy or too paralysed by self-absorption or misery to make the effort we can't help that."

"You're wrong there," sighed Grandfather. "A life, such as mine, that has known God's goodness, should act like a magnet. Yes. I can claim no such triumph of personality and therefore I have failed."

"We can't agree," smiled Jocelyn. "Tell me more of Ferranti. Where he came from, what he wrote, why he failed."

"Dear me, yes," said Grandfather. "I came to talk of

Ferranti and stay to talk of myself. How typical that is of human nature. How typical of my own gross selfishness.... Dear me, now I'm starting on my own gross selfishness.... Yes. Ferranti. Where was I?"

"Where did he come from?" asked Jocelyn.

"He had lived for years abroad, he told me, chiefly in Italy, for he was partly Italian, but that was all I could find out. He had that fanatical, dangerous love of beauty, that 'desire of the moth for the star,' that can be content with nothing but perfection. ... Yes. ... He could not be content, as we must be in this world, to worship beauty amid imperfection. If he had seen a lovely picture in an ugly frame he would, I think, have destroyed picture and frame together in his rage. From his complete loneliness I gathered that he must have turned aside from every human relationship the moment that it failed to satisfy his ideal."

"And his verse?" asked Jocelyn.

"That was his passion. Dear me, yes. It was the way in which he had elected to serve beauty and nothing would turn him aside from it. He had that fatal gift of identifying his whole being with one object only. ... Yes. ... There'a a touch of greatness there, but it's dangerous."

"And as a poet he was a failure?"

"How could he be anything else? He wrote the sort of verse that only supersensitives such as himself could have appreciated. You know what I mean. It dealt with problems that are not problems to normal folk, and tortures they would never be likely to feel, and pleasures too delicate for their apprehension. It was verse that needed interpretation and he had no interpreter."

"Did he want a public or did he not care?"

"Of course he cared. He said to me once, 'At rock bottom living is merely a giving of personality in one form or another. If no one wants what you have to give you might as well hang yourself and have done with it.'"

"That sounds bad," said Jocelyn. "The sort of temperament that would turn melancholic under strain."

"Yes. Yes. And he suffered great strain. He told me one day that he had all the money he needed. Private means, he said. Yet, as I told you, when he disappeared we found that he had run through every penny of it. Pride, you see. Life is an appalling strain for those who are both proud and poor together. . . . The fear that he may have made away with himself haunts me night and day."

"In all that you have told me there are certainly the ingredients for a first-class tragedy," Jocelyn agreed. "But, if it happened, I can't see that it's any fault of yours. And I don't see either," he added gently, "what we can do about it now."

"If he still lives," said Grandfather, "he is not beyond our help. Dear me, no. As I said before, I think that you, living in this house, may yet be able to do something about it."

"Good heavens, what?" asked poor Jocelyn.

"That is for you to find out. You will say that I am shifting my burden on to you. Perhaps I am. But your shoulders are younger than mine. . . . Dear me, it's late. . . . I must get home or your dear grandmother will be seriously displeased."

Jocelyn put his cloak about him, took him to the door, erected his umbrella and bade him good night. "I'll do all I can," he said to the troubled old man, but he spoke as one speaks to a child who has broken a toy beyond hope of repair. . . . For what could he do?

"Well, of all the fantastic nonsense," he said to himself when he was alone in his sitting-room again. "But what a dear old boy Grandfather is!"

He lit a pipe and settled down again, thinking. Grand-father had quoted Shelley and now scraps of Shelley's verse floated through his mind.

> "The desire of the moth for the star,
>   Of the night for the morrow,
>   The devotion of something afar
>   From the sphere of our sorrow."

Yes, that was all right. That was the quest for beauty upon which every soul is engaged; but Ferranti, it seemed, had pursued the spirit of transcendent beauty only, and that way madness lay. Immanent beauty he had missed.

> "Spirit of beauty . . . where art thou gone?
>   Why dost thou pass away and leave our state,
>   This dim vast vale of tears, vacant and desolate?"

Had beauty always been for Ferranti an elusive, flying thing? Had it never, in this lovely city, sat beside him at his own hearth and brought him peace?

V

It grew dark and the world was still. Outside the silent rain muffled every sound and in Jocelyn's room the flames had ceased whispering and lay dead, still glowing rose-pink and in their winding-sheets of grey ash. It was so quiet that surely peace should have sat enthroned with Jocelyn, yet he had no sense of peace. Frustration, regret and sadness seemed to be written in the house. Although there was no sound and no movement anywhere Jocelyn felt that the stillness was that of impotence rather than of quiescence. . . . If the house could have spoken aloud it would have done so.

He got up and moved about the room, putting things away. He did not want to stay in this lonely room by himself and yet neither did he want to go upstairs to bed in the room above, where it would be horribly cold and even lonelier. Unused to loneliness as he was he felt decidedly queer. He was ashamed of himself, but he did. . . . He almost wished he had not come to live here. . . . It was a creepy place.

Then he resolutely lit his candle with his last match. He had told Felicity he would regret nothing. He might go through bad times here but they should not drive him either to turn back or to regret the step that he had taken.

Carrying his candle he went out into the passage. The flame guttered in the draught and the chill damp was overpowering. "Spirit of beauty, where art thou gone?" The words said themselves over in his mind so insistently that he felt the question had been asked before in this house. "Spirit of beauty, where art thou?" As if in answer there was another knock at the front door. Jocelyn, stumbling up the stairs, started and dropped the candlestick, plunging himself in darkness. "Fool!" he said to himself, deeply ashamed of his own jarred nerves.

He groped his way to the door and opened it. The street lamp outside The Green Dragon faintly illumined a slim figure in a mackintosh with a dripping hat jammed down on golden hair.

"Felicity!" gasped Jocelyn. "You're beauty! You ought to have come knocking at this door when poor Ferranti lived here."

"I don't know what you're talking about," said Felicity. "I'm looking a perfect sight. . . . But I've brought you this."

She dumped something soft and nondescript into

Jocelyn's arms and stretched her own in relief. "What a weight!" she groaned. "I've carried him all the way from the station. He wouldn't walk."

A cold, wet nose suddenly shot up into Jocelyn's face and a warm tongue was passed interrogatively over his chin. "Great Scot!" said Jocelyn. "A dog!"

"Black," said Felicity. "Front elevation collie, rear elevation pomeranian. The man I bought him from said he was a spaniel but I think myself that there's a dash of dachshund about the legs. If I were you I should call him Mixed Biscuits."

"Come in, Felicity," implored Jocelyn.

"I should think not, at this time of night. As it is it'll be all over Torminster by nine o'clock to-morrow that I carried a dead body to your house under cover of the darkness. . . . I've been thinking about you all day and wondering if you'd be lonely here, and then I saw him sitting in a cage in a shop window, all by himself, crying, and my course seemed clear. He bit the guard. Good night."

"You're an angel, Felicity," cried Jocelyn into the darkness, but she was gone, the rain and the night taking her. He stumbled along to the kitchen, found some matches, lit the lamp and looked at Mixed Biscuits. The creature had lived only a few months in this world and was apprehensive as to what it might do to him. Fearing the worst he rolled over on his back on the kitchen floor, holding up four bandy legs to heaven and exposing all his tenderest parts, thinking perhaps that an attitude of utter defencelessness was his best policy. He thudded his tail on the floor with a pathetically propitiatory action, rolled pleading dewy eyes and panted, exposing all his baby teeth and hanging out his tongue like a yard of pink ribbon.

"Good fellow!" said Jocelyn encouragingly, and

placed the remains of the cold ham on a plate on the floor, with the blancmange on top as a relish.

There was a wild confusion of flying legs as Mixed Biscuits leapt right way up and attacked his food. With feet planted far apart, tail extended and quivering with ecstasy, body taut, jaws champing and tongue whirling round the plate with a circular motion that made the onlooker dizzy, he was an example of concentration to all. . . . But he was not a tidy eater. . . . Bits of blancmange flew into the air and portions of ham skidded along the floor in all directions. Jocelyn, in the intervals of pursuing them with a kitchen fork, gazed at Mixed Biscuits in astonishment.

He was, as Felicity had said, black. He was also woolly. His nose was long and his mouth large, but Jocelyn thought that viewed from the side he was more like a crocodile than a collie. His ears were immense, and flapped, and his tail was like a housemaid's brush. His poor body was weak and thin, as though good food had not come his way too often, and his legs were a great deal too large for the rest of him.

"Good lord!" said Jocelyn.

Mixed Biscuits polished up his empty plate with sweeping movements of his long pink tongue, sighed, panted, had a drink, sat down and looked at Jocelyn. His limpid eyes were exquisite and a character of unusual loveliness had already set its mark upon his countenance. Jocelyn fondled his silky ears with growing enthusiasm and Mixed Biscuits again flung himself on his back and erected his legs. But this time there was nothing cringing in his attitude. With a slight motion of his right forepaw he invited Jocelyn to scratch his chest. Jocelyn scratched, while Mixed Biscuits closed his eyes and simpered, and mutual affection grew every moment stronger.

"What about bed, old man?" asked Jocelyn at last.

Mixed Biscuits had no objection and they went upstairs together. It was cold, and the candle sent queer shadows leaping over the walls, but Jocelyn was too absorbed in Mixed Biscuits to notice and climbed into bed with a sense of companionship warm about his heart and grateful thoughts of Felicity flocking like birds in his mind, ready to turn into dreams of beauty as soon as sleep gave them wings.

CHAPTER VI

I

JOCELYN'S fears that the shop would be a failure proved groundless. Torminster, rather to its own astonishment, took a pride and pleasure in Jocelyn and his books. There was something flattering in the fact that an intelligent young man from London should think it worth his while to settle down among them and minister to their intellectual needs. It implied that he had the highest opinion of their mental powers and was grieved that residence so far from the Metropolis should debar them from the full exercise of the same.

Everyone, from the Bishop and the Dean downwards, patronized the bookshop. They bought each other presents at it, they borrowed the library books, they discussed what they read with Jocelyn and they started a literary society. Even the tea-parties took on a mental flavour, the people who had read the latest books being careful to bring the conversation round to them and the people who had not saying, "Ah!" in a very profound way, and implying by their wrinkled brows that they were silent only from excess of thought. Grandmother, instead of finding herself looked down upon for having a grandson in trade, was astonished to find herself on a pinnacle as the relative of a literary character. People even asked her advice on books and she said, "Don't ask me, I've no time for such rubbish," but was very pleased all the same.

"It can't last," said Jocelyn to Grandfather. "I'm a new turn, like a performing bear."

"I think it will last," said Grandfather. "In my experience when people once begin to read they go on. They begin because they think they ought to and they go on because they must. Yes. They find it widens life. We're all greedy for life, you know, and our short span of existence can't give us all that we hunger for, the time is too short and our capacity not large enough. But in books we experience all life vicariously."

But Jocelyn became gradually a good deal more to Torminster than just its bookseller, he became its interpreter. He had the gift, born of sympathy and personal humility, of banishing restraints by giving people a good conceit of themselves, and so it happened that people like Mr. Bell the draper and his son Bert summoned courage to drop in in the evenings when the shops were shut and talk books with Jocelyn. In the end so many of them came, and so often, and stayed so long and talked so hard that he began to feel himself the host of a Parisian *salon*.

He was astonished at his success, both social and financial. He seemed popular as a man and secure as a tradesman, with friends in his back room and a balance, if microscopic, at the bank. He had found his niche and it gave him a glorious feeling of security. His feet seemed set firmly on the causeway of which he had spoken to Grandfather and the slough of the world all round him seemed less black.

But it was there. Side by side with his new happiness there lived with him in the house that sadness that had weighed him down on his first night. How could he rejoice whole-heartedly in his own firm footing when another had not found it here? He felt as though the thread of his own life was woven with that of another, a light thread with a dark, and until both of them were light he could not feel at peace.

II

A certain Wednesday in September dawned mellow and still. It was the time of year when Torminster was at its loveliest, a moment when it seemed that the streets of the city were paved with gold. The sky above the town was a stainless blue but below it the faint mist of autumn hung over roofs and towers, a mist that seemed to be of gold dust, as though the sun that burned all day in a glory of raying flame had let fall a distillation of itself that warmed as dew refreshes.

Everywhere there seemed a suggestion of fires burning, orange and red and gold. In the gardens of the Close were scarlet dahlias and yellow chrysanthemums, while the trees on the Tor and the elms on the Cathedral Green were pure gold.

In the utter peace and stillness the world seemed holding its breath, a little apprehensively, drawing near to the fire to warm itself. There was none of that sense of urgeful, pushing life that robs even a calm spring day of the sense of silence; life was over and the year was just waiting, harbouring its strength for the final storms and turmoil of its death. The warmth and the colour of maturity were there, exultant and burning, visible to the eyes, but the prophecy of decay was felt in a faint shiver of cold at morning and evening and a tiny sigh of the elms at midnight when a wandering ghost of a wind plucked a little of their gold away from them.

Jocelyn got up on that Wednesday morning in the best of spirits, for it was early-closing day. This afternoon the shop would be shut and he would be a free man. He loved his new life but its airlessness irked him sometimes and the exercising of Mixed Biscuits was a problem that at times seemed to fill the whole world; especially at night

when Mixed Biscuits, suffering from insomnia for lack
of walks, alternately howled at the moon, chased mice
and slaked his thirst at the water jug.

As he dressed and shaved Jocelyn looked out of the
window. In his tangled garden, as in all the gardens of
Torminster, there was a riot of flaming flowers. The
red-hot pokers were looking especially proud that morning,
spearing up from among their lesser brethren with the
arrogance of the Cathedral towers themselves. Beyond
them the woods and hills were shrouded in mist and beyond
those again the eastern sky was still a gold-barred lattice
window that the sun looked through.

Jocelyn went downstairs, unlocked the front door, sent
Mixed Biscuits into the garden to bark at the blackbirds
and set about getting his breakfast. He did not allow
Martha to come to his assistance until later in the morning,
when old Mary had been arrayed in her petticoats and the
sweet-shop started for the day.

He hummed a tune as he fried his bacon over the oil-
stove, wondering who would come to the shop this morning. The coming and going of customers was a continual
amusement and interest, for unconsciously they revealed
so much of themselves to him that he felt at times as though
he was the audience in a theatre and each ring of his shop-
bell was the ring that sent up the curtain on a human drama.
. . . It was absurd how people showed their character while
shopping. . . . Their decision or their lack of it; their
attitude towards the weather; their taste in books and bindings; the way in which they treated Jocelyn himself,
some of them being aware of his humanity, grateful
for it and courteous towards it, and others regarding him
merely as the Man in the Shop, an automaton whose feelings need not in any way be considered; their reaction to the
fact that an ordered book had not come yet; the way
they behaved if Mixed Biscuits tripped them up on the

doorstep; all these things were straws which showed which way the wind blew, and sometimes Jocelyn felt that what he did not know about the character of every reading man, woman and child in Torminster was not worth knowing.

He had just finished his breakfast when Martha arrived, cheery as ever, with her little black bonnet perched delicately on top of her head and her jet-trimmed mantle hiding the working print dress that she wore beneath it from the gaze of Torminster. . . . For when Martha crossed the Market Place from her house to Jocelyn's she always dressed up as though she were bound for America. . . . Besides the bonnet and mantle she wore gloves, and on windy days a veil, and she carried her apron in a brown paper parcel fastened with safety-pins.

When Jocelyn had greeted her he went out into the Market Place to take down his shutters. This daily opening of the shop was a continual delight to him. As he came out into the sunlight, where the pigeons were whirling softly through the golden air and the sleepy cats were stretching themselves in the sun, he glanced round him to see who else had come out to take their shutters down. . . . Yes, they were all there. . . . The landlord of The Green Dragon, Mr. Bell, Mr. Jones, Mr. Atkins, Mr. Loveday, 'Arriet Kate of the sweet-shop and several others. They glanced at each other across the Market Place and nodded and smiled, for this was their hour of fellowship and in the absence of those whom they served they were conscious of each other as a brotherhood of servers, and then, with a creaking and grinding, the shutters came down and the eyes of the shops were open. Nine o'clock rang out from the Cathedral, mellow and lovely, and the work of the day had begun.

Jocelyn took a duster from his pocket and began polishing his bow-window from the outside. As he

smoothed its face lovingly, going carefully into all the
corners, he remembered how, when he had first seen
this window, even though the shop behind had been
empty, he had thought of it as being bulged outwards
by the wealth behind. . . . Well, the wealth was there
now, rows and rows of it, the greatest treasures of
mankind.

He went into the shop, accompanied by Mixed Biscuits,
and began dusting and rearranging and reading the books,
a job that kept him endlessly happy between the visits
of customers. His desultory reading during the daytime
was giving him a nodding acquaintance with nearly every
author in the shop and during the long evenings when the
shop was closed he picked out a few of them and let the
acquaintance deepen into friendship.

III

But to-day he did not get farther than a few nods and
bows, for the shop-bell tinkled and the curtain rang up
on the drama of the Dean of Torminster. He was a
character. He had a commanding figure, bushy white
side-whiskers and legs especially moulded by Nature to
wear gaiters. Like Mr. Gotobed he always wore a top-
hat, but whereas Mr. Gotobed's hat was always poised
on the back of the head the Dean's was always tipped
forward over the nose, which was in this case aquiline.
The Dean's blood was very blue indeed and his balance
at the bank heavy. These things, he thought, were to his
credit, and the knowledge tinged his bearing and his
high-pitched, nasal, fluting voice with a slight pomposity.
As a Father in God he had his limitations but as a figure-
head he was perfect, and as such Torminster was proud
to wear him on the prow of its ship.

"Fine day, fine day," piped the Dean, as though patron-izing it, and tripped over Mixed Biscuits. "Must this animal take upon himself the duties of a doormat?" he continued in icy and falsetto annoyance, though the catastrophe was just as much his fault as Mixed Biscuits', for why should Mixed Biscuits look out for him any more than he for Mixed Biscuits? But the Dean was one of those who are far more aware of the obligations of others to them than of theirs to others. . . . Mixed Biscuits, unapologized to for a nasty kick on the hind parts, growled and went under the counter. . . . "And might one ask what kind of a dog he is?" went on the Dean, implying that Mixed Biscuits' lack of breeding should prevent him from sunning himself on a respectable doormat.

"I've decided to call him a Rumanian mousehound," said Jocelyn a little coldly.

"Ah!" commented the Dean, "another of these Balkan problems," and became quite sunny again, for no one appreciated his occasional gleams of humour more than he did himself.

"What can I do for you?" asked Jocelyn.

The Dean sat down, readjusted his top-hat and folded his hands on top of his silver-headed stick.

"This annual difficulty of the choir-school prize-giving," he proclaimed through his nose, "will be upon us in a couple of months and I should like to consult with you upon the choice of books for that purpose."

Jocelyn bowed with great solemnity to hide the twinkle in his eyes. He always enjoyed the Dean immensely.

"For the dear boys these are the formative years," con-tinued the Dean, "and I realize the importance of the personal touch. I write each boy's name in his book with my own hand and I trust that the book with its inscription will recall to him throughout life the few words that I may have occasion to speak at the moment of presentation.

But I naturally cannot set my seal to any work but that of the highest quality."

Jocelyn quite saw that.

"The books should be instructive but not heavy," fluted the Dean, "suitable to their tender years yet sufficiently advanced in thought to act as counsellors through life, and of course of irreproachable purity. . . . Difficult. . . . Difficult."

Jocelyn agreed that it was.

"And what would you suggest?"

"Verse," said Jocelyn promptly.

"Eh?" piped the Dean, surprised. "Personally I distrust verse. There is a luxuriance about it that appears to me slightly sensual."

"Why should luxuriance be sensual?" asked Jocelyn. "Look at the seraphim. . . . All that wing."

The Dean thought this remark flippant and waved it aside with the well-kept left hand that wore a diamond ring. "May I inquire your reasons for advising verse?" he asked.

"Children love good poetry," said Jocelyn. "It appeals to their sense of rhythm, I think. . . . You know how a baby loves to watch anything swinging. . . . And grown people love it because its very luxuriance recaptures their youth for them. Therefore verse fulfils one of your requirements and provides something that will appeal throughout life."

"H'm. Yes," said the Dean. "Possibly, possibly."

"And then as regards instruction without heaviness," said Jocelyn. "I have heard it said that real poetry is always the expression of very intense perception. The jog-trot of prose is sufficient for the mere observer to record his observations in but the man who has seen behind an appearance to its significance employs winged verse. He must, like a lark, leap up above the material plane if he

E

is to convey any impression of the significance to which he has penetrated."

"I doubt if I follow you," said the Dean shortly. . . . There were times when he had a very slight suspicion that Jocelyn led him on.

"When an artist, be he poet or painter, has expressed the significance of a thing he has said the inevitable word on that subject and by doing so has created a masterpiece. And surely a masterpiece is instructive? And it is certainly never heavy or, as Anatole France tells us, it could not fly over the ages in the way it does."

"Possibly, possibly," said the Dean. "But we are still left with the need for literature of irreproachable purity. The lives of the poets do not always show that. Shelley, for instance. . . . Regrettable. . . . Regrettable."

"That's got nothing to do with it."

"Eh?"

"You've got no business to inquire into an artist's private life."

The Dean snorted. He enjoyed his talks with Jocelyn, but there were times when the young man presumed.

"It's got nothing to do with you unless you happen to be attending his soul in a professional capacity," continued the intrepid Jocelyn. "What matters to you is what he gives you, not the flaws in a personality that has perhaps been cracked and strained by the effort of giving."

"Possibly, possibly," said the Dean, and then, with a sudden change of tone, "Ah! Spring roses and June sunshine!"

He was gazing out of the window, preening himself slightly and inserting his eyeglass as he did so, for outside in the Market Place was Felicity.

The Dean had an eye for a pretty woman. Never did he allow it to lead him beyond the bounds of propriety, but still, he had it. "Ah!" he said again. "Exquisite! Exquisite!"

Both men gazed, the Dean with the appraising yet detached eye of the connoisseur, Jocelyn with the hunger of the lover.

Felicity was standing by the holy well among the pigeons, feeding them and watching them, engrossed in them, her body taut in its habitual attitude of poised attentiveness, as though she had sent her mind up into the air with the pigeons and her body were just going to take wing to join it. She wore yellow to-day, instead of her usual blue, and looked as though she were spun out of the warm air and the golden light of autumn. The pigeons were strutting round her feet and circling round her head and shoulders, obscuring her gold with the silvery colour of their wings. Jocelyn had not noticed that they flocked round other people as they did round Felicity, but then all birds and animals loved her. Like all happy people she always seemed to be very close to the earth and to all growing, living things. Perhaps her joy in life gave her a special unity with all forms of life, and entry into that state of awareness where self is forgotten and the horizon of love creeps out and out until it embraces all that can be seen and known while the body still hems in the spirit.

"Charming, charming," said the Dean. "A little too thin, perhaps, but very nearly perfection. Do you know the lady?"

"She is Mrs. Jameson's goddaughter."

"I should be honoured by an introduction."

Jocelyn could have cheerfully slain him, for it was a crime to disturb that picture of golden stillness and silvery movement. . . . What was more he was not going to. . . . He strolled to the front door and stood watching, letting the picture of Felicity grave itself so deeply on his mind

that when with the passing of time it would seem to other
people that she had grown old and lost her beauty it would
not seem so to him.

But his attention was too burning not to affect her.
She felt it as a warmth in her secret spot of loneliness
and she swung round towards him as one turns unconsciously towards a fire. "The Dean," said Jocelyn, strolling
towards her, "wishes to be introduced. You're a little
too thin, perhaps, but charming."

Felicity, her eyes twinkling, returned with him to the
shop, where the Dean had risen to his feet and removed
his hat.

The introduction took place, the Dean and Felicity
seated themselves on Jocelyn's two hard shop chairs and
exchanged beautiful Victorian compliments, Felicity rising
to the occasion with amazing histrionic skill.

"Will you convey my compliments to your admirable
godmother," summed up the Dean at the end of a quarter
of an hour, "and my wife and I will be delighted if you will
both drink tea with us on Thursday next."

"I am unfortunately obliged to leave Torminster this
afternoon," said Felicity sweetly, "but I am sure that
my godmother will be most happy to accept your in-
vitation."

The Dean was perturbed. His wife could not stand
Mrs. Jameson and if she were to turn upon Thursday next
undiluted by Felicity he feared that there would be
domestic trouble later. . . . But his courtesy was not
only on the surface. . . . "Delighted, delighted," he
murmured distractedly. "My wife will write. Good day.
Good day."

He shook hands, bowed, re-poised his top-hat over his
aquiline nose and issued out into the Market Place in
some distress of mind, entirely forgetting the choirboys'
books.

"Now that was really wrong of me," said Felicity with contrition. "But it hurts Aunt Adelaide that they never ask her to the Deanery, and now they'll have to."

But Jocelyn was not interested in Aunt Adelaide's feelings. "Are you really going to-day?" he asked.

"Yes. I was coming to say good-bye when you saw me. I've been offered a part in a new play."

Jocelyn felt stricken, the more so that he had not realized until this moment what it would mean if Felicity went away. There was suddenly no warmth in the sunshine and no brightness in the fires of autumn. The chill of it, that sighed at midnight and touched the morning and the evening with icy fingers, struck at him like a sword. . . . These warm lovers of life, born under dancing stars, how without them was life tolerable for those, such as himself, whose bias was towards sadness, their stars cloud-hidden when their spirits woke to life. . . . In this world, surely, there should always be a mating between the lovers of life and the endurers of it, in couples they should find a causeway for their feet and walk it together, the star-shine of the one comforting the darkness of the other.

"When will you be back?" he asked tonelessly.

"If the play is a failure, and it's so clever and beautiful that it's sure to be, I shall be back for Christmas."

"You'll be glad to get back to your work?"

"Yes. I love it."

"Is it so wonderful?" He spoke carelessly, trying to hide his burning eagerness to know just how much her stage life meant to her.

"Of course it's wonderful. It's the only form of art in which you actually feel what you are giving accepted. It gives you a glorious feeling of power."

"And fills every corner of your life?"

"Of course it doesn't. How silly you're being, Jocelyn! It wouldn't fill every corner of me unless I were a genius, and I'm not, I'm only a perfectly ordinary woman gifted with a personality that happens to give pleasure on the stage. And that life has not got the whole of me; there seems to be something of me, the kernel perhaps, that I can't give to it however much I try. I couldn't give up my work, but I want something besides, something deeper that will satisfy deep things in me."

Their eyes met and she hoped she had made herself understood, but feared not, men were so obtuse. . . .

"I wonder what sort of financial condition the shop will be in when you come back," said Jocelyn lightly. Their eyes met again and he hoped he had made her see what he was driving at, but was afraid not. Women being sometimes rather slow at the uptake.

Further mutual enlightenment was impossible for the Dean reappeared, slightly breathless. Half-way home it had occurred to his subconscious mind that if he did not go back and have another good look at Felicity he would not get the chance again for some while to come. This idea, slightly altered in transit, appeared in his conscious mind as a conviction that it was his plain duty to go back to the bookshop and settle the matter of the choirboys' prizes.

"Ah, Miss Felicity!" he proclaimed, hat in hand. "Still here?"

"I'm just going home."

"Then I can have the happiness of offering my escort. Permit me."

He offered his arm with an air, Felicity accepting it with an even greater air.

"I'll see you off at the station," whispered Jocelyn.

"Two-forty-five," whispered Felicity.

"Send up a selection of the poets to the Deanery, Captain Irvin," piped the Dean. Then he and Felicity bowed to Jocelyn, swept from the shop, sailed across the

Market Place and glided superbly towards the Close, exchanging mutual compliments as they went.

Only in Torminster, thought Jocelyn as he watched them, was the world sufficiently leisured for such a display of *la politesse*.

IV

The rest of the day was exhausting. When the Dean and Felicity had disappeared there was a constant stream of ladies to change their library books before the shop shut for the day. Ladies with library books could be very irritating, Jocelyn found. They wanted the perfect book without knowing what it was called or who it was by, and when nothing in the library seemed to be just right they blamed Jocelyn. On the rare occasions when they did know what they wanted it was always out and they again blamed Jocelyn.

"I want a *nice* book," they would say to him.

"What kind?" he would say.

"Oh, just nice. . . . By the way, I didn't like the second book by that man, I can't remember his name but you know who I mean; it was quite different from his first."

"But he couldn't write the same one over again, could he?"

"Well, anyway, I didn't like it and I don't know why you gave it to me. Can't you find me a really *nice* book?"

Or they would say, "I want a book for my husband to read over the week-end."

"What sort of book?" he would say with a little sigh, for week-end husbands were the worst problem of all.

"Something he hasn't read before."

"What has he read before?"

"Really, he reads so many I can't keep pace. *You*

choose. You're a man and you ought to know what men like."

"What did he say about the last one I sent him?"

"He said he wasn't senile yet."

After lunch there was Felicity to be seen off at the station. They travelled down in the bus, accompanied by Henrietta and Hugh Anthony, so that conversation was impossible. The only really private remark that Felicity managed to murmur in a moment's quiet was, "Read that story of Ferranti's before I come back."

"You're as bad as Grandfather," sighed Jocelyn. "I'm a jaded bookseller, not a magician."

Then, when Felicity had gone, Mixed Biscuits had to be exercised. Jocelyn and the children took him round by the Palace, his favourite walk because he could bark at the swans on the moat. At the far end of the Market Place yet another of the archways in which Torminster abounded led to the great trees and green grass that surrounded the moated Bishop's Palace. If the houses in the Close, hidden behind their high walls, could be seen with the eyes of imagination as fortresses the Palace was one in actual fact. Grey, battlemented walls, with loopholes for arrows, surrounded it and its gardens, completely hiding them from sight, and a wide moat, brimful of water, surrounded the walls. The portcullis was still there, and the drawbridge that linked this warlike island to the peace of Torminster.

As they stood watching, the swans obligingly rounded the curve of the moat and sailed royally towards the drawbridge, their necks curving and sinister, their snowy wings graciously folded. Mixed Biscuits barked ecstatically but Henrietta did not like them. "They're like snakes," she said.

The foremost swan turned gracefully towards her and reared his head almost as though he meant to shoot out a fanged, poisoned tongue, but thinking better of it he fixed upon her for a moment the swan's cold, inhuman stare, and then turning from her with beautiful contempt he pulled with his beak the bell-rope that hung from the Palace wall. He rang it once, imperiously, his concubines falling into place behind him, and instantly a human menial showered bread from a window. This ringing of the bell was the superb accomplishment of the swans of Torminster, an accomplishment that had made them world-famous. . . . Indolent black beaks were lowered to the bread and the crescents of curved necks met other, reflected crescents, and formed together flawless circles. . . . Billowy white feathers, lying on blue water, had the snowy softness of cumulus clouds on a summer day.

"They may be lovely," said Jocelyn, "but they're certainly rude birds. Let's look for the kingfisher."

They walked on under the trees until a sudden meteor flash of blue shot over the water and was gone. They stood and blinked but there was nothing there except the unchanging grey walls and their mirrored reflection.

"It's like a falling star," said Henrietta.

"Why?" said Hugh Anthony.

"Well, it's there and then it isn't there."

"Too lovely to be permanent," said Jocelyn gloomily, and wondered if it was true that Felicity had ever been in Torminster.

"We're coming back to tea with you so as to cheer you up," said Henrietta.

"Oh, are you?" said Jocelyn. "Thank you."

"We'll play hide-and-seek all over your house," said Hugh Anthony.

"Oh, will we?" said Jocelyn. "Thank you."

E*

Alone in his sitting-room that evening he found that once again he had to light a fire of apple-wood to banish gloom. He had walked and hidden-and-sought more than his lame leg liked and he was filled with the restlessness and depression of fatigue. He wanted to read, so as to stop himself thinking about Felicity, but he found himself as difficult to please as his library-book ladies. Every book he took up seemed the wrong book and every time he sat down in his chair a spring seemed broken in a different place.'

Resolutely he lit a pipe and opened a new novel. These depressed fits submerged him very often in Torminster and his inability to get the better of them infuriated him, for though he was not naturally joyous he was no pessimist. . . . Sometimes he thought that unhappiness was alive in the house as an actual personality, sometimes seeming a part of the house as on his first night, and sometimes, as to-night, entering into him.

His left foot went to sleep and the novel seemed the stupidest ever written. Getting up for the eighth time he went to his bookcase, envying the unsusceptibility to atmosphere of Mixed Biscuits, who snored in front of the fire in utter content. What *was* he to read? He would have a shot at something he knew almost by heart already. That at least would be no effort. . . . When in doubt choose Shakespeare. . . . His own was upstairs but Ferranti's, that he had never yet opened, was here on the shelf. He carried it to the fire and settled down to read *Hamlet*.

And almost at once his unhappy mood slipped from him and he felt instead dreamy and contented. As his eyes slid over the words the poetry of the opening scene

sang itself in his mind, as though his eyes on the printed
page were fingers gliding over a piano.

> "But look, the morn, in russet mantle clad,
>   Walks o'er the dew of yon high eastward hill."

He turned the pages and with the entrance of Hamlet
himself his new mood of lulled peacefulness turned to
one of tingling interest, for it seemed that Ferranti was
one of those criminals who mark their books. Passage
after passage was pencilled in the margin with strokes
that in places had cut like a knife. Jocelyn had always
declared that if you want insight into a man's state of
mind you have but to look at the marked passages in his
books, and now, as he read, he felt that he was getting
to know Ferranti.

> "O that the Everlasting had not fix'd
> His cannon 'gainst self-slaughter! O God! God!
>   To die: to sleep;
> No more; and by a sleep to say we end
> The heart ache.
> By the o'ergrowth of some complexion,
> Oft breaking down the pales and forts of reason.
>   What is he whose grief
> Bears such an emphasis? Whose phase of sorrow
> Conjures the wandering stars and makes them stand
> Like wonder-wounded heroes? This is I."

These and many others seemed to come to him in the
tones of an actual voice. He read on and on, pity and a
sense of friendship deepening in him, until he came to the
last marked passage of all, where the pencil had scored
the margin twice over.

"O good Horatio, what a wounded name,
  Things standing thus unknown, shall live behind
    me!
  If thou didst ever hold me in thy heart,
  Absent thee from felicity awhile,
  And in this harsh world draw thy breath in pain
  To tell my story."

The book still open on his knees Jocelyn leant back
in his chair and stared at the fire. He felt normal and
alert, both depression and a too painful interest lifted
off his mind so that he could think clearly. He turned
back to the earlier marked passages and read them through
again, although they told him nothing except that Ferranti
had been a tormented man, now in all probability dead
by his own act, who had perhaps found comfort in com-
muning with someone equally tormented yet able to give
him the vicarious relief of self-expression. But why had
he marked the last passage? "And draw thy breath in pain
to tell my story." Who was his Horatio? Who was the
ordinary, normal man who stood beside him as the foil
of his twisted genius and the interpreter of it? . . . Jocelyn
had the feeling that it was himself. . . . But he knew next
to nothing about Ferranti's history, and how could he tell
a story he did not know?

"To tell my story," he murmured to himself, and then,
the one line bringing another to his mind, "Drive my
dead thoughts over the universe." Now where in the world
did that come from? He sat bolt upright, thinking, and
then remembered that Henrietta had murmured it in her
sleep one night and that it came from Shelley's "Ode to
the West Wind."

He shot out of his chair, went to the bookcase
and pulled out Ferranti's Shelley, turning the pages
feverishly.

"Drive my dead thoughts over the universe,
  Like withered leaves to quicken a new birth;
And, by the incantation of this verse,
  Scatter, as from an unextinguished hearth,
  Ashes and sparks, my words among mankind."

It was marked, like the speech in Hamlet, twice over.

Ten o'clock had struck and the fire was dying. Jocelyn went upstairs to his bedroom, sat on the bed and stared at the blank wall opposite his window. Had he seen the Hamlet only he would have thought no more about it but the passage at the end of Hamlet backed by the one in Shelley had taken on the character of a direct command.

"And yet the whole thing's fantastic," he murmured, and suddenly remembered the fantastic dream in which he had read Ferranti's story written on this very wall. Well, it was not written there now. There was nothing on the wall but shadows and a spider. Could Ferranti have left any of his manuscripts behind in the house? No, it had been cleaned and repainted from top to toe and each cupboard had been revealed bare as Mother Hubbard's. What had happened to them all? "I hate waste. I'll buy them to light my fires with." Now who had said that? Good heavens! The crazy Mrs. Jameson!

Jocelyn could not possibly wait till the morning, for goodness only knew with what Mrs. Jameson's housemaid might not have lit the fire by that time. He dashed downstairs as fast as his lame leg would allow, seized his hat and let himself out into the Market Place. There was no moon to-night and as he crossed the Green the Cathedral and the Tor were visible only as dark shapes that blotted out the stars.

"But I think Mrs. Jameson is just going to bed, sir," said the astonished maid who opened the door.

"'Then I must catch her before she gets there," said Jocelyn, and hurried upstairs past the thistles without waiting to be announced.

Mrs. Jameson was still in her drawing-room. She had just given the parrots a lump of sugar each to avert night starvation and was covering them over with embroidered Chinese shawls. It was the season of Trinity and she was dressed in superb green velvet, with green shoes and stockings and emeralds in her lovely hair.

"'Ullo, dearie," remarked the only uncovered parrot, and Mrs. Jameson swung round.

"Captain Irvin," she said calmly. She was not at all startled for like a child she took everything that happened quite for granted. "How nice. Let's have tea."

The astonished maid, appearing at the door at this moment, was sent for tea. "And cakes," said Mrs. Jameson, "and I think I'd like a banana."

They sat down and Jocelyn explained himself slowly and clearly, and found to his relief that Mrs. Jameson had quite understood the essentials. Gabriel Ferranti had been a poet and his poems were lost and it was important that they should be found, and were there any poems among the papers she had bought?

"How am I to know," she asked sweetly, "now that they are burnt?"

"Are you sure they're all burnt?"

"There might be some in the housemaid's cupboard. Shall we go and see? Have you any matches?"

Jocelyn lit two candles in tall silver candlesticks and taking one each they set out, eleven o'clock striking as they went. The cupboard was at the end of a dark passage and in it, beneath brooms and dustpans, was a small pile of very dirty papers. Jocelyn pulled it out with fingers that trembled and saw newspapers and, here and there among them, some pages of manuscript.

"This is all?" he asked huskily.

"That's all. There was a great deal more, of course, before we burnt it. . . . And now shall we have tea?"

At sight of the silver tea-tray and the cakes and bananas Mrs. Jameson lost interest in Ferranti and began to tell Jocelyn some fantastic tale about parrots building nests in banana-trees, and then she asked him to tell her a story and out of pity and gratitude he did his best, relating another of Ferranti's that had come to him via Henrietta. . . . And all the time, perhaps, *the* story lay on his knee.

When he let himself into his own house again it was striking midnight. He went into his sitting-room, re-kindled the lamp and the nearly extinguished fire, and set to work to sort out the papers on the floor. The pages of manuscript, when gleaned from the newspapers, seemed for the most part to be only jotted notes on un-finished poems, and Jocelyn's heart sank as he wondered what had already gone to feed Mrs. Jameson's flames.

But at last, folded between a two-year-old copy of *The Times*, he found a bundle of pages roughly fastened together with a piece of string. He laid them on the table, pulled the lamp towards him and unfastened them, wildly excited, for they seemed to be a long dramatic poem.

And then excitement turned to despair for the thing was almost illegible and in wild confusion. It was written in pencil in a tiny, crabbed handwriting, with gaps and erasions, evidently dashed down in a hurry and never re-read or corrected. And Jocelyn was bitterly disappointed as well as despairing, for it seemed to be some queer symbolic tragedy that had no connection with reality and therefore could not be Ferranti's relation of his own story. . . . That, if the marked passages in the books

were more than chance and it had ever existed, must have
been destroyed. . . . For a mad moment, tired and dis-
couraged, he was on the point of throwing the whole thing
into the fire but then, ashamed of himself, he turned to it
once more and began puzzling over it again.

And now, as he grew more accustomed to the writing,
he found himself deciphering whole consecutive phrases,
and found that they were good. If this was not Ferranti's
own story it was at any rate fine poetry, with here and there
a ring of genius.

"Have I got to make all this out and rewrite it?"
Jocelyn's weary mind inquired of his spirit. "God!
It'll take me months!"

But Jocelyn's real self, that seemed now to be standing
a little apart from the aching body and tired mind that
it used, assured him that he had. Was he not a bookseller, a link between mind and mind? Had he not discovered that he had it in him to interpret genius? He
must try to explain this Ferranti to a world eager for beauty
just as he tried to explain the minds in his front shop to Mr.
Bell and Bert.

One o'clock struck and he put the pages together again
and stretched himself. "The bell then striking one," he
murmured, his mind going back to Hamlet. "This is the
point where the ghost should enter. Are you alive, Ferranti,
or are you dead?"

He put everything away and went upstairs to bed,
lying awake until the bird of dawning awoke the god of
day.

"If you're a ghost, Ferranti," he thought, "you must
go away now and let me sleep. At the cock's warning
the extravagant and erring spirit flies to his confine. Rest,
rest, perturbed spirit! Remember thee? Ay, thou poor
ghost, while memory holds a seat in this distracted globe.
Remember thee!"

CHAPTER VII

I

IN November Torminster Cathedral commemorated its patron saint and benefactors. The Cathedral was great at festivals, each Christmas and Easter and Whitsun marching by in the procession of the days in flower-decked pomp, but in after years it seemed to Henrietta and Hugh Anthony that this particular festival surpassed all the others. It of course lacked the secular excitement of Christmas and Easter, for no one hung up stockings on it or ate pink boiled eggs for breakfast on it, but it had a peaceful and rather wistful beauty that was unforgettable.

It had been led up to by a season of remembrance. In September they had commemorated St. Michael and all the angels. In the Cathedral a great brass pot of michaelmas daisies had been placed under the window in the Lady Chapel that showed the good angels, looking very strong-minded and muscular, heaving the bad angels out of heaven on the end of pitchforks, and at home they had an iced cake for tea and while they ate it Grandfather told them how busy the angels were kept looking after little children. Henrietta felt that what with one thing and another the poor angels were very overworked, and she felt so grateful for their exertions that she made garlands of autumn flowers and hung them round the necks of the cherubs in her bedroom and the seraphim in the spare room.

And then had come All Saints' Day, a lovely, wonderful

day when the choir at evensong sang, "Who are these like
stars appearing?" and the figures on the west front surely
swelled a little to find themselves so appreciated. At
bedtime that night Grandfather told them stories about
the saints. They heard about St. Francis who loved
birds and animals, St. Martin who shared his cloak
with the beggar, St. Cecilia who loved music, St. Elizabeth who told such a shocking lie about the roses in her
apron but was forgiven because she meant well, and St.
Joan whom Grandfather loved best of all because when
people laughed at her for saying she had been guided
she took no notice whatever but just went straight on and
did it.

Henrietta listened in a dreaming silence to these stories,
utterly satisfied by their beauty, but Hugh Anthony was
much exercised by the various points that they raised in
his mind.

"When the saints die," he asked Grandfather, "how
long does it take their souls to get to heaven?"

"Ten minutes," said Grandfather.

"How do they get there?"

"In the arms of their angels."

"What do the angels do with the saints when they
get them there?"

"Give them a thorough cleaning. It is, I believe, painful
but very necessary. Dear me, yes. Not even the saints are
perfect."

"Are you a saint, Grandfather?"

"Dear me, no!"

"Why not?"

Grandfather replied in the words of Falstaff, "I have
more flesh than another man and therefore more frailty."

"What does that mean?"

"It means that I am stout and therefore inclined to
be lazy. I can't help being stout but I ought to help being

lazy and I fear I do not always do so. I go to sleep in the psalms."

"Do saints never go to sleep in the psalms?"

"Dear me, no!"

Hugh Anthony returned to the point that was really worrying him more than he cared to admit. "Are you quite sure that it takes exactly ten minutes to get from earth to heaven?"

"I am absolutely certain," replied Grandfather, meeting Hugh Anthony's searching eyes with a keen, steady glance that brought conviction.

"Really, Theobald!" protested Grandmother, who was sitting by knitting and clicking her tongue in annoyance at Grandfather's flights of fancy. "The things you say! One plain. One purl."

But Grandfather was not penitent for he believed with St. Elizabeth that there are times when a little inaccuracy is not only advisable but right. He was convinced that if a child with a naturally sceptical mind is ever to have faith there must never be any uncertainty about the answers given to his questions. He never said, "I don't know," or "I'm not sure," to his grandson, though very occasionally, when completely floored, he replied to a question in the words used by the Angel Uriel when coping with the insatiable curiosity of the prophet Esdras. "Go thy way, weigh me the weight of the fire, or measure me the blast of the wind, or call me again the day that is past. . . . Thou canst give me no answer. . . . Thine own things, and such as are grown up with thee, canst thou not know; how should thy vessel then be able to comprehend the way of the most Highest?"

II

And so, by way of the archangels and the angels and the saints, they came to the humble benefactors, remembering them in the very middle of St. Martin's summer. . . . And St. Martin played up. . . . But then, Henrietta thought, he would be sure to. That splendid young man who came dashing out of the town on a frosty winter's night, with his scarlet cloak gleaming in the torchlight like a great dahlia and his horse's hoofs striking sparks from the stones, was bound to be lavish in the way of weather. Just as he flung the rich folds of his cloak over the beggar who cowered by the roadside so, year after year, did he fling warm sunshine and a final largesse of autumn flowers over Torminster on its great day. . . . A nice man.

And this year it was lovelier than ever. As soon as she woke up Henrietta scurried to the window to inspect the day. A sky of pale milky blue was tenderly arched over a world misted with silvery dew, and so frail and still and shining that it seemed like a blown soap bubble. Henrietta, leaning out of her window, was almost afraid to breathe lest it should break in spray against her face.

And after breakfast, as she helped Grandfather pick flowers in the garden for the Cathedral decorations, she was still afraid, for the flowers they picked were fragile as rainbows. There had been no cold weather yet and there were actually a few pink roses left, their petals transparent and faintly brown at the edges. The Japanese anemones, folded and hanging their heads after a touch of frost, were fairy lanterns of pearl and lilac that might at any moment vanish, and the scarlet leaves of the virginia-creeper fell at a touch like dead butterflies.

"They'll all come to pieces when we put them on the

graves," mourned Henrietta, laying her spoils tenderly in the basket.

"Never mind," said Grandfather, "the fallen petals are as precious in God's sight as the dust of His dead." He spoke sadly for he was always depressed by the disintegration of autumn.

"Now don't be morbid, Theobald," said Grandmother, issuing out of the front door in her goloshes. "And don't stand about on that wet grass in those shoes. You've no more sense than a child of two. . . . Here's Bates with the chrysanthemums. . . . Give them to Mrs. Elphinstone with my compliments, Theobald, and if she wants any more she can have them, but you must fetch them, mind. I won't have her running about in my garden without a with-your-leave or a by-your-leave, wife of the senior Canon though she may be."

Bates came out from behind the mulberry-tree with a huge bunch of yellow and red chrysanthemums and their colour and sturdiness, together with Grandmother's strong-minded remarks, were somehow exhilarating in this dream-like, vanishing autumn world.

They set off for the Cathedral, Grandfather and Henrietta and Hugh Anthony and Bates and the flowers. Grandmother did not come. She had been decorating churches for festivals for fifty years and had now come to the conclusion that she had had enough of it. . . . Let other women take their turn at keeping the jampots from showing and mopping up the water that the clergy kicked over.

Grandfather and Henrietta walked on ahead, talking softly about the angels, and Hugh Anthony and Bates followed behind discussing horticulture.

"Bates, if I was to pour all the water over one plant in a flower-bed would it run along underneath the ground and make the others wet too?" asked Hugh Anthony.

"No, sir, it wouldn't. If you was to 'ave a drink of beer it wouldn't do me no good."

"Bates, if you planted all the bulbs upside down would they come up in Australia?"

"I couldn't say, sir, I ain't never done such a thing."

"Bates, why do peas grow in pods?"

"I couldn't say, sir, I'm sure. Maybe they're fond of a bit of company."

"Bates, do you like radishes for tea?"

"I'm more partial to a kipper, sir. More tasty."

"Bates, do you believe in God?"

"Yes, sir. I took religion when I started gardening. Wot I say is, 'oo put them peas in them pods and made them flowers so pretty and all?"

III

The Cathedral presented a scene of frantic activity, with all the canons' female dependants scurrying about in overalls with scissors hanging from their waists. Not only had the lectern and the pulpit and the high altar to be flower-decked, as at other festivals, but every single tomb and memorial tablet in the Cathedral, no matter how humble and obscure, must have what Peppercue, the head verger, called its "floral tribute" before three o'clock that afternoon.

There was always a little difficulty as to who should decorate what, all the ladies having the lowest opinion of each other's decorative powers. There was especial difficulty over the side chapel vases. . . . If there is one thing in the world that every woman is quite sure no other woman but herself can do it is vases. . . . The vases on the high altar were of course, as always, the duty of the wife or daughter of the Canon in residence (though goodness knew that poor Nell Roderick could no more make a dahlia stick upright than fly) but the side chapel vases were only filled on benefactors' day and there was no real precedent as to who did them. Mrs. Elphinstone, as wife of the senior Canon, naturally thought she should, and Miss Roderick thought she should because she was doing the high altar vases and might as well do the lot together, and Mrs. Allenby thought she should because she had once been to the Scilly Isles and therefore must know more about flowers than anyone else, and no one knew why Mrs. Phillips, who was only the organist's wife, thought she should. . . . The Archdeacon had no female dependants.

It was at moments such as these that Grandfather came in useful. As he came smilingly up the aisle with his arms full of Japanese anemones it suddenly did not seem to matter very much who did what. For one thing his serene presence smoothed away all disagreement and for another thing he would be quite likely, with his fatal habit of thinking aloud, to repeat later at the Deanery tea-party, saying it over slowly and sadly to himself, any little remark that he had overheard and not liked. . . . They all fell to on something or other and the side chapel vases were left to Mrs. Phillips.

Behind the high altar was the tomb of the patron saint of the Cathedral, a glorious canopy raised over a sculptured figure lying peacefully in his monk's habit with his hands crossed on his breast and his eyes closed. It was a lovely piece of work, the luxuriant carving that had been hewn out of stone and raised over his bones for love of him contrasting touchingly with the simple figure. . . . But, alas, heavy doubts were entertained as to whether his bones were really there at all.

For he had lived in the Torminster valley as long ago as the age of miracles. He had been swineherd to a king whose name no one remembered but whose behaviour had been most distressing. So bad had he been that the whole land had groaned beneath his wickedness, the blue hills hiding their heads beneath the clouds for very shame, and the waters of the streams that ran down to the Torminster valley turning blood-red in horror. And the swineherd, who was a good man, was much upset. It was terrible, he thought, that this lovely valley, lying in the lap of these fair hills, should be so polluted, and one day while he sat beside the well where he watered his herd he earnestly prayed to God, as Grandfather would have done under similar circumstances, that he might be guided. And God in reply sent the Angel Gabriel down to the swineherd to talk the matter over and Gabriel said he thought the best thing to do would be to found a monastery, so that the radiance of the holy lives led by the monks might spread over the valley and conquer the darkness of its wickedness. That's all very well, replied the swineherd, but where am I to find the holy monks? Gabriel made no verbal reply to this but he picked up the stick that the swineherd carried and waved it over the backs of the pigs and over the well, and lo and behold, each pig became on the spot a holy monk while the well, that until now had been rather piggy and secular, became clear and holy, and the swineherd became the first Abbot of Torminster.

Helped by the holy angels, whose images are found carved everywhere in Torminster, he ruled long and wisely, living until the age of one hundred and ten and becoming holier and holier and sterner and sterner, for he was fully determined that never again should there be wickedness in the beautiful Torminster valley. . . . And there never has been. . . . To this day the inhabitants of Torminster are, on the whole and taking everything into consideration, exceptionally well-behaved, so well-behaved indeed that the disciplinary measure practised by the first Abbot, that of walling up alive indiscreet members of the community, has been discontinued.

But no one could ever be quite sure about the Abbot's bones. After his death they took on extraordinary powers. Once a year his tomb was opened and they were displayed and people with whooping-cough who prayed beside them and touched them whooped no more, and other diseases were similarly benefited. This brought great credit upon the monastery and another monastery near-by whose Abbot's bones stayed put and did simply nothing at all was exceedingly jealous, and when there was a terrible fire at the Torminster monastery and vigilance was relaxed the miraculous bones mysteriously disappeared. . . . And plague fell upon the neighbouring monastery. . . . And a parcel of bones was mysteriously returned but, alas, they never cured the whooping-cough again, so were they the same bones?

The twentieth-century ladies of the Close did not know but they gave them the benefit of the doubt and the Deanery hothouse plants.

Lady Lavinia Umphreville, the Dean's wife, did not take any active part in the good work, for decorating tombs is a dusty business and she bought her clothes in Paris and knew what was due to them, but she always put in an appearance, walking very slowly and beautifully up the north choir aisle and down the south choir aisle and then out, bowing and smiling to the ladies of the Close as she went.

She arrived soon after Grandfather and the children, looking very exquisite in grey silk, with a pink ostrich feather in her hat and her grey hair beautifully done with the curling-tongs. . . . She had a ladies' maid and paid her, so Mrs. Allenby said, a fabulous sum, so no wonder she looked as she did. Mrs. Allenby would have looked the same, so she said, had Canon Allenby seen his way to providing her with a ladies' maid too. . . . Lady Lavinia had the willowy grace and dignity that so often go with aristocratic birth and her voice was low and gentle . . . though Henrietta had heard it said that the Dean was henpecked, but then Grandfather said one should not listen to gossip.

In Lady Lavinia's wake followed the Deanery under-gardeners and the footman carrying the hothouse flowers, exotic things that seemed out of keeping with the memory of the simple man who had once kept swine in the valley.

Mrs. Elphinstone was not quite sure whether Grand-father and the children could be entrusted with any really important decorating so she handed over to them an obscure chantry whose interior decorations could not be seen from outside. Its floor was covered with six flat tombstones whose lettering had been so worn away by the passing feet of the generations that it was impossible to make out the names of the dead whose dust lay under one's feet. Though aware that he was being poked into a corner Grandfather was not in the least resentful, for he liked to feel that his flowers were honouring the unknown and this chantry was one of his favourite spots in the Cathedral.

The children loved it too for it was like a fairy house carved out of an iceberg. You went up two steps, opened a door and there you were inside it. The walls and the ceiling were built of very white stone fretted into a hundred intricate shapes of flower and leaf and bird and demon, and so passionately had the sculptor enjoyed himself that he had taken as much trouble with the parts that did not show as the parts that did; you could put your finger round behind a grinning imp and find he had an unseen tail lashing away in the dark. And once upon a time the carving had all been coloured, for its white ness was still stained here and there with patches of rose-pink and azure and lilac, as though the iceberg reflected a rainbow overhead.

The east end was entirely filled up by the huge tomb of the founder of the family in whose honour this chantry had been built. His sculptured likeness lay upon it, a colossal figure in armour with a huge plumed helmet on his head and a hound of no recognizable breed lying at his feet. His legs were crossed in token that he had been to the Crusades and his mailed hands were joined finger-tip to finger-tip as though in prayer. . . . And looked a little awkward like that, as though it were a position not frequently adopted in life.

"Shall we give some flowers to Sir Despard Murgatroyd?" asked Henrietta. This was not really his name but the children had once been taken to see a performance of *Ruddigore* and had been struck with the strong family likeness between the Bad Baronet and the gentleman in the chantry, whose grim face could just be seen below his raised vizor.

"Not too many," said Grandfather. "I don't think he's the kind of man to appreciate flowers on his chest. But we'll make wreaths to lay on the graves of these unknown descendants of his."

"I bet you they're his six wives," said Hugh Anthony, "and I bet you he beat them. If he did a crime every day, like the Murgatroyds, I bet you he beat one every weekday and the dog on Sunday."

"I don't think they're his wives," said Henrietta, standing astride one of the tombs, "I think they're six Saracens that he killed at the Crusades, and he had them pickled and brought home to show that he'd really done it."

"Then if they're Saracens they're not benefactors," said Hugh Anthony, "and it's waste of time decorating them."

"That will do," reproved Grandfather. "Put the flowers down there, please, Bates, and fetch us some jam-pots and water and then you can go home and see about those potatoes."

Mrs. Elphinstone was quite wrong in thinking that Grandfather and the children could not decorate. Grandfather, of course, could not get down on the floor and actually do it because of his rheumatics, but he sat on one of the praying chairs that stood in a row at the back of the chantry and was full of bright ideas which Henrietta and Hugh Anthony carried out with deft fingers.

The chantry looked lovely when they had done. Each wife, or Saracen, had a wreath of virginia-creeper and Japanese anemones, Sir Despard had a rose in his helmet and in all the niches in the walls they put pots of chrysanthemums. It was sad to think that both the rose and the wreaths on the floor would be dead by night, but the people in the tombs were dead too and Grandfather assured them that death did not really matter at all, what mattered was that life while it lasted should be beautiful.

When they had finished decorating, and had cleared up the mess, Grandfather announced that they would now say a prayer for the repose of the souls of Sir Despard Murgatroyd and his relations. So they knelt in a row on the praying-chairs and Grandfather pleaded for Sir Despard, making use of the word Murgatroyd in his prayer in all innocence, for he had entirely forgotten how Sir Despard had originally come by it. . . . "Give rest, O Christ, to Thy servants with Thy saints, where sorrow and pain are no more, neither sighing, but life everlasting," he finished, and the children said "Amen."

"And now we'll go home to dinner," said Grandfather, getting up from his rheumatic knees with a grimace of pain that was hastily repressed lest the children should see it.

"Roast beef," said Hugh Anthony.

"I'll stop a minute," said Henrietta.

Grandfather nodded and left her, taking Hugh Anthony with him. There was something in Henrietta that he loved and respected, a power that she had of attuning herself to the things that are not seen. And it was because of this that he let her do things alone and go about by herself far more than Grandmother thought proper. He knew that she must discover by solitary experiment the way in which she herself could most easily learn to listen to the ditties of no tone that are piped to the spirit. She must learn to say, "Therefore, ye soft pipes, play on," and know that they would obey her.

Left alone Henrietta dived about in the basket and found a long spray of virginia-creeper and three anemones. She twisted them together to form a collar and then, kneeling down in front of the dog who propped Sir Despard's feet up, she slipped it round his neck.

She loved that dog, mongrel though he might be, and ugly into the bargain. The sculptor must have loved him too for he had been carved so realistically that it was hard to realize his tail did not wag. Henrietta stroked his back, where the ribs stuck out under the skin as badly as Mixed Biscuits' had before Jocelyn fed him up, and rubbed him behind the ears in the place where Mixed Biscuits liked to be rubbed and scratched his chest in the place where Mixed Biscuits liked to be scratched, and then she very gently kissed his nose.

Did dogs have immortal souls, she wondered? She had once asked Grandfather but he had been distressingly vague about it. They might, he thought, or they might not. If it was a nice dog one could but hope.

Henrietta was sure this one had been a nice dog. After she had kissed his nose she knelt on with her eyes shut, thinking about him and his master. She doubted if Sir

Despard had gone straight up to heaven to play a harp when he died. . . . He did not look like that. . . . He looked like one of those who went to a place called "the realms of darkness" and had a good deal done to them before they were suitable for harp playing. One of Grandfather's prayers for the dead went like this—"King of majesty, deliver the souls of the departed from the pit of destruction that the grave devour them not; that they go not down to the realms of darkness: but let Michael, the holy standard bearer, make speed to restore them to the brightness of glory." It was a prayer that suited Sir Despard very well, Henrietta thought. She could see him behind her closed lids, a dead man striding down long, black corridors, with his armour clanking and his feet kicking up a lot of dust, down and down into deepening darkness, with his dog at his heels. . . . The dog was frightened by the dark and the dust and the silence of death and had his tail tucked in and his ears back, but he did not dream of leaving his master. . . . And they tramped for hundreds of years until they came out into a great vaulted place like the crypt of the Cathedral and there Michael was waiting for them, with a sword in his hand and looking very grim, and he had a great deal to say to Sir Despard about his behaviour to the wives, or Saracens, before he could make him sorry for it, and a good deal to do to him before he could make him fit for heavenly society. . . . And the poor dog had to sit in the corner and watch, trembling all over and whining but not dreaming of running away. . . . And then at last they went on again, Michael leading and Sir Despard following feeling properly ashamed of himself, but this time they went up and up into deepening light, on and on for hundreds of years, so that the poor dog got terribly exhausted and his tongue hung out and his legs dragged. And so they came to the door of Paradise and Michael

knocked on it with his sword and cried out, "Open!
Bring the prisoner out of his prison house and he that
sitteth in darkness out of the shadow of death!" And
Saint Peter opened the door and Michael and Sir Despard
went in. . . . But the little dog, because he had no soul,
was left crying outside and scratching at the door. . . .
Perhaps he was still there at this moment, after all these
centuries, still trying to get in. . . . Desperately Henrietta
began to pray for him. "Give rest, O Christ, to Thy
servant with Thy saints, where sorrow and pain are no
more; neither sighing, but life everlasting." And behind her
closed eyelids she saw the door open a crack and heard
Saint Peter say, "Come along in and don't make that noise,"
and the little dog ran in, his tail wagging, and disappeared
in a blaze of light.

Henrietta opened her eyes and discovered that tears
were running out of the far corners of them and making
stiff wet tracks down her face in front of her ears. She
wiped them away with the backs of her hands and giggled
at herself, for during the last five minutes she had been
living with that dog as intensely as it is possible to live. . . .
She had thought it was all real. . . . It was odd, she thought,
how that faculty that Grandfather said was called imagination could make one actually see and hear what was not
really happening at all.

Yet surely that story she had imagined was a real thing?
If you created a story with your mind surely it was just
as much there as a piece of needlework that you created
with your fingers? You could not see it with your bodily
eyes, that was all. As she got up and dusted her knees
Henrietta realized how the invisible world must be saturated
with the stories that men tell both in their minds and by
their lives. They must be everywhere, these stories, twisting together, penetrating existence like air breathed into
the lungs, and how terrible, how awful, thought Henrietta,

if the air breathed should be foul. How dare men live, how dare they think or imagine, when every action and every thought is a tiny thread to mar or enrich that tremendous tapestried story that man weaves on the loom that God has set up, a loom that stretches from heaven above to hell below and from side to side of the universe. . . . It was all rather terrifying and Henrietta was glad to hurry home to lunch.

IV

At ten minutes to three Grandmother was sitting in her pew in the choir with the children one on each side of her. She wore her Sunday clothes and carried her best umbrella, that she never used unless it was sure not to rain. She had three umbrellas; one for rain, one for uncertain weather and one for fine weather. Henrietta wore her new red winter coat trimmed with beaver, with a round beaver cap on her head and a little muff hung round her neck on a chain. She was much too hot but she did not mind because she knew she looked very sweet. Hugh Anthony, in his new nautical overcoat with brass buttons, neither knew nor cared what he looked like but was comforted in his heated state by a whistle on a white cord. For years he had been telling his grandparents that a whistle should always accompany marine attire and now at last, just in time for the festival, this remark had sunk in. With his lovely eyes fixed on the altar and an expression of great spiritual beauty on his face he was wondering just when to blow the whistle. Should he accompany the last hymn on it or should he blow one shrill blast in the middle of the Dean's sermon? It was difficult to decide. He must, as Grandfather said one should, wait and be guided.

The ladies of the Close had their pews near the altar

and these were always reserved for them. Lady Lavinia had the front pew on the right with the Palace pew opposite her across the aisle. Behind these were ranged the pews of the Canons' ladies in order of seniority. Barleycorn, the second verger, attired in his black gown and carrying his wand of office, was in charge of these pews and it was his business to see that no presuming stranger dared to sit itself down in the seats of the mighty. It sometimes seemed to Henrietta that Barleycorn thoroughly enjoyed the ejection of a stranger. He would wait until the poor wretch had lowered itself, very tentatively, on to the square of wood sacred to Lady Lavinia and then he would glide swiftly forward with an expression of horror on his face, his gown floating behind him and his wand outstretched like the neck of a hissing swan. There would be a whispered colloquy, and the poor stranger would get up and creep away as though detected in the act of shoplifting, leaving its umbrella behind. . . . On these occasions Henrietta detested Barleycorn, for she hated to see people made to feel ashamed.

But to-day no one sat down where they should not and very soon Barleycorn hurried away, a bell tinkled, they all rose to their feet and far away the choir were heard singing a hymn, "Ye holy angels bright," as they came in procession from the vestry.

And now they had reached the entrance to the choir and were passing under the carved angels of the screen, the sound of their singing swelling gloriously.

Henrietta, her muff swinging and her hands holding her prayer-book upside down, forgot all distractions in her excitement as the procession came up the choir. First came one of the masters of the choir-school holding the great golden cross and after him came the choirboys singing fit to burst themselves, and then the choirmen singing more moderately but yet with extreme heartiness.

"Ye blessed souls at rest,
    Who ran this earthly race,
And now, from sin released,
    Behold the Saviour's face,
His praises sound,
As in His light
With sweet delight
Ye do abound."

After them came another choir-school master carrying the patron saint's banner, a needlework picture embroidered in blues and greens and pinks and purples. It showed the saint, attired in his swineherd's get-up, sitting beside the holy well and brooding sadly over the sins of the Torminster valley. At his feet flowers grew—pansies and violets and cowslips—and behind him were the blue hills, and up in the sky the Angel Gabriel was sitting comfortably on a cloud and holding an architect's model of the cathedral on his left palm. It was a beautiful picture but by some extraordinary oversight the pigs had been omitted.

Behind the banner came Peppercue and Barleycorn, the vergers, followed by the Dean and Canons and the Archdeacon.

The combined ages of the Dean, the four Canons and the Archdeacon at this time came to four hundred and eighty-four, but it was marvellous how they got about. First came the two juniors, Grandfather and the Archdeacon, aged seventy-eight and eighty, who walked quite easily without sticks, then came Canon Allenby aged eighty-two, who used one stick, and Canon Roderick aged eighty-six who used two sticks, and behind them came Canon Elphinstone aged eighty-eight in his bathchair, pushed by his gardener.

The Dean, who was only seventy, came behind the

bathchair, and was apt to complain to his wife that shepherding his Chapter in a procession made him feel exactly like a—er—nursemaid. . . . The Dean never used strong language but in conversation he quite unconsciously left expressive pauses where he would have used it had he not been a clergyman.

Behind the Dean came the Bishop's chaplain carrying the Bishop's pastoral staff and behind him came the Bishop's cope with the Bishop just visible inside it, limping a little because his sciatica was bad that day. Spiritually the Bishop was a very great man but physically he was not, being small and thin and lacking that autocratic bearing that made the Dean such a fine figure of a man at dinner-parties. The Dean and Lady Lavinia always patronized the Bishop a little. The man lacked private means and as a result the soles at his dinner parties were lemon, not Dover. . . . But it was noticeable that people in difficulties always went to the Bishop for help rather than to the Dean.

> "My soul, bear thou thy part,
> Triumph in God above,
> And with a well-tuned heart
> Sing thou the songs of love:
> Let all thy days
> Till life shall end,
> Whate'er He send,
> Be filled with praise."

They all filed singing into their seats and knelt down to pray and Henrietta found to her delight that she was feeling good, a feeling she adored. Tears of happy emotion pricked behind her eyelids, her throat swelled and she was certain that she was never going to be naughty any more. God and His angels were near and one only had to be absolutely good and everything would be perfect. . . . It was all quite easy.

"Shall I blow it now?" whispered Hugh Anthony, nudging her behind Grandmother's back.

"Blow what now?" demanded Henrietta, opening her eyes.

"My whistle."

"You dare blow your beastly whistle! You dare!" she whispered savagely. She was in an ugly rage that tore at her. She stretched across Grandmother, dragged the lanyard roughly over his head and buried it and the whistle in the depths of her muff. "You beast! You beast!" she panted.

"Here, give me that back," said Hugh Anthony loudly. "It's my whistle."

Lady Lavinia, Mrs. Elphinstone, Miss Roderick, Mrs. Allenby and all the ladies of the Close raised their bowed heads and gazed at the couple more in sorrow than in anger. . . . Really, if Mrs. Fordyce must adopt children at her age she could at least make some attempt to keep them in order during divine service.

Grandmother made it, for she was very angry. Her eyes were shining quite dangerously and her mouth, until she opened it, was a thin line. "Be quiet, children! Henrietta, give me that whistle. One more word from either of you and you go straight home. I never saw such an exhibition in all my life!"

The whistle was placed in Grandmother's bag, which was snapped to with a resounding click, and everybody's heads were lowered again. But Henrietta no longer felt good and the tears that trickled down behind her fingers were those of rage instead of sweet piety. . . . How dared Hugh Anthony! . . . Little beast! . . . Just let him wait till they got outside and she would show him!

Hugh Anthony was not at all angry for he was a firm believer in destiny. Things happened because they were ordained to happen. It was interesting to find out by what sequence of cause and effect they did happen but useless to try to avert them. His whistle was gone and he was unlikely to see it again, but never mind; he would now be able to use on Henrietta, in punishment for her theft, a new booby-trap that he had recently invented but lacked opportunity to put into action. During the prayers and psalms he employed himself in working out a few minor touches that would perfect its mechanism. . . . By the time they got to the first lesson he had decided that when he grew up he was going to be an inventor.

The Dean's high, nasal voice piped out from the lectern. "Let us now praise famous men, and our fathers that begat us. . . . Such as found out musical tunes and recited verses in writing. . . . All these were honoured in their generations, and were the glory of their times. . . . And some there be, that have no memorial; who are perished, as though they had never been; and are become as though they had never been born. . . . But these were merciful men, whose righteousness hath not been forgotten. . . . Their bodies are buried in peace; but their name liveth for evermore."

That penetrated Henrietta's rage and she began to feel less wicked. She whispered the words to herself and they were so calming that by the time the final hymn was reached she had quite forgotten what it was she was going to do to Hugh Anthony when she got him outside.

This hymn was the climax of the service and lifted her up into the seventh heaven. The choir, followed by the whole congregation, sang it in procession, going all round the Cathedral and passing by all the decorated graves, leaving none of them out, so that everyone who had loved Torminster, alive or dead, was gathered together in one company.

"For all the saints who from their labours rest,
    Who Thee by faith before the world confessed,
    Thy name, O Jesu, be for ever blessed.
                    Alleluia!"

They were singing that verse as they passed Sir Despard
Murgatroyd's chantry, though he hardly deserved it,
and Henrietta stood on tiptoe trying to see the dog with
his wreath round his neck, but she could not.

"The golden evening brightens in the west:
    Soon, soon to faithful warriors comes their rest;
    Sweet is the calm of paradise the blest.
                    Allelulia!"

She did so hope her little dog was in Paradise, lying
curled round in a ball in a bed of lilies, sleeping off the
fatigue of following Sir Despard through purgatory.

They sang the end of the hymn standing in a group
by the west door.

"From earth's wide bounds, from ocean's farthest coast,
    Through gates of pearl streams in the countless host,
    Singing to Father, Son and Holy Ghost.
                    Alleluia!"

Then they bowed their heads and the Bishop blessed
them. "The peace of God which passeth all understanding keep your hearts and minds in the knowledge and love
of God." Then for a few moments there was silence, a
deep, cool silence like the inside of a well. . . . Peace. . . .
Henrietta was not quite sure what it was but she knew it
was very important. If one wanted it, Grandfather had
told her once, one must not hit back when fate hit hard
but must allow the hammer-strokes to batter out a hollow

place inside one into which peace, like cool water, could flow.

The festival was over for another year and they drifted out through the west door on to the Green. It was dusk now, a smoky orange dusk that made the universe look like a lighted Chinese lantern swinging in space.

"I think I should like to go and help Uncle Jocelyn sell in the shop," whispered Henrietta to Grandmother.

"Aren't you coming to the Deanery tea-party?" whispered Hugh Anthony in astonishment. "There'll be iced cakes, and cream in the tea."

"I want to show Uncle Jocelyn my muff," said Henrietta.

"Very well, dear," said Grandmother, slightly relieved. . . . One child alone at the Deanery party would probably behave itself, but with two together you never knew.

v

Henrietta ran across the Green and into the Market Place. She did not really want to show Jocelyn her muff, but she did not want to face all those people at the party; it would have been an anticlimax. She could not have explained why she ran away, but she knew instinctively that she must let herself down lightly.

It was nice in the Market Place. The chimneys and roofs were sharp and black against the orange sky but below them purple veils had been drawn over unsightly things like dustbins and paper in the gutter, so that the Market Place looked mysteriously beautiful. Here and there a light had been lit in a window, orange to match the sky, and overhead a few stars were like pinholes pricked in the swinging Chinese lantern.

The gas was lit in the bookshop but it was empty, so Henrietta went on to Jocelyn's sitting-room. He was sitting writing, his table strewn with manuscript and a large black pot of tea and a plate of ginger biscuits beside him.

"You ought to be in the shop, Uncle Jocelyn," said Henrietta severely. She herself, on the occasions when Jocelyn allowed her to help sell, was frightfully serious about it.

"No one will come," said Jocelyn. "The laws of commerce command that I shall keep this establishment open till six but with all this to-do over the dead going on I can't expect customers."

"The service was glorious," said Henrietta. "It was dreadful that you couldn't come."

"Tragic," agreed Jocelyn, but he did not seem overwhelmed. "Fetch yourself a cup from the kitchen. And there are chocolate biscuits in that tin with Windsor Castle on it."

Henrietta always enjoyed Jocelyn's haphazard teas. Very strong tea out of a black pot, with heaps of sugar, was much nicer than the milk and water with a dash of tea only that she had at home, and nothing is nicer than a chocolate biscuit held in one hand and a ginger one in the other, with alternate bites taken of each.

"Have you any bullseyes?" she asked, pulling up a chair to sit beside Jocelyn at his table.

"No. Why?"

"They're lovely after ginger biscuits. They cool them down."

"I'll have them next time you come," Jocelyn promised.

Henrietta put her half-eaten biscuits down on his manuscript and had a long pull at her tea, leaving off in the middle of that to show Jocelyn her new clothes.

"Exquisite," said Jocelyn, as she turned slowly round.

She took off her coat so that he could see her dress, green silk smocked by Grandmother, and lifted the skirt a little to show him her new petticoat and frilly knickers. Then she got back into her chair again and finished her biscuits.

She was always very happy with Jocelyn, though his presence gave her a tiny ache somewhere. So much love was showered on her by Grandfather, Grandmother and Hugh Anthony that she did not usually remember that she was an orphan, but when she was with Jocelyn she did remember it. She thought that if she had had a father he might have been rather like Jocelyn; nice and teasing and young enough to feel nearer to her in time than Grandfather did. She finished her tea down to the dregs, scooped up what was left of the sugar in her spoon and ate it, and leant her head against Jocelyn's shoulder.

"I'd like you to be my father," she said. "And Hugh Anthony's father too."

Jocelyn started slightly. This idea had already occurred to Grandfather and fond as he was of both children he was not altogether sure that he relished it.

"You funny little scrap," he said. "If I were your father I'd whack you every day."

Henrietta giggled and then, the pangs of hunger being now satisfied, was at leisure to have her eye caught by the manuscript in front of her.

"It's verses in writing," she said. "Did you write all that, Uncle Jocelyn?"

"Most of it was written by a friend of mine," said Jocelyn, "but he didn't quite finish what he wrote and so I am finishing it for him."

"Is it a story?"

"Yes, it's a sort of fairy story. I'll read it to you on Christmas Day."

"Felicity will be here for Christmas," said Henrietta.

F*

"What?" said Jocelyn, and upset the tin of chocolate biscuits.

"She wrote and told Grandmother. She said we were to tell you, but we forgot."

"Brutes!" said Jocelyn, with quite unnecessary fierceness.

"Will you read the story to all of us on Christmas Day?"

"Yes, if I get it finished in time."

"Verses in writing," repeated Henrietta. "That's what the Dean said in church. 'Such as found out musical tunes and recited verses in writing. Their bodies are buried in peace but their name liveth for evermore.' Is it because you want your friend's name to live that you are finishing his verses for him?"

"That's the idea," said Jocelyn.

"Is he dead?" asked Henrietta.

Jocelyn hesitated a moment and then said, "I think so."

"That's a pity," said Henrietta, "but it can't be helped. Shall we go and sell in the shop?"

No one arrived to buy anything in the shop but that did not worry Henrietta; the mere fact of sitting up behind the counter in the capacity of shop assistant was sufficient for her joy.

And as she perched beside Jocelyn she repeated to him all she could remember of the words of Ecclesiasticus that the Dean had read.

"What a memory you've got!" said Jocelyn in admiration.

"I remember things that I like," said Henrietta. "They go in at my eyes or my ears and down inside and stay there."

Jocelyn got up and went to one of the bookshelves. "There are some rather similar remarks by a gentleman

called Pericles that you might like," he said, and bringing
the book back with him to the counter he read them to
her.

"They received, each for his own memory, praise that
will never die, and with it the grandest of all sepulchres,
not that in which their mortal bones are laid, but a home
in the minds of men, where their glory remains fresh to
stir to speech or action as the occasion comes by. For
the whole earth is the sepulchre of famous men; and their
story is not graven only on stone over their native earth,
but lives on far away, without visible symbol, woven into
the stuff of other men's lives."

When he had finished Henrietta seized the book and
read the last words of the passage to herself several times
over. "That's what I thought this morning," she said.
"All the stories that people tell and live get so mixed up
with other people's stories that they never come to an
end. Now if you finish that story for your friend his life
will be woven with yours, won't it?"

Jocelyn stared at her, remembering how he had felt
himself that the thread of his own life was woven with
that of another, a light thread with a dark. "Henrietta,"
he said, "for a little 'un you're too perspicacious to live."

CHAPTER VIII

I

AS soon as the festival was over St. Martin withdrew his summer and the rain came down in the way peculiar to Torminster, day after day of steady, penetrating downpour that made everybody and everything feel like a saturated sponge. It was very cold in the old, damp bedrooms of the Close. Grandfather got rheumatics very badly in his knees and Grandmother in her hands, and Henrietta sneezed incessantly. Hugh Anthony's health remained unaffected, though he felt the chill of his little bedroom to such an extent that his nightly query was, "Grandmother, need I wash?"

Jocelyn, now that winter was upon them in good earnest, found the discomfort of a house without modern conveniences acute. His morning's cold bath lacked thrill, but to boil enough water in his two little kettles for a hot one took a good hour. A large and loathsome fungus appeared in the corner of his bedroom and the paper in the hall peeled off with the damp. Very few customers came to the shop and he found a dead rat in the bread-bin. Martha Carroway went down with bronchitis and Mixed Biscuits with distemper. Jocelyn himself caught a bad cold through sitting up with Mixed Biscuits at night, and his balance at the bank mysteriously disappeared.

But the worst of all his trials was the mess he was getting into over Ferranti's dramatic poem. The more he worked at it the more convinced he became that it

was amazingly beautiful poetry, but though the plot of
the story was mapped out to the end the actual writing
was only a little more than half finished, and Jocelyn
found himself obliged to fill up the gaps with his own
verse.

And though, like everyone else, he had written pass-
able poetry in his youthful days he did not find it so easy
now that life and its disillusionment had a little dulled
his perception of beauty and his response to it. "How
is it that artists keep their powers of perception even
in the days when life darkens?" he asked himself. Thinking about it and taking as his model Grandfather, an artist
in religion who had given to its study the devotion and
the hours of discipline that a violinist devotes to his instrument, he thought that their perception was born of the
faculty of wonder, deepening to meditation and to penetrating sight and so strong that it could last out a lifetime.
Grandfather wondered, all day and every day, at the wisdom
of God and the beauty of the world, and Ferranti had wondered at the waste and pain and frustration of life.

In him, judging from the scraps of poems that had
been rescued from Mrs. Jameson, wonder had become
a sense of outrage, but it had had its fruits of meditation
and a rather terrible penetration. The verse that expressed
it was vivid as lightning and cruel as a microscope in its
power of enlarging horror.

So Jocelyn too tried to acquire the perceptive outlook,
the outlook of Hamlet when he cried, "This most excellent canopy the air, look you, this brave o'erhanging
firmament, this majestical roof fretted with golden fire."
Even the bitter words that followed, "it appears to me no
other than a foul and pestilent congregation of vapours,"
were the words of an artist, Jocelyn thought, stabbing like
a sword in their quick flash from joy to despair. Night
after night and during every spare moment of the day

he steeped himself in Ferranti's poetry, and in all poetry that seemed to him akin to it, and he tried to feel every trivial happening of the day acutely and see every beauty and sorrow trebly intensified. And, though he reduced himself to a nervous wreck, he had his reward, for his verse became more and more like Ferranti's, lighter and clearer and with a winged quality that Henrietta would have told him, had she heard it, made it jump up like a lark.

Not that Jocelyn thought so. Domestic trials and the weather and his own nervous exhaustion had reduced him to depths of depression as yet unplumbed by him. When at midnight on Christmas Eve he wrote the last word, completely unsatisfied yet knowing that he could not get the thing better, he felt that he had failed Ferranti utterly. . . . This man Ferranti whom he had never seen and yet who, alive or dead, had mysteriously become his friend.

II

Yet when next morning he set out to spend Christmas Day at the Close he had the manuscript under his arm. He had promised Henrietta to read it to them and he would keep his word, even though his additions to Ferranti's original work had, in his opinion, ruined the whole thing. . . . One could not disappoint Henrietta and see the light in her eyes flicker and die out. . . . For Henrietta was very excited about this story. She had told the others that Uncle Jocelyn was finishing a fairy story begun by a friend of his and that he would read it to them on Christmas Day. He should do so, she had ordained, between tea and bed, and Mrs. Jameson and Felicity, who was to arrive at Torminster on Christmas Eve, were to come to tea and listen too.

It had seemed to Jocelyn in anticipation that the hours

until tea, Felicity and the story would be a howling wilderness of impatience, but it proved not to be so, for on his first Christmas Day since his own childhood that he had spent with children he found himself recapturing a glamour that he thought had vanished completely.

For years Christmas Day had been for him a day when one ate too much so as not to disappoint cook, stifled a great many yawns and made a lot of silly jokes to hide an inner sadness that was both a lament for romance and belief that had faded and a vague sense of unsatisfied expectation.

But to-day, in company with Henrietta and Hugh Anthony, romance and belief and satisfaction were vicariously his again. He stood in the Cathedral during morning service with the children one on each side of him and sang, "Hark the herald angels sing," aware that Henrietta, whose eyes were beaming with joy and whose muff was swinging from side to side like a pendulum as her figure swayed in time to the music, was seeing a starlit sky full of wings and a manger with a baby in it, and seeing them with her. Hugh Anthony on his other side was singing the tune a semitone flat with the full force of his lungs, but he looked happily distrait and his left hand was plunged deep in his pocket; it clutched, Jocelyn knew, the knife with two blades, a corkscrew and a thing for getting stones out of one's horse's hoofs (if one happened to have a horse that got into this predicament) that had been in his stocking.... Jocelyn seemed to feel the delightful outside roughness of the knife against the fingers of his own left hand and knew the sensation of satisfaction that it brought.

Beyond Henrietta was Grandmother. She was sitting down with her eyes shut because she was tired with the Christmas preparations, but her mind was thankfully fixed upon the fact of God made man. She was too practical, of necessity too concerned with the details of daily living, to be romantic in her religion like Henrietta, or quixotic like Grandfather, but her faith was the strength of her strong-minded life.

As she sat there she was in that state of detachment and tranquil concentration that brings one mind very near to another, and Jocelyn could distinctly feel her sober certainty reaching him through Henrietta's stars and wings, as though what she and her like believed was the thread strung through the lovely bead of things that Henrietta and her like imagined, giving them form and value.

During the Dean's sermon Jocelyn's thoughts wandered, for the Dean's remarks never brought conviction to sceptical minds. . . . Yet to-day he was almost persuaded by the silence of others, Grandfather, Grandmother, Henrietta and the small, thin Bishop who sat opposite him on his throne. It struck him as he meditated that if these four, whom he held to be his superiors, were believers, then their belief was more likely to be true than his own unbelief. The Bishop, a distinguished scholar with a mind far more able to test and probe than his, Grandfather with his artist's perceptiveness, Grandmother with her every-day common sense and Henrietta, sensitive and romantic, playing so happily with the toys of religion and finding reality through them, had arrived through their different avenues of approach at the same place and who was he, in the face of their evidence, to say that the place did not exist?

III

The Christmas dinner, too, seemed because of the children to take on a new value. The turkey was a noble bird, brought overnight by Father Christmas in his sledge, and the flaming plum-pudding, that they had stirred laboriously in its earlier stages, was alight with the wishes they had wished as the spoon went round.

And then came the ecstasy of present giving, and then a short walk to assist the processes of digestion, and then, at last, it was tea-time and they were sitting in the drawing-room and waiting for Mrs. Jameson and Felicity.

"I'll go down and meet them," said Jocelyn with extreme casualness, as soon as the garden door was heard to click.

"Me too!" yelled the children, but Grandfather quite unaccountably seized one by the slack of his jersey and the other by her sash and seemed not to want to be left.

Jocelyn went downstairs and out into the garden. It was quite dark, with stars burning frostily, and the lantern that Felicity carried swung very gently on its chain, backwards and forwards, as Henrietta's muff had swayed in church, accompanying her singing, as the pendulum of the clock moves, measuring time, as the tides swing in time to the measured movement of the moon. . . . And love too has its rhythm, its partings and its reunions, its times of waiting and its times of movement. . . . And love to-night was on the move. Jocelyn standing still, and Felicity coming a little nearer with every swing of her lantern, both seemed to themselves to be drawing together without any volition of their own.

They were suddenly together in the lighted hall without any very clear idea as to how they had got there. As Jocelyn sat her down on the oak chest and took off her fur coat and goloshes Felicity chattered as a bird sings, joy being with her a thing that must be instantly expressed lest she burst, but Jocelyn did not speak, it being with him a thing that silenced. He took as long as possible over the removal of each golosh so that he could quietly verify all Felicity's high-lights. . . . Her sunflower hair and tawny eyes, her laugh and her gaiety were mercifully unchanged. . . . The velvet frock that reached to her

ankles was a warm brown and she was not so unaware of
her own charms as to forget to lift it a little now and then
so that her orange satin petticoat could be enjoyed by an
admiring world.

"I can't undo this safety-pin," complained Mrs. Jameson
from the shadows.

Their joy had been like four walls that shut out all
remembrance of an outside world but at the sound of
her voice they jumped up in compunction and hurried
to help her, unwrapping the five white shawls that hid
the glory of her festival snow-white velvet dress and icy,
sparkling diamonds.

The two women made a strange contrast as they followed
Jocelyn and his lighted candle up the dark stairs, the one
looking as though she were carved out of the same wintry
grief that had paralysed her mind and the other in her
brown and orange as palpitant with life as the crocuses
when they spear their way through spring earth.

"Henrietta says you're going to tell us a story," said
Mrs. Jameson.

"A story?" said Felicity. "What story?"

Jocelyn on the top stair turned to face her and their
eyes met. Between them the candle-flame danced like a
live thing, reflected in two pin-points of excitement in
Felicity's eyes.

IV

Henrietta never forgot that Christmas tea-party. Grandmother had lit twelve wax candles all round the drawing-
room and there were twenty tiny candles on the small
Christmas-tree that stood in the centre of the tea-table.
The room seemed full of stars and all the stars were singing, like those that sang to the young-eyed cherubim when

Lorenzo and Jessica sat on the bank where the moonlight slept. . . . At least Henrietta thought they sang but perhaps what she heard were the bells ringing for the evensong that no one had time to go to on Christmas Day because of the cake having to be cut.

Hugh Anthony cut it, with Jocelyn applying a little pressure in the background, and it was all that it should be, white icing and fruity inside and all, though the latter was a little plainer than was customary because of Henrietta's weak digestion.

It struck Henrietta as she ate, biting it all up very carefully as Grandmother bade her, that they were all looking extraordinarily beautiful. Grandmother in her lace cap, Mrs. Jameson in her diamonds, Felicity with her lovely petticoat, Hugh Anthony with his flaming hair and Jocelyn smiling with his eyes in the way that she liked. Even Grandfather looked beautiful, with his snowy beard, and his bald head reflecting the candlelight so merrily. . . . How safe they were, she thought. In this warm, cosy place nothing could hurt them. . . . Outside it was cold and frosty but the cold could not get in to them.

V

And then it did.

Tea was finished and cleared away, they pulled their chairs round the fire, the children sitting on the floor at Grandfather's feet with their Sunday playthings, the shells that sounded like the sea when you held them against your ears, ready to hand in case they should be bored, and Jocelyn read them his story.

It began all right and like the nicest kind of fairy story, with a wandering Minstrel playing his flute in the forest, and it went on all right, with the Minstrel engaged on a quest, as all the best fairy-tale heroes should be, but after that it went all wrong and a cold air blew through the room. For this hero was not a homely Dick Whittington, whom you felt at the start was bound to end up as a well-fed mayor, he was someone fine and strange and likely, Henrietta felt, to be a tragic figure just because he was different. And his quest, too, was peculiar, because instead of searching for a sleeping beauty, a tangible person who could be relied on to stay put till found, he was searching for what he called the spirit of perfect beauty, an illusive thing like the will-o'-the-wisp.

Jocelyn related this hero's adventures in verse that sang like Lorenzo's stars but its beauty did not comfort Henrietta, for that unhappy wind was blowing through it all the time. . . . And yet, though she did not altogether understand, she found that she had to listen. . . . She could not do as Hugh Anthony did, close her ears to Jocelyn's story and open them to the song the sea was singing inside the shells, she was obliged to follow the Minstrel on his journey.

At first he tried to find this beauty in his forest, among the trees and the flowers and the nymphs who danced to the music of his flute, but he found that there were snakes coiled on the branches of the trees, and worms and dead bodies under the roots of the flowers, and as the nymphs twisted and turned in the measure of their dance he saw to his horror that there was a satyr prancing about in the middle of them. So he took off the garland of roses that the nymphs had given him and trampled on it, and he turned his back on the woods and the fields and tramped over the mountains until he came to a lovely city set on a hill and here, in the world of man's art, he tried again to find his beauty.

There were lovely things in this city, cathedrals and shrines and pictures and books and statues, but there were none of them quite perfect, sharing as they did the imperfection of the men who had made them, and they did not satisfy the hunger for the absolute that was destroying the Minstrel. Yet he stayed in the city, searching everywhere, until one day he did a dreadful thing. A certain sculptor had just completed a new statue and he invited all the chief artists of his city to come to see it, and among them he invited the Minstrel, who was full of excitement and hope, thinking that perhaps here at last he would find perfection. The party dragged on until at last the great moment came and the veil was taken from the statue. The Minstrel caught his breath and tears of delight came into his eyes as he looked at the figure of a peasant woman. His eyes travelled from the perfectly poised head and the eager face to the arms stretched out in supplication and the figure swaying a little forward as though in a passion of self-giving. . . . And then he saw the feet. . . . The sculptor's inspiration must have flagged when he got to the feet, he must have been bored or drunk or tired, for they were all wrong. The woman should have been poised on tiptoe, as though she were just going to take flight in her eagerness, but these feet were heavy as lead, ugly and shapeless, and planted on the pedestal as though fixed in mud. A sick rage took hold of the Minstrel, he rushed to the statue and flung it on the floor, smashing it into a thousand pieces. All the artists rushed at him like wild beasts and hounded him out of the city.

So he went off on his wanderings again and as he tramped along the road, weary and very sore from the beating he had had, he found that his memory was haunted by the tenderness in the face of the statue he had smashed and he wondered if perhaps he might find perfection in love. The figure he had broken had been a peasant, a woman of the people, and so he looked for the living woman in all the villages along the way. As soon as he came to a village he would go to the cross at its centre and stand there playing on his flute and all the women and children would come running out of the cottages to listen to his tunes. And at last one day he saw her, golden-haired and mysteriously beautiful, standing on the outskirts of the crowd that had collected, with a little black-haired child clinging to her skirts, her figure swaying a little to his music and her hands outstretched in her eagerness. He did not stop his playing but over the heads of the people his eyes met hers and said to her, "Wait."

When he had finished his tune and the crowd had gone she was still there, with the child clinging to her skirts, and he went to her and took her hands and asked her to go with him.

"To the world's end," she said, "I and the child."

"I don't want the child," he said.

She looked at him steadily out of eyes that were much wiser than his. "Love is a child," she said, "and after him as he runs along with his bow and arrows come the pattering feet of little children."

So he gave in and the three of them took the road together. They earned their bread quite easily, for the woman had a lovely voice and sang to the music of his flute, so that in the towns and villages they passed through people flocked to hear them and flung silver and gold into the hat that the black-haired child carried round.

For a little while the Minstrel thought that his quest was ended for his love made the world such a paradise that he thought he had found his perfect beauty; until one day he realized that the woman was not all that he had thought her. She had a quick temper and could say stinging things when she was tired, and she did not always give him the perfect response of sympathy that he demanded. And though her voice remained unchanged her loveliness became tarnished by her hard life, and as her mysterious beauty faded his love faded too. This third failure, far more bitter than the others because he had been nearer to attainment, made him so wretched that it robbed him of the power of clear judgment; he thought his misery was the woman's fault and he was no longer kind to her and the child.

So one day as they played and sang at a village cross another man noticed the figures of the woman and the child. He was a careless, thoughtless man but he thought that the woman looked tired and her faded beauty touched him so much that he went to her and said, "Bring the child and come with me," and because she was proud and hated to stay with the Minstrel when he no longer loved her she obeyed.

Then it seemed to the Minstrel that nothing was left to him but himself. The natural world had failed him and the world of man's art and the world of human relationships, yet perhaps out of himself he could still spin perfection. So the music that had been to him merely a pleasure or a means of livelihood became a passion, the one thing that he lived for. He composed tune after tune for his flute, trying always to achieve perfection, always feeling it elude him by a hair's breadth yet always trying again. . . . But he could no longer earn his living for these new tunes of his, into which he had poured all his longing and passion, did not please people as had the light, gay tunes of the old days, they were too intricate and too sad, and they would not listen to them or put money into the Minstrel's hat. . . . And so one day, as he stumbled along the road faint with hunger, he swooned and fell, and when he came to himself again he found that his flute had been broken by his fall. He picked himself up and went into a green meadow through which a river ran and here he lay down and went to sleep and in a little while he was dreaming.

He dreamed that he was looking at a pattern woven from earth to heaven, a pattern composed of shape and colour and scent and music, and the pattern was perfect beauty. . . . So what he had been searching for was a pattern. . . . For what seemed an eternity he gazed on its satisfying loveliness and then, closing the dazzled eyes that could not look any longer, he tried with his mind to separate the pattern into its component parts. They were a scent of roses, the shapely head and figure of a statue, a woman's voice, the black hair and white face of a child and a few notes from his own music. . . . And suddenly he was awake again and the pattern had vanished.

It was dark now and sitting near the rushing river, and talking to it as though it were a spirit, he tried to think how it was that these random memories of his life could so have combined together as to form perfection. Out of the night there came to him the realization that man while still in the body cannot look upon pure spirit, for the white circle of transcendent beauty would strike him blind, he can apprehend it only when its light is split into coloured fragments by the prism of his own senses. And if it is his senses that apprehend these coloured fragments it is his mind that must pluck them out of the mud that he has strewn about his dwelling-place and form them into a pattern, perfect in its degree, that shall satisfy him by shadowing faintly the perfection of pattern that he cannot see.

Despair seized the Minstrel. The fragments had been there for his taking and what had he done with them? The roses he had trampled underfoot, the statue he had destroyed, the beauty that was in the woman and the child he had driven from him and the stupidity that had caused his bodily weakness had smashed his flute into a hundred pieces. He had destroyed beauty. Beauty was dead and he must follow it, for without it his life was useless to him. His feet carried him through the darkness to the water's edge and the river of death closed over his head.

VI

Jocelyn's voice ceased and Grandmother, who had become bored with the Minstrel at the end of Scene II and had gone to sleep, woke up for a moment to send the children to bed and then dozed off again. Mrs. Jameson had slept throughout and was still sleeping. When the children had been kissed and blessed and dispatched upstairs Grandfather, Felicity and Jocelyn looked at each other strangely and then at the sleeping old ladies.

"Better come downstairs," whispered Grandfather.

They lit a candle and stole down to his study, where they lit the green-shaded oil-lamp, poked up the log fire and pulled their chairs close to it. Books lined the walls and were piled in pyramids on the table. More books lay on the floor and the window-sills and, owing to the difficulty of housework in the study when Grandfather would not allow anything to be touched, a light coating of dust gave to the whole room a rather pleasant neutral tint, like the silvering of dew in early morning. The mingled scent of old leather, damp and burning wood was a singularly studious smell, suggesting the treasures of the past and the torch of learning. . . . The room had the indescribable fascination of all studies, the atmosphere of a room where the life of the mind only is carried on and the fret and business of practical living are shut out.

"When did you find that poem, and how and where?" whispered Felicity.

Jocelyn told her the whole history and when he had finished Grandfather, who had been leaning back in his chair with his hands folded across his stomach, suddenly leant forward. "My dear boy, do you mean to tell me that you wrote only a little less than half of that exquisite poetry yourself?"

"Weren't the joins and patches obvious?" asked Jocelyn.

"No," said Grandfather, and could say no more. There had been times in the past when his children had given him severe shocks by suddenly displaying unguessed-at powers, but none of their shocks had been equal to the earthquake with which his grandson had just shot him skywards. . . . He needed to get his breath.

"Well, Horatio," said Felicity, "you've told that story very well."

"Why do you call me Horatio?" asked Jocelyn, smiling.

"'And in this harsh world draw thy breath in pain to tell my story.' Heavens, how you must have worked! No wonder you look like a dug-up corpse."

"This is only a fairy tale. What makes you think it is Ferranti's own story?" queried Jocelyn.

"Because every word of it digs into you. You know yourself the difference between the poetry of experience and the poetry of imagination. Take the Elizabethan love poetry, it affects you just like a dance tune, tickling awake one's surface pleasure, and compare that with a poem like Emily Brontë's 'If grief for grief can touch thee.' When I first read that I didn't know a thing about Emily, who she was or why she wrote as she did, but it gave me such a wound that I stayed awake at night. . . . This poetry affects one in the same way."

"I can't judge of it from the outside like that because I've identified myself with Ferranti so closely that I feel the whole thing is my own work."

"Yet you think it is his own story?"

"Yes. I didn't at first but I do now."

"Why?"

"You'll laugh," said Jocelyn, "but you told me that Ferranti's story must be written in the house, and Grandfather told me that the print of his personality must be there, and after all they are the same thing, for a man's history is just the shadow thrown by his personality, isn't it?"

"Yes. Well?"

"And I've felt that personality, read the story if you like to put it like that, in several ways. I've felt it internally weaving itself into my own life as though two threads were twisted together, and externally, as though it were part of the house, and it's a frustrated, remorseful thing, the very same person as the Minstrel in that story."

"What do you think?" Felicity asked Grandfather.

"That Minstrel," said Grandfather, "is Ferranti as I knew him."

"Is Ferranti alive or dead?" asked Felicity.

"Dead," said Jocelyn. "The Minstrel followed the beauty he had killed beyond death and at the beginning of his poem Ferranti wrote these words from Shelley's 'Adonais,' 'Die, if thou wouldst be with that which thou dost seek, follow where all is fled.'"

Grandfather made a restless, unhappy movement. Suicide was to him a confession of failure more humiliating to the spirit of man than any other and the thought that his friend had stooped to it hurt him intolerably.

"Alive or dead it doesn't make any difference," said Felicity. "The play must be put on. If he's alive it will bring him back and if he's dead it will also bring him back."

"How?" asked Jocelyn.

"Ferranti once said to me," said Grandfather, "that at rock-bottom living is merely a giving of personality. Therefore if you and Felicity give his personality to the world he lives whether he be alive or dead. Is that right, Felicity?"

Felicity nodded, her face eager and her eyes bright as

her mind grappled delightedly with ways and means, an activity it adored.

"No manager in his senses would put on a tragic dramatic poem," said Jocelyn firmly. "We must try and get it published."

"But the public won't read him," objected Felicity, "they've refused to already. . . . No, it must be acted."

"But I tell you——" began Jocelyn.

Felicity stamped her foot. "Now don't begin to be sensible and defeatist or we'll get nowhere. No one ever does anything in this world until they go a little mad."

"But are there any insane managers in London now? You ought to know."

"Not loose, but there's plenty about this play to appeal to the sane ones," declared Felicity. "The scenes would be an effective spectacle; the dancing nymphs and the satyr, the smashing of the statue and the finding of the woman and the child at the village cross. Then there's a chance for lovely music. . . . I know a composer who would help us there. . . . And there's the poetry; that's not just good, it's great, and spoken rightly it can't fail of its effect; for the public does care for what's great, you know, it's only the just plain good that's not sharp enough to get through its thick skin. And, best of all for commercial purposes, we can advertise Ferranti as dead."

"I never knew that death was commercial before."

"Oh, very. You see it is always the people who are furthest away from us who seem most worth while, and death is a great distancer. And then producers love a dead author because he can't come and interfere."

"What if Ferranti is alive after all and turns up in the middle of rehearsals?"

"Well, we must take the risk."

"What shall we do if no one will put on this play unless we provide a little capital?"

"I shall borrow money from everyone I know, including the Dean."

"But the Dean didn't like Ferranti."

"No, but he likes me."

Grandfather roused himself from the silence that had wrapped him round while they talked. "Go on," he said, "and God guide you, but go carefully. Go mad with circumspection."

VII

Jocelyn and Felicity stood in the dark porch while behind them in the hall Mrs. Jameson was saying goodbye to Grandfather and Grandmother. They were about to embark together on an adventure and they felt taut and excited and very close together.

With a sudden unthinking movement he flung his arms round her and kissed her on the highlights that he loved, her hair and her eyes and her pointed chin, and then as suddenly let go again.

Felicity, smiling and unflurried, returned his kiss gently, aware that the instinctive fling of his arms round her was what his heart knew about his love, while his considered withdrawal was what his mind knew about his bank balance. She was used to being fallen in love with, she had in fact reduced the business of saying no to a fine art, but the art of saying yes she had yet to master and she felt a little afraid. She was capable of earning enough for both of them but if she humiliated him in any way she would upset the balance of their relationship, put the weight of dependence on the wrong side of the scales and strain their love with the drag of it. She would have to go slowly, as Grandfather said, and yield to the madness of love with circumspection.

"Good night, Horatio," she said lightly. "You and I and Ferranti, we're together in this, but Ferranti comes first. Happy people can always wait."

Instantly their positions seemed to Jocelyn rightly adjusted. They stood one on each side of Ferranti, for the moment separated by him. It would be time enough for their positions to change when he no longer needed them.

VIII

A quarter-past ten o'clock and Grandfather was alone in his study, having actually let Grandmother go to bed without him, though of course he had carried up the teapot as usual.

He felt too tired for sleep to be possible. He said compline but even that failed to soothe him. "I will lay me down in peace and take my rest." He was at the end of his life as well as at the end of the day but his over-active conscience caused him to doubt if he deserved rest.

It was the weight of his responsibility for other lives that troubled him most; the children and the grand-children whose lives derived from his and, in a lesser sense, all those other lives that had touched his at any point and been glad or sorry because of their contact.

They seemed to pass him by in a terrible procession. The men, such as Ferranti, in whom he had not kindled faith, the little children whose sorrows he had not comforted, the animals to whom he had not given the full measure of affection.

And his own children. . . . They passed by him in the shadows, grown men and women whose faces were marked by their sorrows and whose eyes were reproachful because they need not have suffered had they not been conceived by his act. . . . And his grandchildren. . . . How would they fare in life? Jocelyn with that streak of sadness in him, Hugh Anthony with his questioning mind, and the other boys and girls each with a seed of danger in their natures that growing crookedly might wreck their lives.

And yet the terrible law of life must be obeyed, that law of which we know nothing but that life must go on, at whatever cost, through whatever darkness, to whatever goal. Our responsibility, thought Grandfather, is not for life but for living and on that may God, Who only knows the end and the beginning, have mercy.

The door opened and closed and Grandfather started up. Henrietta was standing by his chair in her nightgown, her feet bare and her face very white against her black hair. He was reminded for an instant of the child who had flickered across the stage in Ferranti's story.

"Dear me!" he said, and lifting her on to his knee he adjusted his spectacles to have a look at her. Her eyes seemed without light, a sure sign that she was unhappy, and her toes were very cold. He rubbed them, repeating the time-honoured formula, so soothing to cold toes, about the little pigs who went to market, wrapped her up in his old cassock and inquired what the matter was.

"I can't go to sleep because I have a pain here," said Henrietta, laying her hand upon her front.

"That's the cake," said Grandfather, who had suffered similarly, and administered a peppermint lozenge.

"And I have a pain in my mind," she said.

"That's the Minstrel," said Grandfather, who had a pain in his from the same cause.

"I didn't understand," she sighed. . . . She had been terribly out of sorts all the evening, quite unable to enter whole-heartedly into the nightly game with Hugh Anthony, that of seeing who could spit farthest into the fire the skin that they removed with their tongues from the top of their supper glass of hot milk, and crying when she was alone in bed, as though she and the Minstrel were in some way connected. . . . "I didn't understand why the Minstrel was so unhappy."

Grandfather told her the story all over again, explaining it as well as he could, and with clear understanding Henrietta was comforted. Few things upset her when she understood them, she was only disturbed, like every human creature on this earth, by the unexplainable.

"Poor Minstrel," she said sleepily, "I'd like to tell him how silly he was."

"It's only a fairy story," said Grandfather. "How does your inside feel now?"

"Nice and hot," said Henrietta.

He took her upstairs to bed, tucked her up and sat by her till she fell asleep. Just as she was drowsing off she made a rather startling announcement.

"They are both here to-night," she murmured.

"Who?" asked Grandfather.

"The monk who sits in the spare room and paints and the lady with the lovely petticoat who goes tap-tap up and down the stairs."

She was asleep already, her lashes lying on her cheeks and her lids lowered like blinds between her dreaming mind and the created figures of her fancy who moved about the old house. She needed her sleep more than most children, Grandfather thought, needed it to draw the curtain now and again between reality and illusion. . . . When she woke up in the morning she would see only the creatures of flesh and blood who move upon the material plane.

And yet he felt it was right that she, with her sensitive imagination, should grow to womanhood in such a place as Torminster, for imagination, like the honey-sucking bee, creates from what it feeds upon. Surrounded with flowering beauty it creates sweetness, surrounded with harshness and ugliness the fruits of its toil are bitter.

A mood of humble thankfulness descended upon Grandfather, banishing his former sadness. His failures were many but Henrietta was quite certainly a success. In planting this life in the right soil he felt he had done at least one good bit of gardening before the shadows lengthened and his work was done.

CHAPTER IX

I

JOCELYN and Felicity spent the next few days after Christmas feverishly discussing the play. How exactly should it be presented? Was it a tragedy or a romantic fairy tale? Should it be produced with the simplicity suitable to the one or the fantastic splendour demanded by the other? Above all what was the central idea that must link music, scenery, movement and poetry into one unity? They argued with some heat until Torminster itself, that was already so deeply concerned in Ferranti's play, became even more so by providing the answer at the choirboys' annual Christmas party.

This always took place on Holy Innocents' Day and was a great event, for the entire Close, as well as the choirboys, came to it. It took place at the Palace and not at the Deanery because the Bishop liked giving parties for small boys and Lady Lavinia did not. It was regarded by all as an act of reparation made to the choirboys by Torminster. Other small boys tasted the joys of leisure at Christmas time but these sweet innocents were obliged by the exigency of their profession to work harder than ever. Christmas Eve, Christmas Day, Saint Stephen's Day, Saint John the Evangelist's and Innocents' Day followed close upon each other's heels with that singular lack of proportion in the matter of festivals displayed by Mother Church, who might surely have spaced them out a bit, and on all of them the poor children had to attend at the Cathedral twice daily and shout themselves hoarse in anthems, carols, hymns and special psalms. . . . It was hard.

But the party, a gargantuan one, made up for it, and how fitting it was, said those who never came into close contact with the choirboys, that it should take place on Holy Innocents' Day. . . . All those sweet little boys with their round cherubic faces, guileless eyes and clean white collars. . . . It was noticeable that those, such as the organist and the headmaster of the choir-school, who did come into contact with the cherubs, never expressed an opinion on the matter.

The party began soon after three o'clock and lasted for five hours.

Henrietta and Hugh Anthony began dressing for it at twelve o'clock. They wrestled with underclothes from twelve till one, when they had lunch with overalls over the underclothes, and from two onwards, with the assist-tance of the entire household, they coped with the parts that show.

The underclothes of the young at that period were no light matter. The amazing amount of heat that is stored within the bodies of little children was not perhaps realized and it was considered that they must be kept warm. Henrietta wore immensely thick woollen combinations, a woollen liberty-bodice, a woollen vest, a flannel petticoat, a silk petticoat and finally her winter party frock of blue velvet trimmed with fur. Hugh Anthony was not quite so overburdened with clothes, though his pants were tremendous, because Grandmother did not consider the bodies of the male young to be so tender as those of the female of the species, but his brown velvet suit with its frilly collar drove him nearly mad.

"I look a fool," he growled to Henrietta. "Why can't I wear Etons?"

"Grandmother says you can when you've worn out that,"

said Henrietta. "And I think you look sweet. . . . Like Bubbles."

Hugh Anthony made a rude noise in his throat and hurled his shoes across the floor.

Yet when it was time to go his philosophic temperament had come to his rescue. What cannot be helped must be endured and he was not without hope that some untoward accident at the party might ruin his detested suit for ever.

Grandfather, Grandmother and the children started off together, the children carrying their party shoes in brown holland bags and all of them swathed to the eyes in coats and shawls and mufflers.

For it had turned very cold. The stars that had shone so brightly on the evening of Christmas Day had been the first torchbearers in a procession of sparkling days and nights. Every morning the sun rose out of a glowing bed of fire and slowly climbed a sky of cold, brilliant blue. There was not much warmth in the sun, though he was so bright and gay, and he seemed a little aloof from the earth that loved him, but at midday he unbent a little and graciously touched the frosted trees with his fingers so that each grey twig was strung with diamonds. Then he withdrew again, flinging as final largesse an orange glow like a veil over the roofs of the city and painting the shadows of the elm-trees deep blue across the snow. Close at his heels the stars came marching and the moon blazed over the Cathedral towers like a round shield carried on the arm of a giant.

As the four of them crossed the Green the world was at that moment of pause between day and night. Henrietta had already noticed that there was always a haunting, unearthly beauty about this time of transition and that it was very varied. On grey, stormy days it was a gradual strange darkening that blotted out familiar shapes and divorced sound from its cause in a way that terrified. On sunshiny summer days it was a gradual intensification of colour and scent that came near to ecstasy. On other days it was a sudden blaze as of fire, on others a hard, bright flatness as though the earth was a painted picture.

It was this last to-day. The bare branches of the elm-trees were strokes of paint laid on sharply against the primrose wash of the sky. The Cathedral towers stood out hard and black against the sheeted gold of the west and the snow-covered grass stretched smooth and pure. Here and there a sudden speck of colour burned as the painter's brush touched the flat surfaces; an orange square of lamplight leaping out in a dark house, a flash of colour on the snow as a robin hopped across it, a gleam of blue and green as a child in a gay muffler ran home from school. As always on these days when the earth is a painted picture it was very still; the cawing of a rook and the chime of a bell fell sharply as pebbles dropped in a deep well.

They crossed the Green and came to the Market Place, then turned to their left under the great archway that led to the Palace. Here they were overtaken by Mrs. Jameson and Felicity, accompanied by Jocelyn, who had found someone to take charge of the shop till closing time. . . . Grandfather had noticed before that when Felicity was in Torminster Jocelyn found it perfectly easy to leave the shop but when she was not it was a sheer impossibility.

They crossed the drawbridge and passed under the portcullis into the courtyard beyond. In front of them the old walls of the Palace rose majestically, quiet and withdrawn in the evening light, only the windows lighted. They paused to look at it for a moment, for it was very lovely, then scurried hastily to one side as the Dean's carriage and pair swept by them bearing Lady Lavinia in grey velvet, with a purple boa, and the Dean in a new top-hat.

"Do they want to run over us?" inquired Jocelyn with irritation.

"We're not carriage folk," explained Felicity.

II

There was no need to ring at the front door, for it stood hospitably wide open, and Peppercue and Barley-corn, who always assisted the Bishop's decrepit old butler Baggersley on festive occasions, were hovering about to help them off with their coats. The huge stone-floored, vaulted hall was very cold and they parted with their wraps reluctantly. "There are two fires lit in the gallery," whispered Baggersley, with intent to cheer, and totteringly led the way up the lovely carved staircase.

Baggersley was very old, looked like a tortoise and was not of the slightest use. His dress clothes, green with age, hung loosely upon his withered old body and he could not now remember anyone's name, but suggestions that he should be pensioned off were not favourably received by him so the Bishop kept him on. . . . "A dis-grace to the place," the Dean said. "A—er—disgrace."

"Archdeacon Jones and family," quavered Baggersley at the gallery door and the Fordyces, Mrs. Jameson, Felicity and Jocelyn trooped smilingly in.

The Bishop, whose sight was poor, had a moment of confusion until Grandfather whispered hoarsely, "'Smee, Bishop," when he identified them with relief. The short-ness of Baggersley's memory, together with the shortness of his own sight, made the arrival of guests something of a strain.

Few lovelier rooms were to be met with at this time in England than the gallery of the Bishop's Palace at Tor-minster. It stretched the whole length of one wing of the

Palace and was perfectly proportioned for its length. The polished floor shone like dark water and the linen-fold panelling on the walls roused the students of these things to ecstasy. At each end of the gallery a log-fire was blazing, its glow reflected on floor and walls, and in the centre was a Christmas-tree, its top reaching to the ceiling and its branches laden with twinkling candles and presents done up in coloured paper. The choirboys stood in an excited group near the tree, looking terribly clean in their Etons, their faces shining with soap and their eyes with expectation, while near them stood the dignitaries of the Close with their dependents, smiling with the urbanity of those who feel themselves to be in the position of bene-factors but yet have had no bother with the preparations. It was certainly a great occasion, and from the walls of the gallery the former bishops of Torminster looked down upon it from their portraits, the flickering firelight playing queer tricks with their painted faces so that some of them seemed to smile at the happiness, and some to frown at the frivolity, while one gentleman at the far end of the room was dis-tinctly seen by Henrietta to raise a hand in blessing.

The choirboys' presents were given first. Peppercue and Barleycorn mounted two rickety step-ladders and cut them off the tree, calling out the boys' names in stentorian voices, while Baggersley trotted round in circles calling out instructions to Peppercue and Barleycorn, after the manner of those who while doing no work themselves see all the more clearly how it should be done. Paper and string strewed the floor and happy squeals greeted the appearance of knives, watches, whistles, blood-curdling books about Red Indians and boxes of those explosives which, when placed beneath the chairs of corpulent relations, go off with loud and satisfying reports. . . . The Bishop always insisted upon this type of present, disregarding the complaints of the Dean and Lady Lavinia who maintained that they were in no way calculated to improve the morals of the dear boys. "No one," said the Bishop, "wants to be bothered with morals at Christmas"; which the Dean and Lady Lavinia considered such an outrageous remark that they were careful not to repeat it. . . . Delight mounted higher and higher, reaching the peak of ecstasy when the tree caught fire and Barleycorn fell off his step-ladder, Baggersley remarking with acid pleasure that he had said so all along.

Grandfather took advantage of the confusion and howls of joy that ensued to press little packets into the hands of his young grandchildren. He remembered from his own childhood how difficult it is to watch other children receiving presents when you do not get any yourself. You may have a toy-cupboard at home stocked with good things, you may be going to a party every day for a fortnight, but it does not make any difference, for in childhood there is no past and no future, but only the joy or desolation of the moment. The tight, polite smiles that Henrietta and Hugh Anthony were maintaining with difficulty changed in the twinkling of an eye into happy grins as knobbly parcels were slipped into their hot palms from behind. . . . Surreptitiously they opened them. . . . A tiny china teapot and a box of pink pistol-caps numerous enough to turn every day of the next fortnight into a fifth of November.

Looking over their shoulders they saw Grandfather standing with his back to them, gazing with an appearance of great innocence at a portrait of an eighteenth-century bishop with a white wig and sleeves like balloons. . . . They chuckled.

The fire put out and Barleycorn smoothed down they all went downstairs to the banqueting hall for tea.

The original banqueting hall, where kings and queens had feasted, was now a ruin standing out in the Palace grounds in the moonlight, but its name had been transferred to the sombre great room below the gallery, where damp stains disfigured the walls and where the wind always howled in the chimney.

Not that this worried the choirboys for the Bishop's cook had surpassed herself. They sat themselves down round the groaning table and they did not speak again.

But at the buffet at the far end of the room, where the grown-ups balanced delicate sandwiches and little iced cakes in their saucers, there was a polite hum of conversation. Extraordinary, thought Hugh Anthony and Henrietta, who had to-day to be perforce counted among them, how grown-ups talk when they eat. Don't they want to taste their food? Don't they want to follow it in imagination as it travels down that fascinating pink-lined lane to the larder below? Sometimes Henrietta tried to picture that larder. It had shelves, she thought, and a lot of gnomes called "digestive juices" ran about putting things to rights. . . . Or sometimes, unfortunately, forgetting to.

"Please," said Henrietta plaintively to Felicity, "could you hold my cup while I eat my cake? It's so dreadfully difficult not sitting down."

Felicity, who had finished her own tea, was most helpful. She held Henrietta's cup in one hand and with the other she held the saucer below the cake so that Henrietta should not drop crumbs on the carpet.

"Shall I hold yours, Hugh Anthony?" asked Jocelyn, for Hugh Anthony's cup of milk was slopping over into the saucer in the most perilous way.

"No, thank you," said Hugh Anthony, and his eyes were very bright because he had just had a brilliant idea.

Putting it into immediate practice he placed himself and his cup behind the Archdeacon, who was holding forth to Mrs. Elphinstone about total abstinence. Now when the Archdeacon held forth he had a curious habit

G*

of stepping suddenly backwards when he reached his peroration. He did it in the pulpit, frightening everyone into fits lest he should fall over the edge and kill himself, and he did it on his own hearthrug so that in winter his visitors had to keep a sharp look-out and make a dash for it when his coat-tails caught the flames, and he did it now. "Temperance, my dear lady," he said to Mrs. Elphinstone, "is the foundation stone of national welfare," and stepped backwards on top of Hugh Anthony.

Everyone rushed to pick the poor child up. He was patted, soothed, kissed, and the milk that had spilled all over him was mopped up, though it was distressingly evident that his velvet suit was ruined.

The courage with which Hugh Anthony bore the pain of his trampled feet was much admired by everyone but Henrietta, for Henrietta, standing grave-eyed and aloof, knew quite well that he had done it on purpose.

III

"And now," said the Bishop, when the boys could eat no more, "I'm afraid we must go to evensong."

This was not the end of the party but only an interruption to it, and it was not even necessary to go out of doors, for a covered way led from the Palace to the Cloisters and the Cloisters led directly into the Cathedral.

A silence fell upon them all as they entered the Cloisters, for the Cloisters always imposed silence. They were built round three sides of a square, the fourth side being occupied by the Cathedral itself, and in the square the dead were buried; those very same bishops whose pictured faces had smiled and frowned upon the Christmas party, together with deans and canons whose names on the headstones had been washed out by wind and rain. It was bright moonlight now, with a blaze of stars, and the headstones showed up black and sharp against the snow. The feet of the living clanked harshly as they passed and all unconsciously they tried to go on tiptoe. Mr. Phillips, the organist, had gone on ahead with Peppercue and Barleycorn so that when the others came into the Cathedral the candles were already flowering in the darkness and the organ playing softly.

They began with a hymn, "Once in royal David's city," after which evensong pursued its accustomed course until they got to the anthem, and it was here that Felicity and Jocelyn, who had never before attended evensong on the party day, had a shock, for it was Steggall's anthem, "Remember now thy Creator in the days of thy youth."

It was always sung on the party day and Grandfather considered it a most depressing choice, and had said so more than once at Chapter Meetings, but was not listened to because what always had been done at Torminster always was done, suitable or not, and would be till the Day of Judgment, but Felicity and Jocelyn were not concerned with its suitability so much as with its beauty.

Felicity had always considered the twelfth chapter of Ecclesiastes the most haunting poem ever written. She found in it the same beauty, tinged with a feeling of eeriness, that years later she was to find in the poetry of Mr. Walter de la Mare. "Remember now thy Creator in the days of thy youth, while the evil days come not, nor the years draw nigh, when thou shalt say, I have no pleasure in them; while the sun, or the light, or the moon, or the stars, be not darkened, nor the clouds return after the rain." A boy's clear treble rang out in the great Cathedral, where the candlelight fitfully shone on shadowed faces and carved stone and wood dark with age, while above them the pillars soared into darkness and all around them the night pressed in. A strange mutter of voices, quiet but very ominous, took up the next verse. "In the days when the keepers of the house shall tremble, and the strong men shall bow themselves, and the grinders cease because they are few, and those that look out of the windows shall be darkened." This lament for the fate of man, for the passing of his youth and joy and the coming of old age and death, was very queer and frightening, all the more so because one was not quite certain what it was all about. "Vanity of vanities, saith the preacher, all is vanity. . . . The mourners go about the streets. . . . The wheel broken at the cistern." Was that the end of the matter? "The spirit shall return unto God Who gave it." In that word "return" Felicity suddenly found comfort. The fate of man in this world was certainly a thing to be lamented over, a thing of uncertainty and loss and pain, and no amount of easy optimism could alter the facts of the case, yet in death he "returned" to his starting point of sun and moon and stars that are not darkened. Her mind wandering she thought that the writer of this poem, when he chose sun and moon and stars as the supreme givers of joy, must have felt as Ferranti had done that man can best understand the meaning of perfection when he takes as its symbol a circle of white light. They were very akin, Ferranti and this writer whose name she did not know. . . . Suddenly she started and touched Jocelyn's arm as he sat beside her. The mist of sorrow that was in his eyes cleared away as he looked at her and whispered the thought that was in both their minds. "The answer. . . . Our play must be presented as a great lament."

The anthem ended and they knelt down to pray, their lowered eyelids shutting out even the faint candlelight so that each of them was alone in darkness. To Jocelyn, even more deeply depressed than Felicity because depression came more naturally to him, it seemed that the darkness of human life was too great to be endured. The words of the prayers flowed on unheard by him as he sank deeper and deeper into desolation. It seemed that he had touched rock-bottom when Felicity, wise through that knowledge of his thoughts that had come to her through love, put out a hand and gently touched his side. Instantly his spirits rose a little and opening his eyes he saw the candlelight. So often in his experience the minor miseries of life had been eased by the touch of humanity; would the great miseries, when they came, be eased by God's touch? One would have to be old to know and the old, he had noticed, and not the young, were more often the men of faith.

They sang a last hymn and filed silently out of the dark Cathedral and through the moonlit Cloisters. Safely back in the Palace any eerie feelings that might remain were dispelled by Mrs. Phillips' "How those boys can sing like that after all that tea," she said, "beats me."

IV

After this pious interruption the party became secular again. There was snapdragon in the darkened banqueting hall and races in the gallery, followed by the giving of prizes to the winners of the races and a few speeches. It was one of the habits of Torminster, a habit to be deplored, that upon every possible occasion it spoke. There were speeches at the choir-school prize-giving, speeches at the annual missionary sale of work, speeches at drawing-room meetings, speeches at concerts in aid of charity and, as if that was not enough, speeches at the party. Why there should be speeches at the party no one knew, but there always had been speeches at the party and so there always must be.

When the races had all been run, the orange-and-teaspoon race, the three-legged race, the wheel-barrow race, the hopping race and all the others, they sat down, the boys on the floor and the grown-ups on chairs, and the Bishop said a few words.

He made them as brief as possible, hoping that others might follow his example. He merely told his guests what a delight it was to entertain them at the Palace—at this point Baggersley who sometimes, like Grandfather, spoke his thoughts aloud, began to say something forcible to the contrary but his remarks were drowned by a very loud fit of coughing on the part of Barleycorn—hoped the boys had enjoyed themselves and congratulated Binks Major and Minor, Hopkins Minor and Jenkins upon carrying off the prizes. Then he sat down and the Dean got up, clearing his throat and grasping the lapels of his coat in his beautiful hands.

With the light shining on his silvery white hair and whiskers he looked magnificent. His coat was without a crease and on his gaiters every button was done up. His diamond ring sparkled and the toes of his boots, just showing below his gaiters, shone like glass. . . . Torminster glowed with pride. Not every Cathedral city, it thought, had a dean like theirs. You could have put him down anywhere and within two minutes he would have looked as though he owned the place.

"Dear friends and dear boys," fluted the Dean. This party, he felt, always had too worldly a tone—out of the tail of his eye he could see that the prizes the Bishop would soon bestow on Jenkins, Binks Major and Minor and Hopkins Minor were boxes of fireworks and water-pistols —and he always did his best, in this speech, to raise things to a higher level. He did so now for a full quarter of an hour. He told the boys how grave and noble a calling was that of a choirboy. He likened them all to the infant

Samuel serving in the Temple. He went on a long time
about the infant Samuel. Then he warned them very
seriously, with a sidelong glance at the fireworks, of the
pernicious effects upon the character of frivolity. In
the midst of life, he said, we are in death, and we
should not allow pleasures to lull us to forgetfulness
of our sins.

Then he sat down amid loud and prolonged applause,
for really, the boys thought, the old boy had looked splendid
while he gassed, and dear old Canon Roderick, the senior
canon present—for it was impossible to get Canon Elphinstone's bathchair up the Palace stairs—tottered to his feet.
Everyone loved Canon Roderick for he had a face like a
rosy apple and he never saw a child but he gave it sixpence.
Moreover, he always made exactly the same speech, both at
the prize-giving and at the party, so that you knew exactly
where you were and could applaud automatically in the
right place without having to listen too hard. He always
related the histories of his own sons—now elderly men—
for he found, he said, that young people always like to
hear about other young people. They began with Tom
and followed his career through Eton and Sandhurst and
into the army, went with him to India where he won
distinction in a frontier skirmish, scurried at his heels to
South Africa, where he won the V.C.—terrific cheers—
and finally settled down with him in Hampshire where
he was now, would you believe it, a retired general. Loud
cheering, and they passed on to James, a sailor, following
with deep interest and for the twentieth time as he climbed
from midshipman to admiral and greeting his final elevation
with a storm of cheering that nearly brought the roof off.
Charles, a doctor, was a rugger blue—loud cheers—and
Thomas, a schoolmaster, was a double first—rather subdued cheers. Henry was a leading barrister and last of all
Edward, the baby, was actually a bishop. At this point,

the company being what it was, the applause became deafening. Cheers, claps, and even stamping greeted the achievement of Edward. Canon Roderick was helped to his seat, with his rosy face beaming with pride, and the Archdeacon rose to take his place with one of those speeches without which no prize-giving, not even a tiny one, is complete.

He began by saying that people who make long speeches are a great nuisance. Then for ten minutes or longer he explained why it is that they are a nuisance. Then he spoke a few words of congratulation to the boys who were to receive prizes, then a few words of consolation to the boys who would not receive prizes—conveying the impression that on the whole it is better not to receive prizes—followed by a few words to the grown-ups, followed by a peroration during which he suddenly stepped backwards on top of some potted plants and sent them flying.

The choir-school headmaster seized this opportunity to get up and begin his speech, which was always the last to be made at the party, hoping by this ruse to prevent anybody else from saying anything, for time was getting on and the longer they were over the speeches the longer it would be before his wife could get the boys to bed and there would be a little peace. On behalf of the choir he thanked everyone for their kindness and sat down.

It then seemed that Canon Allenby was going to make a speech, for he began to pant and grunt and heave his large person forward in his chair, and the headmaster cast a glance of anguished entreaty at the Bishop, for there was no reason whatever why Canon Allenby should make a speech, and once he started he never stopped. . . . The Bishop got up hastily, while Canon Allenby was still heaving and grunting, and called upon Binks Major and Minor, Hopkins Minor and Jenkins to come and receive their prizes. . . . Henrietta felt unhappy, and she could see that Grandfather felt unhappy too, for it was obvious that Canon Allenby was put out, and the old ought not to be put out. Let the young be put out, thought Grandfather fiercely, for the self-adjustment necessary to getting in again is so good for them. Then both he and Henrietta felt happy once more for they saw the Dean give Canon Allenby a glance of commiseration behind the Bishop's back and Canon Allenby, who adored the Dean and felt exactly as he did about the Bishop, was comforted.

The four boys received their prizes amid renewed applause and it was time for hide-and-seek all over the house.

The ardour of the grown-ups now began to cool a little and those of them who only liked children within reason gradually melted away, leaving behind those who after four hours of a party still liked children; on this occasion Mr. Phillips, Felicity, Jocelyn—though perhaps he only stayed because he liked Felicity—Hugh Anthony, Henrietta, Grandfather and the Bishop. The two latter, when hide-and-seek was well started, sank into chairs before one of the fires in the gallery, stretched their feet to the blaze, folded tired hands and meditated silently upon the amazing vitality of the young.

At eight o'clock the dishevelled children, their heated faces smeared with dirt and their Etons ornamented with cobwebs, were assembled in the banqueting hall and again fed, after which they all went home. . . . It had been a grand party. The Bishop and Baggersley, as they saw their guests off at the hall door, could scarcely stand, while Grandfather did not refuse Jocelyn's offer of an arm home.

Felicity walked behind with the children.

"I've milked my front," said Hugh Anthony triumphantly, "and torn the seat of my trousers."

"You're a wicked boy," said Henrietta, "and your suit will have to be given to the poor. . . . I'm not milked or torn," she continued with pride, and opened her coat for Felicity to see.

It was quite true. She was one of those fortunate people who are never untidy. Whatever Henrietta might do, and to-day she had fished raisins out of the snapdragon, slid down the banisters and hidden in corners that the Palace housemaid, having no mistress, consistently overlooked as a matter of principle, she always emerged at the end of it with unruffled hair and spotless dress. At this moment, in her blue frock in the moonlight, with her opened coat held out like wings and her eyes stars in her tilted face, she looked as much like a little angel as makes no difference.

"Oh, but I love you!" cried Felicity, and the garden door of Number Two the Close being now reached she gave way to that extravagance of action which so annoyed those who did not like her, went down on her knees in the snow and flung her arms round both children. "Don't ever go away from me," she implored them. "Never. Never." Hugh Anthony, kissing her chin politely, wriggled and went away but Henrietta remained, pressing closer.

v

The day after the party was the day chosen by Grandfather for the children's annual lesson on the connection between Faith and Works, and it was a black day. Faith, as understood by Henrietta and Hugh Anthony, was saying your prayers and going to church and this they had no objection to, but Works was giving away your toys to the poor and that was another thing altogether. What connection was there, they demanded indignantly of each other, between kneeling in your nightgown at the side of your bed at night and saying "Our-Father-witchard-in-heaven," followed by "Now-I-lay-me," and parting next day from the dolls' perambulator and the tin helmet? . . . There seemed none.

The giving away of the toys always took place in the afternoon, and in the morning, as soon as breakfast was over, Grandfather and the children withdrew to the little room half-way up the tower where the toy-cupboards were kept. They toiled up the stone stairs, carrying two large baskets and the oil-stove that was to warm them during their melancholy employment, in a depressing silence.

The little room had been given to the children because it was like a room in a fairy tale. It was nearly at the top of the tower and its mullioned window, set in the thickness of the wall, had a lovely view of the Cathedral towers, the Tor and the jumbled roofs of the city. It was quite empty, except for the children's treasures, and in it they were never required to tidy up.

They had a cupboard each whose state, Grandfather thought, was typical of their owners. In Henrietta's cupboard her dolls, together with their garments, furniture, crockery and cooking utensils, were laid out in neat rows on the top shelf. Her books were on the second shelf and treasures such as ribbons, tinsel off the Christmas-tree and boxes of beads were on the third shelf. You could see at once where everything was, and what it was, and when you opened the cupboard door nothing fell out.

With Hugh Anthony's cupboard it was not so, for as soon as the door was opened an avalanche descended. Jumbled up among engines with their wheels off, cricket bats cracked in the middle, headless soldiers and a moth-eaten golliwog who had seen better days, were chestnuts, bits of silver-paper, birds' feathers, the skin of a defunct snake, a mangel-wurzel and, most horrible of all, a baby

chicken with two heads which had been preserved in a
bottle of spirits and given to Hugh Anthony by Bates
two Christmases ago. . . . Hugh Anthony with his scientific
mind adored this chicken and could never understand why
everyone else averted their eyes when it was produced.

Having lit the oil-stove Grandfather sat himself down
on the old rocking-horse and proceeded to superintend.
Each child was required to fill a basket but they were not
required to give away anything they had received this
Christmas. They chose themselves what they should give
away and Grandfather only interfered when he considered
the choice unsuitable.

The cupboards were opened, the avalanche fell and work
began.

Hugh Anthony always started by picking out the
things that he really did not want, the heads of the soldiers,
for instance, and the moth-eaten golliwog, but Grandfather's voice would thunder out behind him, "No, Hugh
Anthony! Rubbish must not be given to God's poor!"
Then Hugh Anthony, after getting no answer to his "Why
not?" which Grandfather considered a rhetorical question
unworthy of answer, would be obliged to choose instead
the soldiers that were very nearly intact and the least beloved of his engines, pistols and bricks. The things that
he cared for most deeply, such as the two-headed chicken
and the skin of the snake, Grandfather mercifully considered
unsuitable.

Henrietta was the stuff of which martyrs are made, for
when she had to give away she always gave what she
loved best. Grandfather, as he watched her dark head
bent sadly over the basket and her dainty fingers slowly
placing her treasures side by side inside it, understood
her and suffered agonies. Yet he never interfered with
the suggestion that Gladys Hildegarde, the least-loved of
Henrietta's dolls, would do just at well to give away as

Irene Emily Jane the worshipped and adored. . . . No. . . .
For who knew what spiritual strength and beauty might
not pass from Henrietta to the sawdust bosom of Irene
Emily Jane, and from thence to the little girl to whom
she would be given?

But the sacrifice of this lady had taken place a year ago
and she was now forgotten, for time heals even the worst
of wounds. Henrietta had this year, so her conscience said,
to part from the snowstorm that Miss Lavender had
given her on her birthday. It was an incomparable toy.
It consisted of a glass globe inside which a red man in a
yellow hat stood on a green field. His cottage stood in the
middle distance while to the right was a fir-tree and to the
left a dog. This in itself was amazing, for how in the world
did the red man, his cottage, his dog, and the fir-tree get
inside the globe? But there was a greater marvel yet to
come for when the globe was held upside down it began to
snow. First a few flakes fell, then a few more, then they
fell so thick and fast that the man and his house and his dog
and the fir-tree were hidden from sight. Then you turned
the globe right way up again and the storm ceased. . . . It
was amazing. . . . Henrietta took it out of the cupboard
and held it in her hands, her head bent. Then for the last
time she held it upside down and watched the snow fall.
Then she placed it in the basket and turned her back on it.

Grandfather watched her with painful attention and
her action seemed to him to take on a mystic meaning.
The globe was the world itself, containing all creation,
trees, animals, man and his works, the earth and the sky,
and Henrietta, it seemed, was one of those rare beings
who, like Catherine Earnshaw, are prepared for love's
sake to see "the universe turn to a mighty stranger."

After she had parted with the snowstorm it seemed to
Henrietta quite easy to part with other things; with her
necklace of blue beads, her set of drawing-room furniture

made by herself out of chestnuts, with pins for legs and pink wool twisted round more pins for the backs of the chairs, her toy sewing-machine and her Dolly Dimple, a cardboard person with twelve sets of cardboard under-clothes, and ten hats.

When the baskets were packed they went downstairs and Grandfather read to them to cheer them up, and after that there was a rather penitential dinner of boiled cod and rice pudding at which Hugh Anthony did not behave well.

"Will you have skin, Hugh Anthony?" asked Grand-mother, for she did not make the children eat milk-pudding-skin if they did not want to.

"No," said Hugh Anthony shortly.

"No, what?" asked Grandmother, who was punctilious about "thank you" being inserted in the proper place.

"No skin," said Hugh Anthony.

VI

After dinner they started out, carrying the baskets and watched with disapproval by Grandmother. It was not that she disapproved of self-sacrifice, in fact she approved of it within limits set by herself, but in this case she feared its after-results. At the worst visiting the poor led to whooping-cough and at the best it resulted in the bringing home of insect life.

It had been snowing and the children insisted upon walking behind Grandfather so as to tread in his footsteps, for he was good King Wenceslas and they were the page who, they decided, was really a twin.

"Couldn't you walk with me?" asked Grandfather, who felt a bit lonely by himself.

"No," they said, but they did not explain why such

a thing was totally out of the question so he went on feeling lonely. They looked very odd, going up the street treading in each other's footsteps, but then Torminster was used to Grandfather and the children looking odd, and took no notice.

Beyond the Close a steep street wound uphill and here lived those people referred to by the Dean as the Lower Orders and by Grandfather as God's Poor. The part of the city where they lived had a fascination for the children because in its own way it was beautiful. The street knew, as the streams know, that it looks ugly to come down a hill in a straight line, and it wound about with stream-like windings so that you never knew what was coming round the corner. The cottages on each side were old, with weather-stained walls and flights of steps leading up to their front doors, and their crinkled roofs made a lovely pattern against the sky. No street that climbs a hill can be unattractive, Henrietta used to say in after years, the irregular line of the climbing roofs sees to that, but an old street on a hillside is one of the loveliest things on earth.

To-day the curious white light of snow was over the world and a stinging cleanliness was in the air. The sky, emptied now of its snowflakes, was a pale grey with jagged rents torn in it through which one saw the blue behind; aquamarine just over the hills, turquoise higher up and sapphire overhead. To their right the trees that covered the Tor showed to perfection the softness of their winter dress. The bare twigs seemed by their interlacing to create colour, the brown of them melting into blue and red and purple. The Tor looked like the breast of a bird, Henrietta thought. It was hard to realize that if you came close to the trees their softness would melt into hardness and their colour into stark black and brown.

Firelight shone ruddily from windows and open doors

and in spite of the cold the elder children were sitting on the steps that led to them, while the babies peered over the wooden boards put across the doors to keep them from hurtling down the steps. Inside the rooms busy mothers could be seen moving backwards and forwards, their figures dark against bright-patterned wall-paper and shining pots and pans.

It was of course difficult to know which cottages they ought to go to, for they could not go everywhere. The only thing to do, Grandfather had said when he first started the annual lesson on Works, was to begin at the bottom of the street and stop whenever they saw children, and next year to begin where they had left off the previous year. There were bound to be complaints, of course, in the cottages where they did not go, but he was primarily concerned with the characters of his own grandchildren so he tried not to think about them.

"Last year," said Henrietta from the rear, "we stopped at the cottage half-way up on the left-hand side where the wicked little boy showed Hugh Anthony how to make a long nose."

Grandfather remembered the regrettable incident, as indeed he might, for Hugh Anthony had been making long noses ever since, no amount of spanking curing him of the habit. That was the worst of Hugh Anthony. The wrong things seemed always to make an indelible impression on him while sweet and good influences ran off him like water off a duck's back. . . . Or so it seemed. . . . Grandfather could only hope and pray that future years might prove it otherwise.

"We'll go and see that little boy again," said Hugh Anthony.

"We will not," said Grandfather firmly. "We will go to the first house beyond him that has respectable-looking children."

The wicked little boy seemed out and they passed the danger point in safety. Beyond were several cottages where there were no children but after that things began to happen.

They began well.

Three little tow-haired girls sat on a flight of steps one behind the other. They wore stout boots and mufflers crossed over their chests and tied in bows behind. The dirt on their faces was only surface dirt, for their necks in contrast with their black faces were white as snow, and they had the eyes of children who have been loved from the beginning. Large handkerchiefs were attached to their persons with safety-pins and they were eating bread and jam. . . . A delightful family. . . . A family after Grandfather's own heart. . . . He smiled at them and they stopped eating bread and jam, wiped their mouths with the backs of their hands—the handkerchiefs being apparently intended for nasal use only—and smiled back at him. Then shyness seized them; they cast down their eyes and squirmed.

But Grandfather had seen behind them a clean, fire-lit kitchen, a cheerful mother and two tow-haired boys, and he led the way in, patting the heads of the girls as he climbed over them.

Inside, in an atmosphere of welcome, he was utterly happy. He sat himself down in a windsor chair, placed his hat on the floor and talked to the cheerful mother as though he had known her all his life. He felt as though the hard, happy days of his parish work were back with him again, those days when he had not felt conscious, as he was always conscious in the Close, of living a segregated life. He hated segregation, inevitable though he knew it to be. He hated the barriers of time and age and class and language. He longed for the time when all the different lights carried by man in the pagentry of life should glow into one.

But his ease was as yet impossible to Henrietta and Hugh Anthony. They stood side by side, stiff and miserable, subjected to the unwinking stare of five pairs of eyes; for the tow-headed little girls had now joined the little boys in a group as far removed as possible from their visitors. The whole width of the kitchen separated the well-dressed from the ill-dressed and it was the well-dressed, weighed down by numbers, who felt themselves at a disadvantage. What makes one feel uncomfortable, they discovered suddenly, is not what one has got or has not got, but being different.

But gradually the situation eased itself. First Henrietta took a step forward, then one of the little girls, and then before they knew where they were the chestnut chairs with the wool backs had been set out on the stone floor, becoming in a flash mahogany upon a marble pavement.

After that the giving of gifts was easy. Hugh Anthony parted almost willingly from an engine with three wheels and a box of soldiers, and Henrietta added to the chestnut chairs her blue bead necklace and Dolly Dimple.

"Isn't 'Arold going to 'ave nothink?" asked the eldest little girl.

"Who's Harold?" asked Grandfather with benign interest.

"My eldest," said the woman. "Upstairs with the measles." She sighed, glancing at the youngest little girl who was sniffling. "They'll all 'ave it now. There's Rosie sneezing already."

Grandfather's eyes popped a little behind his glasses, but he was careful to go quietly on with the conversation until the end, when he rose and thought they ought to be going. A picture book was found for Harold, mutual good-byes were said and they departed.

"I think," said Grandfather, when they were out in

the street again, "that it would be better not to mention the measles to your dear Grandmother."

"Why not?" asked Hugh Anthony.

"It would distress her," said Grandfather, "to think of the poor little boy being ill."

"Oh no, it wouldn't," said Hugh Anthony.

Henrietta privately agreed with him for she had noticed that Grandmother and Clara enjoyed hearing about other people's ups and downs. Whenever anybody's chimney caught on fire, or cook gave notice, or appendix had to come out, Clara would come running to tell Grandmother and Grandmother would say, "Dear me, Clara, you don't say so!" and look almost bright and interested.

They went on up the street, giving toys to the children whom they saw and sometimes going inside their homes, and all went well until they turned a corner and came upon a dingy-looking house from which no firelight shone. The broken window-panes were stuffed with rag, a most unusual sight in Torminster, and over the board across the door there peeped a dirty baby with a cold in its head, and no handkerchief. Grandfather, seeing the cold, would have passed on but as the children were still in single file behind him, treading in the footsteps of Good King Wenceslas, he had no control over them and before he could stop her Henrietta had darted across the pavement to the baby.

She had never seen such a pitiful baby and the sight of it made her feel dreadful. It was dirty all over, from its matted hair to its bare toes, and its poor little upper lip was terribly sore because no one had ever blown its dribbling nose. In a flash Henrietta climbed over the board and blew the nose on her own clean handkerchief, then picking up the scrap in her arms she staggered with it into the gloom beyond.

Inside were dirt and evil smells and dead ashes in the

grate. A horrible-looking old woman, the grandmother perhaps, with greasy strands of grey hair escaping from a man's cap, was peeling potatoes and shouting raucously at the children who seemed swarming all over the place. Henrietta, unseen, stood still and stared, for the children had not got faces like the children she was accustomed to. They had old faces and their eyes did not seem to look at anything steadily. When the old woman hit out at two of the little ones they ducked cleverly, and without fear, but their cunning was somehow horrible. Then they saw Henrietta and came boldly crowding up to her, shouting out things that she did not understand, though she knew they were mocking things. She recoiled a little and found to her relief that Grandfather was just behind her.

"Give them some toys," he said quietly, "and then come away."

But before she had time to do anything a door burst open and a drink-sodden brute of a man was upon them, a man as repellent as it is possible for a human creature to become upon this earth. It was lucky for Henrietta that in her fright she did not see him very clearly, or understand anything of the torrent of abuse that he hurled at Grandfather, except his last shout of, "I'll have none of your damned charity."

"I have no wish to inflict it on you at the moment," said Grandfather sternly, and he moved to the door, pushing Henrietta and Hugh Anthony in front of him and quite unmoved, apparently, by the flung boot that missed his head by inches. . . . This was not the first time in the course of his ministry that boots had been hurled at his head and he supposed it would not be the last, for with the vicar's permission he intended to visit this gentleman again.

Out in the street Henrietta suddenly dived under Grandfather's arm and ran back. When that terrible man had come in she had seen the children all cowering back, as they had not shrunk from their grandmother, and the sight had awakened in her some queer agony of understanding, for these were children who were not wanted. Deep down in Henrietta's mind was a half-formed memory of a time when she herself had not been wanted. It was not a real memory, like the memory of her singing mother, it was only a shadow that spread itself behind the figure of her mother, not emanating from her but from someone else, and faintly darkening those days at the orphanage when she discovered that her mother was dead and that no one would tell her anything about her father. . . . Someone, at some time, had not wanted her, that was all she knew. . . . The horrible man had disappeared again, but the children were still cowering in their corner. She pushed fiercely in among them and took the snowstorm from her basket. "Look!" she cried, and held it upside down. "Look at the snow falling."

Suddenly they were crowding round her, kicking and scuffling, fear and hatred forgotten and their eyes and mouths "ohs" of amazement. One of the boys seized the globe rudely from her and hit out indiscriminately at all the others so that he could have this treasure for himself. His hard fist caught Henrietta in the chest and nearly winded her, but she did not mind. Backing out from among them she ran back to Grandfather at the door, momentarily happy again.

But the swift changes of mood possible to childhood were not possible to Grandfather and he was by no means happy. He had had no idea that Torminster possessed such a family, and he was terribly sorry that the children should have seen it. . . . Henrietta, he knew, would never forget. . . . And he was grieved, too, that she should have parted with her snowstorm when she did, for he had not the slightest doubt that within two hours it would be at the pawnbroker's. Well, for two hours, for the first time and probably the last, those wretched children would possess for their own the world and its beauty, earth and sky, a tree, a cottage, a dog and a red man in a yellow hat.

They visited no more houses that afternoon for there was no more spirit left in them. They trailed rather sadly home, giving away the few toys that were left to the children they met.

When they got to their own garden door the light was fading and the shadows were long across the snow. The Tor woods had lost their colour and the bright patches of blue sky were swallowed up in the grey.

Henrietta and Hugh Anthony ran straight upstairs to Grandmother in the drawing-room, where the warm fire gleamed on dark panelling and coloured china and where the smell of the fresh chrysanthemums was clean and pungent. Grandfather went to his study, shut the door, fell upon his knees and prayed that the dear children might not catch the measles. . . . They did not.

CHAPTER X

I

GRASS might grow in many places but it never grew under Felicity's feet. She threw herself into a fury of activity over Ferranti's play, dragging Grandfather and Jocelyn down with her into the whirlpool. Most of her time was spent in London, interviewing managers, composers, producers, designers of scenery, editors, journalists and gentlemen with money. She made shameless use of her attractions, proving an adorable companion to those whose services she required and smiling over her shoulder in a devastating way at the gentlemen with money.

Jocelyn, constantly summoned to her aid by a stream of telegrams whose number and volubility was at this time a great source of revenue to the government, was obliged to leave the shop to the care of Grandfather, the children and Miss Lavender on at least three days a week. . . . Grandmother was outraged. . . . That she should live to see her own husband on the wrong side of a counter was really the last straw in a married life strewn with straws. "A Canon of the Cathedral serving in a shop," she said indignantly to Jocelyn. "I never heard of such a thing in all my life. What the Dean thinks I don't know and don't want to know. And what your poor grandfather, who has never, let me tell you, been able to subtract a penny from three-halfpence since the day he was born, gives in the way of change I'm sure I don't know."

"Perhaps you could give him arithmetical help in the shop, Grandmother?" suggested Jocelyn mischievously.

"I help in a shop?" exclaimed Grandmother in horror. "Thank you, Jocelyn. You and your poor grandfather may have lost the sense you were born with, but I thank God that I still retain mine."

II

On a certain February evening Jocelyn waited for the London train at Torminster station. . . . That is to say it was known as the London train because people who had left London in the dim past occupied it during the last lap of their journey to the city of dreams, but of what agonies of changes and waits and missing of connections they had passed through before they reached its shelter they were generally too exhausted to give a coherent account. . . . It was quite dark and a soft wind was blowing, a friendly buffeting wind that slapped you on the back in a cheery way, assuring you that winter was over and spring was on the way at last. Jocelyn could almost fancy that the smell of flowers was in the wind, and standing out in the darkness at the far end of the platform, looking at a round green light in the distance, he could think he was walking down the tunnel of winter and coming nearer and nearer to the green light of spring beyond.

Through the wind he could hear the grinding of wheels and see a threaded line of lights winding its way through the valley, that prosaic thing a train transformed by the alchemy of darkness into a jewelled snake. His heart beat a little faster for one of those dots of light represented Felicity.

The train blew its whistle and 'Erb, the beery porter, appeared upon the platform and spat upon his hands in case manual labour of any sort should be required of him.

"Blowy night, sir," he confided.

"Feeling of spring in it," said Jocelyn.

"Ah," said 'Erb profoundly, and then, yelling with the full force of his lungs as the line of lights rounded the last bend and slid into the station, "Tor-min-ster! Tor min-ster!"

To hear him you would have thought the train was full to bursting with strangers from the Antipodes with no idea where they were, yet nothing got out but Felicity and her suitcase and Mr. Wilks and a case of stout.

Felicity looked tired, and in her grey fur coat that had been rained on during the day she seemed a depressed squirrel recently fished up out of a pond. She sighed with relief when she saw Jocelyn, feeling as she always did when she was with him that the burden of two lives fused into one, with the weight shared equally between them.

"You look dead beat," said Jocelyn. "Gotobed's here with the bus. Shall we go up in it?"

"No. Mr. Wilks and his stout are going up in the bus, and Mr. Wilks is a bit cheery. . . . He's been to a licensed victuallers' luncheon. . . . 'Erb shall put in my suitcase and we'll walk."

Mr. Wilks, with his bowler hat on the side of his head and a song on his lips and the stout, a present for Mrs. Wilks, beside him on the seat, was driven off in Cinderella's pumpkin, with Mr. Gotobed joyously cracking his whip on the box to indicate to Torminster the state of mind that Mr. Wilks was in. When they had gone, with the bus creaking from side to side and the lamps swinging, the peace of the windy night seemed intensified to Jocelyn and Felicity, strolling along in the dark.

"What a lovely wind!" murmured Felicity, slipping her arm through Jocelyn's. "It sounds like a big giant laughing up in the hills."

H

"What luck?" asked Jocelyn.

"Everything is practically settled and we hope to open this spring. Rehearsals begin next week and that friend of mine I told you of, Nigel Compton, is composing the loveliest music, with one tune especially that will haunt everyone till their dying day. The scenery and the ballet will be heavenly, I think, and those articles you are writing about Ferranti in the *Evening Journal* are making people quite excited. You're a splendid journalist, Jocelyn. That suggestion of yours that he's probably killed himself for lack of appreciation was first-rate propaganda."

"Who's to play the lead?" asked Jocelyn, slithering modestly away from the subject of his own journalistic efforts of which, as a matter of fact, he was inordinately proud.

"Oliver Standish. He has a lovely singing voice, and though he has the largest appetite of any man I ever met he's slim with it and looks wonderfully ethereal and sad on the stage. That's what we want in the Minstrel; we must give the impression of a lost spirit; something in the wrong place, out of tune with its environment. . . . Man himself. . . . If this play is not a lament for the spirit of man astray in the world it is nothing at all."

"Do they understand that?"

"I've tried to rub it in and the scenery and the music and the dancing are all being designed to that end. . . . It will be a great lament."

"And who," asked Jocelyn, "is to play the golden-haired woman?"

"Felicity Summers."

"I'm glad. I wanted that," said Jocelyn, though his jealousy of Oliver Standish suddenly painted the hitherto blue night a hideous green.

"My singing is not first class but it's adequate, and they say I'm a draw."

Her voice suddenly dragged a little and Jocelyn sensed in her weariness and fear. "Are you afraid, Felicity?"

"For the first time in my life," she whispered. "You see I'm responsible for all this. It's I who've made men risk their money and their reputations over this play. They think it's their own doing but I know it's mine, for they've seen the play through a rosy flame and the flame was my own thoughts about it, burning before their eyes. It's terrible, Jocelyn, to be the sort of person who lights fires. I wish I wasn't."

"It will be all right," Jocelyn comforted her. "I know it will be all right."

But Felicity was still afraid. For the first time she had been realizing the heavy burden to herself that her own strength could be. That her personality could attract her stage experience had proved to her, but she had not known before that her vitality was a dynamic force to inspire others, to guide and control them, and often without their knowledge. In a sudden moment of rather dreadful clarity she saw herself going through life paying the penalty of her vitality. . . . Galvanizing other people into action, making their decisions for them, bearing their burdens, enduring their reproaches when her advice proved wrong, while all the while her ceaselessly tapped strength ebbed from her and her weariness grew. . . . Yet life, said Ferranti, was a giving of personality.

"The human race," said Jocelyn, answering her unspoken thought with that uncanny insight into her mind that was growing on him with his knowledge of her, "is divided into the proppers and the propped. The propped have an easier time, of course, but they do not live so deeply or so excitingly and they get very bored."

Felicity drew gratefully closer to him in the dark street.

If their two lives ran together, as she wanted them to, and this man beside her became her husband she knew just how the propping would be divided. On the surface it would be all hers, he would rely on her to charm away his depression, to light his imagination, to reassure his self-distrust and to lighten his fears and she would sometimes perhaps, as life went on, get rather weary of doing it, yet deep down he had something that she had not got, some sober quality of level-headedness and caution, together with an unchangeable endurance in love and work upon which in her bad times she would be able to rest her whole weight.

The shops were shut and the hum of life stilled. The High Street, as they made their way up it, with the wind pushing jovially behind, was lit only by the sparse street-lamps that shed pools of light here and there in the darkness. The stream that came down from the hills slid from darkness into light and then back into darkness again, talking to itself all the while. As a companion it was unobtrusive and the whole of the dreaming city seemed theirs alone.

III

It had not been only the London gentlemen who had provided the backing for the play, what they alone were willing to give would not have been enough. *The Minstrel* had been written in Torminster by Ferranti and Jocelyn and it seemed to Felicity that the beauty of the city was enshrined in it and that in its verse she could hear the ringing of the bells. Therefore, she argued, the worst financial risk must be taken by Torminster for its own child. Mrs. Jameson gave what she could afford, Grandfather gave what he could not afford, Felicity her-

self gave all she could, pawning all her jewels except her
mother's pearls, and the Dean and the Bishop between
them gave quite a substantial sum.

The evening when she abstracted this from them,
just a week earlier than the night when Jocelyn met her
at the station, was the only really light-hearted evening
that Felicity enjoyed in all that difficult time. She chose
to call upon the Dean after dinner in the evening because
like all women she was quite sure that she looked her
best in evening dress by artificial light. She dressed
with extreme care, putting on a green silk frock
that was girdled at the waist with gold and fell to
her golden shoes in long folds that shimmered like
water when she moved. It had an Elizabethan collar
that rolled softly back from her face and stood up high
behind her yellow head, so that she looked like one of
those wild arum-lilies that children call lords-and-ladies.
. . . Very lordly she looked, very ladylike. . . . She did
not usually wear jewels, and in any case most of hers
were pawned now, but to-night she hung her mother's
pearls in her ears and put a string of them round her
neck because the Dean, she felt sure, liked a woman to
be discreetly jewelled. When she was ready she sat in
front of her mirror and studied the finished work of
art very seriously, as she was wont to do before her stage
appearances.

Wax candlelight, that most flattering of all light to a
woman, lit up her beauty with a mysterious softness
but left the far corners of her bedroom dark, so that
she saw her own reflection in the mirror bright against
the darkness of night. Her gift of unselfconsciousness
had given her a curious sense of detachment regarding
her own beauty. She made use of it in her art, and she
employed it to gain the ends that she wanted, but it
always seemed to her a thing external to herself, a thing

that she picked up and used as she would have used a sword or a rose. But to-night, seeing it so lit against darkness, she felt for the first time the fear that haunts beautiful women. When it left her would she find that it had been more valuable than she knew? Would it leave her with only the darkness? "Shall I miss you?" she asked it. "Will Jocelyn miss you?" It was love, she discovered suddenly, that had brought this fear to birth within her. Jocelyn, she had been so sure, would be a constant lover, but how could she know? How could he know himself? Was there anything in this world of which one could be certain, of which one could take hold and say "This will never forsake me"? The lovely face in the mirror that was herself and beauty too, suddenly smiled at her. "We will be with you always," it seemed to say, "we two." Herself, she would always have herself, that tiny spark that illness or madness or death might hide or distort or torture but would never obliterate because, paradoxically, it was not herself but God. And beauty, she would always have that because, as the Minstrel had discovered, it was not a rose that could fade or a statue that could be broken or a love that could die but the immanent something in all these things that threaded them together into a pattern that would last as long as human life, would last until at death the pattern gave way to the blinding circle of white light and the spark of oneself was absorbed into eternity.

Well, she could not stay meditating here for ever or the mellowing effect of the Dean's nightly glass of port would have worn off. She folded a cloak that was black like the night outside and pink like the dawn inside over her green lordliness and went downstairs and out into the starlight.

IV

The Close, flooded by the moon, was quite deserted and her high-heeled gold shoes went clack-clack along the stone pavement, echoing strangely in the stillness. She held up her skirts carefully on each side and she was careful to step in the centre of each paving-stone and not on the cracks, a habit that she had caught from Henrietta. Why, she asked herself, do children never step on the cracks? Is it because it would do violence to their sense of pattern? Those beautiful paving-stones, shaped like the squares in that game called noughts and crosses, simply cried out for something planted plumb in the middle. She had heard it said that man is a pattern-making animal. For ever, in sound or sight or movement, he must be making patterns. . . . Perhaps, like the Minstrel, he has discovered that in it lies his salvation.

She turned under the great stone archway into the Deanery courtyard.

The Deanery, built of grey stone, old and frowning, took up two sides of a square, the third side being the wall of the stables and the fourth the great wall that held the gateway. At night, with the windows shuttered and the moon behind a cloud, the Deanery was alarmingly like the Bastille.

Felicity crossed the courtyard to a smaller archway in the wall opposite her where, as in some French châteaux, a flight of stone steps led up to a front door that was set right back in the heart of the building. A lamp shone over the door and a great iron bell hung down at one side. Felicity, guessing its unrelenting character, hung on to it with both hands and lifted her feet from the ground for a brief second. The result was a clanging that seemed to be ringing the knell of all the demons in the nether regions.

Wotherspoon, the Deanery butler, was so prompt and outraged in his opening of the door that Felicity retreated a few steps downwards, the black and white curves of his enormous figure looming over her like the prow of a ship intent on bearing her down. What the devil, inquired Wotherspoon's beetling brows and arched nose, did she mean by ringing the bell like that?

"Is the Dean in?" she quavered from below him.

"Have you an appointment, madam?" inquired Wotherspoon with contemptuous dignity. He always asked this question of callers of whom he did not approve; shabby callers who might beg, hungry-looking callers who arrived near lunch-time, timid callers whom it gratified his love of power to frighten out of their wits and impudent callers like Felicity who dared to ring the bell in this outrageous manner.

But Felicity had only been scared for the moment by the suddenness of Wotherspoon's eruption and his tone roused all her fighting spirit. Like a meteor she flashed by him into the lighted hall, the great man unconsciously giving ground, swept off her velvet cloak with a superb gesture of her right arm and held it out to him.

"Miss Summers," she informed him through her nose.

Wotherspoon looked from her proud golden head, rising superbly from the winged, leaf-green collar, to the silken folds of her dress and there was no more spirit left in him. Carefully he laid her cloak on a chair, reverently noting that it must have cost a pretty penny, and signified with a gracious inclination of the head that she might follow him.

It was a long way to the Dean's study and they walked

slowly, as befitted the dignity of them both, Wotherspoon going first, the curves of his person protruding
well in front of him, his shoulders well back and his
arms held rigidly at his sides, and Felicity following, her
chin in the air and her skirts whispering over the thick
pile carpets. Very luxurious the Deanery was, oppressively
warm with blazing fires, scented with hothouse plants
and rich with all the lovely things that strew a house
owned by wealth and taste. Yet Felicity thought defiantly
that she did not like it as much as Grandfather's cold,
monastic house. There were too many things in it.
The distilled loveliness of so many centuries lay here that
one felt as in a picture gallery, confused and tired, one's
attention pulled into small pieces instead of braced into
that one act of concentration that is like a knock flinging
open a door into Paradise.

Wotherspoon opened the door of the study and announced her. She had chosen the moment well for the
Dean had just left the ladies in the drawing-room but
was not yet absorbed in whatever work it was, if any,
that he did till bedtime, and so felt no sense of irritation
in interruption. . . . Not that he would have minded at
any time being interrupted by such a vision.

"Charming! Charming!" he murmured, fixing his
eyeglass more firmly in his eye with one hand and slipping the novel he was reading under a pile of sermons
with the other. Then he rose to his feet with alacrity,
came to her where she stood radiantly under the hanging-
lamp and kissed her hand gallantly, retaining it in his as
he led her to his best arm-chair.

"This is indeed an honour," he piped, and seated himself where he could see her to the best advantage, the
firelight painting roses on her green dress and the whole
of his lovely room disposed around her like the setting
of a jewel. Could she, he wondered, have come to him

H*

for spiritual advice? He was touched, for so few people came to him for spiritual advice, a fact that saddened him. He shot out his snowy white cuffs a little further, a habit of his when bracing himself for any activity and an action performed as unconsciously as 'Erb the porter's when he spat upon his hands.

"I want help," said Felicity, her voice vibrating with the pathos that with her theatrical training she was able to pump into it at will.

"Dear child, tell me," said the Dean, and a richness had come into his voice, as though cream had been poured into skim milk. "You can tell me anything you like with perfect certainty that I shall not abuse your confidence, and I will give you all the help that an old man has in his power to give."

Felicity realized at once that she was going to disappoint him terribly. Here he was waiting to give advice on a matter of conduct and pleased as punch because she had come to ask it of him, while she, mercenary minx that she was, had simply come to ask for money. Suddenly she was conscious of an element of pathos in him. Did he sometimes feel, during that wakeful hour of the night between one and two when sorrows loom too large and the taste of failure is at its most bitter, that as a priest he was not the shining light he had meant to be? Very quickly she rearranged in her mind the appeal that she had to make, so as to give him what he wanted while at the same time getting what she wanted without his knowing it.

"I have done something," she said, "and I don't know if I was right to do it. . . . I'm so worried . . . I thought that perhaps you, with all your wisdom and experience, would be able to advise me. It's not too late to turn back and I will be guided by what you say."

The Dean purred.

Pleating her dress between her fingers in an adorable
assumed shyness she told him the whole story. Had she
done right, she asked pathetically, to make so many
people risk their money and their reputations in a crazy
effort to win appreciation for a man in all probability
dead? With a childlike trustfulness she flung her burden
upon him.

"H'm," said the Dean, and joined finger-tip to finger-
tip, considering, while into his silence she dropped little
remarks calculated to make him give the judgment she
wanted. Surely one should be willing to take any risk,
however great, to help another? She had heard him say
that in a sermon once. She could not help feeling that
the trend of modern literature was becoming distressingly materialistic and immoral. Did he think so? Didn't
he think that artists, such as herself, should put up a
fight for good and pure literature such as this play or
Ferranti's undoubtedly was? She had heard him say
once, in another sermon, that the battle-front of morality
must fling itself out through every department of thought
and action before the victory could be won. "The battle-
front of morality." She had thought that such a stirring
phrase of his.

Her little remarks, dropped so unobtrusively that
they were hardly noticed, yet built themselves up as
banks to guide the stream of the Dean's thoughts. After
a long pause he told her that she had done right. "Quite
right, dear child," he said. "That is my considered
and unbiased judgment, given you for what it is
worth."

Felicity rose to her feet with a sigh of relief. "Thank
you," she murmured tremulously. "Thank you so very
much. You don't know how much you have helped
me."

"This fight of yours to keep your art pure, dear child,"

he said, "is a noble fight, and it is a delight to an old man to see nobility and beauty so allied."

Felicity drooped her lovely head and again her fingers pleated her shining skirt in that pathetically childish action.

"If only," she whispered, "I had not got to carry on the fight with other people's money." She flung up her head in a challenging way. "If only I could back the play myself. Those horrible men I have had to beg from! If you could see them!"

Was there a suspicion of tears in her tawny eyes that they shone so brilliantly? The Dean was not sure but the mere idea was enough to turn his mind into a veritable battle-ground. . . . Though he had so much money he found it, as he grew older, increasingly difficult to part with it. . . . He seated himself at his exquisite, inlaid writing-desk and began to make jerky remarks about the weather while his plump left hand, with its gleaming diamond ring, groped uncertainly over its drawers.

Felicity watched in an agony of uncertainty. . . . His fingers touched the first drawer. . . . His keys would be in that. . . . They touched the second drawer. . . . Unanswered letters would be there. . . . They touched the third drawer, that sacred third drawer where methodical people always kept their cheque-books, and she made a swift movement as though to go. "I know!" she exclaimed in sudden delight, "I'll sell my pearls! And now I really must go. Thank you so very much for all the help you have given me."

If there is one thing that an admirer of beautiful ladies dislikes more than another it is the idea of a woman selling her pearls. Like a flash that third drawer flew open and the Dean extracted his cheque-book. "Wait!" he cried triumphantly, "Wait!" and he wrote feverishly.

Felicity gasped at the amount. He would not miss it but even so his generosity amazed her and made her feel ashamed of her deceitful ways. . . . And yet if she had not behaved so badly he would never have won that sharp, miser's battle. . . . Was one perhaps justified in doing evil that good might come? In any case she was so over-whelmed between gratitude and shame that her thanks were a display of female sensibility that nearly stirred the Dean, deeply moved as he already was by his own generosity, to tears.

"The Bishop of Torminster," announced Wotherspoon.

The Bishop limped in, looking very small and insig-nificant. "About a living for that poor fellow Brown," he began at once, being a man who never wasted time or words.

"You know Miss Felicity Summers?" piped the Dean. "But of course you do, she was at the Christmas party. She is one of our leading actresses and frequently honours Torminster with her presence."

"Intensely grateful to you for your labours at the party," said the Bishop, and gave Felicity a kind smile and a grip of the hand, but seemed not really to want to notice her. He rather fought shy of women, as indeed a man who has succeeded through sheer strength of will in being both a bachelor and a clergyman for forty-five years is bound to do. "He can't support six children on a curate's stipend and he's perfectly suitable for that living in the Chapter gift," he went on, and subsided into a chair.

But the Dean was still absorbed by his recent magnifi-cent behaviour and could not be side-tracked.

"Bishop," he proclaimed, "under the guidance of this dear young lady I have this moment become a dabbler in theatrical affairs."

"Rather you than me," said the Bishop. "Now about Brown——"

"We are to produce a play of Ferranti's," went on the

Dean inexorably. "You remember Ferranti? That crazy fellow who lived in the Market Place."

"Ferranti?" said the Bishop quickly, and putting Brown on the shelf for the moment he turned to Felicity. "Tell me about it," he demanded.

Felicity told him, quickly and accurately, employing a method of narration so different from that used with the Dean that had he not been sunk in his arm-chair in that happy, dreamy state that comes after a well-fought battle he would surely not have recognized it for the same story.

"Good luck to you," said the Bishop, and felt in his pocket.

"Did you know Ferranti?" asked Felicity.

"Met him once up in the Tor woods, talked to him and liked him. Wouldn't come and see me. Funny fellow. He haunted one. A reflection on us all that he apparently made away with himself." He took something crumpled out of his pocket and began writing.

"I'm backing the play," proclaimed the Dean.

"No more than you ought to do," said the Bishop. "So am I," and he handed a cheque to Felicity.

"Thank you," said Felicity quietly.

The Dean passed behind Felicity's chair ostensibly to adjust the lamp, and so was able by sheer chance to see how much the cheque was made out for. . . . Twice as much as his.

"Bishop!" he exclaimed, outraged and reproachful, "you can't afford it."

Only last week he had again dined with the Bishop and the soles had still been lemon, not Dover.

"That's my affair," said the Bishop.

"But how do you know," smiled Felicity, "that the play is a suitable one for a bishop to back?"

"Take Canon Fordyce's word for it. Finest man I know. . . . Good night, Miss Summers, and good luck. . . . Now, Dean, about that living."

The Dean was obliged to ring for Wotherspoon to show Felicity out, feeling, as he often did, that at times the Bishop was rather a thorn in the flesh.

V

Out in the moonlit Close again Felicity's shoes went clack-clack along the deserted pavement, stepping this time on the cracks and not in the centres of the paving-stones, so as to make a change. Her cloak, lined with the dawn, floated out behind her because she could not hold it, both hands being occupied with cheques.

She looked from one to the other, the Dean's so sleek and shining, the Bishop's crumpled and smelling of cheap tobacco, and smiled wickedly.

"Where will your influence stop, Ferranti?" she asked. "You were a stone thrown into Torminster as though into a pond and the ripples go out and out."

High over her head the two gentlemen with bushy hair and square caps stirred out of their habitual torpor and struck the bell ten times.

VI

One of the big days of Henrietta's life came only a few weeks later. It was the occasion of her and Hugh Anthony's annual visit to the dentist, which was a great occasion, for they patronized a London dentist and were obliged also, owing to the peculiarities of the Torminster train service, to spend a night either with Jocelyn's mother or at a respectable hotel opposite the British Museum. . . . A very respectable hotel indeed, temperance, patronized by clergymen and their wives and daughters from country parishes and Cathedral towns who were always a little disappointed, at dinner in the evening, when they hoped and expected to see a little life, at seeing only each other.

"Perfect nonsense," Grandmother said, "spending all this money going to London when there's an adequate dentist at your very door."

But Grandfather thought otherwise. Mr. Algernon Royde, who had his torture-chamber over Mr. Loveday the undertaker's, had an excellent moral character and there was doubtless great good in him professionally as well as morally, though Grandfather had not personally been able to test his capabilities because of having no teeth, but only the best dentist in England, Grandfather considered, was fit to touch the precious pearls upon which his beloved grandchildren relied for mastication. . . . So to London the three of them went annually, the visit to the dentist washed down, so to speak, by a visit to the zoo. They enjoyed it all immensely, except the dentist, but that did not last long and by concentrating their minds upon the monkey-house they were able to forget about it beforehand.

The excitement of it all was much increased by the fact that they arose at dawn so as to catch the milk-train. Grandmother did not get up, of course, but she woke up, and with a lace cap tied over her curl papers and a pink woolly shawl round her shoulders and her bedroom door open she issued directions about the children's clothes and food to Sarah and Ellen, who had scarcely slept all night with all the anxiety of early breakfast and one thing and another.

They wore their best clothes of course. Henrietta had

on her red coat and green silk dress and beaver cap and muff, Hugh Anthony wore naval attire and Grandfather had on the least green of his overcoats and his best round clerical hat, which was only six years old, rather than his everyday one that he could not remember how long he had had.

Mr. Gotobed, with a bunch of the first snowdrops in his buttonhole, fetched them in the bus. Very extravagant to have the bus, Grandfather said, but Grandfather did not want the dear children's legs to ache. Their legs, and his too for that matter, must be kept for the zoo.

In the train the three of them sat very still because they were so excited. The children sat one on each side of Grandfather, holding his hands, facing the way they were going, with the carpet-bag containing their night things on the seat opposite them. It was wonderful to see the Torminster hills just showing like opals against the pale blue sky, and the cows standing knee-deep in mist. The early morning was very nice, Henrietta thought, and it was lovely to see the world all misted over with the dreams of the night. The dreams that people dreamed were not visible when they came down to breakfast, except sometimes as a shadow in their eyes, but the dreams of the earth clung about her till the sun was up, soft and filmy and rainbow-tinted. . . . What did she dream of? . . . Perhaps of the days to come when men would have eyes to see her beauty and minds that would not pollute it.

The changes were enjoyable because Grandfather gave them a penny each to spend at the slot-machines, and chocolate out of a slot-machine tastes so much nicer than chocolate bought at a shop because of the risk that you run in procuring it. . . . For how are you to know, when you poke your penny into the slot, that something will not go wrong with the machinery and the chocolate never appear at all? . . . You cast your bread upon the waters and it returneth after many seconds, terrible seconds during which you listen agonizedly to those curious clicking sounds inside the machine, your eyes glued to the place where the chocolate will, perhaps, appear, and your mouth ajar and watering.

VII

They reached London at one o'clock and to Grandfather the journey had seemed to take a long time, because travelling always made his head ache and did not do his rheumatism any good, but to the children it had passed like a few seconds. They had lunch at the station in a great room packed full of people and gleaming with glass and silver that they thought must be as wonderful as Buckingham Palace, and were waited on by a real live waiter. Grandfather said they might choose what they liked to eat and they chose pork and ices. He was a little nervous about their choice and the waiter, who had children at home, said tentatively that the mutton and semolina pudding were both particularly good that day. But Henrietta and Hugh Anthony had minds of their own and knew them and Grandfather consoled himself by remembering that there is something in the atmosphere of a festive occasion which acts as a digestive. He himself could at the Deanery dinner-parties eat without any unfortunate after-effects food which if partaken of at home would have put him to bed for a week.

When they could not eat any more Grandfather unfastened the carpet-bag and took out a tooth mug, two toothbrushes and a tube of toothpaste and the children went to the cloakroom and cleaned their teeth, because

Grandfather did not think it would be polite to Mr. Arbuthnot, their kind dentist, to give him teeth to look at that had pork in the corners. And anyhow, Grandfather said, one must always be as clean in the parts of one that are not seen, such as one's soul and one's back teeth, as one is in the parts that are seen, such as face and hands.

Then they took a hansom-cab to Mr. Arbuthnot's.

Twenty years later, when they were grown up, Henrietta and Hugh Anthony used to try to recapture in imagination the London of their childhood, that London of hansom-cabs and horse buses, with barrel-organs and monkeys in every square, and flower-girls and crossing-sweepers at every corner. . . . In memory it seemed a very magical city. . . . It seemed to be always spring there, with a yellow sun shining in a blue sky and a river of colour flowing before one's enchanted eyes; scarlet coats of little brown monkeys, bunches of yellow daffodils, bales of coloured silk and baskets of tomatoes in shop windows, gleaming chestnut coats of trotting horses and here and there flashes of silver and gold where the sun caught the metal on their harness. And in retrospect the smell of London had been good in those days, the mingled smell of horses and flowers and that delicious smell a dusty street has just after a water-cart has passed along it. . . . And the noise of London in those days. . . . At the time people used to complain about it but twenty years later the alchemy of time had transformed it into a symphony. The clip-clop of the horses' hoofs, the rattle of the hansom-cabs, the cracking of the whips wielded by the jovial bus-drivers, the cries of the paper-boys, the soft swish of the crossing-sweepers' brooms, and sounding through it all, weaving the sounds together into one piece of music, a melody from Verdi's *Il Trovatore* played on the barrel-organ.

And to-day it was all at its best and the children's hearts beat high in their hansom-cab. . . . Surely a chariot of the gods, this hansom-cab. . . . The glorious thrill of it, bowling along at a great pace driven by someone you could not even see; the genius shown in the design of the thing, two wheels only, so that you swayed as in a rocking-chair, the graceful curve of the hood over your head, the slanting shutters that were slapped down over your knees, shutting you as firmly in as though you were about to turn a somersault, the trap-door through which you could if you wished hold converse with the god in the sky who drove you. And this god! Always his eyes were blue and twinkling and his nose was red and his hair was ginger; he wore a bowler hat on the side of his head and a flower in his buttonhole and when you peeped at him through the trap-door he winked one eye.

With a final breath-taking swirl round a corner they clattered to a standstill, swaying frantically, and the joyous drive was over. It had lasted, it seemed, for one second only but in it they had flown over the moon and girdled the earth in forty minutes. They got out, too depressed now even to smile at the jovial god in the sky, and suddenly the world was darkened and all the colour and gallantry of London dwindled to a flight of ominous stone steps, and a huge expanse of shining front door with a brass plate on it inscribed with the name of Mr. Arbuthnot.

Grandfather rang the bell that pealed far away, funereally, like the bell that rings up the curtain on a tragedy. . . . Silence.

"Perhaps he's gone out," whispered Henrietta hoarsely.

"Perhaps he's dead," said Hugh Anthony with sudden hope.

But his hope was a tiny flower, nipped in the bud as

soon as born, for the door was flung open by a bright young man smiling that excessively large-hearted smile that is only to be met with on the faces of dentists' assistants. . . . They went in.

Henrietta and Hugh Anthony were on the whole good children, trained to courage. To see them sitting motionless on two chairs in the dentist's waiting-room, holding copies of the *Illustrated London News* stiffly before their unseeing eyes, you would never have guessed how bad they felt. It was only Grandfather who showed traces of emotion. His hands trembled and his old head wobbled nervously. . . . These dear children and their teeth. . . . What would they not suffer before they reached that haven that he had now reached, that harbour of a top and bottom plate? He felt at that moment in his own heart every pang of dentistry that they would suffer throughout the whole course of their lives. To steady himself he pulled out his office-book and began to say evensong, though it was only two o'clock. "O Lord, open Thou our lips and our mouth shall show forth Thy praise." Surely, he thought, God Who created our mouths that they should praise Him did not intend that we should so suffer in them? Surely toothache is of the devil?

The bright young man reappeared, grinning like the Cheshire cat. "Master and Miss Fordyce," he said.

They went upstairs, the bright young man going first and Grandfather following sadly in the rear with the carpet-bag, and it was astonishing how quickly they got there.

Mr. Arbuthnot, very black and tall and slim, with grey hair and glasses and a jovial smile that showed all his flashing white teeth, was washing his hands in a high, light room where everything was very bright and shining, especially the rows of instruments set out on trays. A black chair that could move magically up and down, and should have proved attractive but did not, stood in the window and beside it was a round white basin with a fountain splashing into it that ought to have been fascinating but somehow was not.

Mr. Arbuthnot, as he dried his hands, chatted charmingly about this and that but met with very little response.

"What about a ride in the chair?" he asked. "Or do you prefer that afterwards?"

"I think," said Grandfather, "that they prefer it afterwards."

"Right," said Mr. Arbuthnot. "Ladies first?"

Without a word, and with the calm dignity of Mary Stuart on the scaffold, Henrietta removed her cap and muff and coat, climbed into the chair and opened her mouth. Mr. Arbuthnot tucked a white napkin round her neck in case she should dribble over her best frock, that he admired very much, and it began.

"Shan't hurt you," said Mr. Arbuthnot—though how could he possibly know—"A little wider please."

But he did hurt. He hurt very much indeed. Three teeth did he fill and scraped off a lot of tartar, but Henrietta never moved or made a sound, though she felt pain more than most children, and felt, too, the awful indignity that it is to a woman to have a member of the opposite sex who is in no way related to her poking about in the inside of her mouth.

"Teeth decay very easily," said Mr. Arbuthnot in an undertone to Grandfather. "She'll have trouble later."

"Dear me!" sighed Grandfather and looked dreadfully unhappy.

"Good girl," said Mr. Arbuthnot when he had done. "Now, sir, your turn."

Hugh Anthony felt these things less than Henrietta, indeed after the first minutes were over he almost enjoyed it because of his interest in seeing how things were done. Every time an instrument was removed from his mouth he asked a question. "Why is that one curved like that? Why do you have that flame burning? What's stopping made of? Must one be clever to be a dentist? Could I be a dentist? Why do you have that fountain playing into that basin?"

"Now look here, young man," said Mr. Arbuthnot. "If you don't hold your tongue I'll put stopping into it."

Hugh Anthony said no more and his tartar was removed in silence.

"This fellow will never have much trouble," said Mr. Arbuthnot in an undertone to Grandfather. "Sound teeth. No nerves."

It was over and they had rides in the chair, that had suddenly become a thing of fascination, while the fountain was a fountain playing in a fairy tale.

VIII

Out in the street, to their astonishment, they found Jocelyn waiting for them. He had come up to London the night before, leaving Miss Lavender in charge of the shop, and was to have travelled back to Torminster with them in the morning but they had not expected to see him that afternoon.

"Are you coming to the zoo with us?" asked Hugh Anthony.

"If you don't mind," said Jocelyn, "Felicity wants you to give up the zoo and come to a rehearsal at the theatre instead."

They did not mind, indeed they were delighted, for they thought that actors and actresses rehearsing would probably be even funnier than the monkey-house and would, too, be something quite new in the way of an entertainment.

As there was not room for four in a hansom they went to the Firebird Theatre on top of a horse bus. It lacked the excitement of a hansom-cab but had an enchantment all its own, for one felt one was riding over the turbulent sea of London in a golden galleon. It was thrilling to hang over the edge and watch the figures below sway backwards and forwards like weeds under the water.

"We get down here," said Jocelyn.

They turned up a dark alley like a cave and went through a narrow opening marked "Stage Door." It was very dark and rather mysterious to the children.

"They're rehearsing in the studio," said Jocelyn. "It's a long way up I'm afraid."

They seemed to climb for ever, up long stone staircases and along stone passages. Grandfather got very puffed and thought the zoo preferable, but Henrietta's lively imagination transformed the ugly place into the inside of an enchanted mountain where the gnomes with their pickaxes had hollowed out a city, the sort of mountain to which the Pied Piper had taken the children. . . . With a sudden leaping up of her heart she wondered if she would find the Pied Piper inside this mountain, the Pied Piper with Ferranti's face. . . . As if in answer a thin thread of music came creeping through the passages to meet them, a lilting tune played on the flute.

"The Pied Piper! The Pied Piper!" she cried, and pummelled Jocelyn in the back.

"What?" said Jocelyn. "Oh, that's only Oliver Standish. Listen, Grandfather, you can hear Felicity now."

A clear voice that sang as effortlessly as a blackbird had taken up the tune. It was a wonderful tune, beauti-

ful with the beckoning beauty of woods in the spring
yet sad as a man's heart when the clouded years are upon
him and he stands between birth and death with empty
hands.

Grandfather stopped on the steps so suddenly that his
following grandchildren nearly toppled over backwards.
There had come to him one of those moments of quiet
despair that lie in wait for even the happiest. Stealthy-
footed they leap upon us, as we walk along the street,
as we sit at evening with fruit and wine upon the table
and laughter on our lips, as we wake suddenly from sleep
in the hour before dawn; neither at our work nor our
play nor our prayers are we safe, those moments can
leap at any time out of the blackness around human life
and suddenly the colours that we have nailed to our
mast are there no longer and all that we have grasped
is dust.

For a moment it was so with Grandfather, then he
reaffirmed his faith in the existence of God by an ejacu-
latory prayer and blew his nose. "That tune," he murmured to Jocelyn, "that tune."

"Isn't it amazing?" said Jocelyn. "He's a genius, that
fellow Compton. If that tune alone doesn't take London
by storm I don't know what will."

"But so sad," said Grandfather.

"This play is a lament, remember. A lament for the
spirit of man astray in the world."

"But have we any right," asked Grandfather, "to let
such sadness loose?"

"I don't think it saddens people to have their heartache
expressed for them in art," said Jocelyn. "It relieves
them as a burst of tears would."

"Please are we going to stay here all the afternoon?"
asked Hugh Anthony plaintively, and they went on.

The blackbird's voice came to them clearer and louder

as they climbed, strengthening and deepening as though bird after bird were joining in the dawn chorus, until at last they found themselves in the doorway of a barn of a room under the roof. At one end of it steps led up to a platform, and here Felicity stood singing, accompanied on a cracked piano by a stout man who swore under his breath whenever he struck a faulty note. Near her, with a flute in his hand, stood a dark young man with his back to them, and at sight of him, with his height and his grace and his black hair, Henrietta's heart gave another leap. . . . It was the Pied Piper. It was Ferranti. . . . But then a short-tempered man who was standing below the platform with pages of typescript in his hand shouted out disagreeably, "Oliver, must you stand like a lamppost? If you have a waist, man, turn this way and use it," and the dark young man, turning and using it, revealed himself as a quite ordinary stranger.

Henrietta's heart ceased pounding and she was able to notice the other ladies and gentlemen who sat about on chairs near her, the men either yawning or reading books and the women knitting or sewing. They all looked dreadfully bored and the room was very dusty and bare. . . . The zoo would have been much nicer, Hugh Anthony thought, and Grandfather thought how incredible it seemed that a beautiful play could ever flower out of these dusty beginnings.

Then they came right into the room and the ladies and gentlemen stopped looking bored and looked intensely amused instead. Grandfather and the children were never in the least put out when their appearance together caused twinkles to leap into the eyes of strangers. They did not know why they were funny but if they were, and it gave pleasure, no one was more delighted than they. They would have agreed with Herman Melville that "a good laugh is a mighty good thing and if any one man in his own proper person afford stuff for a good joke to anybody, let him not be backward, but let him cheerfully allow himself to spend and be spent in that way." Grandfather, his round clerical hat in one hand and his carpet-bag in the other and his bald head shining, beamed on the company as though they were all his own dear children. Hugh Anthony, his hair like a flame in the general dinginess, grinned, and Henrietta hurled her muff madly from hand to hand, a habit of hers when excited. "Darlings!" cried Felicity and leaped from the stage like a kangaroo. . . . The rehearsal came to an abrupt stop and they were all introduced.

The short-tempered man was Miles Harpenden the producer, the stout man who swore was, incredibly, Nigel Compton the composer of that glorious tune. . . . Though how a man who looked like that could have written a tune that sounded like that it was impossible to say. . . . The dark young man who looked so romantic from behind but was a little disappointing from the front was the Minstrel and all the other ladies and gentlemen would one day be nymphs, artists, villagers and a satyr, though it was difficult to believe it. The satyr was the nicest of them and told Henrietta he had two little girls just her age at home. "Twins," he said, "and they go to St. Paul's day school for girls."

"You see, Grandfather," Felicity was explaining, "Flossie has chickenpox and we can't find any other child who would look the part as Henrietta does."

Henrietta, talking to the satyr about his little girls, suddenly realized that something of great importance to her was being discussed. Felicity was looking eager and Grandfather distressed.

"Her dear grandmother wouldn't like it," he said. "She disapproves of the theatre in any case and if a grandchild of her own——"

"It would only be for a little while," pleaded Felicity. "Just till Flossie is well again. And Henrietta is perfect for the part, she's so luminous, just the sort of child to represent an idea rather than a person. Look, Miles," and she pulled Henrietta towards Miles Harpenden and took off her beaver cap.

Miles, his habitual short temper by no means lengthened by the sight of Henrietta, grunted. "Can she act?" he asked disagreeably.

"My good man, she doesn't need to. It's the tiniest part. And she has—oh, I don't know how to say it—a grace and a swiftness that are a part of beauty. . . . Henrietta, take off your coat and go and walk across that platform."

Henrietta did not quite understand what it was all about, and she was very frightened, but she was a disciplined child and she did what she was told. Half-way across the platform, when she was feeling at her worst, the satyr made a sudden funny face at her and she smiled, her own particular brand of smile that was like a light lit behind alabaster.

"H'm," said Miles Harpenden when he saw it. "Can she be relied on to smile like that to order?"

"It's the smile she always uses," said Felicity. "Now dance, Henrietta. Just anything."

This was worse, but Nigel Compton bounced to the piano and played such a glorious jigging tune that her feet had to run after it, like two kittens after a coloured ball. And after the first few minutes she was not really frightened for these watching people below her seemed to call out from her a power that she did not know she had. She realized afterwards that achievement is born of circumstances, a certain response that would never be called out but for a certain challenge.

The tune stopped and her feet stopped too and she

found that she wanted to cry. "Darling!" cried Felicity, and ran to her and lifted her down. "What did I say?" she cried to the others over Henrietta's head.

"Good," said Miles Harpenden. "Good. Done."

"I don't think I can allow it," said Grandfather miserably. "It might be bad for her character."

"Why?" asked Felicity. "Is it bad for people to develop the talent that's in them? Can't you see that she has talent? And it will only be for a very little while and she shall live with me. Have you no trust in me?"

"Yes, dear," said Grandfather. "But what would her grandmother say?"

No one knew.

"Let her choose for herself," suggested the satyr.

"Yes," said Grandfather, brightening. "The dear child will know what is right for herself to do."

So the situation was explained to Henrietta and when she understood what she might do if she wished she jigged for joy. She too was to become a part of this lovely thing that her friend Mr. Ferranti had made. She was not to be shut out of this stone mountain, as the boy in the story of the Pied Piper had been shut out, she too was one of the company who had followed the lilting of a tune inside its fastnesses. . . . Yet where was he himself, the Pied Piper who had brought them here? . . . Perhaps if they sang the song that he had taught them he would come back, following them as they now were following him.

CHAPTER XI

I

JOCELYN opened the door of the box and ushered
them in, Grandfather and Grandmother, Mrs. Jameson,
Miss Lavender and Hugh Anthony. They had come up
that day from Torminster to attend the first night of
The Minstrel and, Jocelyn's mother being away, were
spending the night at the respectable temperance hotel
opposite the British Museum. Jocelyn regarded them
with an affectionate twinkle, wondering if quite such an
extraordinary party had ever before occupied a box at
the Firebird Theatre on a first night. Grandfather in his
dinner-jacket, the one that had been let out with fresh
material so that it looked stripy, Grandmother in her
black silk, lace fichu, locket and corkscrew curls, Miss
Lavender in grey silk and black mittens, Hugh Anthony
in his sailor suit, and Mrs. Jameson, it being the season
of Lent, in purple velvet with a tiara of amethysts.

Grandmother, though she highly disapproved of the
whole thing, and had only come to keep an eye on Grandfather, was nevertheless enjoying herself very much. She
seated herself well to the front of the box, bolt upright,
severe, bright-eyed and alert. She polished and adjusted
her glasses, and Jocelyn put a cushion behind her back and
saw that her smelling-salts were ready to her hand, so that
she could disapprove in comfort of the fashionable crowd
already filing into the stalls below her. Miss Lavender,
frightened by this unusual excitement, shrank into the

shadows, but Mrs. Jameson, childishly eager to show her lovely clothes, seated herself superbly beside Grandmother and raised the lorgnette that hung round her neck by a purple ribbon. Hugh Anthony, dropping on to his hands and knees, crawled through the old ladies' skirts and popped up in front of them, his blazing red head appearing like a jack-in-the-box over the edge of the box.

Grandfather sat in the shadows beside Miss Lavender. He was miserable and kept nervously clasping and unclasping his hands. He had said evensong in the train and compline in the cab but nothing seemed to him any good. For one thing he was attending a theatrical performance on a Friday in Lent, a crime that he had never in his wildest moments dreamed of committing, and for another thing he was so anxious about the play itself. He could not imagine how it had all come about, though he felt sure that he had had something to do with it, though he could not now remember what, and it seemed to him a very desperate undertaking. . . . What if it failed. . . . All this money and trouble wasted. . . . And these dear children, Jocelyn, Felicity, Henrietta and Gabriel Ferranti, the success or otherwise of this evening might make the whole difference to their lives. . . . Terrible to think what little things could affect the fate of men and women. . . . Terrible. . . . Yet he could not but think that they had been guided and his lips moved silently as he clasped and unclasped his hands for the hundredth time.

"I don't know if your poor grandfather expects a blessing on this ridiculous performance," said Grandmother to Jocelyn. "What the Bishop would say if he knew we were all sitting like this in a devil's playhouse on a Friday in Lent I'm sure I don't know."

"The Bishop is in the stalls, dear," said Grandfather mildly.

"You don't say so, Theobald!" cried Grandmother, and polished her spectacles frantically.

"Why, so he is!" cried Mrs. Jameson loudly. "Bishop! Bishop! Hi!" and she leaned right out of the box and waved her lorgnette. The Bishop waved his programme jovially back and the stalls were all agog with amusement.

"You and the Bishop, Theobald," said Grandmother severely, "should be ashamed of yourselves. I can only hope the Dean won't come to hear of it."

"The Dean and Lady Lavinia," said Miss Lavender gently, "are in the dress-circle."

"I don't know," said Grandmother in despair, "what the Church is coming to."

"Look, dear Mrs. Fordyce," cried Mrs. Jameson, "that woman below us. Her lips are painted and I am quite sure that her hair is dyed."

"Where?" exclaimed Grandmother eagerly. "Where? Oh, I see. Disgraceful!"

"Let me see too," whispered Miss Lavender, creeping forward.

They were all quite happy now, except Grandfather, who would not be till the thing was safely over, and Jocelyn left them and went round behind to Felicity's dressing-room.

It was a warm, glowing room curtained in pink, its air heavy with the scent of cosmetics and the bouquets of flowers that filled its every corner. Felicity in a silk dressing-gown, with her dresser Mrs. Baker hovering behind her, was sitting in front of her looking-glass intent on her face. She smiled at him in the glass but she did not speak and he sat down in one of her arm-chairs to wait until she was free. Somehow he felt a little strange with this new Felicity. She looked so different in this luxurious setting, with her altered face and her strained smile, that he had that feeling, intolerable to love, of being shut out.

"Uncle Jocelyn," said a voice, and there, standing beside him, was Henrietta. She was dressed in a little green frock, the dress of a peasant girl, and her dark hair lay over her shoulders in two plaits. Mrs. Baker had not made up her face yet and her jasmine whiteness was just the same.

"You do look grand," she whispered, regarding his brand-new dress-clothes from Savile Row and the carnation in his buttonhole. "Does it make you feel better inside to look grand outside?"

"Much better," said Jocelyn. "It's a great thing to have an outside that one must live up to, don't you think?"

Henrietta nodded gravely. "I was afraid last week," she said in her calm, deep voice, "that I was going to have a pimple on my nose. But it's all right, I haven't."

"Are you frightened?" he asked her.

"Only a little," she said. "You see, nothing can really go wrong because this is the inside of an enchanted mountain. And I mustn't be frightened, Felicity says, or I shall hurt Mr. Ferranti's play. . . . And it's your play, too."

"Hush!" said Jocelyn, one eye on Mrs. Baker. His own share in this play was a secret that he had kept from the world at large. It was being given to London as the work of Gabriel Ferranti only. . . . That poet whom this very same London had hounded to death by its neglect. . . . So he had told London.

"That will do for the moment, Mrs. Baker," said Felicity, and Mrs. Baker tactfully withdrew.

Felicity stood up and slipped off her dressing-gown. Under it she wore a peasant's blue dress, cornflower colour, and her feet and her arms were bare. Her hair, freshly washed and burnished, seemed a blaze of light, and she

I

had used a make-up that made her look sunburnt. She was the beauty of the earth incarnate, Jocelyn thought extravagantly.

"You look perfect," he told her.

"I dare say," said Felicity peevishly, "but I can't find my gargle."

His sense of being shut out vanished as he hunted through the bottles on her dressing-table, and when he knocked something over and she snapped, "Idiot!" at him he felt positively comforted. . . . When one is sufficiently intimate with the beloved to be snapped at one is intimate indeed.

He found it and she gargled, pausing at intervals to be sorry because she had been so cross.

"I feel awful, Jocelyn," she said in excuse. "I've never felt so awful on a first night before. . . . What if we fail?"

"We won't fail," he rallied her. "Buck up, Felicity. You told Henrietta she mustn't be frightened and now you're frightened yourself."

She looked at him, a little surprised at his cheerfulness, a little surprised at finding him the stronger and the more courageous of the two of them. In his new clothes he looked amazingly handsome and trim and erect. His habitual shyness and self-distrust seemed to have vanished, he was laughing and confident, the hidden strength in him called out by strain. She laughed back at him, her courage leaping to meet his so that a taut wire caught and held between them, her delight in him lifting her up like a wave.

"I didn't know you were so good in danger," she said, holding out her hands. "Do you realize that this is our first adventure together?"

"It won't be our last," he laughed, "and you so wildly impulsive as you are."

The shrill voice of the call-boy echoed down the corridors. "Beginners in ten minutes, please!"

"Good-bye! Good luck!" they cried to each other.

Henrietta, watching like a mouse in her corner, thought they must have hurt themselves, they gripped each other's hands so hard.

Jocelyn tore along the passage and knocked at Oliver's door.

"Come in, damn you."

Oliver stood in the middle of his dressing-room glowering. He was dressed, at the suggestion originally of Henrietta, though the designer of the scenery and dresses thought it was his own idea, like the Pied Piper, in particoloured tights, with a cloak that was half of yellow and half of red. He looked very tall and thin, very charming and romantic and unearthly, and appallingly bad-tempered. Jocelyn, in spite of his confidence, felt a stab of apprehension. This man was the Minstrel himself and everything depended on him. He carried the weight of the whole thing on his shoulders. . . . And he was being exceedingly temperamental.

"Good luck," said Jocelyn cheerfully.

"Rotten bad play," growled Oliver.

Jocelyn fought down his rage. "Only you could make a success of it," he agreed. "Without you there'd be no hope."

The voice of the call-boy was heard again. "Beginners for the first act, please!"

His cry was like the pistol-shot that transforms the crouching athlete into a creature of fire and grace, a swiftly moving spirit that is hardly a human being. "Get out of the way," snapped Oliver, and pushed Jocelyn away from the door. Gone was the disagreeable, glowering young man of a moment ago and in his place there swept past Jocelyn the spirit of all young men; eager, adventurous, a little wild, foredoomed to tragedy by the very greatness of his hope. His feet made no sound as he ran down the steps, his cloak floating behind him, yellow and red like poppies in the corn.

Jocelyn went slowly back to the box, dimly aware of the subdued stir going on behind the stage. Harpenden in his shirt-sleeves swearing softly, looming shapes of scenery, moving figures of silent men and women, that behind-world packed with activity and vibrating with it like a great hive. The orchestra was playing the overture and in and out of it there ran the haunting tune that Grandfather had heard Felicity singing. It came louder and clearer as Jocelyn drew nearer to the unseen orchestra and it seemed curiously one with the yellow and red figure that had just vanished.

Back in the box he gave a little gasp as he realized the change that had come over the auditorium since he left it. From floor to ceiling it was packed with silent figures. The lights had been lowered and one saw them only as phantom shapes filling a great cavern of darkness (what had Henrietta said about this being the inside of a mountain?) all the more ominous because of their ghostliness. . . . . That army of witnesses. . . . All that activity behind the stage, all those strained nerves, all the weeks of hard work and travail of creation that lay behind them, all Ferranti's tortured thoughts, all his own wakeful nights had been directed to one end, the pleasing of this unseen, critical multitude. . . .

"Full house," whispered Grandfather, by whom he unexpectedly found himself sitting. "Curtain's going up."

II

Never had Nigel Compton's genius been shown more clearly than in the way in which, as the curtain rose, the overture melted into the play. Imperceptibly, with the sobbing of wind in the branches of a forest, the music died away. One hardly realized it had ceased, or that the curtain was up, before one was in the heart of that wood, soundless now except for the haunting tune that had slipped from the first violin to the flute that the Minstrel was playing under an oak-tree, an enchanted oak-tree that shone faintly silver against a dim green background.

Then the tune passed from the flute to the Minstrel himself and the voice that had already made Oliver Standish famous rang out into the dark cavern full of listening phantoms, singing words of inimitable poetry that were Ferranti's own, and the best he could do. In and out among the phantoms crept that song, now ringing out like a bell, now whispering like wind among the grasses, weaving that curious spell that destroys the sense of distance in a theatre, as though the stage itself moved forward and stood in the very heart of the audience.

Jocelyn leant back in his chair with a sigh of relief. . . . They had begun well. . . . Acutely sensitive as he was to every sensation that swept the audience he could feel, as though balm were laid on a wound, that they were touched, interested, aroused, those twin ogres of boredom and censoriousness banished at the very outset.

The orchestra was playing again, a dance tune with an undercurrent of fear in it that grew in volume as one after the other the nymphs danced through the trees, reaching its full loveliness as they came together, swaying, parting, converging, yet always keeping visible to the audience, but hidden from the Minstrel, that hideous prancing satyr in their midst.

Jocelyn began to be able to notice things; the dim loveliness of that mysterious wood, the rainbow colouring of the nymphs' dresses, very soft and faint so that the brilliant red and yellow of the Minstrel's cloak flamed out like reality against illusion, that stark reality that man seems to himself to be against the background whose very existence apart from himself he cannot even prove.

The scene moved on to its horrible conclusion, the satyr made visible to the Minstrel and the skeletons hidden under the fair earth rising again to pollute it. The undercurrent of fear that had been in the dance tune swelled until it seemed that the figures in the dance were moving in time to the chanting of death. Oliver could act, it seemed, as well as sing, for his horror and despair caused even Jocelyn, who had written the words in which he expressed it, to shiver a little. . . . The curtain came down, the lights went up and there was a silence, the confused silence of a dreamer waking suddenly to daylight, before the thunder of applause rang out.

"That's all right," said Jocelyn to Grandfather.

"Dear me. Is it?" murmured Grandfather distractedly. "How is it that that young man is now so like Ferranti? His looks, his voice, everything. . . . He wasn't like him on the day of the rehearsal. . . . It's uncanny."

"The character he is acting has taken possession of him, that's all."

"I think it's a dreadful play," said Miss Lavender. "Those horrible skeletons! It's too terrible to think we shall all look like that one day!"

"We shan't know it, my dear," Grandmother consoled sharply. "We aren't put into our coffins with a looking-glass."

Mrs. Jameson was weeping softly into a white hand-kerchief with a purple border. The theme had upset her, the skeletons had upset her, everything had upset her, reminded her as it all did of the late Mr. Jameson and his end.

"I liked that satyr," said Hugh Anthony. "I liked his legs. Could I be a satyr?"

"The next act will cheer you up quite a lot," Jocelyn informed them.

And it did. The adventures of the Minstrel in the city that man had made were comic rather than tragic. The artists, attired in outrageous overalls stiff with smears of oil-paint and all of them in their make-up caricatures of famous artists and musicians of the day, including Nigel Compton who appeared in person as a caricature of himself, were amusingly grotesque against the back-ground of beauty that they had themselves created; and the scene of the sculptor's party, where everyone reached that stage of intoxication which, like the amateur Hamlet, is funny without being vulgar, sent ripples of laughter over the audience. How comic a creature is man, cried the whisper of music that was all this scene was allowed, an ant of a creature who can yet create cathedrals and pictures and music that may live a thousand years after he is dust. How pitiful a thing he is, with his squabbles and his meanness and his cruelty, and yet how great is the vitality that raises him to life again and again when the blows of his fate strike him down.

Jocelyn was rather proud of this scene for he had written most of it. The verse had the same superb rhythm as the poetry of the rest of the play but the matter of it was comic, an echo of the motif of the scene, the contrast between man and his works.

But the ending of the act, the smashing of the statue, the cruel rage of the artists and the hounding of the

Minstrel out of the city, was Ferranti's own and terrible. Ferranti seemed to say that in man, grotesque, creative, mean and courageous, there lives still the cruelty of the jungle, and who should know better than Ferranti who had felt himself to be hounded out of the life of men?

"Will it be Felicity and Henrietta now?" asked Hugh Anthony in the next interval.

"It's them next," said Jocelyn, and the expectation of the little party in the box was roused to fever pitch.

The orchestra played a country dance, the lights dimmed, the curtain rose on a village green and Jocelyn entered upon one of the most curious experiences of his life, an experience for which at the time he could find no practical explanation.

During the last few months he had thought ceaselessly about Ferranti, while he had been re-writing *The Minstrel* he had identified himself with him, while he had watched the first two acts of the play he had felt increasingly conscious of the fact that he was sitting where Ferranti ought to have been sitting, feeling probably as Ferranti would have felt had he been here, and now, during the third act, he lost all consciousness of being himself and became his friend. . . . He was Ferranti. . . . And he was watching not a scene in a play but a scene of his own life, and watching it in an anguish of love and remorse that was harder to bear than almost anything he had endured yet.

The act was the central one of the play, and the longest, and through its several scenes was traced the tragic course of human love. Its glorious birth, with the woman the incarnation of the mystery of beauty to the man, and the man a god to the woman, and each of them to the other the fulfilment of all longing. And then the gradual realization that human longing is too vast a thing to be satisfied by anything that the earth holds, human love like natural beauty can comfort but it cannot satisfy.

Gradually the beauty of the woman ceased to have any mystery for the man and the end of the mystery was the end of love. With the woman it was not so. To find her god only a man roused in her not disgust but a passionate maternity. Over his faults she mourned as over the bruises of a little child but such mourning was wearisome to him, striking at the very roots of his pride and turning the remnants of his love to hatred. Her fault, he cried, if he was but a bruised creature after all, her fault for tricking him to his fall by the lure of a mystery that was no mystery and a promise of satisfaction that was unfulfilled.

With a terrible sense of helplessness Jocelyn watched his own cruelty to the woman he had once loved; watched the growth of her bitter pride that would not humble itself to woo him again, watched her go with the careless, thoughtless man who was her second lover and who, he knew, would give her no happiness; felt anew, when she and the child had gone, the terrible sense of loss and loneliness that had nearly overwhelmed him before. . . . Fool that he had been. . . . Fools that they both had been. . . . Unable to take human love for what it is, man's chief support in his search for the unattainable but not its satisfaction, and so losing that inimitable comfort. . . . Jocelyn clenched his hands together. . . . It was terrible to see it happen all over again and, because it was the past, be unable to alter the march of events.

And the child! She was so delicious with her swift, graceful movements and her white face like a jasmine flower against her dark hair. Why had he not realized how lovable she was? Her hurt look when she realized he did not want her stabbed him. She had a luminous quality that was like moonlight and in her way she was as beautiful as that incomparable woman with her golden voice and her aureole of burnished hair. Together they

were sunshine and moonlight and without them his life
was a pitch-black night. He looked at himself in his
desolation, crouching alone on the steps of a village
cross, wrapped in his torn and tarnished cloak; that cloak
that once had been half of yellow and half of red, the
colours of divinity and humanity, yellow for the sunshine
of God in man's soul that he calls idealism, red for the
marching song of a young man's blood in his veins that
he calls romance. He looked at himself and no hatred
that he had ever felt was like his hatred of that crouching,
contemptible figure.

The stage darkened round that desolate man, a lament
of music was born in the shadows, grew into a tumult
of despair and died. The curtain fell slowly and from
far away Jocelyn heard Grandfather's voice, speaking in
the drawing-room at Torminster. "I should like to see
Felicity and Henrietta together. . . . Sunshine and moonlight."

Felicity and Henrietta? But that woman and child had
not been Felicity and Henrietta! Or had they? The lights
were up in the auditorium, a hum of conversation was
rising from its crowded seats and in the box the three old
ladies were chattering like starlings. "How lovely Felicity
looked! And how beautifully she sang. Dear little
Henrietta! She was so sweet and calm. If she was
frightened no one knew it. The two of them together
were quite perfect."

While the old ladies were admiring Henrietta Grandfather was painfully puzzling over her. How could she,
with her inexperience, portray so poignantly the sorrow
of an unwanted child? "That house where she gave away
her snowstorm," he muttered. "She has remembered
it and the wretched children. I should not have taken
her there."

He raised his voice and spoke aloud to Jocelyn. "I

did not know Felicity could act like that. . . . I did not know. . . . That was a painful scene, that last one. Dear me. Very painful."

Jocelyn blinked like an owl and found he was as cold as ice but yet had perspiration on his forehead as though it were eighty in the shade. He felt for his handkerchief and tried to readjust himself to reality. He, Jocelyn Irvin, had been sitting in a box at a London theatre and watching Oliver Standish and Felicity Summers, the popular actor and actress whose countenances were well known to the *Daily Mail*, acting very superbly in a play partly written by himself. His own little adopted niece, Henrietta Fordyce, had also had a tiny part to play and very taking she had been in it. . . . But it had all been nothing to do with him. . . . He was neither Ferranti nor the Minstrel, he was Jocelyn Irvin who loved Felicity Summers and would do till he died. . . . Had he had a fit, or what?

The last act was a difficult one and its production had taxed every ounce of ingenuity possessed by Miles Harpenden, Nigel Compton, Oliver and Jocelyn. The first scenes showed the Minstrel striving to spin perfection out of his own music and for the second time rejected by men. The tunes that Nigel Compton had composed as the Minstrel's own were very haunting, expressing his longing and despair and as different from the tunes that he had played in his hey-day as the songs of nightingale and robin. The last scene was played in the semi-dark beside the river of death. Behind the Minstrel as he slept moved the figures of his dream, the beauty he had rejected; the nymphs and their flowers, the statue of the peasant that he had smashed and the woman and the child, their figures forming into a pattern as they moved. The figure of the Minstrel was very dim now, his torn cloak a dull grey in colour. At the beginning of the play he had been bright reality against a dim background, utterly sure of himself

in his arrogant youth, but now it was the background that
stood out gloriously as his figure faded. "We are such
stuff as dreams are made on," sobbed the music, "and
our little life is rounded with a sleep."

The dream faded, the dark-winged spirit of death was
present with the Minstrel and the music died as they
spoke together of the circle of transcendent beauty, of
the pattern of immanent beauty, of the murder of beauty
by man and the despair of the murderer. It was a curious
dialogue, Ferranti at his most obscure and only partially
illumined by Jocelyn, but it was great poetry and the
audience, though with minds completely baffled, were
yet lifted by it into that clear air where we lose consciousness of ourselves. Like the Minstrel they lost their sense
of their own reality, and the things that in broad daylight
are shadowy and dim became in that enchanted cavern
where they sat the things that mattered.

As the voices ceased the orchestra began softly lamenting and as the Minstrel's feet carried him over the grass
to the water's edge and darkness blotted out the scene it
broke into a dirge as wild as the Highland coronach.
Played in the pitch-dark it was a strange and fearful ending to what the critics afterwards described as "the most
peculiar play ever produced in London."

III

But it was a success. Within three minutes the anxious
ears of the actors heard a ripple of cheering breaking
through the storm of clapping that had broken out as soon
as the lights were up. When the curtains parted to show
the whole company grouped together the roar that met
them was like a great wave breaking in their faces. For
a moment they were breathless with astonished relief

and then, on the faces of Miles Harpenden, Nigel Compton and Oliver, there dawned the sleek expression, seen so often upon the countenance of a cat absorbing cream, of a man who is taking to himself the entire credit. . . . But Felicity did not look sleek. She shot a swift glance to the right, towards the nearest box, and her eyes met Jocelyn's. Humility was in their look, for between them stood a ghost.

Then followed what seemed to Jocelyn, overwrought as he was, the intolerable absurdity of a first-night finale. Cheers. Excitement. Speeches. Felicity and Oliver taking call after call as though no one had ever seen them before or was ever likely to see them again. Then more excitement behind the stage. Mutual congratulations. Felicity snowed under by flowers. Henrietta kissed until she was quite sure the surface of her face must be worn away. Inability to find a cab for the Torminster party. Cab found. Inability to find Torminster party. Torminster party found and despatched to the respectable hotel opposite the British Museum. A party on the stage at which everyone got noisier and noisier and Oliver was quite intolerable. Inability to find a cab to take Felicity home in. Oliver's offer of his own brougham in which he himself, by himself, would take Felicity home rejected by Jocelyn with the utmost rudeness. Finding of a cab by the satyr in which Jocelyn and Felicity departed together, Felicity crying the whole way and extremely cross because she was so dreadfully tired. . . . And, at last, Jocelyn alone on the embankment with the dark river running by him and the stars over his head.

One o'clock struck from all the churches in London. . . . One o'clock. . . . Jocelyn remembered how it had struck from Torminster Cathedral on that wakeful night when he had first agonized over the manuscript of *The Minstrel*. How incredible it seemed that the great work

of art that had just come to full-grown life in the city of
London, the combined work of poet, artist, composer
and actors, had flowered from the seed of a few dirty pages
of manuscript found in a housemaid's cupboard in a
small cathedral town.

"The bell then striking one," he murmured, as he had
murmured on that other night. "This is the point where
the ghost should enter. Are you alive, Ferranti, or are
you dead?"

There was no answer; only a whisper of wind that swept
little bits of paper along the dry pavement and ruffled
the surface of the dark river.

CHAPTER XII

I

THE MINSTREL and Felicity remained in London as the successes of the season while Jocelyn and Henrietta, Flossie recovering from the chickenpox in due course, went back to Torminster and took up again the quiet lives that had been so strangely interrupted. It was typical of them both that they did this without difficulty. Henrietta, at heart a contemplative person, enjoyed alarums and excursions for a short while only. For her a background of quiet was essential to happiness. It had been fun to stay with Felicity, to be petted and spoiled by all her friends, to be applauded by big audiences in a crowded theatre, to have lovely things to eat and go to the zoo whenever she liked, but it had completely upset her equilibrium and she had felt as though she had been turned upside down so that everything that was worth while in her mind fell out. She, like everyone else, had to find out by experience in what mode of life she could best adjust herself to the twin facts of her own personality and the moment of time in which destiny had planted it, and she was lucky perhaps that she found out so early.

The day when she returned to Torminster was another of her great days.

Felicity's Mrs. Baker took her as far as the last change before Torminster but from there home she travelled alone in the care of the guard, Mr. Ebenezer Wilbraham, a cousin of Mr. Bates, a nice man with a grey beard and thirteen grandchildren.

This in itself was epoch-making for she had never before been alone in a railway-carriage. It was true that at every stop Mr. Wilbraham came along, poked his head in, gave her a peppermint lozenge and inquired, "All serene? Eh?" but as he immediately went away again upon perceiving her still intact he did not really disturb her lovely loneliness.

There was no one in the carriage with her so she was able to taste to the full that delicious feeling of moving through space by oneself. Why it should be so delicious it is hard to say but the pilot alone in his plane, the motorist solitary at the wheel of his car and the lark mounting towards the sun will all tell you that it is.

Henrietta thought there was no adventure like it. Here she was, being flung from the world of London to the world of Torminster, belonging at the moment to neither of them and so untrammelled by their cares and worries. It was lovely until she began to wonder what would happen if she never arrived. . . . What if she fell between one world and the other and went down into space. . . . She was just beginning to feel a bit frightened when the train swung round a bend, the blue hills parted like a curtain and the city of Torminster was visible.

With a squeal of delight she jumped to her feet and leaned out of the window, which she had faithfully promised Felicity she would not do, many disobedient little girls having met their end in that way, according to Felicity. It was her first return home after her first long absence from all that she loved and the joy of it was like nothing that she had ever felt before or ever would feel again.

There it was, Torminster, her home, the place that she

loved as she would love no other place all her life long. There were the old roofs and chimneys and the church spires, the smoke lying over them like a mist, and there, towering up above the smoke, was the grey rock of the Cathedral with its three towers. Her heart seemed to turn right over and she found that she was laughing and crying at the same time.

Who would meet her, she wondered; would the entire family come? She hung out of the window at the most perilous angle, only the tips of her toes touching the floor, until she could see the platform and a small dark blue figure with a flaming red head, his hands in his pockets and his legs wide apart. . . . Hugh Anthony had come to meet her by himself.

Instantly she knew that this was just as it should be. No one was nearer to her than Hugh Anthony and what she felt for Torminster only he in the years to come would understand; because he was a child when she was a child and had lived with her, within it, in the same enchanted land.

"Hugh Anthony!" she screamed, and falling headlong out of the carriage as soon as 'Erb had got the door open she flung her arms round his neck.

"Hullo," said Hugh Anthony, "I've got a guinea-pig," and he gave her a wet kiss.

Henrietta was enchanted. That he should kiss her like that in front of 'Erb and the station-master and Mr. Gotobed was an overwhelming proof of his affection. "I *do* love you, Hugh Anthony," she cried.

"If you hold it up by its tail its eyes fall out," said Hugh Anthony. "Your luggage is to go up in the bus, but we can walk if we want to."

"Did you ask if you could come along to meet me?" asked Henrietta.

"Mm."

"Why?" she asked, in trembling eagerness to hear him express his love for her.

"I thought it would be nice for Solomon to have a walk."

"Who's Solomon?"

"The guinea-pig, silly."

"Is he here?"

"Mm. In the ticket-office."

Mr. Gotobed took charge of the luggage while they hurried to the ticket-office, where Solomon was awaiting them in a perforated cardboard hat-box tied up with string.

"He's lovely," breathed Henrietta, squinting at him through the perforations.

"I haven't held him up by his tail yet," said Hugh Anthony magnanimously. "I waited till you came back."

"Oh, but you mustn't," wailed Henrietta. "It would be awful if his eyes fell out."

"But how are we to know if it's true that his eyes will fall out unless we hold him up by his tail to see?" asked Hugh Anthony.

Henrietta sighed, for this was not the first time that this type of problem had confronted her. How, for instance, could one prove that there was life after death unless one died to see? And it would be such a pity to be dead, just as it would be such a pity for poor Solomon to lose his eyes.

"What does Grandfather say?" she asked.

"Grandfather says that the situation is an opportunity for the exercise of simple faith. . . . I don't know what he means."

"Not to hold up the guinea-pig," said Henrietta firmly. "Come on."

Carrying Solomon between them they slowly traversed

the enchanted streets of the city. It did not look to them as it did to the grown-ups hurrying by. To them the houses seemed very tall, reaching nearly to heaven, so that the angels could pace along the tops of the curly old roofs if they wished; and very mysterious because of the unknown things that happened inside them. The little stream that ran down the side of the High Street seemed very wide to them, almost a river. It had waves in it, with jewelled fish in the curves of them, and its waters were crystal-clear. The pigeons in the Market Place all had human voices and they cried, "We are glad you are back, Henrietta, we are glad you are back," and on the Cathedral Green the birds in the elm-trees were singing like mad.

They stopped under the west front and Henrietta looked up at the ranks of kings and queens and saints. They were gazing out over her head towards the hills, as they had gazed for hundreds of years, and they did not seem to notice that she had come home. They looked very superior and they made her feel small and insignificant, human beings like herself though they were, and she turned from them to the Christ Child over the west door. His eyes met hers and suddenly He laughed, leaning His head back against His mother's shoulder and clapping His hands.

"Look, look, Hugh Anthony!" cried Henrietta, "the Baby is laughing!"

Hugh Anthony looked from the grave, unsmiling statue to Henrietta's rapt face and hoped, not for the first or the last time in his life, that his Henrietta wasn't going funny in the head. "Duffer!" he said. "He isn't!"

"No more He is," said Henrietta, looking again. "But it's funny," she continued, following Hugh Anthony homewards, "that human people can make one feel mean and small when God, Who is so much greater, doesn't."

At home there was a joyous reunion with Grandfather and Grandmother, Sarah, Ellen and Bates, and then there was high tea, followed by unpacking, and then at last she was alone in her scented bedroom with the carved angels, standing on the bare floor in her nightgown and listening to a spring shower pattering down on the garden path outside her window. . . . And mingling with the shower was the sound of footsteps coming clack-clack up the stairs and along the passage.

Henrietta smiled, for she knew who it was. It was the lovely lady with the powdered hair and the great billowing rosy skirt and the green petticoat, who had rings on her fingers and a black patch on her chin and pattered up and down the stairs in the evening when the house was quiet. Henrietta opened her door very softly and peeped out but she could not see anything, or hear anything now but a mouse. It was funny how she could never see that lady with her bodily eyes but only with the eyes of her mind, and that so clearly that she could describe her appearance down to the smallest detail.

She tiptoed down the passage and opened the door of the spare-room. No one was sleeping there now and the furniture was shrouded with dust-sheets and the curtains drawn. The light was so dim that it must have been difficult for the man who sat there painting to see what he was doing. She could hardly see him herself though she knew so well what he looked like. . . . He had a kind, lined face and a circular bald patch on the top of his head, and he wore a long brown robe that reached to his toes and a rope round his middle. . . . He was painting a book, ornamenting its pages with purple pansies and ivory roses and queer little animals with long legs and scarlet tongues. . . . It was strange that she knew all about that book though she only saw it in the dark.

She went back to her room, happy and unafraid in her sense of companionship, and stood listening again. The shower had stopped and she found herself listening only to the lovely silence and it seemed to her that in it she came right way up again and her dreams, that had deserted her in London, came flocking back, so that with joy she flung open the doors of her mind and welcomed them in. Never again, she vowed, would she live a noisy life that killed her dreams. They were her reason for living, the only thing that she had to give to the world, and she must live in the way that suited them best.

II

Next day she and Hugh Anthony went to tea with Martha and Mary of the sweet-shop on the occasion of the latter's ninetieth birthday.

It was suggested by Henrietta at breakfast that it would be a good idea if lessons that morning took the form of Nature study, so that they could go up to the Tor woods and pick wild flowers as a present for old Mary. Incidentally she was not feeling like staying indoors that morning, not even to do English literature, for after weeks of London the Tor woods were pulling at her feet and whispering in her ears. As she sat at breakfast she could almost hear the sounds that soft, furry beasts make as they slip through the undergrowth, and the tap-tap of a tree-creeper's beak on dry bark and the whisper of the wind in the branches that met one at the top of the hill.

Grandfather, reading her thoughts in her eyes, was amenable. Producing his writing-pad he wrote a note to Miss Lavender in his beautiful spidery handwriting. "Dear Miss Lavender, I find that Nature study commends itself to the young as a branch of learning to be studied on this May morning. Henrietta is certainly a little pale after London and fresh air will do her good. Yours, my dear Miss Lavender, in gratitude, Hilary Theobald Fordyce."

He handed this epistle to Grandmother to see if it met with her approval. He always asked her opinion about what he did or wrote, though if it did not coincide with what he felt to be right he was careful not to let it influence him in any way.

"H'm," said Grandmother, handing it back. "The children will never learn anything."

"Nature study is lessons, Grandmother," explained Henrietta.

"H'm," said Grandmother. "Poking about in the mud," and she went to the kitchen to tell Ellen what she thought of the consistency of last night's cutlets.

Miss Lavender, on receiving the note, was delighted, for she loved a country walk with the dear children. She had no clear idea what Nature study was, or how it should be pursued, but she thought they were doing their duty if they took with them a volume called *Wild Life Shown to the Children*, and then when they found any queer-looking fauna or flora they hunted through the book and found they were not there. . . . Which, after all, was not their fault.

The Tor woods were reached by taking a sharp turn to the right at the bottom of the street where the Lower Orders—or God's Poor—lived. Henrietta could never pass that street without a sick feeling inside her, for she had never forgotten that terrible house and the children who were not wanted. Every night upon the stage of the Firebird, when the Minstrel turned from her and abandoned her, she had remembered them, and every night the look on her face said something to those people in the audience who had eyes that saw. . . . Had those children still got the snowstorm, she wondered, and the little yellow and red man who was like the Minstrel?

The road they had taken was one of several roads that wound up from the city to the hills. Macadamized surfaces were unknown in those days and the roads varied with the weather; in winter they were slippery with a sticky brown mud that was peculiar to the Torminster valley and in dry summers they were deep in white dust. They were bad for walking, no doubt, and when bicycling was fashionable they made skidding a thing that happened with tedious regularity, but in after years Henrietta found herself regretting them, for their mud was tender to horses' hoofs and in summer their gleaming whiteness, seen in the distance against green fields, was good to look at.

They followed the road a little way and then climbed a stile to their left and found themselves on the steep path that led up through the Tor woods. . . . And the Tor woods in May were Paradise.

The primroses and violets were faded but the wood anemones were sprinkled over the dark earth like stars. Here and there a shaft of sunlight pierced through the new green leaves overhead and touched their whiteness to a shimmering silver, and sometimes a puff of wind made them all shiver and stir, as though they were bright points of light on water. That poised look, peculiar to them, as of something so frail that it might at any moment blow away, made them look more like butterflies than flowers whose roots were in the earth.

Miss Lavender and the children stood staring, each of them crying out in their different ways to this moment,

"Stay a little. Stay a little." It did not stay, but as they turned and walked on, the magic of the woods gathering round them and penetrating them, other moments almost as good came in its place. They looked and listened and sniffed, seeing the crumpled green leaves over their heads laid like blobs of paint against a bright blue sky where the clouds were racing before a west wind, hearing the twitter of birds and the scuffling of rabbits in the bushes, smelling the scent of wet earth and moss and ferns. The sunshine seemed to get inside their eyes, brightening them, and the colour that flooded the world seemed to be clothing them too so that they all three felt supremely beautiful; indeed for fully five minutes Miss Lavender quite forgot that she was an elderly spinster and thought she was the young girl that she used to be. Funny, she thought, coming to herself again, how the spring can create this illusion that one is oneself lovely. . . . Until one suddenly remembers that one is not. . . . She stumbled over a stone, for her sight was not what it was, and Hugh Anthony called out, "Hold up, Miss Lavender," and removed a small twig from her path with a gallantry that she thought most touching in the dear boy.

"I don't think it's fair," said Henrietta from the rear, "that the earth should be made new again every year when we aren't. I think God ought to spring-clean us too."

Miss Lavender, stumbling again and feeling her lumbago in her back, heartily, though silently, agreed with her.

"Could God spring-clean us every year if He wanted to?" asked Hugh Anthony.

"Yes, dear," said Miss Lavender.

"Then why doesn't He do it?"

"Look! A squirrel!" cried Miss Lavender, and heaved

a sigh of relief as Hugh Anthony charged off into the undergrowth. The advantage of Nature study over other forms of instruction was that the young mind could always be distracted from theological argument to something more interesting to it.

They climbed slowly higher, getting with every step deeper into the wood. Over their heads the leaves gathered closer and all round them the trunks of the trees soared upwards like the pillars in the Cathedral.

Hugh Anthony was very happy poking about among the roots of the trees and then running back to Miss Lavender to ask questions about the treasures he had found; a woolly caterpillar that he thought at first was a baby hedgehog, a salmon-pink toadstool, stones and mosses. Miss Lavender gave very inaccurate replies, culled at a moment's notice from *Wild Life Shown to the Children*, but he took it all for gospel and was happy.

But Henrietta, when the trees began to thin towards the top of the hill, suddenly went off by herself. Loneliness was at times a necessity to her in the woods because then she could go mad. There was a queer streak in her nature that had come to her from her unknown ancestry and was completely at variance with the rest of her. There were two Henriettas, the orderly child whom Grandfather was training so carefully and another one, a wild thing who came to life at unexpected times and behaved like a kitten at twilight, a creature who was more of a pixy than a human being.

The orderly person was for the moment left behind on the path with Miss Lavender and Hugh Anthony, an unseen presence, and it was the wild Henrietta who took to her heels and ran, leaping over stones and fallen branches and dodging round the trunks of the trees, nimble and sure-footed as a wild animal. Every now

and then she looked up at the clouds over her head and
felt that she was running with them before the wind.
She could run faster than they if she wanted to, she felt,
she could run right over the rim of the world and get
to the place where they were going before they did. She
stretched her arms wide as she ran and cried out aloud,
queer, high calls that sounded more fairy than human
and that would have startled Grandfather if he had heard
them. For pagan magic had entered into her body through
her flying feet that touched the earth, and leaped, and
touched again, and into her mind from the air and the
light and the clouds, and she had lost all touch with time
and place.

With a bound she leaped to the top of a hill and looked
down into a dell carpeted with bluebells. She checked
and paused, still poised on her toes with her arms stretched
out. The bluebells ran down the sides of the dell in
rivulets and gathered at the bottom into a pool of azure.
The sun that smote through the trees overhead gathered
up their scent, so that it brimmed the dell like wine
in a cup, and when the wind blew the slender stalks
near Henrietta leaned all one way, bending their blue
heads.

She paused for a moment only, then she raced down the
side of the dell and fell face downwards into the azure
pool. The bluebells, very tall down here because they
had to reach up to the sun, yielded sweetly to the pressure
of her body, then seemed to gather round as though to
hide her. She stretched out her bare arms through them
and felt their stalks and leaves smooth and cool against
her skin, and she buried her face in the moss, sniffing
its pungent, wet scent. The sun was warm on her back
and she felt happy with an almost savage happiness.
Something that she had heard Grandfather quote slipped
into her mind.

> "I hold him happiest
> Who, before going quickly whence he came,
> Hath looked ungrieving on these majesties,
> The world-wide sun, the stars, waters and clouds
> And fire. Live, Parmeno, a hundred years
> Or a few weeks, these thou wilt always see,
> And never, never, any greater thing."

Those words had been written by a heathen poet,
Grandfather had said, and so they were not quite true,
but Henrietta at this moment felt that they were. The
earth was greater and lovelier than anything else and to
be one with it, as she was one with it now, her body
pressing against it, its scent in her nostrils and its colour
blinding her eyes, was to be supremely happy; there was
nothing greater than this.

Suddenly the pixy vanished, as the queer spirit that
takes possession of the kitten vanishes, and she was her
sober self again. She got up, surprised at herself,
straightened her twisted socks and picked bits of stick
out of her hair. When Miss Lavender and Hugh Anthony
joined her she was picking bluebells and anemones for
old Mary and was once more the tidy, orderly Henrietta
whom they knew. . . . They had no idea, of course, that
the other one existed.

III

At four o'clock the children presented themselves at
Mary and Martha's. It was early-closing day so they did
not go in through the shop but through the door at the
side. It was opened to them by Martha, dressed in her
best black alpaca, with a crochet shawl folded across her
chest, and chattering away all of a twitter about the honour

of a visit from the Close and Grandfather's great condescension in letting them come. Henrietta could not
see how they could be conferring an honour upon Martha
and Mary by eating up their food, the honour, she thought,
was the other way round, and she did not understand
the meaning of the word condescension, though she
often heard it used in reference to the behaviour of the
people who lived in the Close. She had once told Grandfather that she did not know what it meant and he had
snorted and said he was thankful to hear it, and had not
enlightened her.

Hugh Anthony did not require enlightening about
these things. He had become aware early in life that there
were differences of class and sex and that his own position
in regard to them was happy. He belonged to the
Governing Class, he had discovered, and the Dominant
Sex, and like the Dean he thought these things were to
his credit. . . . In after years both he and the Dean were
most determined opponents of the suffrage movement.
. . . So now, as he stalked down the dark passage after
Martha and Henrietta, knowing himself to be conferring
a benefit upon these women, he bore a marked resemblance
to Napoleon in his more affable moments.

Old Mary sat in her big arm-chair beside the little
fire that was always burning in her parlour, summer or
winter, dressed in all her petticoats and her best dress of
maroon silk. She was surrounded by the china ornaments she had collected during ninety years of life, and
by the photographs of all the masters and mistresses who
had known her devotion since she first took service with
the then Bishop of Torminster at the age of ten. By
her side was the inevitable basket of kittens—the sweet-
shop cat kittened with a regularity and profusion that
no other Torminster cat could get anywhere near—and
on her lap were the birthday presents and letters that

she had received from all her masters and mistresses still living, and also from the Bishop, to whose ears it had somehow come that eighty years ago the Palace saucepans had been washed by one of the greatest saints, always excepting Grandfather and the first Abbot, that Torminster had ever harboured. . . . She had not let these precious treasures out of the sight of her old eyes and the touch of her old hands all day, and was not likely to until sleep overtook her.

Yet she was not too absorbed in them not to be deeply touched by the gift of wild flowers from the children. "The pretty dears," she murmured, caressing the cheeks of the children and the petals of the flowers with her finger-tips.

"They're lovely in the Tor woods," said Henrietta. "Up there they look like butterflies and blue water."

"They won't last," said Hugh Anthony the realist. "Is tea ready?"

It was ready on the table in the window and was a thoroughly satisfactory tea, including four kinds of sugar cake and three jams.

"Will Master Anthony say grace?" asked Martha.

Hugh Anthony took up a Napoleonic attitude, closed his eyes tightly and came out with a long Latin grace that Grandfather used on state occasions, such as when visiting clergy came to dinner and the day when they had the annual goose.

"Latin!" said Martha. "Well, I never!"

"He doesn't understand a word," explained Henrietta. "He's just copied it from Grandfather like parrots do."

Hugh Anthony gave Henrietta a pained glance. She was always so anxious that no one should labour under a misapprehension but personally he could not see that it did them any harm. Lying, of course, was wrong, and he never lied, but the same results could often be obtained by judicious silence. . . . He must explain this to Henrietta.

There are occasions in life when it is not only a pleasure but a duty to overeat and this was one of them, for Martha and Mary would have been disappointed if full justice had not been done to the tea they had provided. Both children understood this and even Henrietta, though she disliked excess, ate a great deal more than she really had room for. Every time she took a fresh spoonful of jam, or Hugh Anthony reached for yet another cake, a glance of pleasure passed between the two old ladies. It seemed cruel to have to put an end to these glances but the time came when even Hugh Anthony was obliged to shake his head speechlessly.

Any sort of movement was for the present impossible so they sat on the floor at old Mary's feet, with the clawing squeaking kittens spread-eagled on their chests, and listened while old Mary dilated on the glories of old.

The days of Mary's youth had been, according to her, the great days of Torminster. In those days, such was the wealth of the Church, not only the dean but every canon in the Close had had his carriage and pair. It had been grand, Mary said, to see them driving out, the reverend gentlemen so fine in their top-hats and their ladies beside them in their smart bustled dresses.

"What's a bustle?" asked Hugh Anthony. "I thought it was what you got into when you ran for a train."

"It sticks out at the back below the waist, dearie," explained Mary. "Or it did when I was young. I remember when I was parlourmaid at Archdeacon Dobson's and was waiting at my first dinner-party—nervous I was—I let the dish of potatoes slip in my hand and two of them fell out and lodged in Lady Maria Jefferson's bustle. I *was* in a taking, but I picked them up careful-like in my fingers and her ladyship was none the wiser."

"*My* lady," said Henrietta dreamily, "has a bustle all the way round, front and sides as well as back. . . . It's pink, though her petticoat is green."

"Who's she, dearie?" asked old Mary.

But Henrietta, absorbed in unhooking a particularly prickly kitten, did not answer.

"Please," said Hugh Anthony, "may we see your Little Things?"

This was the great moment of the afternoon. A tender smile dawned on old Mary's face and Martha, who had been sitting opposite to them knitting, and jogging Mary's memory when she went astray in her stories, got up and almost ran to a cupboard in the corner. From it she produced a wooden stand covered with a glass shade and carried it triumphantly to the table at Mary's elbow, removing the kittens to a safe distance.

On the stand stood every kind of miniature object that Mary had been able to collect throughout her life. There were tiny chairs carved out of ivory, a Bible the size of your thumb-nail which could be actually read with a magnifying glass, a silk purse with tiny coins inside, a tea-set of Bristol china, a bottle of shells the size of pins' heads, a little telescope through which you could look and see a picture of Brighton, and many other treasures, thirty of them altogether, all of them works of art and not a single one of them bigger than an acorn. Martha lifted off the shade and the children gloated, as they had gloated many times before and would gloat again, kneeling reverently on their knees and not daring to touch until Mary gave them leave. . . . But she did give them leave. . . . She picked up the treasures one by one in her transparent, blue-veined hands and handed them to the children, telling them the history of each one, how she had come by it, how long she had had it and what the people of importance to whom she had shown it had said about it.

Hugh Anthony was deeply interested for the workmanship of the Little Things presented all sorts of practical problems to his mind, but Henrietta was more than interested, she was uplifted. The thought of so much patience and skill poured out upon the making of things so tiny gave her a feeling of liberation. The sight of perfection was like a gate that let one out into freedom, and if one could make small things so lovely then it seemed that one had not got to go very far or own very much to be free. "I could be bounded in a nutshell and count myself a king of infinite space." It was not the size of things that mattered but their perfection, it was not what one had that was important but what one made.

She laid down an exquisite carved ivory spinning-wheel on her lap and looked at her own hands, small brown shapely hands, and for the first time she was aware of them in connection with her dreams. A consciousness of power welled up in her. One day she too would make something and it should be beautiful. She would make it out of her two selves, her pixy self and her sober self. The one should give form to the magic of the other.

"When I die, my dear, these shall be yours."

Old Mary's voice seemed to come from a long way off. Looking up from the treasure in her lap it seemed to Henrietta that Mary, so old and frail, was already slipping away behind the mists that hid the dead from the living. Her eyes, bright and amused and tender, rested on the little girl. She seemed to be already enjoying, in a far country, the pleasure she had left behind her by the gift of thirty Little Things under a glass shade.

"Thank you," said Henrietta, and she said it very clearly and with all her heart so that it should reach to Mary.

Their time was up and they said a loving good-bye to both the old ladies and all the kittens. Even Hugh Anthony, who embraced seldom and with reluctance, offered Mary one of his wet kisses with politeness and respect. . . . In spite of himself her dignity and great age impressed him.

When they came out into the Market Place again the glorious May day was drawing towards evening. The wind had dropped and the great cauliflower clouds, touched here and there with gold, were moving very slowly across the sky.

"I haven't looked in the holy well since I came home," cried Henrietta, and raced across the Market Place towards it, Hugh Anthony at her heels. She ran up the steps and leaned over the parapet. The water seemed blacker than ever, deep and mysterious, and her own face looked back at her from it, flushed and eager and more alive than usual as though the mind behind it had woken into new life. She laughed and nodded at herself and held out her hands over the water so that she saw them reflected like two starfish. . . . Her hands that would one day take the thoughts of her mind and form them into visible beauty. . . . Again that sense of power welled up in her and she looked forward to the achievement of the future as a time of wonder and glory.

A cloud passed over the sun and the picture in the well dimmed. Hugh Anthony had been disturbing the pigeons and now there was a flapping of wings behind her as though a dark spirit passed. In the sudden darkening she remembered the Minstrel and his broken flute. . . . Men did not always achieve; sometimes they failed. . . . Her heart ached with pity for him because he was dead and could not begin again to make things. She wanted him to come alive again. In the play he had not wanted her, and that had hurt her, but then he had not

K

understood how like himself she was. If he could have come to her now in Torminster then he would have understood and they could have made things together. . . . Then she remembered, blinking confusedly, that he was only a man in a play.

Sighing, she climbed down the steps and went home with Hugh Anthony.

CHAPTER XIII

I

JOCELYN, too, one of those steady people whom the ebbing tide of excitement leaves unchanged, returned thankfully to Torminster and the vocation of a book-seller. Yet he found that his life had widened for he was now not only the interpreter between mind and mind in Torminster only. Popularity, that twin sister of the fickle jade fortune, who had never until now had one glance to bestow upon Ferranti, was now all smiles. He was the rage of the moment, a gold piece buried under the dust that must at all cost be dug up, his worth intensified by the labour of digging. Must the human race always wait, queried Jocelyn, until its poets and painters are buried beneath neglect and the dust of death before it realizes their worth? Is it a human instinct to think that buried gold is richer than the treasure that lies ready to hand? All the better, thought Jocelyn, for those deputed to do the digging.

For his articles on Ferranti had challenged attention and a suggestion that he should collect and edit Ferranti's poems came to him from the chief publishing house in London.

It was a task after his own heart and he laboured at it evening after evening. Two volumes of poetry, that had appeared years ago and perished immediately, were resurrected and to them he added the poems that had been with the manuscript of *The Minstrel* in Mrs. Jameson's

287

cupboard. They all of them needed finishing, polishing and explaining but after his labours on *The Minstrel* this seemed comparatively easy. In a very short while the book was out and was an immediate success. It was followed by a novel of Ferranti's that had failed on its first appearance, one of those imaginative books that are rejected as nonsense or reverenced as brilliant fantasy according as their writer is, or is not, the mode of the moment.

And Jocelyn began to do some writing on his own account. If he could interpret his friend Ferranti, he asked himself, why not his other friends? He had made so many of them in his bookshop, scraping acquaintance with them during odd minutes in the day and pursuing it through long evenings. It was true that most of these friends of his were already beloved friends of the human race, well known and already interpreted and re-interpreted by writers more skilled than he, yet surely something fresh could still be found to say about them? No man, Jocelyn argued, is quite the same person to each of his friends, one will call out one quality, one another. In the meeting of two people each is altered, like wine and water mingling. It was not too conceited of him, he hoped, to think that in his friendship with Shelley the mingling of their minds had revealed to him some shade of colour in the thought of his friend that he only could have discovered. . . . In any case he wrote a series of articles on the Victorian poets for the *Sunday Post* that made even his brother Hubert realize to the full that a prophet is frequently without honour in his own country.

Felicity, reading them, purred. She had thought Jocelyn love-worthy when he was a shabby young man whose name nobody knew, and would have continued to think so whatever he had done or not done, but it was nevertheless pleasant to have her opinion endorsed. With Felicity playing nightly in Ferranti's play and Jocelyn pursuing his vocation at Torminster they met only during the week-ends when he rushed up to London to see her, yet all the while it seemed to them that their intimacy deepened.

"I am making money now," he would tell her. "Book-selling alone was not enough but the shop and my writing together are making an embryo breadwinner of me. . . . A bit dull, bread-winning for oneself alone. . . . Just a bit longer and the embryo stage will be over."

Felicity, after commenting upon the beauty of Kensington Gardens, their usual meeting place on a Sunday, one day replied with apparent irrelevance, "I get tired of not feeling rooted. I have a wonderful life, of course, but it gives me no feeling of permanence. One wants something besides one's work, don't you think, some existence apart from it that links one up deep down with the earth itself." Her eyes went from the summer foliage of the trees to their roots that reached down into quiet places that one could not see, quiet places where the mystery of birth took place.

Jocelyn, who was engaged at the moment on an article on Keats, replied softly, "Keep a bower quiet for us, and a sleep full of sweet dreams, and health, and quiet breathing."

"Keats didn't say that of marriage," said Felicity impulsively, and then, with a sidelong twinkle at Jocelyn, hastily bit her lip.

"He said it," said Jocelyn, returning the twinkle with interest, "of anything that will never pass into nothingness."

At that moment, in spite of the inadequacy of his bank balance, he might have launched out into a beautiful Edwardian proposal of marriage, but Felicity murmured something about, "when the run of the play is over," and then stopped. . . . There was still that ghost between them.

II

For still nothing was heard of Ferranti. Felicity thought his silence was the silence of death, and Grandfather sadly agreed with her, for if he was alive, they argued, he must surely have come back to rejoice in the recognition that was his at last. But Jocelyn had become convinced that he was alive, though he seemed unable to tell them why. . . . Not even to Felicity could he speak of that curious experience in the theatre but he could explain it to himself in no other way than as thought transference. Ferranti himself had been in the theatre and the thoughts of his mind had passed to Jocelyn.

He thought about that experience more and more, though the culmination of his thinking did not come until a night in August. It had been stiflingly hot as Torminster could be at its worst. The hills all round them kept away any breeze there was and it seemed impossible even to breathe. Under a brazen sky the elm-trees on the Green stood still and exhausted and in the gardens of the Close the flowers drooped their heads.

His day's labour over Jocelyn set to work to water the garden. He was very proud of his garden that year. With the help of Bates he had dug it all up and replanted it and made of it a blaze of concentrated colour. He envied no one their garden, not even the Dean with his terraced walks and great lawns and innumerable hot-houses. His might be the size of a pocket handkerchief but he loved it as Jacob loved Joseph and the coat of many colours that he had woven for it was perfect in his eyes.

To-night the apples hung among their wet leaves like words fitly spoken, apples of gold in pictures of silver. The grass under them, drenched with water by Jocelyn every night, was still bright green and round the roots of the trees golden nasturtiums grew. All round the wall were hollyhocks, pink and yellow and deep crimson, and in the patchwork of flower-beds near the house were asters, carnations, late roses, mignonette, rosemary and lavender.

The sun had dipped behind the hills now and a delicious coolness stole into the garden as Jocelyn watered. The scent of the flowers, that the heat of the sun had stolen from them during the day, came back like an almost visible presence. "A bower quiet for us," murmured Jocelyn, and thought of Felicity in London standing at this moment on the stage of a stifling theatre. How hot she must be, and how tired. He sent out from his mind thoughts of this cool garden to refresh her and hoped they would arrive. . . . As they hadn't got to travel by that dawdling train they conceivably might.

Thoughts of the theatre brought him back again to remembrance of that queer experience. It had convinced him, if further proof were necessary, that *The Minstrel* was biography and that Ferranti had in very truth driven a wife and child away from him, and suffered afterwards an agony of remorse.

What had this wife and child been like, he wondered? Had they been in real life as Ferranti had described them in the play? Had the woman had golden hair and a singing voice like a blackbird's and had the child had the black hair and the white face that were Ferranti's own?

His watering over he drifted indoors and sat down by the open window of his sitting-room, as full now of the scent of his flowers as though it were a basket crammed with blossoms. He supposed that he ought to start work on his article on Byron, commissioned by the *Sunday Post*, which had to be done in a fortnight and wasn't even started, but he didn't want to. Somehow he could never get up any enthusiasm for Byron; he was not a friend but an acquaintance whom he was always tempted to cut; and to-night he was thinking so much of Felicity and the play that there seemed no room in his mind for Byron. . . . At this moment, he thought, glancing at his watch, she would be singing that haunting song, her blackbird's voice rippling out into the stifling darkness of the auditorium, cool and clear like the water that had refreshed his flowers. "There be none of Beauty's daughters with a magic like thee." A picture rose in his mind's eye of a boat on a moonlit lake and a woman sitting in it and singing. . . . Singing to Byron. . . . Clare Claremont about whom Byron had written one of his loveliest lyrics and then, her usefulness over, abandoned.

The thought of that lyric, one of the few lesser things of Byron's that he really liked, made him feel that he could start that article after all. He got up languidly and strolled into the dark, shuttered bookshop to look for a copy of Byron. . . . He used the books that ought to have been kept untouched for customers in the most shameless way, considering that sellers in shops should have their perquisites. He had heard that the girls who worked in sweet-shops were allowed to stuff as many sweets as they liked into their insides, so why shouldn't he stuff his wares into his mind if he wanted to? The only difference in their cases being that the girls got sick and stopped while he got well nourished and went on.

As he hunted along the dark shelves, lighting match after match, Jocelyn found himself murmuring the lyric, one of those haunting things that once read are memorized unconsciously.

> "There be none of Beauty's daughters
>   With a magic like thee;
> And like music on the waters
>   Is thy sweet voice to me:
> When, as if its sound were causing
>   The charmed ocean's pausing,
> The waves lie still and gleaming
> And the lull'd winds seem dreaming:
>
> And the midnight moon is weaving
>   Her bright chain o'er the deep;
> Whose breast is gently heaving
>   As an infant's asleep:
> So the spirit bows before thee,
>   To listen and adore thee;
> With a full but soft emotion,
> Like the swell of summer's ocean."

The sixth match burnt his fingers and he dropped it impatiently, plunging himself into darkness again. He must either go upstairs and fetch a candle, which he felt far too lazy to do, or leave that article till to-morrow. Taking the line of least resistance he strolled back to his sitting-room again, the smell of carnations and mignonette welcoming him and the evening light picking out the reds and blues and greens of his own books on their shelf as though they themselves were the flowers whose scent filled the room. They all had gay bindings, except those three tattered ones of Ferranti's.

Ferranti's Byron! Wasn't one of the three a Byron? Of course it was; Shakespeare, Shelley and Byron. It

K*

would now be possible to start work without going upstairs and Jocelyn settled himself happily at the table in the window with paper, pencil and the Byron. He turned to the lyric first of all, idly anxious to see if he had memorized it correctly. . . . It was pencilled in the margin.

Gone were all thoughts of Byron himself, of the article, of anything at all except Ferranti. Once before his friend had spoken to him in this room, using the words of Hamlet, and now he was speaking again with Byron's voice.

Jocelyn rapidly turned the pages, looking for more of those pencil marks that told him so much. Surely Byron and Ferranti had had much in common. Both had driven a wife and child away from them and Byron had lost as well the little daughter of Clare Claremont whom he had loved with a love that actually endured. He turned to Byron's lament for his wife and child and found it marked. He turned to the two laments for a dead girl and found those marked too; for if Ferranti's child was not actually dead yet she was dead to him.

> "For life is but a vision—what I see
>   Of all which lives alone is life to me,
>   And being so—the absent are the dead,
>   Who haunt us from tranquillity, and spread
>   A dreary shroud around us, and invest
>   With sad remembrances our hours of rest."

That passage too was marked and he read it over and over again. Then he turned back to the lyric and read that again, yet after all what did they tell him? Nothing but that the painful third act of the play was, as he knew already, the tragedy of a personal love as well as of the impersonal love of man and woman. He remembered again the misery of remorse that he had felt as he watched the Minstrel drive Felicity and Henrietta away from him and he felt again, for the second time, that curious sense of identification with Ferranti himself. He closed the book and sat very still, leaning back in his chair, his eyes shut to the glorious afterglow of sunset that filled the room, and gradually the thought of Felicity and Henrietta filled his mind to the exclusion of all else.

He felt for them both a passionately protecting love stronger than any emotion he had felt yet. He wanted to spend the whole of his life, from now until death, in their service. He wanted that service to be an act of atonement for the desertion of that other man who seemed so curiously to be himself. He would be able to give Felicity what she wanted for he knew what she wanted; that he, rather than she, should be the home-maker, that he should create for her quietness and permanence as a background for her busy life. But what kind of service would Henrietta want of him? The same, perhaps. Merely the creation of that quietness which is the essence of home. He smiled, remembering his dismay when Grandfather had first suggested that he should be Henrietta's father. Well, he felt no dismay now, only a sense of inevitability. Queer little Henrietta, with her stillnesses, her sudden emotions, her perceptiveness and her precocity, if she didn't grow up into something startling he'd be surprised. He wondered where on earth she had come from. He supposed Grandfather knew.

Suddenly he felt that he must know at once all that there was to know about Henrietta. Laziness had made going upstairs to fetch a book a sheer impossibility but now in his excitement a walk to the Close seemed not only possible but desirable.

Although it was August that brilliant afterglow still lingered. The world was utterly still and a planet blazed in the sky. Other people besides Jocelyn had been watering their gardens and the whole town seemed flower-scented. If quiet was what Felicity and Henrietta would want of him it struck him that in all the world he would be able to find no more peaceful city in which to build their home. At the west front he paused for a moment. The carved figures were very dark to-night, brooding and a little terrible, as though they stood in their ranks waiting for the last trump to call them to judgment. Jocelyn found himself, though with no intention of irreverence, addressing his Maker rather flippantly. "If You ask me at the Last Day what I did with my life," he said, "I shall reply, 'I was a nursemaid to the artists.'"

III

"Dear me," said Grandfather, looking up from the book he was writing, Grandmother having gone to bed early that night and not needing his companionship in the drawing-room. It was called *The Faith of a Sinner* and it was his apologia. He had a great desire to state in writing the faith that was in him and to which it seemed to him that he had failed utterly in giving expression in living. He had been writing his book in his odd minutes for the last forty years but he couldn't seem to get it finished because of interruptions. The moment he put pen to paper somebody came to see him.

"Dear me," he said to Jocelyn, as he had said to other interrupters a thousand times before, "can I do anything for you?" And he patiently laid his writing aside, put the cork in his bottle of ink, changed his spectacles from his reading to his looking-at-people ones, leant back in his chair with his hands folded over his stomach and gave his visitor his whole attention. This series of movements had been performed so often that they happened, so to speak, all in one breath.

"I felt," said Jocelyn, "that I would like to hear all you can tell me about Henrietta."

"What for?" asked Grandfather.

"It's a funny thing," said Jocelyn, "but I feel more and more that Henrietta is my own child."

Grandfather beamed. "I hoped," he said, "that you would be guided to feel that. If you remember, dear boy, on the first day you came I said——"

"I know," interrupted Jocelyn, "but if I am one day to be Henrietta's father——"

"And Hugh Anthony's," said Grandfather firmly.

"Er—what?" said Jocelyn. "Oh, yes, I suppose so. But he'll be mostly at boarding school, thank God, and then at Oxford, heaven help it, and then I should think the Canadian mounted police, or an exploration to the North Pole. . . . But Henrietta. . . . I should like to know about her."

"There's very little to know," said Grandfather. "Henrietta's mother was a singer, a woman who called herself Miriam Raymond. She earned her living singing at concerts and during the last year of her life her permanent home was in two rooms in London. My good friend Miss Balfour, who is now the matron of the orphanage from which I took Henrietta, was at that time a district nurse in London and became friendly with this poor Miriam and her four-year-old baby girl. The mother died very suddenly, exactly a week after Miss Balfour was appointed to the orphanage, and she was able to take the poor little child with her when she went."

"Poor Miss Balfour must have hated you for taking Henrietta away."

"I don't think so. She cares only for tiny children and has long ceased to take a personal interest in Henrietta.

By the way, it was Miss Balfour who had the child baptized Henrietta. Her mother, who had never had her baptized, had called her Gabrielle but Miss Balfour thought that too French and fanciful."

"Who was the child's father? Didn't Miss Balfour know?"

"Miriam told Miss Balfour that her husband was a Welshman called Jones who had met her when she was living in Italy. I am afraid that he was a worthless fellow, for their marriage lasted a few months only, and Miss Balfour had no way of tracing him. . . . You see, Jones is not an unusual Welsh name."

"I refuse to believe," said Jocelyn explosively, "that Henrietta is the child of a Welshman called Jones. Who was Miriam with before she took up with this wretched Jones?"

Grandfather looked infinitely distressed. It had never occurred to him that Henrietta was not the child of Miriam's Welshman. He had always thought tenderly of Miriam, the beautiful mother of his beloved Henrietta, and he hated to think that she was perhaps—perhaps—his mind refused to follow this train of thought and he turned rather sternly on Jocelyn.

"You have no right, Jocelyn, to suggest that Miriam did not tell the truth to Miss Balfour."

"She would naturally wish to appear as a respectable married woman," said Jocelyn.

"Miriam was a good woman," said Grandfather fiercely. "I have her photo and it shows what she was. When she was dying she gave it to Miss Balfour to be given to Henrietta when she was older. It was a photo of her, she said, that had once been treasured by Henrietta's father."

"If you have it here may I see it?" asked Jocelyn gently.

Grandfather opened a drawer and took it out, unwrapping the paper that he had put round it. "Very soon now," he said, "I shall give it to Henrietta. I did not want her to have it until I felt she was old enough to have the questions that it will make her ask about her father truthfully answered."

Jocelyn took the faded, old-fashioned photograph mounted on stiff board and looked at it eagerly. He saw what he expected, a young and beautiful woman with a mass of fair hair. Not even the horrors of Victorian photography, the basket of paper flowers that she carried, a rickety Greek temple behind her, the fur rug under her feet and the cracked sundial that supported her elbow, could detract from her rather challenging charm. There was something independent about her figure, something proud in the carriage of her head, and her face, as Grandfather had said, was the face of a good woman. Jocelyn tilted the photo a little, so as to get the light from Grandfather's lamp fully on it, and caught sight of some writing on the back. He turned it over, looked, and found the room revolving round him, for on the back of the photo of Henrietta's mother Byron's lyric had been written out in the tiny, crabbed handwriting that, to his cost, he knew better than any other handwriting in the world.

For the moment he did not say anything to Grandfather, he laid the photo back on the table and leant back in his chair, trying to bring his whirling thoughts into order.

"There now," said Grandfather triumphantly, "you see. Is that the face of a woman who would go from man to man?"

Jocelyn pulled himself together and tried to answer. "Many a good woman, if she is not a Christian bound by the Christian laws of marriage, and if she is proud, will go from man to man."

"Jocelyn!" exclaimed Grandfather.

"Did you," asked Jocelyn, "despise that woman in Ferranti's play? She went from the man who did not want her to the man who did."

"But she was only a figure of fantasy," said Grandfather.

"Not at all. She was a real woman." He tapped the photo. "That woman was this woman."

"What do you mean?"

"Grandfather, did you ever see Ferranti's handwriting?"

"No, dear boy, I can't say I did. The poems of his that he showed me were in print; those same poems that you have lately been reprinting."

"Well, that's it," said Jocelyn, and pushed the photo, lyric upwards, towards Grandfather.

It was a long time before Grandfather could quite understand. First he had to change back again from his looking-at-people spectacles to his reading ones, and then he had to read the lyric over and over again, and then he had to have Jocelyn explain things to him over and over again, but at last he grasped it.

"And to think," he said, "that I saw those two together time and again and it never even occurred to me—it never even occurred to me——"

"How should it?" said Jocelyn. "You had the Welshman Jones firmly fixed in your mind as Henrietta's father and you had no idea that Ferranti had ever had a wife and child. . . . Come to think of it we have no definite evidence even now; only some marked passages in a book, a similarity between handwritings and a conviction, for which we have no real foundation, that *The Minstrel* is biography."

"And in any case," sighed Grandfather, "Ferranti is dead."

"No."

"So you insist, but you can give no reason for your insistence."

Jocelyn fidgeted. He would never be able to tell any-one, not even Felicity, about that experience in the theatre. . . . . No one but Ferranti himself.

"I do not see," said Grandfather sadly, after a little more talk, "that there is anything we can do about it at the moment. We must just wait for guidance. Good night, dear boy."

Left alone Grandfather found it impossible to return to his book. He sat looking at the face of Henrietta's mother, identifying her with the woman of Ferranti's play, thinking about her and now and then turning the photo over to re-read the poem on the back. "There be none of Beauty's daughters with a magic like thee." Perhaps she too, like Byron's Clare, had sat in a boat on an Italian lake and sung to the man who, for the moment only, loved her. The rippling of calm lake water was in the rhythm of the poem, he thought, unstable water that flows away so quickly. . . . Unstable. . . . Unstable. . . . The word seemed to cry out in the night and the Cathedral clock, striking eleven, rang a knell for the passing of love. Poor Clare and poor Miriam. How alike was all human experience. The same bitter thing over and over again. Yet those two lived on, the one in a poem and the other in a play, their hour of love endowed with immortality by the very men who had destroyed it. . . . A paradox, thought Grandfather, lighting his bedroom candle, the perpetual reply of life to death. "This shall die," says death, his sickle laid to a blade of wheat in its glory and the love of a man in his pride; and the fallen seed is a green shoot and the dead love a poem.

IV

"We must wait for guidance," said Grandfather, but Jocelyn, after his latest discoveries, had no intention of doing anything of the sort. Ferranti, he considered, had made a fool of himself for quite long enough. He was now thirty-five, or more, and hadn't behaved rationally yet. Perhaps rationality couldn't be expected of geniuses but they might at least put themselves into a position where they could be guided for their good by their friends.

Jocelyn bribed Bert the draper's son to look after the unfortunate shop, went up to London and put up at a cheap pub near the theatre. He told Grandfather and Felicity that he was going for a few days' fishing with a friend. It was mad of him, Felicity thought, to desert the shop just when it was doing so well, but then in her opinion fishing itself was a form of lunacy. . . . To stand for hour after hour in the rain, in Jocelyn's case chiefly on one leg, like a stork, because of the weakness of the other, gazing at a few yards of sullen water and catching nothing at all, or, worse still, having to eat what you'd caught. . . . That this appealed to Jocelyn only proved to Felicity that even the sanest of human beings have a kink in them somewhere.

Jocelyn salved his conscience by telling himself that he *was* going fishing. . . . For Ferranti.

Of two things about Ferranti he felt certain. He had been in the theatre on the first night and so had been, and perhaps was still, in London, and he wished for some reason to remain in obscurity. And yet if he had seen the play once he would surely want to see it again and yet again for it is not in human nature for a parent not to gloat over the triumph of his own child. If Ferranti was to be found anywhere, argued Jocelyn, it would be, some night or other, in the pit of the Firebird theatre; or refreshing himself later in the bar of the cheap pub. Any hesitation that Jocelyn might have felt in breaking into Ferranti's privacy was banished by the discovery of his fatherhood. . . . The man had no right to continue in desertion.

If it was hot in Torminster it was worse in London. The sky, that was blue in Torminster, was here a dirty yellow hanging low over the roofs, heavy with its weight of thunder. Flies crawled over everything and people in the buses sat well forward, not leaning backwards in case they should stick. The traffic went dead slow and all the milk turned sour. For a week Jocelyn boiled in the gallery, baked in the pit or stewed in his little room at the pub, varying his sufferings now and then by drinking bad beer in the bar. But he never saw, either in the theatre or the pub or the streets, the tall thin man who lived and died nightly upon the stage of the Firebird.

Hot and tired and sleepless Jocelyn began to feel as though he were in a nightmare, pursuing down endless corridors a mysterious something that was nothing but a figment of his own brain. Had Ferranti ever existed, he wondered, or was he something that they had all imagined, the spirit of man that had no tangible existence? Next Wednesday, he decided, he would give up, and on Tuesday night he went to see *The Minstrel*, by Gabriel Ferranti, for the last time.

As usual, he stood in the pit queue, his eyes going now only mechanically up and down the line of figures. He was abominably dressed, with his hat pulled over his eyes, so that Felicity as she passed him on her way to the stage door did not recognize him. . . . And he hardly recognized her. . . . She looked thin and hollow-eyed, her vitality drained from her by hard work and the heat. How much longer was this wretched play going on, Jocelyn asked himself savagely? How much longer before the figure of Ferranti was no longer between them and they could get away somewhere together? Somewhere cool and quiet where he could fish for proper fish and she could laugh at him for it.

He found a seat in the stuffiest part of the pit and sat wedged between a stout lady eating oranges and a stout gentleman eating bananas. Once more, and for the last time, he watched the curtain rise upon that dim wood, with the figure of the Minstrel splashed in brilliant yellow and red upon its mystery, and once again he heard that wonderful tune stealing out into the theatre, weaving its spell over the hot, silent multitude. But it wove no spell over Jocelyn. Familiarity and heat had bred contempt and he could no longer find anything in this play but boredom. The first act seemed to him crude and the second act tedious. Even the third act, which had given him those strange moments of poignant experience and had never after-wards failed to move him, left him to-night quite cold. Felicity's vivacity seemed forced and her voice not quite true. Oliver, by this time sick to death of his part, was over-acting and Flossie, who had never at any time been equal to Henrietta, looked like a congealed suet dumpling.

In the interval before the last act Jocelyn decided that he had had enough of this boring play and rose to go but the lady of the oranges, over whose bulk he would have had to climb to reach the exit, gave him a look of such hatred upon perceiving his intentions that he sat down again. . . . He shut his eyes and prepared to drowse through it, for his head was aching with the heat and the menace of thunder.

But gradually, as the act went on and the shadows of death crept nearer to the Minstrel, he found his apathy banished by a growing feeling of horror. "I cannot get back," cried the Minstrel on the stage. Until to-night Jocelyn had felt it to be the cry of every man longing to re-live his life in the light of the wisdom that is his in the shadow of death, but to-night that cry came to him with a quite different meaning. . . . No, it did not come to him for he was crying it himself. . . . "I cannot get back." He had left a certain mode of life and chosen another and between that life and this a river ran, as impassable as the river of death. And now he wanted to get back to the world he had left, but he couldn't. He wanted to get back madly, desperately, but he couldn't, not even though he knew that the river was nothing but the inhibitions of his own mind. . . . A man who has lived utterly alone for a long time ceases to be normal. A solitary who has cut himself off from human contact comes to have a terror of his fellow humans. A coward who has abandoned all responsibility is afraid to shoulder it again. A failure cannot trust to success. A sufferer who has been broken by life dare not be friends with it again. . . . It was only his own mind that kept him back but a man's mind can be his greatest friend or his greatest enemy, according as it serves or binds his will, and his was his enemy. Its terrors controlled him. He was bound hand and foot by his own weakness. It was no use. He was as good as dead. "I cannot get back."

Darkness blotted out the scene on the stage, the lamenting music broke into the dirge and the first peal of thunder rolled over London. Then the lights went up and there was a wild stampede for the exits, each member of the audience intent upon nothing but getting home before the storm broke.

It would have been impossible for Jocelyn to linger in the theatre. He was lifted almost off his feet by the surging crowd and before he knew where he was he had passed

through the few streets that separate theatre-land from
the Embankment and was standing, as he had stood after
the first night of *The Minstrel*, by the river.

v

Gradually he came to himself. . . . It had happened
again. . . . Once more Ferranti's thoughts had been his.
As before he had understood his remorse so now he understood the mental chains that had imprisoned him. The
poor wretch could not move. Misery had become apathy
and apathy had brought the inevitable paralysis of the
will.

Fury with himself gripped Jocelyn. Ferranti must
have been in the theatre and he, Jocelyn, had not even
attempted to find him, instead he had given himself up
to the crowd to be carried whither they would, as help-
less in his bewilderment as Ferranti himself. . . . Somehow it had never even occurred to Jocelyn that he would
not recognize Ferranti if he saw him. Ferranti was one
of the best friends that he had and one does not fail to
recognize one's friends.

For some while the lightning had been flickering over
London, passing like a searchlight over the sky and caressing the water with waves of light. Now a puff of hot
wind sent the scraps of straw and paper whirling over
the pavement, sounding in the darkness like an army
of gnomes scampering to shelter. A few great drops
of rain splashed down and it seemed that London turned
over like a fevered sleeper and gasped, praying for relief.

Jocelyn turned away from the river with some wild
idea of going back to the theatre but he had not gone
far when the rain began, coming down as though the
bottom had fallen out of an overhead reservoir. Turning

up the collar of his coat he hurried up one of the steep streets that lead citywards from the Embankment and collided violently at a corner with a flying figure. The stranger swore and Jocelyn, sent spinning into the gutter, was not behindhand with retort.

"Look where you're going, can't you!" snapped the stranger.

"Look yourself," said Jocelyn, and in getting to his feet nearly fell again, for his sudden journey to the gutter had twisted his lame leg.

"Are you drunk, or what?" asked the stranger nastily.

"I've a game leg," said Jocelyn, enraged, "and if you have to cart me home it's your own fault."

The crispness of his irritated utterance was that of complete sobriety and the stranger, already poised for further flight, thought better of it and came nearer. "Far to go?" he asked.

"A goodish way," said Jocelyn. "I'll get a cab."

"You can't. They're all gone by this time." He paused, apparently fighting some sort of battle with himself. "Better come to my room and shelter," he growled, with a savagery that made Jocelyn think it cost him as much to offer shelter as it would have cost a miser to offer gold.

Yet Jocelyn yielded. The pain in his leg was bad and the weather worse and he wanted nothing but a chair and a roof over his head.

They were in a street of mean shops. The stranger fitted a key into a door and opened it and they were in a dark passage. To their left a door led into a newspaper shop and in front of them were rickety stairs.

"I can't get up there," said Jocelyn firmly but the stranger, without a word, flung a strong arm round him and heaved him upwards. It was a short flight leading to a dusty store-room over the shop with a small room behind that was the stranger's own. A flash of lightning revealed it as they came in, with its bare floor and walls and broken window, its camp bed, deal table, wooden chair, tin wash-basin and shelf of books.

The stranger deposited Jocelyn wordlessly and rudely upon the bed, lit the evil-smelling gas jet, sat himself down on his chair, which lacked a leg, and gazed at his find.

Jocelyn realized that he was being looked at as though he were a new kind of wild beast, looked at with both curiosity and fear. His captor was a tall man, and very thin, yet he looked physically strong and Jocelyn remembered that his arm had felt like steel. His dark hair was streaked with grey and his sallow, seamed face roughened by exposure to weather. It was a sensitive face, though weak and a little effeminate, and made a strange setting for his dark, haunted eyes, the eyes of a man who is perpetually seeing a nightmare. His clothes were the clothes of a man in the street, and he had a scarf twisted round his throat to hide the absence of a collar, yet his hands were well tended and his face well shaven and his voice, when he had condescended to speak, had been the voice of a gentleman. The queer lighting of the room, flickering gaslight and forked lightning, was the lighting of a nightmare and seemed to bring the queer face now very close to his own and now very far away, like the faces that waver backwards and forwards in dreams. Jocelyn, tired and confused and in pain, had never before felt so unreal, so utterly unable to grasp the situation in which he found himself. The silence between them deepened and they seemed to be drifting apart. He made a desperate effort to say something.

"Awfully good of you to give me shelter."

The stranger opened and shut his mouth like a fish but if he said anything a peal of thunder drowned it.

"You've made this room nice," said Jocelyn. It was quite true. It was scrupulously clean and the cotton quilt on the bed was actually pretty. A curtain in the corner hid the cooking utensils and the few books on the shelf had the upright, happy look of books that are dusted and cared for every day.

"I sell papers in the shop below. The boss lets me have this room cheap. He's one of the few really decent human beings I've ever met." The information was jerked out with effort and was evidently a desperate attempt to be courteous. As in all first intercourse between shy strangers each difficult sentence that they spoke seemed a rope flung across the chasm that separated them from each other. Jocelyn pulled himself together and leant forward. He was drawn to this man and he wanted to bridge the chasm. He in his turn flung across his information.

"We're much in the same line of business. I keep a bookshop."

"In London?"

"No, in a Cathedral town called Torminster. . . . My name is Jocelyn Irvin."

"My name is Richardson."

The room was momentarily dim and the stranger's face in shadow. There was a long, difficult pause. "You write for the papers," he said at last, and his voice seemed curiously dulled. "I've sold the papers in which your articles appear. You write for the *Evening Journal*."

"Not now," said Jocelyn. "I wrote a few articles for it on Gabriel Ferranti before his play appeared."

"I read them."

"Did you like them?"

"No."

Intercourse seemed again at a standstill and Jocelyn made another effort. "When we collided with each other

I'd just been down to the river for a breath of fresh air after, I should think, my tenth visit to the Firebird Theatre."

"Do you care for that rotten play so much then?"

"Yes. Have you seen it?"

"Twice."

That laconic "twice" was like the crack of a whip scourging Jocelyn's mind to attention. His intuition, upon which he had relied, had been dulled by the confusion of their meeting but now it was in command again. He gripped the edge of the bed with both hands and steadied himself. . . . He must go carefully.

"To-night?" he asked casually.

"To-night and the first night."

"It's curious," said Jocelyn, "how one can feel friends with a man one has never met. I like that fellow Ferranti. Personally I don't believe him dead."

Again came that pause. "Had he been living," said the dulled voice again, "wouldn't he have turned up? He's the fashion now and most men like being made a fool of. . . . And then there's money owing to him, and most men care for money."

"I think I can understand," said Jocelyn, "how a man of his type might not turn up. An unpractical solitary who has suffered gets afraid of practicality, of responsibility, even the responsibility of money, of the whole damn machinery of living. Worst of all he loses his faith in his fellow men." He glanced up sharply at his companion. "You ought to understand that. You said just now that your boss was one of the few decent human beings you'd ever met. . . . That doesn't sound like a man who has much faith in humanity."

The other man's face looked as though carved out of stone. There was no expression in it, and no life.

"That's wrong, of course," said Jocelyn. "We're all

too apt to think that things are as we feel them to be, forgetting that they have an objective value apart from what we feel about them. An embittered mind colours the world black for its owner yet that does not alter the fact that the world is a treasure house of beauty and love."

"Also of disease and loss and pain. Your outlook is the outlook of youth, to which one can never get back."

"'I cannot get back,'" quoted Jocelyn. "The Minstrel in Ferranti's play was mistaken, for it is possible to be born again as a little child. Many men and women have been, though I grant you they have been the greatest of us. The Minstrel made the mistake of choosing death rather than birth. . . . It is easier of course."

"Easier?"

"The dying man, though he may suffer, only has to let go, while the child in the womb has to fight for its life."

The difficult, painful dialogue, that had almost taken on the quality of a wrestling bout, ceased for a moment, for both men were exhausted. The storm was passing, only a mutter of thunder left of it. The lightning and the rain had ceased and through the broken window Jocelyn could see two stars. A coolness stole in from the night and he took great breaths of it.

"In that first birth," said the stranger hoarsely, "the fighting child has every help that love can give."

"And so has the fighting man."

"No. He's utterly alone."

"No man is utterly alone. Even Hamlet had his Horatio."

The stranger gave a sudden movement. "What makes you mention Hamlet?" he asked.

"I should never have found or re-written Ferranti's play had it not been for Hamlet."

"It was you who re-wrote it? It was you?" The

question flashed out suddenly, the man's painful reserve breaking for a moment.

"I'll tell you," said Jocelyn, and quietly and steadily he told the whole tale of his life at Torminster. Only of Henrietta he made no mention. It was too early for that, he thought, it would only confuse the issue. When he had finished there was silence, broken by the clocks of London striking one.

"It is morning now," sighed Jocelyn. "A new day."

"Hadn't you better go now?" asked the stranger harshly. "The storm's over."

"These last ten days," said Jocelyn, "I've dropped right out of normal life. I've been living at a disreputable pub and haunting the pit and the gallery of the Firebird."

"Why?"

"Looking for Ferranti."

"You would not know him if you saw him."

"One knows one's friends. If not at first sight, then very soon."

"Well?"

"We are both, so to speak, out of life now. I don't think I want to return to it unless you come with me, Ferranti."

Ferranti jumped up, his broken chair crashing behind him.

"Now that's nonsense," said Jocelyn sharply. "You knew quite well, some while back, that I knew you."

Ferranti leant against the wall. He looked beaten and hopeless and Jocelyn felt almost overwhelmed by the mixture of pity and exasperation that were always to be part of his love for this man. "Well?" he asked.

"I can't," said Ferranti.

"I am not going back to Torminster without you."

"You have no right to force me," said Ferranti fiercely. "Isn't my life my own?"

"Yes," said Jocelyn slowly, "I suppose it is and, as you say, I have no right to force you." He sat silent for a little, thinking, then coming to a decision he rose stiffly to his feet. Ferranti's eyes, he noticed, were following his every movement with close attention. "I'll go back to Torminster," he said, "and wait for you there. . . . And I'll keep your secret from the world at large. . . . Come to me if you want to, if not, don't. I suppose we can find some way of getting the money you've earned to you without your reappearance. . . . You've got to decide between birth and death and if you choose death you'll be a criminal fool."

"My choice concerns no one but myself," snapped Ferranti.

"I don't agree with you. At every death there are mourners. You might remember that old man, my grandfather. . . . And I've always felt so sorry for Horatio."

At the door he stopped and held out his hand. Ferranti took it reluctantly yet at their grip it seemed to Jocelyn that the chasm between them was bridged.

"If you don't believe in re-birth," he said, "why did you mark that passage in your Shelley? 'Drive my dead thoughts over the universe, like withered leaves to quicken a new birth.' I tried to do what you told me."

He dropped Ferranti's hand and stumbled painfully down the dark stairs. Ferranti did not offer to come with him and had savagely crashed the door shut behind him.

Next day, travelling back to Torminster with a splitting headache, he felt that the whole thing had been a dream. That queer midnight interview in a thunderstorm had assumed the vagueness of a dream and he could not even remember what he had said. . . . Whatever he had said he was sure it was entirely wrong. . . . He had made a hash of the whole thing and Ferranti was lost for the second time.

He was so wretched that he could hardly respond to the jovial greeting of Mr. Gotobed and climbed into the bus as though it were a hearse.

By nine o'clock that night it was all over Torminster that poor Captain Irvin had caught no fish at all upon his holiday.

CHAPTER XIV

I

LATE September, the season of Torminster's greatest loveliness, was with them again and the city seemed to Jocelyn to have become royal in its beauty. Golden elms and scarlet dahlias wove a garment fit for a king and the Cathedral, towering against the brilliant blue sky, gave to its lovers who looked upon it that gift of self-forgetfulness that is at the same time both awe and peace.

Jocelyn, standing one late afternoon at the door of his shop and looking across the golden Market Place to the three grey towers that rose above the old roofs, realized with a shock of surprise that for a few minutes the anxiety that tormented him had vanished, leaving his mind as serene as the beauty he looked at. Very lovely, he thought, are the sudden moments of relief that come in the midst of strain, those moments of forgetfulness when we are "teased out of thought" by a bird or a flower or the sight of old roofs in the sun; lovely though so transient, the reversal of those brief moments of misery that visit us even in the midst of joy.

For Jocelyn was in a pitiable condition of worry. Last night the run of *The Minstrel* had ended. It had played for five months to full houses and then suddenly failed. It had appealed to that limited number of theatregoers who turn to the theatre for artistic and mental satisfaction but it had not appealed beyond them to that larger multitude who want amusement only. . . . And so it was over. . . .

But nevertheless it was reckoned a success, one of those plays with the stuff of eternity in them that are revived again and again.

And this evening an exhausted Felicity was returning to Torminster to recuperate.

Yet Jocelyn, with success in work and love both within his reach, was miserable, for Ferranti had not turned up. All day and a good part of the night he cursed himself. . . . He should have refused to leave Ferranti. . . . He had acted on intuition and his intuition here had failed him. He had thought on that nightmare night that if Ferranti was to make a success of new life he must come to it of his own free will, not of coercion. What we are made to do we seldom do well, what we do of our own choice we make a success of for very pride. So he had argued; and he had not doubted that Ferranti, once he knew that he had friends who would help him to break his chains, would choose life rather than death. . . . For surely he must want to make that pattern. . . . Well, he had argued wrong. Ferranti's chains had proved too much for him.

Realizing this he had gone up to London only a week ago and had made his way to the newspaper shop, but a stranger had served him with the *Daily Mail*. As he expected, the man called Richardson had gone away, leaving no address. He dared not tell Grandfather, the old man would be heartbroken at their failure. He would be able to tell Felicity perhaps, but not Grandfather.

The silence was broken by the rattle of wheels and the empty bus swung round the corner and disappeared down the High Street, Mr. Gotobed cracking his whip and singing his favourite song, "Gaily the Troubadour." He was going to meet the London train which was what, thought Jocelyn, he himself should be doing, for on the

London train would be Felicity. . . . Yet he had no heart
to meet Felicity. . . . The acknowledgment of love, which
should have been so sweet, would now have a flavour
of bitterness in it, and a ghost would be between them
always.

He went back to the shop and began dusting the books.
On his shelves were twelve shop volumes of Shakespeare,
six of Shelley and one only of the unpopular Byron.
Never, thought Jocelyn, would he be able to look those
three friends in the face again. They had tried so hard
to help him and by his own idiocy he had rendered their
help futile. Never again would he be able to endure to
read Hamlet. "The rest is silence" was an epitaph that
seemed to him to be written on his own heart.

He dusted with a sort of concentrated hate, directed
against himself, until he heard the wheels of the returning
bus. He peeped over the books in his bow-window,
expecting to see it swerve round and drive towards the
Close, but instead it clattered magnificently round the
Market Place and drew up with a flourish at his very
door. Mr. Gotobed, seeing Jocelyn through the window,
hummed "Love's Young Dream" and lowered one eyelid, then leapt from the box and assisted Felicity to alight.

"Take my boxes to the Close, please, Gotobed," said
Felicity, "and tell Mrs. Jameson I'm walking up immediately."

"I wouldn't so perjure meself, miss," said Mr. Gotobed
meaningly. "But I'll tell them you're to be expected in
an hour or two." And turning to Jocelyn, who had come
out, he lowered the other eyelid.

"Gotobed," said Felicity hotly, when he had clattered
off singing "Drink to me only with thine eyes," "is becoming impossible."

"He's privileged," said Jocelyn. "He and the Dean
are the Punch and Judy of Torminster, our mascots so to

L

speak. They both know that without them, trying as they are, we should be desolate. . . . Come in and have tea."

"Haven't you had it yet? It's six o'clock."

"I forgot."

Martha had put Jocelyn's tea ready in the sitting-room an hour ago and the tea, as on the day when Henrietta had tea with Jocelyn, was in consequence very strong. There was no bread and butter, for Jocelyn considered bread and butter overrated, but there were still chocolate biscuits in the tin with Windsor Castle on it.

They sat by the window and Felicity poured out. To be sitting together in this beloved little house that was now, to both of them, home, was comforting but not the joy that it should have been.

"Do you remember," said Felicity, looking through the window at Jocelyn's trim dahlias and chrysanthemums, "the first day we sat here together? The garden was in such a mess then that the flowers and weeds and apple trees seemed all twisted together, but now you've got them all disentangled. . . . You're a wonderful disentangler."

"I don't think," said Jocelyn with difficulty, "that any of my disentangling has been very successful," and bending his head he gloomily examined his nails, a habit with all reserved Englishmen when trying to express themselves.

Felicity impulsively thrust her chocolate biscuit down Mixed Biscuits' gaping and expectant throat and ran round the table to sit on the arm of Jocelyn's chair.

"But we've done all we could," she comforted. "We've done what we said we would, we've made Ferranti live again."

"No."

"I didn't mean in a physical sense. We can't do that when he's dead."

"He isn't dead."

"So you say, but that's just your nonsense, Jocelyn."

Slowly, with close attention to his nails, Jocelyn told her, while she helped him with the unobtrusive little remarks and questions with which she always abstracted information or guided a conversation. When he had finished he sat silent, waiting for her blame. Instead she flung her hat into a corner of the room and slithered off the arm of the chair on to his sound knee.

"I should have done the same," she announced.

There is nothing more consoling than to be told by someone whose judgment you trust that they would have done the same. Instantly you feel that they *have* done the same and that the thing is as much their fault as yours.

"But isn't it hateful to have lost him like this, Felicity?"

"Hateful, but it's his own fault."

"I must have gone wrong somewhere or I wouldn't have failed."

"If your right, meeting another man's wrong, is deflected and goes astray that doesn't make your right any the less right," consoled Felicity.

"Perhaps not, but the thing has still gone astray."

"Astray, but not lost. . . . And in any case, even if Ferranti does not come back, he knows now that he has achieved something. I should imagine, Jocelyn, that whatever a man might have to suffer in after years the knowledge that he'd once done something good would make life seem worth while."

"Yes," said Jocelyn. "Perhaps."

Felicity turned the conversation to all that *The Minstrel* had done for its other makers. Nigel Compton's name was made, Oliver had won fresh laurels and was more conceited than ever and Miles Harpenden's temper was much improved by success.

"And you?" asked Jocelyn.

"*The Minstrel* has done a lot for me," said Felicity gravely. "All this responsibility and hard work has taught me to know myself better. You know what I mean. I know better where I'm strong and where I'm weak. I've got both more confidence and more humility. . . . And you?"

"If Ferranti would only come back I should be happier than I ever believed possible."

"He will yet. I feel in my bones that he will. . . . Now I must go. Come and see me to-morrow afternoon."

Martha, peering round the door to see if they had finished tea, noted where Felicity had chosen to sit. When Felicity had gone and Jocelyn was back in the shop she washed up the tea things in less time than it takes to tell, donned her bonnet, her jet trimmed mantle and her gloves and ran across the Market Place to tell Mary. . . . By nine o'clock that night it was all over Torminster that Jocelyn and Felicity were to be married at Christmas, and Mr. Bell even went so far as to order a fresh supply of grey silk and white velvet for Mrs. Fordyce's and Mrs. Jameson's dresses for the wedding.

II

Jocelyn, unaware of the expense to which he was putting Mr. Bell, went sadly to bed. He was not cheered by the conviction of Felicity's bones that Ferranti would come back, for like most female convictions it seemed to him to lack foundation. In fact so little cheered was he that he deliberately, as he lay down to sleep, gave up hope. . . . Useless now to watch the post, useless to listen for the step of a tall, thin man on the pavement outside the shop. . . . Because of his very hopelessness he fell at once, for the first time in all these anxious weeks, into a dreamless sleep.

So deep was it that when the barking of Mixed Biscuits woke him he felt as though he were being dragged up from the depths of the sea. Heavy with sleep he raised himself on an elbow and listened stupidly. What had disturbed Mixed Biscuits? The night was dark in his curtained room and quite silent until one o'clock struck from the Cathedral. "The ghost," he muttered unthinkingly. "Shut up, Mixed Biscuits," and dropped down on his pillows again, his eyes closing.

Then an unmistakable sound jerked them open. . . . Someone was knocking at the front door. . . . In a moment his sleep had fallen from him as though it were a cloak and he had bounded out of bed and hurried to one of the unused bedrooms that looked out on the Market Place. He opened the window noiselessly. In the faint starlight he could just make out a tall figure propped against the bow-window beside the door. As he looked, it straightened sagging limbs and turned wearily away.

"Hi! Stop, Ferranti!" shouted Jocelyn, and it turned back silently.

When Jocelyn opened the door he found Ferranti leaning against the bow-window again. "At last," said Jocelyn. "Come in, man."

Ferranti slouched after him down the passage and extended his long limbs in the arm-chair while Jocelyn lit the lamp. He looked utterly disreputable and was grey with dust from head to foot.

"Walked," he explained briefly.

"From London?"

"Yes."

"Will you promise not to disappear," asked Jocelyn, "if I go and get some clothes on and heat up some coffee?"

"Get the fire going if you like," volunteered Ferranti.

"Right. You'll find wood and paper in that cupboard."

"I know. That's where I always kept it."

When Jocelyn came back with coffee and food he found Ferranti crouched over a fire of yellow flames. The scent of apple-wood filled the little room, as it had done when Ferranti first spoke to him in the words of Hamlet, and it seemed very natural to see him sitting there; he was only the presence that had always been in the house made visible at last.

Jocelyn sat silent while Ferranti satisfied a ravenous hunger. A curious sense of peace had descended on the room. Mixed Biscuits who, after his first protest, had taken Ferranti quite for granted, was lying on the hearth-rug gazing unblinkingly at the fire. Was it, Jocelyn wondered, because the three of them would sit like this on so many nights to come that it seemed to him they had sat like this before? So often a certainty of what is to come makes one feel that it has already happened.

"What next?" asked Jocelyn. "Bed, or a pipe?"

"A pipe," smiled Ferranti.

He was looking very different, Jocelyn noticed. He was no longer the haunted creature of their first meeting. He had the calm look of a man who has fought and won a battle and his eyes, happily bright in spite of his fatigue, were exactly like Henrietta's.

"After you'd gone," he told Jocelyn, "I nearly went mad with indecision. It's useless to try and explain. Normal people like yourself could never understand how, under certain circumstances, one's will can become useless. Any sort of action, even the action you want to take, seems impossible."

"I understand," said Jocelyn and remembering those few awful moments during the last act of *The Minstrel* he did understand.

"I left the paper shop and took to the streets," went

on Ferranti, "for it seemed to me that I couldn't think when I had work to do. I just wandered about all day and slept at doss-houses at night."

"Well?"

"Then I saw in a paper that *The Minstrel* was coming to an end and so I went to see it for the last time. I realized, as I don't think I had quite realized before, how amazingly well you had re-written it. I couldn't imagine how you had managed, so to speak, so to suit your stride to mine. . . . It seemed to me that there must be some very close link between us."

"There is. Friendship is an unexplainable thing."

"Then I remembered what you'd said. 'I've always felt so sorry for Horatio.' Somehow I couldn't let you down. . . . I had to walk because I'd spent most of my money. I'm sorry I'm in such a mess."

"You'd better have my bed for the rest of the night," said Jocelyn. "To-morrow we'll talk."

III

To-morrow was, by the mercy of Providence, a Sunday, and also by the mercy of Providence Martha did not come on Sundays, or Ferranti's return would have been all over Torminster within five minutes. No one would have guessed, looking at the shuttered front of the house with the green door, that in the garden behind it, hidden behind the ramparts of the hollyhocks, two men were having one of those intimate talks that are achieved only once or twice in a lifetime.

"What made you mark those passages in your books?" asked Jocelyn. "The Hamlet and the Shelley?"

"I did it on the night before I left Torminster. I was in a queer state, partly physical illness, partly despair at the uselessness of my life and its irreparable mistakes. I meant to kill myself, but not in Torminster for fear of upsetting your grandfather. To steady myself, that last night before I left Torminster, I began reading Hamlet. There's nothing so steadying, when you're in pieces, as reading something fine that you know very well. It seemed to me that night that Hamlet was myself; all that he felt I felt. . . . The paralysis, the indecision, the torment, the disgust with life, the knowledge that one's misery is caused by one's own mind. 'The o'ergrowth of some complexion, oft breaking down the pales and forts of reason.' The longing to get rid of this self that so poisons the universe. . . . I marked the passages as I came to them and when I came to the last passage of all, the command to Horatio, I marked that out of sheer envy. Hamlet could leave behind him at death someone who could explain to the world that he hadn't meant to make such a mess of things. 'Let my disclaiming from a purposed evil free me so far in your most generous thoughts.' He would not have done what he did if all had not been 'so ill about his heart' . . . But I had no one. . . . Or so I thought."

"And the Shelley?"

"Then I read a little Shelley. I was taking a last leave of my books, you see, because I was leaving everything I had behind me to pay my debts. I marked the 'West Wind' passage for the same reason—envy. Shelley could believe in new birth, I couldn't."

"You didn't connect that verse with the play you had written, as I did?"

"No. I wrote *The Minstrel* just before I left Torminster in a fit of remorse and then flung it aside. It never occurred to me that it was any use."

"Why didn't you kill yourself after all?"

"Your grandfather. We'd always argued together and though I was far too apathetic to be convinced by any of

his arguments I remembered them because of my affection
for him. One of them was that nothing whatsoever,
not even the existence of God to His lovers, can be
proved, but that every man, if he is to live at all finely,
must deliberately adopt certain assertions as true, and
those assertions should, for the sake of the enrichment
of the human race, always be creative ones. He may,
as life goes on, modify his beliefs, but he must never
modify them on the side of destruction. It may be
difficult, in the face of the problem of human suffering,
to believe in God, he said, but if you destroy God you
do not solve your problem but merely leave yourself
alone with it. . . . A ghastly loneliness. . . . The same,
he said, with your belief in your own soul. To deny it is
to degrade yourself to the level of an animal and to lose
your reverence for the human race; for if man's existence
is to be measured by the span of this life only then he is a
paltry, inconsiderable thing. What he said about creation
haunted me when I wanted to 'shuffle off this mortal coil'
for I had flattered myself that as a writer I was a creator,
if an unsuccessful one, and it seemed to me that in crush-
ing out my life, as I would have crushed a wasp or a worm
on the garden path, I should be denying all that my life
had hitherto stood for. . . . I don't say I was in a state of
mind to remember, as I am remembering now, his reason-
ing, but his parrot cry of 'never destroy' was like a bell
ringing in my head, and I didn't kill myself. . . . Instead
I made a little money as a waiter in a restaurant and went
back to Italy, where I used to live."

"But you didn't stay there," said Jocelyn.

"No. I found I hated it because it was the scene of
the worst of my sins. You know all about that. It's in
The Minstrel."

"You mean your treatment of your wife?"

"She was never my wife. At that time I believed that

L*

freedom consisted in avoiding all shackles of any sort, and so I avoided the shackles of marriage. It was one of those undisciplined love affairs that burn like a bonfire and then die." He smiled affectionately at Jocelyn. "I don't think you would ever love like that and your way is the more admirable, the way that I admire. 'Give me that man that is not passion's slave, and I will wear him in my heart's core, ay, in my heart of heart, as I do thee.' Didn't Hamlet say that to Horatio?"

"And you had a child?" murmured Jocelyn, approaching the kernel of their conversation with a beating heart.

"Yes, a girl. I didn't want her, for I'd no use for children in those days, but Miriam did. Gabrielle was only a year old when she and Miriam left me. . . . Now that I'm middle-aged I care for children very much. . . . One changes."

"And you never knew what happened to them?"

"No. They went to Wales I believe."

"But why didn't you look for them? The marked passages in your Byron showed that you regretted them."

"So you found those too? . . . Miriam had left me in anger and I had no legal rights over either her or the child. But I would give a good deal to know what happened to them."

"Later," said Jocelyn huskily, "Miriam Raymond went to London and died there."

Ferranti went white under his tan. "What?" he whispered.

Jocelyn, examining his nails, told the story. Ferranti listened, immovable. Then he got up abruptly and went down to the bottom of the garden, returned to gasp out a few questions and returned again.

Jocelyn went indoors and waited patiently.

When Ferranti at last came in every emotion seemed to have left him except an almost comic dismay at the thought of his own fatherhood. "God in heaven," he gasped, "I'm no more capable of being a parent than an earwig."

"They're excellent parents," said Jocelyn. "The best parents in the insect world. Didn't you know that?"

"What am I to do?" moaned Ferranti.

"Didn't you like Henrietta?" asked Jocelyn.

"Like her? I adored her. But I'm no more capable of bringing her up than—than—to begin with I've got wandering in my blood now. I'm incapable of staying in one place."

"You couldn't take her from Grandfather while he lives," consoled Jocelyn, "and when he's dead shall I go halves with you in Henrietta?"

"What do you mean?"

"Has it ever struck you," smiled Jocelyn, "that Hamlet and Horatio together make one extremely fine man? Horatio was a dull sort of fellow but he had the stability that Hamlet needed, while Hamlet had the fire and spirit that Horatio lacked. Why shouldn't you and I combine?"

"But how?"

"I am hoping to get married. This shall be our home, and yours and Henrietta's, and you shall come and go as you please. I will give Henrietta the stability that stays at home and you will give her the Puck-like fire and spirit that girdles the earth in forty minutes."

"And you've arranged all this with your unfortunate prospective bride?"

"No, I haven't proposed to her yet."

"Well, I've heard it said that the more a man demands of a wretched woman the more she loves him but I think the whole situation ought, in fairness, to be explained very carefully prior to proposal."

"She knows that marriage with me is imminent, in fact she's practically suggested it herself several times, but we were waiting till you came back from the dead. She has worked for you as hard as I have. She is Felicity Summers."

Ferranti gasped. "The girl who played the part of Miriam? That girl who was Henrietta's mother?" He was silent a moment. "If you devote yourself to those two," he murmured, "you will be making atonement for my sins."

"*You* will," said Jocelyn softly, "if we are one."

They were silent for a long time in the flower-scented room.

"What does it feel like," asked Jocelyn at last, "to be born again?"

Ferranti looked at him with one of his flashing, charming smiles. "I feel as a little child does," he said, "I'm as scared of what's in front of me as a child climbing the dark stairs to bed but yet at the same time the world looks to me as it does to children, amazingly bright and shining and full of wonder. Death has cleared my eyes I suppose. To the dying, the sky is a foul and pestilential congregation of vapours, but to the newly born it is a brave, o'erhanging firmament."

IV

At lunch-time, Ferranti having eaten the Sunday supplies overnight, Jocelyn went into The Green Dragon to purchase a loaf of bread, a German sausage and a pint of beer.

"May I, sir," said Mr. Wilks, wrapping up the sausage, "congratulate you."

"What on?" asked Jocelyn.

"Your engagement, sir. The happy event is to take place at Christmas, I understand."

"Oh, er, yes, thank you," murmured Jocelyn, and grasping the beer and the sausage he fled, leaving the bread behind him.

After lunch he excused himself to Ferranti. "I'll have to leave you this afternoon," he said. "It's highly necessary that I should become engaged to Felicity immediately."

"Between lunch and tea?"

"Yes. You see, Torminster has decided that we shall be married at Christmas and I think that Felicity had better hear about it from me first. Torminster is like that; it is a city that relieves one of all personal responsibility. It decided that I should open a bookshop, so I did. Now it says I am to marry at Christmas, so I shall. . . . Good-bye."

He found Felicity stretched in a deck-chair on the moss-grown path under the nut-trees in Mrs. Jameson's vegetable garden. It was the same path where they had once walked up and down and talked about the bookshop. The moss was as thick and green as ever and the inter-laced leaves all round them were still like lacquered screens put up to ensure their privacy. Stirring and shifting in the sunshine they made a diapered pattern all over Felicity's white dress.

She was lying with her eyes shut, letting the peace of the garden sink into her very bones. Gone was the roar of London and the turmoil of the theatre that had been with her for months. There was no sound now but the rustling of the leaves, the chirp of a robin who was hop-ping up and down beside her, and the conversation of philosophic blackbirds in the currant-bushes outside her leafy bower. Yet, in spite of the robin, she felt lonely. Inside her there was a little room and it was empty and cold. There were lots of other rooms in the house of her life, full of warm fires and laughter and singing, but nothing that happened there could make any lasting difference to the chill of the little room because it was a thing apart. As she lay under the green leaves, half asleep and dreaming, it seemed to her that she was standing in this room feeling very forlorn and listening to the chirp of a robin on the window-sill outside. Then some-one rattled the latch, the door opened a little way, creaking and grinding because this was the first time that it had been opened, and a rosy light came flooding through the crack. The difference that it made was extraordinary. The room that had been cold and grey, like a garden in the rain, began to change. The floor became golden and the ceiling rosy and the walls were lined with a rainbow, while in the grey ash on the hearth geranium-coloured flames unfolded. The glow only lasted a minute, and Felicity's dream only lasted a minute. Then she opened her eyes and found Jocelyn looking down at her.

"Felicity, you must marry me," he announced. The proposal was more abrupt than was usual in Edwardian days but the storm of his eagerness was carrying him along so quickly that he could not stop to look for words.

Felicity sat up and looked at him, rubbing the sleep out of her eyes. He was standing very erect, with triumph blazing in his eyes.

"Ferranti has come back," she said.

"Last night. There's nothing between us now. Will you marry me?"

"Of course, but I can't get out of this deck-chair."

He pulled her up so that she stood beside him on the moss that nature had so thoughtfully arranged as a carpet for them in their hour. Only the robin saw them but the blackbirds outside heard them laughing softly in pride and joy. . . . Laugh, said the philosophic black-birds, and remember your laughter, for it does not come again.

V

Sunday afternoon in the Torminster Close was devoted
to the consideration of religious problems with the eyes
shut. It was not "the thing" to pay calls in Torminster
on Sunday afternoon, so that even the maids whose
Sunday in it was, could, when they had washed up the
dinner things, safely doze off in the kitchen rocking-
chair in happy certainty that the front-door bell would
not ring.

Grandmother, on Sunday afternoons, always retired to
her room with her spectacles and a book of sermons.
Arrived there this Sunday she drew her curtains, removed
her grey silk dress and her lace cap, wrapped herself in
her pink shawl and climbed thankfully upon her bed. . . .
And indeed she needed her rest for she had already, at
the age of eighty-one, attended two services and would
attend yet another before the day was over. . . . She
plumped up her pillows, tied a scarf over her head to keep
her corkscrew curls in place, adjusted her spectacles and
opened her book at a sermon on hell.

Grandmother believed firmly in hell and deplored the
modern tendency to think that there was no such place.
She took her Bible literally and moreover she had a tidy
mind and liked to bestow everyone in their right place,
and hell was the only place she could think of for certain
historical persons she was able to mention by name.
Caligula, for instance, and Judas, and the Borgia creature
who poisoned the wine of those he did not care for.
Grandfather once pleaded weakly that doubtless there
was great good in Caligula but when asked sharply
"What?" was unable to make a satisfactory reply. There
were other people, such as the young man Ferranti, whom
Grandmother was unable to place, and this worried her,

for she was reluctant to send a young man who had drunk tea with her in her own drawing-room down below, and yet where else could he go to, heathen that he was, and a great trouble first and last to her poor husband? Grandmother was unwilling to believe in purgatory, for Roman Catholics believed in it and she did not hold with Roman Catholicism, yet without some intermediate state it was difficult to see what could be done with the likes of the young man Ferranti . . . Perhaps there was purgatory here and now. . . . Perhaps the unfortunate young man had already experienced it. . . . Perhaps even in this life there was such a thing as new birth. . . . Perhaps. . . . Grandmother's book slipped from her hands and her eyelids, faintly shadowed with purple like parma violets, slid down over her bright eyes.

Grandfather and the children, meanwhile, were going in procession to the kitchen-garden for the Sunday lesson that always preceded the Sunday siesta. On fine days the lesson always took place beneath the cedar-tree, no one quite knew why, unless it had something to do with the cedars of Lebanon.

The cedar-tree was glorious. It grew on a patch of grass in the middle of the potatoes and was so big that it was more like a mountain than a tree. Its trunk and branches were a deep red-brown that glowed like fire when the setting sun touched them and the rest of it was a heavenly blue-green, almost the colour of rock-pools when the shadow of night is over them. It was the easiest tree to climb in the world, for the great boughs branched out from the trunk the whole way up it in a series of steps, so that a child could climb to its top in perfect safety. . . . And if they were good at the Sunday Lesson they did climb it.

Grandfather led the procession carrying a deck-chair, his Bible and the *Church Times*, and the children followed carrying cushions and their Sunday picture-books. Hugh Anthony wore his white sailor suit and Henrietta her pink Sunday frock and the inevitable sailor hat. In the cool shade of the cedar-tree they sat down, the children one on each side of Grandfather, and instruction began.

"Let's have about Jezebel and the dogs eating her," said Hugh Anthony.

"No, let's have about Solomon and his apes and peacocks," said Henrietta.

"No, let's have about the lady knocking nails into the gentleman's head," said Hugh Anthony.

"No, that's nasty," said Henrietta, "let's have about the trumpets blowing and the walls falling down."

"If you remember," said Grandfather firmly, "we are on these Sunday afternoons studying the parables of the New Testament."

The children sighed. Grandfather was devotedly attached to the New Testament but they themselves preferred the Old. It was more colourful and full of suggestions for glorious games. However, there was no help for it, and opening their picture-books they turned as instructed to the parable of the prodigal son. It was Grandfather's favourite parable and so deeply did he love it that as he told the story and explained its meaning his eyes shone behind their glasses and he waved his fat hands in positive excitement. "For this my son was dead, and is alive again," he said, "was lost and is found," and his voice seemed suddenly to sound like a trumpet.

Hugh Anthony did not pay much attention for he had found a colony of bachelor's buttons, those fascinating insects like minute tortoises, behind Grandfather's chair, and was busy touching them with his fingers and watching them draw in their legs and roll themselves up into balls, but Henrietta watched Grandfather spellbound.

He looked like a prophet, she thought, foretelling something lovely that was going to happen. She thought that Elijah must have looked just like Grandfather, only possibly he didn't wear spectacles.

"It's a lovely story, Grandfather," she said when he had finished. "It's the loveliest of all. . . . Can we go up the cedar-tree now?"

Grandfather, nodding, removed his glasses and polished them, finding to his surprise that he had quite upset himself by his own eloquence. He was above all things father and grandfather and had been all his life, from the days when his children were two white mice and a canary until now in his old age when it needed a moment's attention to arithmetic to remember just how many descendants he had. No other relationship, not even that of husband and wife, had meant as much to him as that of father and child, and in it he had found his greatest joy and his greatest pain. And his children had not been only those of his body, there had been others who had been as dear to him, all the dearer perhaps that they had sometimes flouted his fatherhood. . . . Ferranti, for instance. . . . If only he could know what had happened to him.

Shouts from overhead interrupted his melancholy thoughts.

"Is it peace?" called Henrietta, mounted on the watch-tower of Jezreel.

"No!" yelled Hugh Anthony. "The driving is like the driving of Jehu the son of Nimshi for he driveth furiously."

Then there were shouts and scramblings in the tree and Hugh Anthony bellowed at the full force of his lungs, "Who is on my side? Who? Throw her down!" The Sunday picture-books fell heavily into the potatoes and Henrietta's voice lamented, "So they threw her down, and he trod her under foot, and the dogs ate her."

Grandfather sighed. Not a single word of his Sunday lesson had sunk in, he supposed, not a single word, but he was to be blamed in that he had allowed them Bibles of their own at too tender an age. . . . Trust the young to fasten instantly upon what you would prefer them not to fasten upon. . . . Well, there was great good in Jezebel. For magnificent courage she was hard to beat. . . . But teaching the young was difficult. . . . Difficult. . . . Unfolding the *Church Times* he placed the advertisements over his head, the sermon wrong way round over his knees and followed Grandmother into the land of dreams.

Henrietta and Hugh Anthony, having buried what was left of Jezebel, climbed to the top of the tree and were the ark perched on Ararat. Hugh Anthony was Noah and Henrietta was the animals and all round them rolled a waste of waters.

"They're going down!" shouted Hugh Anthony. "Look, you can see the hills poking out. . . . Now where did I put that dove?"

Henrietta, hastily making all the animal noises she could think of, looked and saw how the waters quieted and sank sobbing to sleep while out of them there rose fold after fold of misty hills beneath the arch of a rainbow.

"I'll just go down and tell Ham in the hold," said Noah, and slid downwards, greening the seat of his trousers as he went.

Henrietta stayed where she was, gazing, for as the water subsided what she saw was not the Old Testament land but the country round Torminster, and close to her Torminster itself. The top of the cedar-tree was so high that she could see it all spread out like a picture. Beyond the city and the Tor were the further hills. Henrietta knew all about those hills because the Torminster people often drove up to them in their dog-carts and victorias for picnics. Far up on the heights that were almost hidden now in mist, where the grass was cropped short by the sheep and the wild thyme grew, were the old burying places and encampments of people who had lived there hundreds of years ago, even longer ago than the first Abbot and his pigs. From here, standing on tiptoe on top of a grassy mound, you could see the sea, a blue streak so lovely that it took away your breath.

Below these bare, empty places the woods began, and the fields where the moon-daisies grew. In spring the woods were filled with primroses, in summer with wild roses, in the autumn with scarlet hips and blackberries and at all times with ferns that dipped themselves into the streams that ran there. These streams were everywhere, sometimes disappearing underground, sometimes threading their way through meadow grass and sometimes running broad and clear down the sides of the lanes. It was they who fed the moat of the Bishop's Palace and the holy well, and one of them could be traced all the way down from the heights where the encampments were, to the Torminster High Street. In the folds of the hills were prosperous farms where they gave you glorious teas of blackberry jam and rich yellow cream, and the lanes that led to them had white violets in them in the spring.

Henrietta knew that all this beauty lay hidden in the mists and it seemed to her that she could see it and that it was spread out like a painted background for the city of Torminster. That she could see clearly. The great Cathedral set in the centre with the jumbled roofs clustering below it, pressing close like children to their mother, and the Church towers and tall elm-trees a little misted by the smoke that curled lazily up from the old chimneys. She could pick out from among them the roof of the house with the green door, with its wavy tiles and cushions of green moss. Now and then some faint sound, the bark of a dog or the clip-clop of a horse's hoofs, told that life went on in the city, that children were born and men and women lived and loved and sorrowed and then died, their bodies absorbed into the earth that upheld their city and their souls made one with the power that shaped their hills.

As Isaiah in the Temple so Henrietta in her tree saw a vision. She saw all things that are ranged one behind the other in a series of great flat surfaces, as though curtain were hung behind curtain, each greater and mightier than the other. And the things that were near at hand were the clearest to her sight, and the least enduring, while the things that were behind became with each step back harder to see and nearer to eternity. Closest to her was the life of man on this earth, a thing gone in a flash, while behind it was its background of houses and churches that will last out the life of a man and that of his children's children yet crumble at last into dust. And behind the towers and roofs, very faint in the mist, were the hills that we call unchanging but that yet have risen from chaos and will sink to it again. And behind the hills was spread the blue mystery of the sky, set with the sun and moon and stars and hung with the clouds of heaven. Behind that curtain of space Henrietta's eyes could not see, yet in imagination she beheld an even greater that was formed of wings and crowns and the cleansed robes of the saints, and beyond that again was a great white light.

The bang of the garden door awoke her so suddenly that she nearly fell out of her tree. By craning her neck she could look over the roof of the house and she saw

that it was Jocelyn who had come in. Something must
have happened, she thought, for he was hatless and he
charged straight through the flower-beds in the front
garden and rounded the water-butt at the corner of the
house at the double, making for Grandfather beneath the
cedar-tree.

Hugh Anthony had disappeared to some private game
of his own that he played behind the rubbish heap and
only Henrietta, peering out of the cedar-tree, saw and
heard their interview.

"Grandfather!" shouted Jocelyn, but Grandfather only
snorted.

"Grandfather!" shouted Jocelyn again, and tweaked
the *Church Times* off his relative's head.

Grandfather started and awoke, blinking confusedly
at his grandson's transfigured face. "Dear me," he said.
"Has anything happened?"

"Ferranti has come back," said Jocelyn with great
suddenness.

"What?" said Grandfather, his eyes popping out of
his head. "What? What? What?"

With a snapping of twigs, and a slithering sound as of
a very young avalanche, something pink fell upon Grandfather and Jocelyn from the tree. Without a word it picked
itself up and ran.

"Henrietta," said Jocelyn from the recumbent position
into which her descent upon his head had put him. "She
heard."

"Tell me, Jocelyn," implored Grandfather, polishing
his glasses with trembling fingers, "what it is all about,
and try to be coherent, dear boy."

At the end of the kitchen-garden there was a sunny
wall where the peach-trees grew and here they walked up
and down while Jocelyn, too excited to keep still, poured
out a flood of information.

Grandfather took it all very quietly, Jocelyn thought; indeed, except for an occasional "Dear me" he hardly spoke at all. Shock, Jocelyn supposed, and wondered if he had broken the news as quietly and gradually as he had intended. The news of his own engagement, he decided, he must lead up to slowly.

"I'm to be married at Christmas," he burst out.

But this, it seemed, was no news to Grandfather. "So Clara told me last night," he said. "She had it from the postman. Your dear grandmother does not know yet, as Clara thinks it better you should tell her yourself. You remember there was previously a little difficulty when she heard of your shop by way of the grocer."

"You are glad about everything, Grandfather?"

"I have no words," said Grandfather feebly. "I have no words."

"You'll forgive me if I go now, Grandfather? I promised Felicity."

"God forgive me," said Grandfather with sudden depression, "if I should shorten by one moment this period of your love. Nothing like it will happen to you again."

It was what the blackbirds had said, but Jocelyn had not listened to the blackbirds, and did not now, as he once more charged through the flower-beds, pay any attention to Grandfather.

Left alone the old man sat down suddenly on an up-turned flowerpot and blinked at the sun. As always when some anxiety is suddenly removed his first reaction had been a feeling of melancholy. It is hard to know why this should be, he often thought, unless the sudden lifting of a burden makes one conscious of the tiredness one has suffered in the bearing of it. But melancholy did not last long. As he sat there, warmed by the sun, it seemed that the gates of his soul slowly swung open to let in joy. He

thought that he had never felt so happy. Everything that
he had longed for for his children seemed now to be
theirs. . . . Love and work for Jocelyn. Love and a home
waiting for Henrietta and Hugh Anthony when he himself
should die. Ferranti re-born to accept and enjoy new
life. . . . He had not realized until this moment how
much he had loved that strange young man or how deeply
he had mourned his loss.

Hugh Anthony, peeping out from behind the rubbish-
heap, heard him talking to himself. "For this my son
was dead and is alive again, was lost and is found."

VI

Gabriel Ferranti, meanwhile, dozed in the garden of
the house with the green door. Jocelyn had said that
from Felicity he would go on to tell Grandfather, but he
had promised Ferranti to let him down gently and not
"to bring the whole tribe of them" down on him till
to-morrow. "Give me time to get my breath," Ferranti
had said.

So, meditating in a comfortable chair with his eyes
shut, like nearly everyone else in Torminster at that
moment, he got it. He felt like a runner who has just
completed a race in a series of races and lying on the
grass resting between one effort and another looks back
along the way he has come.

It seemed strange to him, looking back, that he could
have lived through so much in so short a time. As a
young man his greedy passion for the experience that he
felt was necessary to an artist had led him to seize upon
all experience, good or bad, with a passion that now
seemed to him almost lunatic. . . . Not so, he thought,

would he live now. . . . In old days he had clutched life with such violence that the juice of it ran out between his fingers and was lost, but now he would touch it delicately, thankful for the good and accepting the ills with patience.

After the greed the satiety, after the satiety the misery. He could not understand now how it was that the misery had so overwhelmed him. He supposed he was one of those unfortunates born with a great capacity for suffering. . . . He opened his eyes a moment and they were dark with fear, for only one race was run as yet and there might be many others. . . . Then his new-born courage came back to him and he accepted his suffering as the price he must pay for the gift of creation that was his. And suffering, he had discovered, could be the gateway to renewal, than which no more glorious experience can be man's on earth.

These last few days when, his battle fought and his decision taken, he had tramped from London to Torminster had been amongst the most wonderful he had ever known, comparable only, as he had said to Jocelyn, to those days of childhood when the world is shining bright and full of wonder. "Only the greatest of us are born again," Jocelyn had said, and he had thought smilingly that he had proved Jocelyn a liar, and yet wondered humbly, as he tramped the hills near Torminster, if St. Paul after his blindness had felt as he did, or the poet Cowper when he rose from madness.

Sitting with shut eyes he saw again the lovely country through which he had tramped on the day he reached Torminster, the same hills and woods and fields and lanes that his daughter was seeing at this moment in her tree-top, seeing because she was his daughter and because he had the power to transfer the thoughts of his mind to the minds of those who loved him. These things, he thought, with the city they enshrined, were now a part of him, a part of the pattern he must set up as a symbol of the perfect beauty that was his god.

He saw this pattern now as a series of lovely things hung one behind the other like great curtains. Closest to him was the life of men with the moving figures of those he must love, an old man and a little girl and a husband and wife whose generosity would make their home his. Then came the city of bells and towers, then the blue hills behind it, then the sky that was now to him a rich, o'erhanging firmament. And behind that? He was no imaginative child and his vision of wings and crowns was not as clear as Henrietta's, but behind the things that are seen he was aware now of the things that are not seen and in his new-made pattern they were the warp.

VII

As he dreamed Henrietta was running through the Close, running impetuously as she had run on another autumn day, her legs twinkling so fast that they could hardly be seen and her pink dress lifted out behind her by the wind of her going. Under the clock she crashed into the Archdeacon and going off at the rebound without a word tore down the steps on to the Green. The elm-trees stood in a golden stillness to watch her go and the kings and queens on the west front stared in astonishment at the little pink thing who flew so fast, but she took no notice of any of them. She crossed the Market Place, disturbing the pigeons at the holy well in their afternoon siesta, dashed up the two worn stone steps and beat with her fists on the green front door.

Ferranti heard the knocking but took no notice. If it

was the milk for tea, he thought lazily, let it knock.
Then a scrambling sound made him start and look up.

Through the hollyhocks he could see his daughter
hung up on the other side of the garden wall, kicking
violently in an effort to get over. Her sailor hat had
slipped backwards and encircled the back of her head
like a halo and her face looked as though a lamp had
been lit inside. "Here! Quick!" she shouted.

Ferranti ran over to her, reached a long arm over the
wall and gripped her pink smock in the small of the back.
Henrietta on her side scrambled with her toes and in a
minute she was on top of the wall and he had lifted her
down.

But for a few moments he did not let go of her. Her
body under its Sunday frills was warm and palpitating in
his arms, like the body of a feathered little bird when
you hold it in your hands. It gave him a queer thrill to
feel that she was his child, her warmth lit from his and her
life a part of his life.

They sat on the grass together, as they had sat long ago,
and laughed, and he remembered how he had told her a
tale of a city where the streets were not paved with noisy
cobbles but with silent, silver water, and where the sun
was so hot that it could melt the ice out of your heart
and the pain out of your mind. No one ever grew old
in that city, he had told her, and love never died, and
she had believed every word he said, her faith in him
the first shaft of light in his darkness. He thought now,
looking at her upturned, glowing face, that one day he
would take her to Venice and watch her eyes widen
in wonder, and to Athens and see her glow in delight,
and to cities of France and Belgium where the bells would
ring as they rang in Torminster. They would wander
over the world together and life would be sweet.

Henrietta, gazing at him in adoration he had done

nothing whatsoever to deserve, half shy and half eager, did not know yet that he was her father, she knew only that the Pied Piper had come back. He was a magic man, a fairy-tale man, and it seemed to her quite natural that he should have got lost, for fairy-tale people are always easily mislaid, but warm inside her was the certainty that now at last he was found for good.